ROUND UP
THE STORIES OF
RING W. LARDNER

ROUND UP
THE STORIES OF
RING W. LARDNER

NEW YORK
CHARLES SCRIBNER'S SONS
1934

CONTENTS

CONTENTS

ROUND UP
THE STORIES OF
RING W. LARDNER

I

THE MAYSVILLE MINSTREL

MAYSVILLE was a town of five thousand inhabitants and its gas company served eight hundred homes, offices and stores.

The company's office force consisted of two men—Ed Hunter, trouble shooter and reader of meters, and Stephen Gale, whose title was bookkeeper, but whose job was a lot harder than that sounds.

From the first to the tenth of the month, Stephen stayed in the office, accepted checks and money from the few thrifty customers who wanted their discount of five percent, soft-soaped and argued with the many customers who thought they were being robbed, and tried to sell new stoves, plates and lamps to customers who were constantly complaining of defects in the stoves, plates and lamps they had bought fifteen or twenty years ago.

After the tenth, he kept the front door locked and went all over town calling on delinquents, many of whom were a year or more behind and had no intention of trying to catch up. This tiring, futile task usually lasted until the twenty-seventh, when Hunter started reading meters and Stephen copied the readings and made out the bills.

On the twenty-ninth, Hunter usually got drunk and Stephen had to hustle out and read the unread meters and hustle back and make out the rest of the bills.

When Townsend, the Old Man, who owned the business and five other gas businesses in larger towns, paid his semimonthly visit to Maysville, Stephen had to take a severe bawling out for failing to squeeze blood from Maysville's turnips and allowing Hunter to get drunk.

All in all, Stephen earned the $22.50 per week which he had been getting the eight years he had worked for the gas company.

He was now thirty-one. At twelve, he had been obliged to quit school and go to work as a Western Union messenger boy. His father was dead and his mother, who established herself, without much profit, as a dressmaker, easily could use the few dollars Stephen drew from the telegraph company. Later on he had jobs as driver of a grocery wagon, soda clerk in a drug store and freight wrestler at the Lackawanna depot.

3

The $22.50 offer from the gas office was manna from somewhere; it topped his highest previous salary by seven dollars and a half.

Stephen's mother died and Stephen married Stella Nichols, to whom lack of money was no novelty. But they had a couple of children and soon fell into debt, which made Stephen less efficient than ever as a collector of the company's back bills. He couldn't blame other people for not settling when he was stalling off creditors himself.

All he could do was wish to heaven that the Old Man would come across with a substantial raise, and he knew there was as much chance of that as of Stella's swimming the English Channel with a kid under each arm.

The Gales were too poor to go to picture shows; besides, there was no one to leave the children with. So Stephen and Stella stayed at home evenings and read books from the town library. The books Stephen read were books of poetry.

And often, after Stella had gone to bed, he wrote poetry of his own.

He wrote a poem to Stella and gave it to her on one of her birthdays and she said it was great and he ought to quit the darn old gas company and write poetry for a living.

He laughed that off, remarking that he was as poor now as he cared to be.

He didn't show Stella his other poems—poems about Nature, flowers, the Lackawanna Railroad, the beauties of Maysville, et cetera—but kept them locked in a drawer of his desk at the gas office.

There was a man named Charley Roberts who traveled out of New York for an instantaneous water-heater concern. For years he had been trying to sell old Townsend, but old Townsend said the heater ate up too much gas and would make the customers squawk. They squawked enough as it was. Roberts was a determined young man and kept after Townsend in spite of the latter's discouraging attitude.

Roberts was also a wise-cracking, kidding New Yorker, who, when at home, lunched where his heroes lunched, just to be near them, look at them and overhear some of their wise-cracks which he could repeat to his fellow drummers on the road. These heroes of his were comic-strip artists, playwrights and editors of humorous columns in the metropolitan press.

His favorite column was the one conducted by George Balch in the Standard and when he was in the small towns, he frequently clipped silly items from the local papers and sent them to George, who substituted his own captions for Charley's and pasted them up.

Charley had a tip that Old Man Townsend would be in Maysville on a certain day, and as he was in the neighborhood, he took an interurban car thither and called at the gas office. Stephen had just got back from a fruitless tour among the deadheads and was in the shop, behind the office, telling Ed Hunter that Mrs. Harper's pilot-light wouldn't stay lighted.

Roberts, alone in the office, looked idly at Stephen's desk and saw a book.

It was a volume of poems by Amy Lowell. A moment later Stephen reentered from the shop.

" Hello there, Gale," said Roberts.

" How are you, Mr. Roberts? " said Stephen.

" I heard the Old Man was here," said Roberts.

" You've missed him," said Stephen. " He was here yesterday afternoon and left for Haines City last night."

" Will he be here tomorrow? "

" I couldn't tell you. He's hard to keep track of."

" He's hard to sell, too. But I'll run over there and take a chance. I notice you've been reading highbrow poetry."

" I got this from the library."

" How do you like it? "

" I'm not strong for poetry that don't rhyme," said Stephen.

" I guess it's easier to write," said Roberts.

" I don't believe so. It isn't much trouble rhyming if you've got it in you. Look at Edgar Guest."

" How do you know he doesn't have trouble? "

" His works don't read like it," said Stephen, and after a pause: " Besides, I've tried it myself."

" Oh, so you're a poet, are you? " asked Roberts.

" I wouldn't exactly claim that, but I've written a few verses and it was more like fun than work. Maybe other people would think they were rotten, but I get pleasure writing them just the same."

" I'd like to read them, Gale," said Roberts eagerly.

" I don't know if I'd like you to or not. And I don't know if I've saved any. I wrote a poem to my wife on her birthday three years ago. She thought it was pretty good. I might let you read that, only I don't know if I've got a copy of it around here."

He knew very well he had a copy of it around there.

" See if you can find it," said Roberts.

Stephen looked in two or three drawers before he unlocked the one that contained his manuscripts.

"It's just a little thing I wrote for my wife on her birthday. You'll probably think it's rotten. It's called 'To Stella.' That's my wife's first name."

Charley Roberts read the poem:

> Stella you today are twenty-three years old
> And yet your hair is still pure gold.
> Stella they tell me your name in Latin means a star
> And to me that is what you are
> With your eyes and your hair so yellow
> I rate myself a lucky fellow Stella.
> You know I cannot afford a costly gift
> As you know it costs us all I make to live
> And as you know we are already in debt,
> But if you will stay well and healthy
> Until I am rich and wealthy
> Maybe I will be more able then to give you a present
> Better than I can at present.
> So now Stella good-by for the present
> And I hope next year I can make things more pleasant.
> May you live to be old and ripe and mellow
> Is my kind birthday wish for you Stella.

"Do you mean to tell me," said Roberts, "that it was no trouble to write that?"

"It only took me less than a half-hour," said Stephen.

"Listen," said Roberts. "Let me have it."

"What do you want with it?"

"I can get it published for you."

"Where at?"

"In the New York Standard. I've got a friend, George Balch, who would run it in his column. He doesn't pay anything, but if this was printed and your name signed to it, it might attract attention from people who do pay for poetry. Then you could make a lot of money on the side."

"How much do they pay?"

"Well, some of the big magazines pay as high as a dollar a line."

"I forget how many lines there is in that."

Roberts counted them.

"Seventeen," he said. "And from what I've seen of old Townsend, I bet he doesn't pay you much more a week."

"And it only took me less than a half-hour to write," said Stephen.

" Will you let me send it to Balch ? "

" I don't know if I've got another copy."

" Your wife must have a copy."

" I guess maybe she has."

He wasn't just guessing.

" I'll mail this to Balch tonight, along with a note. If he prints it, I'll send you the paper."

" I've got one that's even longer than that," said Stephen.

" Well, let's have it."

" No, I guess I'd better hang onto it—if your friend don't pay for them."

" You're absolutely right. A man's a sucker to work for nothing. You keep your other stuff till this is published and you hear from some magazine editor, as I'm sure you will. Then you can sell what you've already written, and write more, till you're making so much dough that you can buy the Maysville Gas Company from that old skinflint."

" I don't want any gas company. I want to get out of it. I just want to write."

" Why shouldn't you ! "

" I've got to be sure of a living."

" Living ! If you can make seventeen dollars in half an hour, that's thirty-four dollars an hour, or—— How many hours do you put in here? "

" Ten."

" Three hundred and forty dollars a day ! If that isn't a living, I'm selling manicure sets to fish."

" I couldn't keep up no such a pace. I have to wait for inspiration," said Stephen.

" A dollar a line would be enough inspiration for me. But the times when you didn't feel like doing it yourself, you could hire somebody to do it for you."

" That wouldn't be square, and people would know the difference anyway. It's hard to imitate another man's style. I tried once to write like Edgar Guest, but it wouldn't have fooled people that was familiar with his works."

" Nobody can write like Guest. And you don't need to. Your own style is just as good as his and maybe better. And speaking of Guest, do you think he's starving to death? He gives away dimes to the Fords."

Stephen was wild to tell Stella what had happened, but he was afraid this Balch might not like the poem as well as Roberts had; might not think it worth publishing, and she would be disappointed.

He would wait until he actually had it in print, if ever, and then show it to her.

He didn't have to wait long. In less than a week he received by mail from New York a copy of the Standard, and in George Balch's column was his verse with his name signed to it and a caption reading " To Stella—A Maysville Minstrel Gives His Mrs. a Birthday Treat."

For the first time in his career at the gas office, Stephen quit five minutes early and almost ran home. His wife was as excited as he had hoped she would be.

" But why does he call you a minstrel? " she asked. " He must have heard some way about that night at the Elks."

Stephen told her the rest of the story—how Roberts had predicted that the poem would attract the attention of magazine editors and create a demand for his verses at a dollar a line. And he confessed that he had other poems all ready to send when the call came.

He had brought two of them home from the office and he read them aloud for her approval:

" 1. The Lackawanna Railroad.

" The Lackawanna Railroad where does it go?
It goes from Jersey City to Buffalo.
Some of the trains stop at Maysville but they are few
Most of them go right through
Except the 8:22
Going west but the 10:12 bound for Jersey City
That is the train we like the best
As it takes you to Jersey City
Where you can take a ferry or tube for New York City.
The Lackawanna runs many freights
Sometimes they run late
But that does not make so much difference with a freight
Except the people who have to wait for their freight.
Maysville people patronize the Interurban a specially the farmers
So the Interurban cuts into the business of the Lackawanna,
But if you are going to New York City or Buffalo
The Lackawanna is the way to go.
Will say in conclusion that we consider it an honor
That the City of Maysville is on the Lackawanna.

"2. The Gas Business.

"The Maysville Gas Co. has eight hundred meters
The biggest consumer in town is Mrs. Arnold Peters
Who owns the big house on Taylor Hill
And is always giving parties come who will.
Our collections amount to about $2600.00 per month
Five per cent discount if paid before the tenth of the month.
Mr. Townsend the owner considers people a fool
Who do not at least use gas for fuel.
As for lighting he claims it beats electricity
As electric storms often cut off the electricity
And when you have no light at night
And have to burn candles all night.
This is hardly right
A specially if you have company
Who will ask you what is the matter with the electricity.
So patronize the Gas Company which storms do not effect
And your friends will have no reason to object."

Stella raved over both the poems, but made a very practical suggestion.

"You are cheating yourself, dear," she said. "The poem about the railroad, for instance, the way you have got it, it is nineteen lines, or nineteen dollars if they really pay a dollar a line. But it would be almost double the amount if you would fix the lines different."

"How do you mean?"

She got a pencil and piece of paper and showed him:

> The Lackawanna Railroad
> Where does it go?
> It goes from Jersey City
> To Buffalo.

"You see," she said, "you could cut most of the lines in half and make thirty-eight dollars instead of nineteen."

But Stephen, with one eye on profit and the other on Art, could only increase the lines of "The Lackawanna" from nineteen to thirty and those of "The Gas Business" from seventeen to twenty-one.

Three days later a special delivery came for Stephen.

It said:

Dear Mr. Gale:

On September second there was a poem entitled "To Stella" in the New York Standard. The poem was signed by you. It impressed me greatly and if you have written or will write others as good, our magazine will be glad to buy them, paying you one dollar a line.

Please let me hear from you and send along any poems you may have on hand.

Sincerely,

Wallace James,

Editor, " James's Weekly,"

New York City.

Stephen had never heard of " James's Weekly " and did not notice that the letter was postmarked Philadelphia and written on the stationery of a Philadelphia hotel.

He rushed to his house, addressed and mailed the railroad and gas verses, and after a brief and excited conference with Stella, decided to resign his job.

Old Man Townsend, dropping into Maysville the following morning, heard the decision and was not a bit pleased. He realized he never could get anyone else to do Stephen's work at Stephen's salary.

" I'll raise you to twenty-four dollars," he said.

" I'm not asking for a raise. I've got to quit so I can devote all my time to my poetry."

" Your poetry ! "

" Yes, sir."

" Do you mean to say you're going to write poetry for a living? " asked the Old Man.

" Yes, sir."

" You'll starve to death."

" Edgar Guest is still alive."

" I don't care if he is or not," said the Old Man. "It's the twelfth of the month and Hunter can tend to his job and yours both for a couple of weeks. If you want to come back at the end of that time, I'll raise you to twenty-three dollars."

It was Stephen's intention to polish up some of his older poems and write one or two fresh ones so his supply would be ready for " James's " demand.

But he found it next to impossible to write while the fate of the two verses he had sent in was uncertain and, deciding to leave the old manuscripts as they were, he was able to make only a feeble start on a new one:

The Delaware River.

Not a great many miles from Maysville is the Delaware River
But there is no fish in this part of the River.

> The upper part of the River is narrow and shallow
> But they claim it is much wider near Philadelphia.

On the twentieth the envelope containing " The Lackawanna Railroad " and " The Gas Business " was returned from New York. There were several inscriptions stamped and written on it, such as " Not Found " and " Not in Directory."

And it dawned on Stephen that he was the victim of quite a joke.

To the accompaniment of Stella's sobs, he proceeded to tear up all his manuscripts save " To Stella," which she had hidden away where he couldn't find it.

" Mr. Townsend came in on the eight-thirty interurban," he said. " I'll have to go see him."

" All right," said the Old Man when Stephen walked into the office. " I'll take you back at your old salary, but don't let's have no more foolishness. Get out now and try and coax a little money out of that Harper woman. She ain't paid a nickel for eight months."

" I wanted to speak to you about those instantaneous water-heaters," said Stephen.

" What about them? "

" I was going to advise you not to buy them. They eat up too much gas."

" Thanks for your advice, but I ordered some from Roberts in Haines City. I told him to send half a dozen of them here," said the Old Man.

" Will he be here to demonstrate them? " asked Stephen grimly.

" He said he would."

" I hope he will."

But even as he spoke, Stephen realized there was nothing he could do about it.

II

I CAN'T BREATHE

I AM staying here at the Inn for two weeks with my Uncle Nat and Aunt Jule and I think I will keep a kind of a diary while I am here to help pass the time and so I can have a record of things that happen though goodness knows there isn't lightly to anything happen, that is anything exciting with Uncle Nat and Aunt Jule making the plans as they are both at least 35 years old and maybe older.

Dad and mother are abroad to be gone a month and me coming here is supposed to be a recompence for them not taking me with them. A fine recompence to be left with old people that come to a place like this to rest. Still it would be a heavenly place under different conditions, for instance if Walter were here, too. It would be heavenly if he were here, the very thought of it makes my heart stop.

I can't stand it. I won't think about it.

This is our first seperation since we have been engaged, nearly 17 days. It will be 17 days tomorrow. And the hotel orchestra at dinner this evening played that old thing " Oh how I miss you tonight " and it seemed as if they must be playing it for my benefit though of course the person in that song is talking about how they miss their mother though of course I miss mother too, but a person gets used to missing their mother and it isn't like Walter or the person you are engaged to.

But there won't be any more seperations much longer, we are going to be married in December even if mother does laugh when I talk to her about it because she says I am crazy to even think of getting married at 18.

She got married herself when she was 18, but of course that was " different," she wasn't crazy like I am, she knew whom she was marrying. As if Walter were a policeman or a foreigner or something. And she says she was only engaged once while I have been engaged at least five times a year since I was 14, of course it really isn't as bad as that and I have really only been really what I call engaged six times altogether, but is getting engaged my fault

13

when they keep insisting and hammering at you and if you didn't say yes they would never go home.

But it is different with Walter. I honestly believe if he had not asked me I would have asked him. Of course I wouldn't have, but I would have died. And this is the first time I have ever been engaged to be really married. The other times when they talked about when should we get married I just laughed at them, but I hadn't been engaged to Walter ten minutes when he brought up the subject of marriage and I didn't laugh. I wouldn't be engaged to him unless it was to be married. I couldn't stand it.

Anyway mother may as well get used to the idea because it is " No Foolin' " this time and we have got our plans all made and I am going to be married at home and go out to California and Hollywood on our honeymoon. December, five months away. I can't stand it. I can't wait.

There were a couple of awfully nice looking boys sitting together alone in the dining-room tonight. One of them wasn't so much, but the other was cute. And he——

There's the dance orchestra playing " Always," what they played at the Biltmore the day I met Walter. " Not for just an hour not for just a day." I can't live. I can't breathe.

July 13

This has been a much more exciting day than I expected under the circumstances. In the first place I got two long night letters, one from Walter and one from Gordon Flint. I don't see how Walter ever had the nerve to send his, there was everything in it and it must have been horribly embarrassing for him while the telegraph operator was reading it over and counting the words to say nothing of embarrassing for the operator.

But the one from Gordon was a kind of a shock. He just got back from a trip around the world, left last December to go on it and got back yesterday and called up our house and Helga gave him my address, and his telegram, well it was nearly as bad as Walter's. The trouble is that Gordon and I were engaged when he went away, or at least he thought so and he wrote to me right along all the time he was away and sent cables and things and for a while I answered his letters, but then I lost track of his itinery and couldn't write to him any more and when I got really engaged to Walter I couldn't let Gordon know because I had no idea where he was besides not wanting to spoil his trip.

And now he still thinks we are engaged and he is going to call me up tomorrow from Chicago and how in the world can I explain things and get him to understand because he is really serious and I like him ever and ever so much and in lots of ways he is nicer than Walter, not really nicer but better looking and there is no comparison between their dancing. Walter simply can't learn to dance, that is really dance. He says it is because he is flat footed, he says that as a joke, but it is true and I wish to heavens it wasn't.

All forenoon I thought and thought and thought about what to say to Gordon when he calls up and finally I couldn't stand thinking about it any more and just made up my mind I wouldn't think about it any more. But I will tell the truth though it will kill me to hurt him.

I went down to lunch with Uncle Nat and Aunt Jule and they were going out to play golf this afternoon and were insisting that I go with them, but I told them I had a headache and then I had a terrible time getting them to go without me. I didn't have a headache at all and just wanted to be alone to think about Walter and besides when you play with Uncle Nat he is always correcting your stance or your swing or something and always puts his hands on my arms or shoulders to show me the right way and I can't stand it to have old men touch me, even if they are your uncle.

I finally got rid of them and I was sitting watching the tennis when that boy that I saw last night, the cute one, came and sat right next to me and of course I didn't look at him and I was going to smoke a cigarette and found I had left my lighter upstairs and I started to get up and go after it when all of a sudden he was offering me his lighter and I couldn't very well refuse it without being rude. So we got to talking and he is even cuter than he looks, the most original and wittiest person I believe I ever met and I haven't laughed so much in I don't know how long.

For one thing he asked me if I had heard Rockefeller's song and I said no and he began singing " Oil alone." Then he asked me if I knew the orange juice song and I told him no again and he said it was " Orange juice sorry you made me cry." I was in hysterics before we had been together ten minutes.

His name is Frank Caswell and he has been out of Darthmouth a year and is 24 years old. That isn't so terribly old, only two years older than Walter and three years older than Gordon. I hate the name Frank, but Caswell is all right and he is so cute.

He was out in California last winter and visited Hollywood and met everybody in the world and it is fascinating to listen to him.

He met Norma Shearer and he said he thought she was the prettiest thing he had ever seen. What he said was " I did think she was the prettiest girl in the world, till today." I was going to pretend I didn't get it, but I finally told him to be sensible or I would never be able to believe anything he said.

Well, he wanted me to dance with him tonight after dinner and the next question was how to explain how we had met each other to Uncle Nat and Aunt Jule. Frank said he would fix that all right and sure enough he got himself introduced to Uncle Nat when Uncle Nat came in from golf and after dinner Uncle Nat introduced him to me and Aunt Jule too and we danced together all evening, that is not Aunt Jule. They went to bed, thank heavens.

He is a heavenly dancer, as good as Gordon. One dance we were dancing and for one of the encores the orchestra played " In a cottage small by a waterfall " and I simply couldn't dance to it. I just stopped still and said "Listen, I can't bear it, I can't breathe " and poor Frank thought I was sick or something and I had to explain that that was the tune the orchestra played the night I sat at the next table to Jack Barrymore at Barney Gallant's.

I made him sit out that encore and wouldn't let him talk till they got through playing it. Then they played something else and I was all right again and Frank told me about meeting Jack Barrymore. Imagine meeting him. I couldn't live.

I promised Aunt Jule I would go to bed at eleven and it is way past that now, but I am all ready for bed and have just been writing this. Tomorrow Gordon is going to call up and what will I say to him? I just won't think about it.

July 14

Gordon called up this morning from Chicago and it was wonderful to hear his voice again though the connection was terrible. He asked me if I still loved him and I tried to tell him no, but I knew that would mean an explanation and the connection was so bad that I never could make him understand so I said yes, but I almost whispered it purposely, thinking he wouldn't hear me, but he heard me all right and he said that made everything all right with the world. He said he thought I had stopped loving him because I had stopped writing.

I wish the connection had been decent and I could have told him how things were, but now it is terrible because he is planning to get to New York the day I get there and heaven knows what I will do because Walter will be there, too. I just won't think about it.

Aunt Jule came in my room just after I was through talking to Gordon, thank heavens. The room was full of flowers. Walter had sent me some and so had Frank. I got another long night letter from Walter, just as silly as the first one. I wish he would say those things in letters instead of night letters so everybody in the world wouldn't see them. Aunt Jule wanted me to read it aloud to her. I would have died.

While she was still in the room, Frank called up and asked me to play golf with him and I said all right and Aunt Jule said she was glad my headache was gone. She was trying to be funny.

I played golf with Frank this afternoon. He is a beautiful golfer and it is thrilling to watch him drive, his swing is so much more graceful than Walter's. I asked him to watch me swing and tell me what was the matter with me, but he said he couldn't look at anything but my face and there wasn't anything the matter with that.

He told me the boy who was here with him had been called home and he was glad of it because I might have liked him, the other boy, better than himself. I told him that couldn't be possible and he asked me if I really meant that and I said of course, but I smiled when I said it so he wouldn't take it too seriously.

We danced again tonight and Uncle Nat and Aunt Jule sat with us a while and danced a couple of dances themselves, but they were really there to get better acquainted with Frank and see if he was all right for me to be with. I know they certainly couldn't have enjoyed their own dancing, no old people really can enjoy it because they can't really *do* anything.

They were favorably impressed with Frank I think, at least Aunt Jule didn't say I must be in bed at eleven, but just not to stay up too late. I guess it is a big surprise to a girl's parents and aunts and uncles to find out that the boys you go around with are all right, they always seem to think that if I seem to like somebody and the person pays a little attention to me, why he must be a convict or a policeman or a drunkard or something queer.

Frank had some more songs for me tonight. He asked me if I knew the asthma song and I said I didn't and he said " Oh, you must know that. It goes yes, sir, asthma baby." Then he told me about the underwear song, " I underwear my baby is tonight." He keeps you in hysterics and yet he has his serious side, in fact he was awfully serious when he said good night to me and his eyes simply shown. I wish Walter were more like him in some ways, but I mustn't think about that.

July 15

I simply can't live and I know I'll never sleep tonight. I am in a terrible predicament or rather I won't know whether I really am or not till tomorrow and that is what makes it so terrible.

After we had danced two or three dances, Frank asked me to go for a ride with him and we went for a ride in his car and he had had some cocktails and during the ride he had some drinks out of a flask and finally he told me he loved me and I said not to be silly, but he said he was perfectly serious and he certainly acted that way. He asked me if I loved anybody else and I said yes and he asked if I didn't love him more than anybody else and I said yes, but only because I thought he had probably had too much to drink and wouldn't remember it anyway and the best thing to do was humor him under the circumstances.

Then all of a sudden he asked me when I could marry him and I said, just as a joke, that I couldn't possibly marry him before December. He said that was a long time to wait, but I was certainly worth waiting for and he said a lot of other things and maybe I humored him a little too much, but that is just the trouble, I don't know.

I was absolutely sure he was tight and would forget the whole thing, but that was early in the evening, and when we said good night he was a whole lot more sober than he had been and now I am not sure how it stands. If he doesn't remember anything about it, of course I am all right. But if he does remember and if he took me seriously, I will simply have to tell him about Walter and maybe about Gordon, too. And it isn't going to be easy. The suspense is what is maddening and I know I'll never live through this night.

July 16

I can't stand it, I can't breathe, life is impossible. Frank remembered everything about last night and firmly believes we are engaged and going to be married in December. His people live in New York and he says he is going back when I do and have them meet me.

Of course it can't go on and tomorrow I will tell him about Walter or Gordon or both of them. I know it is going to hurt him terribly, perhaps spoil his life and I would give anything in the world not to have had it happen. I hate so to hurt him because he is so nice besides being so cute and attractive.

He sent me the loveliest flowers this morning and called up at ten and wanted to know how soon he could see me and I hope the girl wasn't listening in because the things he said were, well, like Walter's night letters.

And that is another terrible thing, today I didn't get a night letter from Walter, but there was a regular letter instead and I carried it around in my purse all this afternoon and evening and never remembered to read it till ten minutes ago when I came up in the room. Walter is worried because I have only sent him two telegrams and written him one letter since I have been here, he would be a lot more worried if he knew what has happened now, though of course it can't make any difference because he is the one I am really engaged to be married to and the one I told mother I was going to marry in December and I wouldn't dare tell her it was somebody else.

I met Frank for lunch and we went for a ride this afternoon and he was so much in love and so lovely to me that I simply did not have the heart to tell him the truth, I am surely going to tell him tomorrow and telling him today would have just meant one more day of unhappiness for both of us.

He said his people had plenty of money and his father had offered to take him into partnership and he might accept, but he thinks his true vocation is journalism with a view to eventually writing novels and if I was willing to undergo a few hardships just at first we would probably both be happier later on if he was doing something he really liked. I didn't know what to say, but finally I said I wanted him to suit himself and money wasn't everything.

He asked me where I would like to go on my honeymoon and I suppose I ought to have told him my honeymoon was all planned, that I was going to California, with Walter, but all I said was that I had always wanted to go to California and he was enthusiastic and said that is where we would surely go and he would take me to Hollywood and introduce me to all those wonderful people he met there last winter. It nearly takes my breath away to think of it, going there with someone who really knows people and has the entrée.

We danced again tonight, just two or three dances, and then went out and sat in the tennis-court, but I came upstairs early because Aunt Jule had acted kind of funny at dinner. And I

wanted to be alone, too, and think, but the more I think the worse
it gets.

Sometimes I wish I were dead, maybe that is the only solution
and it would be best for everyone concerned. I *will* die if things
keep on the way they have been. But of course tomorrow it will
be all over, with Frank I mean, for I must tell him the truth no
matter how much it hurts us both. Though I don't care how much
it hurts me. The thought of hurting him is what is driving me
mad. I can't bear it.

July 18

I have skipped a day. I was busy every minute of yesterday
and so exhausted when I came upstairs that I was tempted to fall
into bed with all my clothes on. First Gordon called me up from
Chicago to remind me that he would be in New York the day I
got there and that when he comes he wants me all to himself all
the time and we can make plans for our wedding. The connection was bad again and I just couldn't explain to him about
Walter.

I had an engagement with Frank for lunch and just as we were
going in another long distance call came, from Walter this time.
He wanted to know why I haven't written more letters and sent
him more telegrams and asked me if I still loved him and of
course I told him yes because I really do. Then he asked if I had
met any men here and I told him I had met one, a friend of Uncle
Nat's. After all it was Uncle Nat who introduced me to Frank.
He reminded me that he would be in New York on the 25th which
is the day I expect to get home, and said he would have theater
tickets for that night and we would go somewhere afterwards and
dance.

Frank insisted on knowing who had kept me talking so long
and I told him it was a boy I had known a long while, a very
dear friend of mine and a friend of my family's. Frank was
jealous and kept asking questions till I thought I would go mad.
He was so serious and kind of cross and gruff that I gave up the
plan of telling him the truth till some time when he is in better
spirits.

I played golf with Frank in the afternoon and we took a ride
last night and I wanted to get in early because I had promised
both Walter and Gordon that I would write them long letters, but
Frank wouldn't bring me back to the Inn till I had named a
definite date in December. I finally told him the 10th and he
said all right if I was sure that wasn't a Sunday. I said I would

have to look it up, but as a matter of fact I know the 10th falls on a Friday because the date Walter and I have agreed on for our wedding is Saturday the 11th.

Today has just been the same thing over again, two more night letters, a long distance call from Chicago, golf and a ride with Frank, and the room full of flowers. But tomorrow I am going to tell Frank and I am going to write Gordon a long letter and tell him, too, because this simply can't go on any longer. I can't breathe. I can't live.

July 21

I wrote to Gordon yesterday, but I didn't say anything about Walter because I don't think it is a thing a person ought to do by letter. I can tell him when he gets to New York and then I will be sure that he doesn't take it too hard and I can promise him that I will be friends with him always and make him promise not to do anything silly, while if I told it to him in a letter there is no telling what he would do, there all alone.

And I haven't told Frank because he hasn't been feeling well, he is terribly sunburned and it hurts him terribly so he can hardly play golf or dance, and I want him to be feeling his best when I do tell him, but whether he is all right or not I simply must tell him tomorrow because he is actually planning to leave here on the same train with us Saturday night and I can't let him do that.

Life is so hopeless and it could be so wonderful. For instance how heavenly it would be if I could marry Frank first and stay married to him five years and he would be the one who would take me to Hollywood and maybe we could go on parties with Norman Kerry and Jack Barrymore and Buster Collier and Marion Davies and Lois Moran.

And at the end of five years Frank could go into journalism and write novels and I would only be 23 and I could marry Gordon and he would be ready for another trip around the world and he could show me things better than someone who had never seen them before.

Gordon and I would separate at the end of five years and I would be 28 and I know of lots of women that never even got married the first time till they were 28 though I don't suppose that was their fault, but I would marry Walter then, for after all he is the one I really love and want to spend most of my life with and I wouldn't care whether he could dance or not when I was that old. Before long we would be as old as Uncle Nat and Aunt Jule and I certainly wouldn't want to dance at their age

when all you can do is just hobble around the floor. But Walter
is so wonderful as a companion and we would enjoy the same
things and be pals and maybe we would begin to have children.

But that is all impossible though it wouldn't be if older people
just had sense and would look at things the right way.

It is only half past ten, the earliest I have gone to bed in weeks,
but I am worn out and Frank went to bed early so he could put
cold cream on his sunburn.

Listen, diary, the orchestra is playing "Limehouse Blues."
The first tune I danced to with Merle Oliver, two years ago. I
can't stand it. And how funny that they should play that old
tune tonight of all nights, when I have been thinking of Merle
off and on all day, and I hadn't thought of him before in weeks
and weeks. I wonder where he is, I wonder if it is just an accident or if it means I am going to see him again. I simply mustn't
think about it or I'll die.

July 22

I knew it wasn't an accident. I knew it must mean something,
and it did.

Merle is coming here today, here to this Inn, and just to see
me. And there can only be one reason. And only one answer. I
knew that when I heard his voice calling from Boston. How could
I ever had thought I loved anyone else? How could he ever have
thought I meant it when I told him I was engaged to George
Morse?

A whole year and he still cares and I still care. That shows
we were always intended for each other and for no one else. I
won't make *him* wait till December. I doubt if we even wait till
dad and mother get home. And as for a honeymoon I will go with
him to Long Beach or the Bronx Zoo, wherever he wants to take
me.

After all this is the best way out of it, the only way. I won't
have to say anything to Frank, he will guess when he sees me with
Merle. And when I get home Sunday and Walter and Gordon call
me up, I will invite them both to dinner and Merle can tell them
himself, with two of them there it will only hurt each one half as
much as if they were alone.

The train is due at 2:40, almost three hours from now. I can't
wait. And what if it should be late? I can't stand it.

III

HAIRCUT

I GOT another barber that comes over from Carterville and helps me out Saturdays, but the rest of the time I can get along all right alone. You can see for yourself that this ain't no New York City and besides that, the most of the boys works all day and don't have no leisure to drop in here and get themselves prettied up.

You're a newcomer, ain't you? I thought I hadn't seen you round before. I hope you like it good enough to stay. As I say, we ain't no New York City or Chicago, but we have pretty good times. Not as good, though, since Jim Kendall got killed. When he was alive, him and Hod Meyers used to keep this town in an uproar. I bet they was more laughin' done here than any town its size in America.

Jim was comical, and Hod was pretty near a match for him. Since Jim's gone, Hod tries to hold his end up just the same as ever, but it's tough goin' when you ain't got nobody to kind of work with.

They used to be plenty fun in here Saturdays. This place is jam-packed Saturdays, from four o'clock on. Jim and Hod would show up right after their supper, round six o'clock. Jim would set himself down in that big chair, nearest the blue spittoon. Whoever had been settin' in that chair, why they'd get up when Jim come in and give it to him.

You'd of thought it was a reserved seat like they have sometimes in a theayter. Hod would generally always stand or walk up and down, or some Saturdays, of course, he'd be settin' in this chair part of the time, gettin' a haircut.

Well, Jim would set there a w'ile without openin' his mouth only to spit, and then finally he'd say to me, " Whitey,"—my right name, that is, my right first name, is Dick, but everybody round here calls me Whitey—Jim would say, "Whitey, your nose looks like a rosebud tonight. You must of been drinkin' some of your aw de cologne."

So I'd say, " No, Jim, but you look like you'd been drinkin' somethin' of that kind or somethin' worse."

Jim would have to laugh at that, but then he'd speak up and say, " No, I ain't had nothin' to drink, but that ain't sayin' I

23

wouldn't like somethin'. I wouldn't even mind if it was wood alcohol."

Then Hod Meyers would say, "Neither would your wife." That would set everybody to laughin' because Jim and his wife wasn't on very good terms. She'd of divorced him only they wasn't no chance to get alimony and she didn't have no way to take care of herself and the kids. She couldn't never understand Jim. He *was* kind of rough, but a good fella at heart.

Him and Hod had all kinds of sport with Milt Sheppard. I don't suppose you've seen Milt. Well, he's got an Adam's apple that looks more like a mushmelon. So I'd be shavin' Milt and when I'd start to shave down here on his neck, Hod would holler, "Hey, Whitey, wait a minute! Before you cut into it, let's make up a pool and see who can guess closest to the number of seeds."

And Jim would say, "If Milt hadn't of been so hoggish, he'd of ordered a half a cantaloupe instead of a whole one and it might not of stuck in his throat."

All the boys would roar at this and Milt himself would force a smile, though the joke was on him. Jim certainly was a card!

There's his shavin' mug, settin' on the shelf, right next to Charley Vail's. "Charles M. Vail." That's the druggist. He comes in regular for his shave, three times a week. And Jim's is the cup next to Charley's. "James H. Kendall." Jim won't need no shavin' mug no more, but I'll leave it there just the same for old time's sake. Jim certainly was a character!

Years ago, Jim used to travel for a canned goods concern over in Carterville. They sold canned goods. Jim had the whole northern half of the State and was on the road five days out of every week. He'd drop in here Saturdays and tell his experiences for that week. It was rich.

I guess he paid more attention to playin' jokes than makin' sales. Finally the concern let him out and he come right home here and told everybody he'd been fired instead of sayin' he'd resigned like most fellas would of.

It was a Saturday and the shop was full and Jim got up out of that chair and says, "Gentlemen, I got an important announcement to make. I been fired from my job."

Well, they asked him if he was in earnest and he said he was and nobody could think of nothin' to say till Jim finally broke the ice himself. He says, "I been sellin' canned goods and now I'm canned goods myself."

You see, the concern he'd been workin' for was a factory that made canned goods. Over in Carterville. And now Jim said he was canned himself. He was certainly a card!

Jim had a great trick that he used to play w'ile he was travelin'. For instance, he'd be ridin' on a train and they'd come to some little town like, well, like, we'll say, like Benton. Jim would look out the train window and read the signs on the stores.

For instance, they'd be a sign, " Henry Smith, Dry Goods." Well, Jim would write down the name and the name of the town and when he got to wherever he was goin' he'd mail back a postal card to Henry Smith at Benton and not sign no name to it, but he'd write on the card, well, somethin' like " Ask your wife about that book agent that spent the afternoon last week," or " Ask your Missus who kept her from gettin' lonesome the last time you was in Carterville." And he'd sign the card, " A Friend."

Of course, he never knew what really come of none of these jokes, but he could picture what *probably* happened and that was enough.

Jim didn't work very steady after he lost his position with the Carterville people. What he did earn, doin' odd jobs round town, why he spent pretty near all of it on gin and his family might of starved if the stores hadn't of carried them along. Jim's wife tried her hand at dressmakin', but they ain't nobody goin' to get rich makin' dresses in this town.

As I say, she'd of divorced Jim, only she seen that she couldn't support herself and the kids and she was always hopin' that some day Jim would cut out his habits and give her more than two or three dollars a week.

They was a time when she would go to whoever he was workin' for and ask them to give her his wages, but after she done this once or twice, he beat her to it by borrowin' most of his pay in advance. He told it all round town, how he had outfoxed his Missus. He certainly was a caution!

But he wasn't satisfied with just outwittin' her. He was sore the way she had acted, tryin' to grab off his pay. And he made up his mind he'd get even. Well, he waited till Evans's Circus was advertised to come to town. Then he told his wife and two kiddies that he was goin' to take them to the circus. The day of the circus, he told them he would get the tickets and meet them outside the entrance to the tent.

Well, he didn't have no intentions of bein' there or buyin' tickets or nothin'. He got full of gin and laid round Wright's poolroom

all day. His wife and the kids waited and waited and of course
he didn't show up. His wife didn't have a dime with her, or nowhere else, I guess. So she finally had to tell the kids it was all
off and they cried like they wasn't never goin' to stop.

Well, it seems, w'ile they was cryin', Doc Stair came along
and he asked what was the matter, but Mrs. Kendall was stubborn and wouldn't tell him, but the kids told him and he insisted
on takin' them and their mother in the show. Jim found this out
afterwards and it was one reason why he had it in for Doc Stair.

Doc Stair come here about a year and a half ago. He's a
mighty handsome young fella and his clothes always look like he
has them made to order. He goes to Detroit two or three times a
year and w'ile he's there he must have a tailor take his measure
and then make him a suit to order. They cost pretty near twice
as much, but they fit a whole lot better than if you just bought
them in a store.

For a w'ile everybody was wonderin' why a young doctor like
Doc Stair should come to a town like this where we already got old
Doc Gamble and Doc Foote that's both been here for years and all
the practice in town was always divided between the two of them.

Then they was a story got round that Doc Stair's gal had
throwed him over, a gal up in the Northern Peninsula somewheres, and the reason he come here was to hide himself away
and forget it. He said himself that he thought that he wasn't nothin' like general practice in a place like ours to fit a man to be a
good all round doctor. And that's why he'd came.

Anyways, it wasn't long before he was makin' enough to live on,
though they tell me that he never dunned nobody for what they
owed him, and the folks here certainly has got the owin' habit,
even in my business. If I had all that was comin' to me for just
shaves alone, I could go to Carterville and put up at the Mercer
for a week and see a different picture every night. For instance,
they's old George Purdy—but I guess I shouldn't ought to be
gossipin'.

Well, last year, our coroner died, died of the flu. Ken Beatty,
that was his name. He was the coroner. So they had to choose
another man to be coroner in his place and they picked Doc Stair.
He laughed at first and said he didn't want it, but they made him
take it. It ain't no job that anybody would fight for and what
a man makes out of it in a year would just about buy seeds for
their garden. Doc's the kind, though, that can't say no to nothin'
if you keep at him long enough.

But I was goin' to tell you about a poor boy we got here in

town—Paul Dickson. He fell out of a tree when he was about ten years old. Lit on his head and it done somethin' to him and he ain't never been right. No harm in him, but just silly. Jim Kendall used to call him cuckoo; that's a name Jim had for anybody that was off their head, only he called people's head their bean. That was another of his gags, callin' head bean and callin' crazy people cuckoo. Only poor Paul ain't crazy, but just silly.

You can imagine that Jim used to have all kinds of fun with Paul. He'd send him to the White Front Garage for a left-handed monkey wrench. Of course they ain't no such a thing as a left-handed monkey wrench.

And once we had a kind of a fair here and they was a baseball game between the fats and the leans and before the game started Jim called Paul over and sent him way down to Schrader's hardware store to get a key for the pitcher's box.

They wasn't nothin' in the way of gags that Jim couldn't think up, when he put his mind to it.

Poor Paul was always kind of suspicious of people, maybe on account of how Jim had kept foolin' him. Paul wouldn't have much to do with anybody only his own mother and Doc Stair and a girl here in town named Julie Gregg. That is, she ain't a girl no more, but pretty near thirty or over.

When Doc first come to town, Paul seemed to feel like here was a real friend and he hung round Doc's office most of the w'ile; the only time he wasn't there was when he'd go home to eat or sleep or when he seen Julie Gregg doin' her shoppin'.

When he looked out Doc's window and seen her, he'd run downstairs and join her and tag along with her to the different stores. The poor boy was crazy about Julie and she always treated him mighty nice and made him feel like he was welcome, though of course it wasn't nothin' but pity on her side.

Doc done all he could to improve Paul's mind and he told me once that he really thought the boy was gettin' better, that they was times when he was as bright and sensible as anybody else.

But I was goin' to tell you about Julie Gregg. Old Man Gregg was in the lumber business, but got to drinkin' and lost the most of his money and when he died, he didn't leave nothin' but the house and just enough insurance for the girl to skimp along on.

Her mother was a kind of a half invalid and didn't hardly ever leave the house. Julie wanted to sell the place and move somewheres else after the old man died, but the mother said she was born here and would die here. It was tough on Julie, as the young people round this town—well, she's too good for them.

She's been away to school and Chicago and New York and different places and they ain't no subject she can't talk on, where you take the rest of the young folks here and you mention anything to them outside of Gloria Swanson or Tommy Meighan and they think you're delirious. Did you see Gloria in Wages of Virtue? You missed somethin'!

Well, Doc Stair hadn't been here more than a week when he come in one day to get shaved and I recognized who he was as he had been pointed out to me, so I told him about my old lady. She's been ailin' for a couple years and either Doc Gamble or Doc Foote, neither one, seemed to be helpin' her. So he said he would come out and see her, but if she was able to get out herself, it would be better to bring her to his office where he could make a completer examination.

So I took her to his office and w'ile I was waitin' for her in the reception room, in come Julie Gregg. When somebody comes in Doc Stair's office, they's a bell that rings in his inside office so as he can tell they's somebody to see him.

So he left my old lady inside and come out to the front office and that's the first time him and Julie met and I guess it was what they call love at first sight. But it wasn't fifty-fifty. This young fella was the slickest lookin' fella she'd ever seen in this town and she went wild over him. To him she was just a young lady that wanted to see the doctor.

She'd came on about the same business I had. Her mother had been doctorin' for years with Doc Gamble and Doc Foote and without no results. So she'd heard they was a new doc in town and decided to give him a try. He promised to call and see her mother that same day.

I said a minute ago that it was love at first sight on her part. I'm not only judgin' by how she acted afterwards but how she looked at him that first day in his office. I ain't no mind reader, but it was wrote all over her face that she was gone.

Now Jim Kendall, besides bein' a jokesmith and a pretty good drinker, well, Jim was quite a lady-killer. I guess he run pretty wild durin' the time he was on the road for them Carterville people, and besides that, he'd had a couple little affairs of the heart right here in town. As I say, his wife could of divorced him, only she couldn't.

But Jim was like the majority of men, and women, too, I guess.

He wanted what he couldn't get. He wanted Julie Gregg and worked his head off tryin' to land her. Only he'd of said bean instead of head.

Well, Jim's habits and his jokes didn't appeal to Julie and of course he was a married man, so he didn't have no more chance than, well, than a rabbit. That's an expression of Jim's himself. When somebody didn't have no chance to get elected or somethin', Jim would always say they didn't have no more chance than a rabbit.

He didn't make no bones about how he felt. Right in here, more than once, in front of the whole crowd, he said he was stuck on Julie and anybody that could get her for him was welcome to his house and his wife and kids included. But she wouldn't have nothin' to do with him; wouldn't even speak to him on the street. He finally seen he wasn't gettin' nowheres with his usual line so he decided to try the rough stuff. He went right up to her house one evenin' and when she opened the door he forced his way in and grabbed her. But she broke loose and before he could stop her, she run in the next room and locked the door and phoned to Joe Barnes. Joe's the marshal. Jim could hear who she was phonin' to and he beat it before Joe got there.

Joe was an old friend of Julie's pa. Joe went to Jim the next day and told him what would happen if he ever done it again.

I don't know how the news of this little affair leaked out. Chances is that Joe Barnes told his wife and she told somebody else's wife and they told their husband. Anyways, it did leak out and Hod Meyers had the nerve to kid Jim about it, right here in this shop. Jim didn't deny nothin' and kind of laughed it off and said for us all to wait; that lots of people had tried to make a monkey out of him, but he always got even.

Meanw'ile everybody in town was wise to Julie's bein' wild mad over the Doc. I don't suppose she had any idear how her face changed when him and her was together; of course she couldn't of, or she'd of kept away from him. And she didn't know that we was all noticin' how many times she made excuses to go up to his office or pass it on the other side of the street and look up in his window to see if he was there. I felt sorry for her and so did most other people.

Hod Meyers kept rubbin' it into Jim about how the Doc had cut him out. Jim didn't pay no attention to the kiddin' and you could see he was plannin' one of his jokes.

One trick Jim had was the knack of changin' his voice. He

could make you think he was a girl talkin' and he could mimic any man's voice. To show you how good he was along this line, I'll tell you the joke he played on me once.

You know, in most towns of any size, when a man is dead and needs a shave, why the barber that shaves him soaks him five dollars for the job; that is, he don't soak *him*, but whoever ordered the shave. I just charge three dollars because personally I don't mind much shavin' a dead person. They lay a whole lot stiller than live customers. The only thing is that you don't feel like talkin' to them and you get kind of lonesome.

Well, about the coldest day we ever had here, two years ago last winter, the phone rung at the house w'ile I was home to dinner and I answered the phone and it was a woman's voice and she said she was Mrs. John Scott and her husband was dead and would I come out and shave him.

Old John had always been a good customer of mine. But they live seven miles out in the country, on the Streeter road. Still I didn't see how I could say no.

So I said I would be there, but would have to come in a jitney and it might cost three or four dollars besides the price of the shave. So she, or the voice, it said that was all right, so I got Frank Abbott to drive me out to the place and when I got there, who should open the door but old John himself! He wasn't no more dead than, well, than a rabbit.

It didn't take no private detective to figure out who had played me this little joke. Nobody could of thought it up but Jim Kendall. He certainly was a card!

I tell you this incident just to show you how he could disguise his voice and make you believe it was somebody else talkin'. I'd of swore it was Mrs. Scott had called me. Anyways, some woman.

Well, Jim waited till he had Doc Stair's voice down pat; then he went after revenge.

He called Julie up on a night when he knew Doc was over in Carterville. She never questioned but what it was Doc's voice. Jim said he must see her that night; he couldn't wait no longer to tell her somethin'. She was all excited and told him to come to the house. But he said he was expectin' an important long distance call and wouldn't she please forget her manners for once and come to his office. He said they couldn't nothin' hurt her and nobody would see her and he just *must* talk to her a little w'ile. Well, poor Julie fell for it.

Doc always keeps a night light in his office, so it looked to Julie like they was somebody there.

Meanw'ile Jim Kendall had went to Wright's poolroom, where they was a whole gang amusin' themselves. The most of them had drank plenty of gin, and they was a rough bunch even when sober. They was always strong for Jim's jokes and when he told them to come with him and see some fun they give up their card games and pool games and followed along.

Doc's office is on the second floor. Right outside his door they's a flight of stairs leadin' to the floor above. Jim and his gang hid in the dark behind these stairs.

Well, Julie come up to Doc's door and rung the bell and they was nothin' doin'. She rung it again and she rung it seven or eight times. Then she tried the door and found it locked. Then Jim made some kind of a noise and she heard it and waited a minute, and then she says, " Is that you, Ralph? " Ralph is Doc's first name.

They was no answer and it must of came to her all of a sudden that she'd been bunked. She pretty near fell downstairs and the whole gang after her. They chased her all the way home, hollerin', " Is that you, Ralph? " and " Oh, Ralphie, dear, is that you? " Jim says he couldn't holler it himself, as he was laughin' too hard.

Poor Julie! She didn't show up here on Main Street for a long, long time afterward.

And of course Jim and his gang told everybody in town, everybody but Doc Stair. They was scared to tell him, and he might of never knowed only for Paul Dickson. The poor cuckoo, as Jim called him, he was here in the shop one night when Jim was still gloatin' yet over what he'd done to Julie. And Paul took in as much of it as he could understand and he run to Doc with the story.

It's a cinch Doc went up in the air and swore he'd make Jim suffer. But it was a kind of a delicate thing, because if it got out that he had beat Jim up, Julie was bound to hear of it and then she'd know that Doc knew and of course knowin' that he knew would make it worse for her than ever. He was goin' to do somethin', but it took a lot of figurin'.

Well, it was a couple days later when Jim was here in the shop again, and so was the cuckoo. Jim was goin' duck-shootin' the next day and had came in lookin' for Hod Meyers to go with him. I happened to know that Hod had went over to Carterville and wouldn't be home till the end of the week. So Jim said he hated to go alone and he guessed he would call it off. Then poor Paul spoke up and said if Jim would take him he would go along. Jim thought a w'ile and then he said, well, he guessed a half-wit was better than nothin'.

I suppose he was plottin' to get Paul out in the boat and play some joke on him, like pushin' him in the water. Anyways, he said Paul could go. He asked him had he ever shot a duck and Paul said no, he'd never even had a gun in his hands. So Jim said he could set in the boat and watch him and if he behaved himself, he might lend him his gun for a couple of shots. They made a date to meet in the mornin' and that's the last I seen of Jim alive.

Next mornin', I hadn't been open more than ten minutes when Doc Stair come in. He looked kind of nervous. He asked me had I seen Paul Dickson. I said no, but I knew where he was, out duck-shootin' with Jim Kendall. So Doc says that's what he had heard, and he couldn't understand it because Paul had told him he wouldn't never have no more to do with Jim as long as he lived.

He said Paul had told him about the joke Jim had played on Julie. He said Paul had asked him what he thought of the joke and the Doc had told him that anybody that would do a thing like that ought not to be let live.

I said it had been a kind of a raw thing, but Jim just couldn't resist no kind of a joke, no matter how raw. I said I thought he was all right at heart, but just bubblin' over with mischief. Doc turned and walked out.

At noon he got a phone call from old John Scott. The lake where Jim and Paul had went shootin' is on John's place. Paul had came runnin' up to the house a few minutes before and said they'd been an accident. Jim had shot a few ducks and then give the gun to Paul and told him to try his luck. Paul hadn't never handled a gun and he was nervous. He was shakin' so hard that he couldn't control the gun. He let fire and Jim sunk back in the boat, dead.

Doc Stair, bein' the coroner, jumped in Frank Abbott's flivver and rushed out to Scott's farm. Paul and old John was down on the shore of the lake. Paul had rowed the boat to shore, but they'd left the body in it, waitin' for Doc to come.

Doc examined the body and said they might as well fetch it back to town. They was no use leavin' it there or callin' a jury, as it was a plain case of accidental shootin'.

Personally I wouldn't never leave a person shoot a gun in the same boat I was in unless I was sure they knew somethin' about guns. Jim was a sucker to leave a new beginner have his gun, let alone a half-wit. It probably served Jim right, what he got. But still we miss him round here. He certainly was a card!

Comb it wet or dry?

IV

ALIBI IKE

I

His right name was Frank X. Farrell, and I guess the X stood for "Excuse me." Because he never pulled a play, good or bad, on or off the field, without apologizin' for it.

"Alibi Ike" was the name Carey wished on him the first day he reported down South. O' course we all cut out the "Alibi" part of it right away for the fear he would overhear it and bust somebody. But we called him "Ike" right to his face and the rest of it was understood by everybody on the club except Ike himself.

He ast me one time, he says:

"What do you all call me Ike for? I ain't no Yid."

"Carey give you the name," I says. "It's his nickname for everybody he takes a likin' to."

"He mustn't have only a few friends then," says Ike. "I never heard him say 'Ike' to nobody else."

But I was goin' to tell you about Carey namin' him. We'd been workin' out two weeks and the pitchers was showin' somethin' when this bird joined us. His first day out he stood up there so good and took such a reef at the old pill that he had everyone lookin'. Then him and Carey was together in left field, catchin' fungoes, and it was after we was through for the day that Carey told me about him.

"What do you think of Alibi Ike?" ast Carey.

"Who's that?" I says.

"This here Farrell in the outfield," says Carey.

"He looks like he could hit," I says.

"Yes," says Carey, "but he can't hit near as good as he can apologize."

Then Carey went on to tell me what Ike had been pullin' out there. He'd dropped the first fly ball that was hit to him and told Carey his glove wasn't broke in good yet, and Carey says the glove could easy of been Kid Gleason's gran'father. He made a whale of a catch out o' the next one and Carey says "Nice work!" or somethin' like that, but Ike says he could of caught the ball with his back turned only he slipped when he started after it and, besides that, the air currents fooled him.

"I thought you done well to get to the ball," says Carey.

"I ought to been settin' under it," says Ike.

"What did you hit last year?" Carey ast him.

"I had malaria most o' the season," says Ike. "I wound up with .356."

"Where would I have to go to get malaria?" says Carey, but Ike didn't wise up.

I and Carey and him set at the same table together for supper. It took him half an hour longer'n us to eat because he had to excuse himself every time he lifted his fork.

"Doctor told me I needed starch," he'd say, and then toss a shoveful o' potatoes into him. Or, "They ain't much meat on one o' these chops," he'd tell us, and grab another one. Or he'd say: "Nothin' like onions for a cold," and then he'd dip into the perfumery.

"Better try that apple sauce," says Carey. "It'll help your malaria."

"Whose malaria?" says Ike. He'd forgot already why he didn't only hit .356 last year.

I and Carey begin to lead him on.

"Whereabouts did you say your home was?" I ast him.

"I live with my folks," he says. "We live in Kansas City—not right down in the business part—outside a ways."

"How's that come?" says Carey. "I should think you'd get rooms in the post office."

But Ike was too busy curin' his cold to get that one.

"Are you married?" I ast him.

"No," he says. "I never run round much with girls, except to shows onct in a wile and parties and dances and roller skatin'."

"Never take 'em to the prize fights, eh?" says Carey.

"We don't have no real good bouts," says Ike. "Just bush stuff. And I never figured a boxin' match was a place for the ladies."

Well, after supper he pulled a cigar out and lit it. I was just goin' to ask him what he done it for, but he beat me to it.

"Kind o' rests a man to smoke after a good work-out," he says. "Kind o' settles a man's supper, too."

"Looks like a pretty good cigar," says Carey.

" Yes," says Ike. " A friend o' mine give it to me—a fella in Kansas City that runs a billiard room."

" Do you play billiards? " I ast him.

" I used to play a fair game," he says. " I'm all out o' practice now—can't hardly make a shot."

We coaxed him into a four-handed battle, him and Carey against Jack Mack and I. Say, he couldn't play billiards as good as Willie Hoppe; not quite. But to hear him tell it, he didn't make a good shot all evenin'. I'd leave him an awful-lookin' lay-out and he'd gather 'em up in one try and then run a couple o' hundred, and between every carom he'd say he'd put too much stuff on the ball, or the English didn't take, or the table wasn't true, or his stick was crooked, or somethin'. And all the time he had the balls actin' like they was Dutch soldiers and him Kaiser William. We started out to play fifty points, but we had to make it a thousand so as I and Jack and Carey could try the table.

The four of us set round the lobby a wile after we was through playin', and when it got along toward bedtime Carey whispered to me and says:

" Ike'd like to go to bed, but he can't think up no excuse."

Carey hadn't hardly finished whisperin' when Ike got up and pulled it:

" Well, good night, boys," he says. " I ain't sleepy, but I got some gravel in my shoes and it's killin' my feet."

We knowed he hadn't never left the hotel since we'd came in from the grounds and changed our clo'es. So Carey says:

" I should think they'd take them gravel pits out o' the billiard room."

But Ike was already on his way to the elevator, limpin'.

" He's got the world beat," says Carey to Jack and I. " I've knew lots o' guys that had an alibi for every mistake they made; I've heard pitchers say that the ball slipped when somebody cracked one off'n 'em; I've heard infielders complain of a sore arm after heavin' one into the stand, and I've saw outfielders tooken sick with a dizzy spell when they've misjudged a fly ball. But this baby can't even go to bed without apologizin', and I bet he excuses himself to the razor when he gets ready to shave."

" And at that," says Jack, " he's goin' to make us a good man."

" Yes," says Carey, "unless rheumatism keeps his battin' average down to .400."

Well, sir, Ike kept whalin' away at the ball all through the trip till everybody knowed he'd won a job. Cap had him in there regular the last few exhibition games and told the newspaper boys a week before the season opened that he was goin' to start him in Kane's place.

"You're there, kid," says Carey to Ike, the night Cap made the 'nnouncement. "They ain't many boys that wins a big league berth their third year out."

"I'd of been up here a year ago," says Ike, "only I was bent over all season with lumbago."

II

It rained down in Cincinnati one day and somebody organized a little game o' cards. They was shy two men to make six and ast I and Carey to play.

"I'm with you if you get Ike and make it seven-handed," says Carey.

So they got a hold of Ike and we went up to Smitty's room.

"I pretty near forgot how many you deal," says Ike. "It's been a long wile since I played."

I and Carey give each other the wink, and sure enough, he was just as ig'orant about poker as billiards. About the second hand, the pot was opened two or three ahead of him, and they was three in when it come his turn. It cost a buck, and he throwed in two.

"It's raised, boys," somebody says.

"Gosh, that's right, I did raise it," says Ike.

"Take out a buck if you didn't mean to tilt her," says Carey.

"No," says Ike, "I'll leave it go."

Well, it was raised back at him and then he made another mistake and raised again. They was only three left in when the draw come. Smitty'd opened with a pair o' kings and he didn't help 'em. Ike stood pat. The guy that'd raised him back was flushin' and he didn't fill. So Smitty checked and Ike bet and didn't get no call. He tossed his hand away, but I grabbed it and give it a look. He had king, queen, jack and two tens. Alibi Ike he must have seen me peekin', for he leaned over and whispered to me.

"I overlooked my hand," he says. "I thought all the wile it was a straight."

"Yes," I says, "that's why you raised twice by mistake."

They was another pot that he come into with tens and fours. It was tilted a couple o' times and two o' the strong fellas drawed ahead of Ike. They each drawed one. So Ike throwed away his little pair and come out with four tens. And they was four treys against him. Carey'd looked at Ike's discards and then he says:

"This lucky bum busted two pair."

"No, no, I didn't," says Ike.

"Yes, yes, you did," says Carey, and showed us the two fours.

"What do you know about that?" says Ike. "I'd of swore one was a five spot."

Well, we hadn't had no pay day yet, and after a wile everybody except Ike was goin' shy. I could see him gettin' restless and I was wonderin' how he'd make the get-away. He tried two or three times. "I got to buy some collars before supper," he says.

"No hurry," says Smitty. "The stores here keeps open all night in April."

After a minute he opened up again.

"My uncle out in Nebraska ain't expected to live," he says. "I ought to send a telegram."

"Would that save him?" says Carey.

"No, it sure wouldn't," says Ike, "but I ought to leave my old man know where I'm at."

"When did you hear about your uncle?" says Carey.

"Just this mornin'," says Ike.

"Who told you?" ast Carey.

"I got a wire from my old man," says Ike.

"Well," says Carey, "your old man knows you're still here yet this afternoon if you was here this mornin'. Trains leavin' Cincinnati in the middle o' the day don't carry no ball clubs."

"Yes," says Ike, "that's true. But he don't know where I'm goin' to be next week."

"Ain't he got no schedule?" ast Carey.

"I sent him one openin' day," says Ike, "but it takes mail a long time to get to Idaho."

"I thought your old man lived in Kansas City," says Carey.

"He does when he's home," says Ike.

"But now," says Carey, "I s'pose he's went to Idaho so as he can be near your sick uncle in Nebraska."

"He's visitin' my other uncle in Idaho."

"Then how does he keep posted about your sick uncle?" ast Carey.

"He don't," says Ike. "He don't even know my other uncle's sick. That's why I ought to wire and tell him."

"Good night!" says Carey.

"What town in Idaho is your old man at?" I says.

Ike thought it over.

" No town at all," he says. " But he's near a town."

" Near what town? " I says.

" Yuma," says Ike.

Well, by this time he'd lost two or three pots and he was desperate. We was playin' just as fast as we could, because we seen we couldn't hold him much longer. But he was tryin' so hard to frame an escape that he couldn't pay no attention to the cards, and it looked like we'd get his whole pile away from him if we could make him stick.

The telephone saved him. The minute it begun to ring, five of us jumped for it. But Ike was there first.

" Yes," he says, answerin' it. " This is him. I'll come right down."

And he slammed up the receiver and beat it out o' the door without even sayin' good-by.

" Smitty'd ought to locked the door," says Carey.

" What did he win? " ast Carey.

We figured it up—sixty-odd bucks.

" And the next time we ask him to play," says Carey, " his fingers will be so stiff he can't hold the cards."

Well, we set round a wile talkin' it over, and pretty soon the telephone rung again. Smitty answered it. It was a friend of his'n from Hamilton and he wanted to know why Smitty didn't hurry down. He was the one that had called before and Ike had told him he was Smitty.

" Ike'd ought to split with Smitty's friend," says Carey.

" No," I says, " he'll need all he won. It costs money to buy collars and to send telegrams from Cincinnati to your old man in Texas and keep him posted on the health o' your uncle in Cedar Rapids, D. C."

III

And you ought to heard him out there on that field! They wasn't a day when he didn't pull six or seven, and it didn't make no difference whether he was goin' good or bad. If he popped up in the pinch he should of made a base hit and the reason he didn't was so-and-so. And if he cracked one for three bases he ought to had a home run, only the ball wasn't lively, or the wind brought it back, or he tripped on a lump o' dirt, roundin' first base.

They was one afternoon in New York when he beat all records. Big Marquard was workin' against us and he was good.

In the first innin' Ike hit one clear over that right field stand, but it was a few feet foul. Then he got another foul and then the count come to two and two. Then Rube slipped one acrost on him and he was called out.

"What do you know about that!" he says afterward on the bench. "I lost count. I thought it was three and one, and I took a strike."

"You took a strike all right," says Carey. "Even the umps knowed it was a strike."

"Yes," says Ike, "but you can bet I wouldn't of took it if I'd knew it was the third one. The score board had it wrong."

"That score board ain't for you to look at," says Cap. "It's for you to hit that old pill against."

"Well," says Ike, "I could of hit that one over the score board if I'd knew it was the third."

"Was it a good ball?" I says.

"Well, no, it wasn't," says Ike. "It was inside."

"How far inside?" says Carey.

"Oh, two or three inches or half a foot," says Ike.

"I guess you wouldn't of threatened the score board with it then," says Cap.

"I'd of pulled it down the right foul line if I hadn't thought he'd call it a ball," says Ike.

Well, in New York's part o' the innin' Doyle cracked one and Ike run back a mile and a half and caught it with one hand. We was all sayin' what a whale of a play it was, but he had to apologize just the same as for gettin' struck out.

"That stand's so high," he says, "that a man don't never see a ball till it's right on top o' you."

"Didn't you see that one?" ast Cap.

"Not at first," says Ike; "not till it raised up above the roof o' the stand."

"Then why did you start back as soon as the ball was hit?" says Cap.

"I knowed by the sound that he'd got a good hold of it," says Ike.

"Yes," says Cap, "but how'd you know what direction to run in?"

"Doyle usually hits 'em that way, the way I run," says Ike.

"Why don't you play blindfolded?" says Carey.

"Might as well, with that big high stand to bother a man," says

Ike. "If I could of saw the ball all the time I'd of got it in my hip pocket."

Along in the fifth we was one run to the bad and Ike got on with one out. On the first ball throwed to Smitty, Ike went down. The ball was outside and Meyers throwed Ike out by ten feet.

You could see Ike's lips movin' all the way to the bench and when he got there he had his piece learned.

"Why didn't he swing?" he says.

"Why didn't you wait for his sign?" says Cap.

"He give me his sign," says Ike.

"What is his sign with you?" says Cap.

"Pickin' up some dirt with his right hand," says Ike.

"Well, I didn't see him do it," Cap says.

"He done it all right," says Ike.

Well, Smitty went out and they wasn't no more argument till they come in for the next innin'. Then Cap opened it up.

"You fellas better get your signs straight," he says.

"Do you mean me?" says Smitty.

"Yes," Cap says. "What's your sign with Ike?"

"Slidin' my left hand up to the end o' the bat and back," says Smitty.

"Do you hear that, Ike?" ast Cap.

"What of it?" says Ike.

"You says his sign was pickin' up dirt and he says it's slidin' his hand. Which is right?"

"I'm right," says Smitty. "But if you're arguin' about him goin' last innin', I didn't give him no sign."

"You pulled your cap down with your right hand, didn't you?" ast Ike.

"Well, s'pose I did," says Smitty. "That don't mean nothin'. I never told you to take that for a sign, did I?"

"I thought maybe you meant to tell me and forgot," says Ike.

They couldn't none of us answer that and they wouldn't of been no more said if Ike had of shut up. But wile we was settin' there Carey got on with two out and stole second clean.

"There!" says Ike. "That's what I was tryin' to do and I'd of got away with it if Smitty'd swang and bothered the Indian."

"Oh!" says Smitty. "You was tryin' to steal then, was you? I thought you claimed I give you the hit and run."

"I didn't claim no such a thing," says Ike. "I thought maybe you might of gave me a sign, but I was goin' anyway because I thought I had a good start."

Cap prob'ly would of hit him with a bat, only just about that time Doyle booted one on Hayes and Carey come acrost with the run that tied.

Well, we go into the ninth finally, one and one, and Marquard walks McDonald with nobody out.

"Lay it down," says Cap to Ike.

And Ike goes up there with orders to bunt and cracks the first ball into that right-field stand! It was fair this time, and we're two ahead, but I didn't think about that at the time. I was too busy watchin' Cap's face. First he turned pale and then he got red as fire and then he got blue and purple, and finally he just laid back and busted out laughin'. So we wasn't afraid to laugh our-selfs when we seen him doin' it, and when Ike come in everybody on the bench was in hysterics.

But instead o' takin' advantage, Ike had to try and excuse him-self. His play was to shut up and he didn't know how to make it.

"Well," he says, "if I hadn't hit quite so quick at that one I bet it'd of cleared the center-field fence."

Cap stopped laughin'.

"It'll cost you plain fifty," he says.

"What for?" says Ike.

"When I say 'bunt' I mean 'bunt,'" says Cap.

"You didn't say 'bunt,'" says Ike.

"I says 'Lay it down,'" says Cap. "If that don't mean 'bunt,' what does it mean?"

"'Lay it down' means 'bunt' all right," says Ike, "but I un-derstood you to say 'Lay on it.'"

"All right," says Cap, "and the little misunderstandin' will cost you fifty."

Ike didn't say nothin' for a few minutes. Then he had another bright idear.

"I was just kiddin' about misunderstandin' you," he says. "I knowed you wanted me to bunt."

"Well, then, why didn't you bunt?" ast Cap.

"I was goin' to on the next ball," says Ike. "But I thought if I took a good wallop I'd have 'em all fooled. So I walloped at the first one to fool 'em, and I didn't have no intention o' hittin' it."

"You tried to miss it, did you?" says Cap.

"Yes," says Ike.

"How'd you happen to hit it?" ast Cap.

"Well," Ike says, "I was lookin' for him to throw me a fast one and I was goin' to swing under it. But he come with a hook and I met it right square where I was swingin' to go under the fast one."

"Great!" says Cap. "Boys," he says, "Ike's learned how to hit Marquard's curve. Pretend a fast one's comin' and then try to miss it. It's a good thing to know and Ike'd ought to be willin' to pay for the lesson. So I'm goin' to make it a hundred instead o' fifty."

The game wound up 3 to 1. The fine didn't go, because Ike hit like a wild man all through that trip and we made pretty near a clean-up. The night we went to Philly I got him cornered in the car and I says to him:

"Forget them alibis for a wile and tell me somethin'. What'd you do that for, swing that time against Marquard when you was told to bunt?"

"I'll tell you," he says. "That ball he throwed me looked just like the one I struck out on in the first innin' and I wanted to show Cap what I could of done to that other one if I'd knew it was the third strike."

"But," I says, "the one you struck out on in the first innin' was a fast ball."

"So was the one I cracked in the ninth," says Ike.

IV

You've saw Cap's wife, o' course. Well, her sister's about twict as good-lookin' as her, and that's goin' some.

Cap took his missus down to St. Louis the second trip and the other one come down from St. Joe to visit her. Her name is Dolly, and some doll is right.

Well, Cap was goin' to take the two sisters to a show and he wanted a beau for Dolly. He left it to her and she picked Ike. He'd hit three on the nose that afternoon—off'n Sallee, too.

They fell for each other that first evenin'. Cap told us how it come off. She begin flatterin' Ike for the star game he'd played and o' course he begin excusin' himself for not doin' better. So she thought he was modest and it went strong with her. And she believed everything he said and that made her solid with him— that and her make-up. They was together every mornin' and eve- nin' for the five days we was there. In the afternoons Ike played the grandest ball you ever see, hittin' and runnin' the bases like a fool and catchin' everything that stayed in the park.

I told Cap, I says: " You'd ought to keep the doll with us and he'd make Cobb's figures look sick."

But Dolly had to go back to St. Joe and we come home for a long serious.

Well, for the next three weeks Ike had a letter to read every day and he'd set in the clubhouse readin' it till mornin' practice was half over. Cap didn't say nothin' to him, because he was goin' so good. But I and Carey wasted a lot of our time tryin' to get him to own up who the letters was from. Fine chanct!

" What are you readin'? " Carey'd say. " A bill? "

" No," Ike'd say, " not exactly a bill. It's a letter from a fella I used to go to school with."

" High school or college? " I'd ask him.

" College," he'd say.

" What college? " I'd say.

Then he'd stall a wile and then he'd say:

" I didn't go to the college myself, but my friend went there."

" How did it happen you didn't go? " Carey'd ask him.

" Well," he'd say, " they wasn't no colleges near where I lived."

" Didn't you live in Kansas City? " I'd say to him.

One time he'd say he did and another time he didn't. One time he says he lived in Michigan.

" Where at? " says Carey.

" Near Detroit," he says.

" Well," I says, " Detroit's near Ann Arbor and that's where they got the university."

" Yes," says Ike, " they got it there now, but they didn't have it there then."

" I come pretty near goin' to Syracuse," I says, " only they wasn't no railroads runnin' through there in them days."

" Where'd this friend o' yours go to college? " says Carey.

" I forget now," says Ike.

" Was it Carlisle? " ast Carey.

" No," says Ike, " his folks wasn't very well off."

" That's what barred me from Smith," I says.

" I was goin' to tackle Cornell's," says Carey, " but the doctor told me I'd have hay fever if I didn't stay up North."

" Your friend writes long letters," I says.

" Yes," says Ike; " he's tellin' me about a ball player."

" Where does he play? " ast Carey.

" Down in the Texas League—Fort Wayne," says Ike.

" It looks like a girl's writin'," Carey says.

" A girl wrote it," says Ike. " That's my friend's sister, writin' for him."

" Didn't they teach writin' at this here college where he went? " says Carey.

" Sure," Ike says, " they taught writin', but he got his hand cut off in a railroad wreck."

" How long ago? " I says.

" Right after he got out o' college," says Ike.

" Well," I says, " I should think he'd of learned to write with his left hand by this time."

" It's his left hand that was cut off," says Ike; " and he was left-handed."

" You get a letter every day," says Carey. " They're all the same writin'. Is he tellin' you about a different ball player every time he writes? "

" No," Ike says. " It's the same ball player. He just tells me what he does every day."

" From the size o' the letters, they don't play nothin' but double-headers down there," says Carey.

We figured that Ike spent most of his evenin's answerin' the letters from his " friend's sister," so we kept tryin' to date him up for shows and parties to see how he'd duck out of 'em. He was bugs over spaghetti, so we told him one day that they was goin' to be a big feed of it over to Joe's that night and he was invited.

" How long'll it last? " he says.

" Well," we says, " we're goin' right over there after the game and stay till they close up."

" I can't go," he says, " unless they leave me come home at eight bells."

" Nothin' doin'," says Carey. " Joe'd get sore."

" I can't go then," says Ike.

" Why not? " I ast him.

" Well," he says, " my landlady locks up the house at eight and I left my key home."

" You can come and stay with me," says Carey.

" No," he says, " I can't sleep in a strange bed."

" How do you get along when we're on the road? " says I.

" I don't never sleep the first night anywheres," he says. " After that I'm all right."

" You'll have time to chase home and get your key right after the game," I told him.

" The key ain't home," says Ike. " I lent it to one o' the other fellas and he's went out o' town and took it with him."

" Couldn't you borry another key off'n the landlady? " Carey ast him.

" No," he says, " that's the only one they is."

Well, the day before we started East again, Ike come into the clubhouse all smiles.

" Your birthday? " I ast him.

" No," he says.

" What do you feel so good about? " I says.

" Got a letter from my old man," he says. " My uncle's goin' to get well."

" Is that the one in Nebraska? " says I.

" Not right in Nebraska," says Ike. " Near there."

But afterwards we got the right dope from Cap. Dolly'd blew in from Missouri and was goin' to make the trip with her sister.

V

Well, I want to alibi Carey and I for what come off in Boston. If we'd of had any idear what we was doin', we'd never did it. They wasn't nobody outside o' maybe Ike and the dame that felt worse over it than I and Carey.

The first two days we didn't see nothin' of Ike and her except out to the park. The rest o' the time they was sight-seein' over to Cambridge and down to Revere and out to Brook-a-line and all the other places where the rubes go.

But when we come into the beanery after the third game Cap's wife called us over.

" If you want to see somethin' pretty," she says, " look at the third finger on Sis's left hand."

Well, o' course we knowed before we looked that it wasn't goin' to be no hangnail. Nobody was su'prised when Dolly blew into the dinin' room with it—a rock that Ike'd bought off'n Diamond Joe the first trip to New York. Only o' course it'd been set into a lady's-size ring instead o' the automobile tire he'd been wearin'.

Cap and his missus and Ike and Dolly ett supper together, only Ike didn't eat nothin', but just set there blushin' and spillin' things on the table-cloth. I heard him excusin' himself for not havin' no appetite. He says he couldn't never eat when he was clost to the ocean. He'd forgot about them sixty-five oysters he destroyed the first night o' the trip before.

He was goin' to take her to a show, so after supper he went upstairs to change his collar. She had to doll up, too, and o' course Ike was through long before her.

If you remember the hotel in Boston, they's a little parlor where the piano's at and then they's another little parlor openin' off o' that. Well, when Ike come down Smitty was playin' a few chords and I and Carey was harmonizin'. We seen Ike go up to the desk to leave his key and we called him in. He tried to duck away, but we wouldn't stand for it.

We ast him what he was all duded up for and he says he was goin' to the theayter.

" Goin' alone ? " says Carey.

" No," he says, " a friend o' mine's goin' with me."

" What do you say if we go along ? " says Carey.

" I ain't only got two tickets," he says.

" Well," says Carey, " we can go down there with you and buy our own seats; maybe we can all get together."

" No," says Ike. " They ain't no more seats. They're all sold out."

" We can buy some off'n the scalpers," says Carey.

" I wouldn't if I was you," says Ike. " They say the show's rotten."

" What are you goin' for, then ? " I ast.

" I didn't hear about it bein' rotten till I got the tickets," he says.

" Well," I says, " if you don't want to go I'll buy the tickets from you."

" No," says Ike, " I wouldn't want to cheat you. I'm stung and I'll just have to stand for it."

" What are you goin' to do with the girl, leave her here at the hotel ? " I says.

" What girl ? " says Ike.

" The girl you ett supper with," I says.

" Oh," he says, " we just happened to go into the dinin' room together, that's all. Cap wanted I should set down with 'em."

" I noticed," says Carey, " that she happened to be wearin' that rock you bought off'n Diamond Joe."

" Yes," says Ike. " I lent it to her for a wile."

" Did you lend her the new ring that goes with it ? " I says.

" She had that already," says Ike. " She lost the set out of it."

" I wouldn't trust no strange girl with a rock o' mine," says Carey.

" Oh, I guess she's all right," Ike says. " Besides, I was tired o' the stone. When a girl asks you for somethin', what are you goin' to do? "

He started out toward the desk, but we flagged him.

" Wait a minute! " Carey says. " I got a bet with Sam here, and it's up to you to settle it."

" Well," says Ike, " make it snappy. My friend'll be here any minute."

" I bet," says Carey, " that you and that girl was engaged to be married."

" Nothin' to it," says Ike.

" Now look here," says Carey, " this is goin' to cost me real money if I lose. Cut out the alibi stuff and give it to us straight. Cap's wife just as good as told us you was roped."

Ike blushed like a kid.

" Well, boys," he says, " I may as well own up. You win, Carey."

" Yatta boy! " says Carey. " Congratulations! "

" You got a swell girl, Ike," I says.

" She's a peach," says Smitty.

" Well, I guess she's O. K.," says Ike. " I don't know much about girls."

" Didn't you never run round with 'em? " I says.

" Oh, yes, plenty of 'em," says Ike. " But I never seen none I'd fall for."

" That is, till you seen this one," says Carey.

" Well," says Ike, " this one's O. K., but I wasn't thinkin' about gettin' married yet a wile."

" Who done the askin'—her? " says Carey.

" Oh, no," says Ike, " but sometimes a man don't know what he's gettin' into. Take a good-lookin' girl, and a man gen'ally almost always does about what she wants him to."

" They couldn't no girl lasso me unless I wanted to be lassoed," says Smitty.

" Oh, I don't know," says Ike. " When a fella gets to feelin' sorry for one of 'em it's all off."

Well, we left him go after shakin' hands all round. But he didn't take Dolly to no show that night. Some time wile we was talkin' she'd came into that other parlor and she'd stood there and heard us. I don't know how much she heard. But it was enough. Dolly and Cap's missus took the midnight train for New York. And from there Cap's wife sent her on her way back to Missouri.

She'd left the ring and a note for Ike with the clerk. But we didn't ask Ike if the note was from his friend in Fort Wayne, Texas.

VI

When we'd came to Boston Ike was hittin' plain .397. When we got back home he'd fell off to pretty near nothin'. He hadn't drove one out o' the infield in any o' them other Eastern parks, and he didn't even give no excuse for it.

To show you how bad he was, he struck out three times in Brooklyn one day and never opened his trap when Cap ast him what was the matter. Before, if he'd whiffed oncet in a game he'd of wrote a book tellin' why.

Well, we dropped from first place to fifth in four weeks and we was still goin' down. I and Carey was about the only ones in the club that spoke to each other, and all as we did was remind ourself o' what a boner we'd pulled.

"It's goin' to beat us out o' the big money," says Carey.

"Yes," I says. "I don't want to knock my own ball club, but it looks like a one-man team, and when that one man's dauber's down we couldn't trim our whiskers."

"We ought to knew better," says Carey.

"Yes," I says, "but why should a man pull an alibi for bein' engaged to such a bearcat as she was?"

"He shouldn't," says Carey. "But I and you knowed he would or we'd never started talkin' to him about it. He wasn't no more ashamed o' the girl than I am of a regular base hit. But he just can't come clean on no subjec'."

Cap had the whole story, and I and Carey was as pop'lar with him as an umpire.

"What do you want me to do, Cap?" Carey'd say to him before goin' up to hit.

"Use your own judgment," Cap'd tell him. "We want to lose another game."

But finally, one night in Pittsburgh, Cap had a letter from his missus and he come to us with it.

"You fellas," he says, "is the ones that put us on the bum, and if you're sorry I think they's a chancet for you to make good. The old lady's out to St. Joe and she's been tryin' her hardest to fix things up. She's explained that Ike don't mean nothin' with his talk; I've wrote and explained that to Dolly, too. But the old lady says that Dolly says that she can't believe it. But Dolly's still stuck on this baby, and she's pinin' away just the same as Ike. And the old lady says she thinks if you two fellas would write to the girl and explain how you was always kiddin' with Ike and leadin' him on, and how the ball club was all shot to pieces since Ike quit hittin', and how he acted like he was goin' to kill himself, and this and that, she'd fall for it and maybe soften down. Dolly, the old lady says, would believe you before she'd believe I and the old lady, because she thinks it's her we're sorry for, and not him."

Well, I and Carey was only too glad to try and see what we could do. But it wasn't no snap. We wrote about eight letters before we got one that looked good. Then we give it to the stenographer and had it wrote out on a typewriter and both of us signed it.

It was Carey's idear that made the letter good. He stuck in somethin' about the world's serious money that our wives wasn't goin' to spend unless she took pity on a " boy who was so shy and modest that he was afraid to come right out and say that he had asked such a beautiful and handsome girl to become his bride."

That's prob'ly what got her, or maybe she couldn't of held out much longer anyway. It was four days after we sent the letter that Cap heard from his missus again. We was in Cincinnati.

" We've won," he says to us. " The old lady says that Dolly says she'll give him another chance. But the old lady says it won't do no good for Ike to write a letter. He'll have to go out there."

" Send him to-night," says Carey.

" I'll pay half his fare," I says.

" I'll pay the other half," says Carey.

" No," says Cap, " the club'll pay his expenses. I'll send him scoutin'."

" Are you goin' to send him to-night? "

" Sure," says Cap. " But I'm goin' to break the news to him right now. It's time we win a ball game."

So in the clubhouse, just before the game, Cap told him. And I certainly felt sorry for Rube Benton and Red Ames that afternoon! I and Carey was standin' in front o' the hotel that night when Ike come out with his suitcase.

" Sent home? " I says to him.

" No," he says, " I'm goin' scoutin'."

" Where to? " I says. " Fort Wayne? "

" No, not exactly," he says.

" Well," says Carey, " have a good time."

"I ain't lookin' for no good time," says Ike. "I says I was goin' scoutin'."

"Well, then," says Carey, "I hope you see somebody you like."

"And you better have a drink before you go," I says.

"Well," says Ike, "they claim it helps a cold."

V

LIBERTY HALL

My husband is in Atlantic City, where they are trying out "Dear Dora," the musical version of "David Copperfield." My husband wrote the score. He used to take me along for these out-of-town openings, but not any more.

He, of course, has to spend almost all his time in the theater and that leaves me alone in the hotel, and pretty soon people find out whose wife I am and introduce themselves, and the next thing you know they are inviting us for a week or a weekend at Dobbs Ferry or Oyster Bay. Then it is up to me to think of some legitimate-sounding reason why we can't come.

In lots of cases they say, "Well, if you can't make it the twenty-second, how about the twenty-ninth?" and so on till you simply have to accept. And Ben gets mad and stays mad for days.

He absolutely abhors visiting and thinks there ought to be a law against invitations that go beyond dinner and bridge. He doesn't mind hotels where there is a decent light for reading in bed and one for shaving, and where you can order meals, with coffee, any time you want them. But I really believe he would rather spend a week in the death house at Sing Sing than in somebody else's home.

Three or four years ago we went around quite a lot with a couple whom I will call the Buckleys. We liked them and they liked us. We had dinner together at least twice a week and after dinner we played bridge or went to a show or just sat and talked.

Ben never turned down their invitations and often actually called them up himself and suggested parties. Finally they moved to Albany on account of Mr. Buckley's business. We missed them a great deal, and when Mrs. Buckley wrote for us to come up there for the holidays we were tickled pink.

Well, their guest-room was terribly cold; it took hours to fill the bathtub; there was no reading-lamp by the bed; three reporters called to interview Ben, two of them kittenish young girls; the breakfasts were just fruit and cereal and toast; coffee was not served at luncheon; the faucets in the wash-basin were the kind that won't run unless you keep pressing them; four important keys on the piano were stuck and people were invited in every

53

night to hear Ben play, and the Buckley family had been augmented by a tremendous police dog, who was "just a puppy and never growled or snapped at anyone he knew," but couldn't seem to remember that Ben was not an utter stranger.

On the fourth awful day Ben gave out the news—news to him and to me as well as to our host and hostess—that he had lost a filling which he would not trust any but his own New York dentist to replace. We came home and we have never seen the Buckleys since. If we do see them it will be an accident. They will hardly ask us there unless we ask them here, and we won't ask them here for fear they would ask us there. And they were honestly the most congenial people we ever met.

It was after our visit to the Craigs at Stamford that Ben originated what he calls his "emergency exit." We had such a horrible time at the Craigs' and such a worse time getting away that Ben swore he would pay no more visits until he could think up a graceful method of curtailing them in the event they proved unbearable.

Here is the scheme he hit on: He would write himself a telegram and sign it with the name Ziegfeld or Gene Buck or Dillingham or George M. Cohan. The telegram would say that he must return to New York at once, and it would give a reason. Then, the day we started out, he would leave it with Irene, the girl at Harms', his publishers, with instructions to have it sent to him twenty-four hours later.

When it arrived at whatever town we were in, he would either have the host or hostess take it over the telephone or ask the telegraph company to deliver it so he could show it around. We would put on long faces and say how sorry we were, but of course business was business, so good-by and so forth. There was never a breath of suspicion even when the telegram was ridiculous, like the one Ben had sent to himself at Spring Lake, where we were staying with the Marshalls just after "Betty's Birthday" opened at the Globe. The Marshalls loved musical shows, but knew less than nothing about music and swallowed this one whole:

Shaw and Miss Miller both suffering from laryngitis Stop Entire score must be rewritten half tone lower Stop Come at once Stop.

C. B. Dillingham.

If, miraculously, Ben had ever happened to be enjoying himself, he would, of course, have kept the contents of his message a secret or else displayed it and remarked swaggeringly that he guessed he wasn't going to let any so-and-so theatrical producer spoil his fun.

Ben is in Atlantic City now and I have read every book in the house and am writing this just because there doesn't seem to be anything else to do. And also because we have a friend, Joe Frazier, who is a magazine editor and the other day I told him I would like to try my hand at a short story, but I was terrible at plots, and he said plots weren't essential; look at Ernest Hemingway; most of his stories have hardly any plot; it's his style that counts. And he—I mean Mr. Frazier—suggested that I write about our visit to Mr. and Mrs. Thayer in Lansdowne, outside of Philadelphia, which Mr. Frazier said, might be termed the visit that ended visits and which is the principal reason why I am here alone.

Well, it was a beautiful night a year ago last September. Ben was conducting the performance—" Step Lively "—and I was standing at the railing of the Boardwalk in front of the theater, watching the moonlight on the ocean. A couple whom I had noticed in the hotel dining-room stopped alongside of me and pretty soon the woman spoke to me, something about how pretty it was. Then came the old question, wasn't I Mrs. Ben Drake? I said I was, and the woman went on:

" My name is Mrs. Thayer—Hilda Thayer. And this is my husband. We are both simply crazy about Mr. Drake's music and just dying to meet him personally. We wondered if you and he would have supper with us after the performance tonight."

" Oh, I'm afraid that's impossible," I replied. " You see when they are having a tryout, he and the librettists and the lyric writers work all night every night until they get everything in shape for the New York opening. They never have time for more than a sandwich and they eat that right in the theater."

" Well, how about luncheon tomorrow? "

" He'll be rehearsing all day."

" How about dinner tomorrow evening? "

" Honestly, Mrs. Thayer, it's out of the question. Mr. Drake never makes engagements during a tryout week."

" And I guess he doesn't want to meet us anyway," put in Mr. Thayer. " What use would a genius like Ben Drake have for a couple of common-no-account admirers like Mrs. Thayer and myself! If we were ' somebody ' too, it would be different! "

"Not at all!" said I. "Mr. Drake is perfectly human. He loves to have his music praised and I am sure he would be delighted to meet you if he weren't so terribly busy."

"Can you lunch with us yourself?"

"Tomorrow?"

"Any day."

Well, whatever Ben and other husbands may think, there is no decent way of turning down an invitation like that. And besides I was lonesome and the Thayers looked like awfully nice people.

I lunched with them and I dined with them, not only the next day but all the rest of the week. And on Friday I got Ben to lunch with them and he liked them, too; they were not half as gushing and silly as most of his "fans."

At dinner on Saturday night, they cross-examined me about our immediate plans. I told them that as soon as the show was "over" in New York, I was going to try to make Ben stay home and do nothing for a whole month.

"I should think," said Mrs. Thayer, "it would be very hard for him to rest there in the city, with the producers and publishers and phonograph people calling him up all the time."

I admitted that he was bothered a lot.

"Listen, dearie," said Mrs. Thayer. "Why don't you come to Landsdowne and spend a week with us? I'll promise you faithfully that you won't be disturbed at all. I won't let anyone know you are there and if any of our friends call on us I'll pretend we're not at home. I won't allow Mr. Drake to even touch the piano. If he wants exercise, there are miles of room in our yard to walk around in, and nobody can see him from the street. All day and all night, he can do nothing or anything, just as he pleases. It will be 'Liberty Hall' for you both. He needn't tell anybody where he is, but if some of his friends or business acquaintances find out and try to get in touch with him, I'll frighten them away. How does that sound?"

"It sounds wonderful," I said, "but——"

"It's settled then," said Mrs. Thayer, "and we'll expect you on Sunday, October eleventh."

"Oh, but the show may not be 'set' by that time," I remonstrated.

"How about the eighteenth?" said Mr. Thayer.

Well, it ended by my accepting for the week of the twenty-fifth and Ben took it quite cheerfully.

"If they stick to their promise to keep us under cover," he said, "it may be a lot better than staying in New York. I know that Buck and the Shuberts and Ziegfeld want me while I'm 'hot' and they wouldn't give me a minute's peace if they could find me. And of course if things aren't as good as they look, Irene's telegram will provide us with an easy out."

On the way over to Philadelphia he hummed me an awfully pretty melody which had been running through his head since we left the apartment. " I think it's sure fire," he said. " I'm crazy to get to a piano and fool with it."

" That isn't resting, dear."

" Well, you don't want me to throw away a perfectly good tune ! They aren't so plentiful that I can afford to waste one. It won't take me five minutes at a piano to get it fixed in my mind."

The Thayers met us in an expensive-looking limousine.

" Ralph," said Mrs. Thayer to her husband, " you sit in one of the little seats and Mr. and Mrs. Drake will sit back here with me."

" I'd really prefer one of the little seats myself," said Ben and he meant it, for he hates to get his clothes mussed and being squeezed in beside two such substantial objects as our hostess and myself was bound to rumple him.

" No, sir ! " said Mrs. Thayer positively. " You came to us for a rest and we're not going to start you off uncomfortable."

" But I'd honestly rather——"

It was no use. Ben was wedged between us and throughout the drive maintained a morose silence, unable to think of anything but how terrible his coat would look when he got out.

The Thayers had a very pretty home and the room assigned to us was close to perfection. There were comfortable twin beds with a small stand and convenient reading-lamp between; a big dresser and chiffonier; an ample closet with plenty of hangers; a bathroom with hot water that was hot, towels that were not too new and faucets that stayed on when turned on, and an ash-tray within reach of wherever you happened to be. If only we could have spent all our time in that guest-room, it would have been ideal.

But presently we were summoned downstairs to luncheon. I had warned Mrs. Thayer in advance and Ben was served with coffee. He drinks it black.

" Don't you take cream, Mr. Drake ? "

" No. Never."

" But that's because you don't get good cream in New York."

" No. It's because I don't like cream in coffee."

" You would like our cream. We have our own cows and the cream is so rich that it's almost like butter. Won't you try just a little? "

" No, thanks."

" But just a little, to see how rich it is."

She poured about a tablespoonful of cream into his coffee-cup and for a second I was afraid he was going to pick up the cup and throw it in her face. But he kept hold of himself, forced a smile and declined a second chop.

" You haven't tasted your coffee," said Mrs. Thayer.

" Yes, I have," lied Ben. " The cream is wonderful. I'm sorry it doesn't agree with me."

" I don't believe coffee agrees with anyone," said Mrs. Thayer. " While you are here, not doing any work, why don't you try to give it up? "

" I'd be so irritable you wouldn't have me in the house. Besides, it isn't plain coffee that disagrees with me; it's coffee with cream.'

" Pure, rich cream like ours couldn't hurt you," said Mrs. Thayer, and Ben, defeated, refused to answer.

He started to light a Jaguar cigaret, the brand he had been smoking for years.

" Here! Wait a minute! " said Mr. Thayer. " Try one of mine."

" What are they? " asked Ben.

" Trumps," said our host, holding out his case. " They're mild and won't irritate the throat."

" I'll sample one later," said Ben.

" You've simply got to try one now," said Mrs. Thayer. " You may as well get used to them because you'll have to smoke them all the time you're here. We can't have guests providing their own cigarets." So Ben had to discard his Jaguar and smoke a Trump, and it was even worse than he had anticipated.

After luncheon we adjourned to the living-room and Ben went straight to the piano.

" Here! Here! None of that! " said Mrs. Thayer. "I haven't forgotten my promise."

" What promise? " asked Ben.

" Didn't your wife tell you? I promised her faithfully that if you visited us, you wouldn't be allowed to touch the piano."

" But I want to," said Ben. " There's a melody in my head that I'd like to try."

"Oh, yes, I know all about that," said Mrs. Thayer. "You just think you've got to entertain us! Nothing doing! We invited you here for yourself, not to enjoy your talent. I'd be a fine one to ask you to my home for a rest and then make you perform."

"You're not making me," said Ben. "Honestly I want to play for just five or ten minutes. I've got a tune that I might do something with and I'm anxious to run it over."

"I don't believe you, you naughty man!" said our hostess. "Your wife has told you how wild we are about your music and you're determined to be nice to us. But I'm just as stubborn as you are. Not one note do you play as long as you're our guest!"

Ben favored me with a stricken look, mumbled something about unpacking his suitcase—it was already unpacked—and went up to our room, where he stayed nearly an hour, jotting down his new tune, smoking Jaguar after Jaguar and wishing that black coffee flowed from bathtub faucets.

About a quarter of four Mr. Thayer insisted on taking him around the place and showing him the shrubbery, something that held in Ben's mind a place of equal importance to the grade of wire used in hairpins.

"I'll have to go to business tomorrow," said Mr. Thayer, "and you will be left to amuse yourself. I thought you might enjoy this planting more if you knew a little about it. Of course it's much prettier in the spring of the year."

"I can imagine so."

"You must come over next spring and see it."

"I'm usually busy in the spring," said Ben.

"Before we go in," said Mr. Thayer, "I'd like to ask you one question: Do tunes come into your mind and then you write them down, or do you just sit at the piano and improvise until you strike something good?"

"Sometimes one way and sometimes the other," said Ben.

"That's very interesting," said Mr. Thayer. "I've often wondered how it was done. And another question: Do you write the tunes first and then give them to the men who write the words, or do the men write the words first and then give them to you to make up the music to them?"

"Sometimes one way and sometimes the other," said Ben.

"That's very interesting," said Mr. Thayer. "It's something

I'm glad to know. And now we'd better join the ladies or my wife will say I'm monopolizing you."

They joined us, much to my relief. I had just reached a point where I would either have had to tell " Hilda " exactly how much Ben earned per annum or that it was none of her business.

" Well! " said Mrs. Thayer to Ben. " I was afraid Ralph had kidnapped you."

" He was showing me the shrubbery," said Ben.

" What did you think of it? "

" It's great shrubbery," said Ben, striving to put some warmth into his voice.

" You must come and see it in the spring."

" I'm usually busy in the spring."

" Ralph and I are mighty proud of our shrubbery."

" You have a right to be."

Ben was taking a book out of the bookcase.

" What book is that? " asked Mrs. Thayer.

" ' The Great Gatsby,' " said Ben. " I've always wanted to read it but never got around to it."

" Heavens! " said Mrs. Thayer as she took it away from him. " That's old! You'll find the newest ones there on the table. We keep pretty well up to date. Ralph and I are both great readers. Just try any one of those books in that pile. They're all good."

Ben glanced them over and selected " Chevrons." He sat down and opened it.

" Man! Man! " exclaimed Mrs. Thayer. "You've picked the most uncomfortable chair in the house! "

" He likes straight chairs," I said.

" That's on the square," said Ben.

" But you mustn't sit there," said Mrs. Thayer. " It makes me uncomfortable just to look at you. Take this chair here. It's the softest, nicest chair you've ever sat in."

" I like hard straight chairs," said Ben, but he sank into the soft, nice one and again opened his book.

" Oh, you never can see there! " said Mrs. Thayer. " You'll ruin your eyes! Get up just a minute and let Ralph move your chair by that lamp."

" I can see perfectly well."

" I know better! Ralph, move his chair so he can see."

" I don't believe I want to read just now anyway," said Ben, and went to the phonograph. " Bess," he said, putting on a record, " here's that ' Oh! Miss Hannah! ' by the Revelers."

Mrs. Thayer fairly leaped to his side, and herded Miss Hannah back into her stall.

" We've got lots later ones than that," she said. " Let me play you the new Gershwins."

It was at this juncture that I began to suspect our hostess of a lack of finesse. After all, Gershwin is a rival of my husband's and, in some folks' opinion, a worthy one. However, Ben had a word of praise for each record as it ended and did not even hint that any of the tunes were based on melodies of his own.

" Mr. Drake," said our host at length, " would you like a gin cocktail or a Bacardi? "

" I don't like Bacardi at all," said Ben.

" I'll bet you will like the kind I've got," said Mr. Thayer. " It was brought to me by a friend of mine who just got back from Cuba. It's the real stuff! "

" I don't like Bacardi," said Ben.

" Wait till you taste this," said Mr. Thayer.

Well, we had Bacardi cocktails. I drank mine and it wasn't so good. Ben took a sip of his and pretended it was all right. But he had told the truth when he said he didn't like Bacardi.

I won't go into details regarding the dinner except to relate that three separate items were highly flavored with cheese, and Ben despises cheese.

" Don't you care for cheese, Mr. Drake? " asked Mr. Thayer, noticing that Ben was not exactly bolting his food.

" No," replied the guest of honor.

" He's spoofing you, Ralph," said Mrs. Thayer. " Everybody likes cheese."

There was coffee, and Ben managed to guzzle a cup before it was desecrated with pure cream.

We sat down to bridge.

" Do you like to play families or divide up? "

" Oh, we like to play together," said I.

" I'll bet you don't," said Mrs. Thayer. " Suppose Ralph and you play Mr. Drake and me. I think it's a mistake for husbands and wives to be partners. They're likely to criticize one another and say things that leave a scar."

Well, Mr. Thayer and I played against Ben and Mrs. Thayer and I lost sixty cents at a tenth of a cent a point. Long before the evening was over I could readily see why Mrs. Thayer thought it was a mistake to play with her husband and if it had been possible I'd have left him a complete set of scars.

Just as we were getting to sleep, Mrs. Thayer knocked on our door.

"I'm afraid you haven't covers enough," she called. "There are extra blankets on the shelf in your closet."

"Thanks," I said. "We're as warm as toast."

"I'm afraid you aren't," said Mrs. Thayer.

"Lock the door," said Ben, "before she comes in and feels our feet."

All through breakfast next morning we waited in vain for the telephone call that would yield Irene's message. The phone rang once and Mrs. Thayer answered, but we couldn't hear what she said. At noon Ben signalled me to meet him upstairs and there he stated grimly that I might do as I choose, but he was leaving Liberty Hall ere another sun had set.

"You haven't any excuse," I reminded him.

"I'm a genius," he said, "and geniuses are notoriously eccentric."

"Geniuses' wives sometimes get eccentric, too," said I, and began to pack up.

Mr. Thayer had gone to Philadelphia and we were alone with our hostess at luncheon.

"Mrs. Thayer," said Ben, "do you ever have premonitions or hunches?"

She looked frightened. "Why, no. Do you?"

"I had one not half an hour ago. Something told me that I positively must be in New York tonight. I don't know whether it's business or illness or what, but I've just got to be there!"

"That's the strangest thing I ever heard of," said Mrs. Thayer. "It scares me to death!"

"It's nothing you need be scared of," said Ben. "It only concerns me."

"Yes, but listen," said Mrs. Thayer. "A telegram came for you at breakfast time this morning. I wasn't going to tell you about it because I had promised that you wouldn't be disturbed. And it didn't seem so terribly important. But this hunch of yours puts the matter in a different light. I'm sorry now that I didn't give you the message when I got it, but I memorized it and can repeat it word for word: 'Mr. Ben Drake, care of Mr. Ralph Thayer, Lansdowne, Pennsylvania. In Nile song, second bar of refrain, bass drum part reads A flat which makes discord. Should it be A natural? Would appreciate your coming to theater tonight to straighten this out as harmony must be restored in orchestra if troupe is to be success. Regards, Gene Buck.'"

"It sounds silly, doesn't it?" said Ben. "And yet I have known productions to fail and lose hundreds of thousands of dollars just because an author or composer left town too soon. I can well understand that you considered the message trivial. At the same time I can thank my stars that this instinct, or divination, or whatever you want to call it, told me to go home."

Just as the trainmen were shouting "Board!" Mrs. Thayer said:

"I have one more confession to make. I answered Mr. Buck's telegram. I wired him. 'Mr. Ben Drake resting at my home. Must not be bothered. Suggest that you keep bass drums still for a week.' And I signed my name. Please forgive me if I have done something terrible. Remember, it was for you."

Small wonder that Ben was credited at the Lambs' Club with that month's most interesting bender.

VI

ZONE OF QUIET

" WELL," said the Doctor briskly, " how do you feel? "

" Oh, I guess I'm all right," replied the man in bed. " I'm still kind of drowsy, that's all."

" You were under the anesthetic an hour and a half. " It's no wonder you aren't wide awake yet. But you'll be better after a good night's rest, and I've left something with Miss Lyons that'll make you sleep. I'm going along now. Miss Lyons will take good care of you."

" I'm off at seven o'clock," said Miss Lyons. " I'm going to a show with my G. F. But Miss Halsey's all right. She's the night floor nurse. Anything you want, she'll get it for you. What can I give him to eat, Doctor? "

" Nothing at all; not till after I've been here tomorrow. He'll be better off without anything. Just see that he's kept quiet. Don't let him talk, and don't talk to him; that is, if you can help it."

" Help it! " said Miss Lyons. " Say, I can be old lady Sphinx herself when I want to! Sometimes I sit for hours—not alone, neither—and never say a word. Just think and think. And dream.

" I had a G. F. in Baltimore, where I took my training; she used to call me Dummy. Not because I'm dumb like some people—you know—but because I'd sit there and not say nothing. She'd say, ' A penny for your thoughts, Eleanor.' That's my first name—Eleanor."

" Well, I must run along. I'll see you in the morning."

" Good-by, Doctor," said the man in bed, as he went out.

" Good-by, Doctor Cox," said Miss Lyons as the door closed.

" He seems like an awful nice fella," said Miss Lyons. " And a good doctor, too. This is the first time I've been on a case with him. He gives a girl credit for having some sense. Most of these doctors treat us like they thought we were Mormons or something. Like Doctor Holland. I was on a case with him last week. He treated me like I was a Mormon or something. Finally,

I told him, I said, ' I'm not as dumb as I look.' She died Friday night."

" Who? " asked the man in bed.

" The woman; the case I was on," said Miss Lyons.

" And what did the doctor say when you told him you weren't as dumb as you look? "

" I don't remember," said Miss Lyons. " He said, ' I hope not,' or something. What *could* he say? Gee! It's quarter to seven. I hadn't no idear it was so late. I must get busy and fix you up for the night. And I'll tell Miss Halsey to take good care of you. We're going to see ' What Price Glory?' I'm going with my G. F. Her B. F. gave her the tickets and he's going to meet us after the show and take us to supper.

" Marian—that's my G. F.—she's crazy wild about him. And he's crazy about her, to hear her tell it. But I said to her this noon—she called me up on the phone I said to her, ' If he's so crazy about you, why don't he propose? He's got plenty of money and no strings tied to him, and as far as I can see there's no reason why he shouldn't marry you if he wants you as bad as you say he does.' So she said maybe he was going to ask her tonight. I told her, ' Don't be silly! Would he drag me along if he was going to ask you? '

" That about him having plenty of money, though, that's a joke. He told her he had and she believes him. I haven't met him yet, but he looks in his picture like he's lucky if he's getting twenty-five dollars a week. She thinks he must be rich because he's in Wall Street. I told her, I said, ' That being in Wall Street don't mean nothing. What does he do there? is the question. You know they have to have janitors in those buildings just the same like anywhere else.' But she thinks he's God or somebody.

" She keeps asking me if I don't think he's the best looking thing I ever saw. I tell her yes, sure, but between you and I, I don't believe anybody'd ever mistake him for Richard Barthelmess.

" Oh, say! I saw him the other day, coming out of the Algonquin! He's the best looking thing! Even better looking than on the screen. Roy Stewart."

" What about Roy Stewart? " asked the man in bed.

" Oh, he's the fella I was telling you about," said Miss Lyons. " He's my G. F.'s B. F."

" Maybe I'm a D. F. not to know, but would you tell me what a B. F. and G. F. are? "

"Well, you *are* dumb, aren't you!" said Miss Lyons. "A G. F., that's a girl friend, and a B. F. is a boy friend. I thought everybody knew that.

"I'm going out now and find Miss Halsey and tell her to be nice to you. But maybe I better not."

"Why not?" asked the man in bed.

"Oh, nothing. I was just thinking of something funny that happened last time I was on a case in this hospital. It was the day the man had been operated on and he was the best looking somebody you ever saw. So when I went off duty I told Miss Halsey to be nice to him, like I was going to tell her about you. And when I came back in the morning he was dead. Isn't that funny?"

"Very!"

"Well," said Miss Lyons, "did you have a good night? You look a lot better, anyway. How'd you like Miss Halsey? Did you notice her ankles? She's got pretty near the smallest ankles I ever saw. Cute. I remember one day Tyler—that's one of the internes—he said if he could just see our ankles, mine and Miss Halsey's, he wouldn't know which was which. Of course we don't look anything alike other ways. She's pretty close to thirty and —well, nobody'd ever take her for Julia Hoyt. Helen."

"Who's Helen?" asked the man in bed.

"Helen Halsey. Helen; that's her first name. She was engaged to a man in Boston. He was going to Tufts College. He was going to be a doctor. But he died. She still carries his picture with her. I tell her she's silly to mope about a man that's been dead four years. And besides a girl's a fool to marry a doctor. They've got too many alibis.

"When I marry somebody, he's got to be a somebody that has regular office hours like he's in Wall Street or somewhere. Then when he don't come home, he'll have to think up something better than being 'on a case.' I used to use that on my sister when we were living together. When I happened to be out late, I'd tell her I was on a case. She never knew the difference. Poor sis! She married a terrible oil can! But she didn't have the looks to get a real somebody. I'm making this for her. It's a bridge table cover for her birthday. She'll be twenty-nine. Don't that seem old?"

"Maybe to you; not to me," said the man in bed.

"You're about forty, aren't you?" said Miss Lyons.

" Just about."

" And how old would you say I am? "

" Twenty-three."

" I'm twenty-five," said Miss Lyons. " Twenty-five and forty. That's fifteen years' difference. But I know a married couple that the husband is forty-five and she's only twenty-four, and they get along fine."

" I'm married myself," said the man in bed.

" You would be! " said Miss Lyons. " The last four cases I've been on was all married men. But at that, I'd rather have any kind of a man than a woman. I hate women! I mean sick ones. They treat a nurse like a dog, especially a pretty nurse. What's that you're reading? "

" ' Vanity Fair,' " replied the man in bed.

" ' Vanity Fair.' I thought that was a magazine."

" Well, there's a magazine *and* a book. This is the book."

" Is it about a girl? "

" Yes."

" I haven't read it yet. I've been busy making this thing for my sister's birthday. She'll be twenty-nine. It's a bridge table cover. When you get that old, about all there is left is bridge or cross-word puzzles. Are you a puzzle fan? I did them religiously for a while, but I got sick of them. They put in such crazy words. Like one day they had a word with only three letters and it said ' A e-longated fish ' and the first letter had to be an *e*. And only three letters. That *couldn't* be right. So I said if they put things wrong like that, what's the use? Life's too short. And we only live once. When you're dead, you stay a long time dead.

" That's what a B. F. of mine used to say. He was a caution! But he was crazy about me. I might of married him only for a G. F. telling him lies about me. And called herself my friend! Charley Pierce."

" Who's Charley Pierce? "

" That was my B. F. that the other girl lied to him about me. I told him, I said, ' Well, if you believe all them stories about me, maybe we better part once and for all. I don't want to be tied up to a somebody that believes all the dirt they hear about me.' So he said he didn't really believe it and if I would take him back he wouldn't quarrel with me no more. But I said I thought it was best for us to part. I got their announcement two years ago, while I was still in training in Baltimore."

" Did he marry the girl that lied to him about you? "

" Yes, the poor fish! And I bet he's satisfied! They're a match for each other! He was all right, though, at that, till he fell for her. He used to be so thoughtful of me, like I was his sister or something.

" I like a man to respect me. Most fellas wants to kiss you before they know your name.

" Golly! I'm sleepy this morning! And got a right to be, too. Do you know what time I got home last night, or this morning, rather? Well, it was half past three. What would mama say if she could see her little girl now! But we did have a good time. First we went to the show—'What Price Glory?'—I and my G. F.—and afterwards her B. F. met us and took us in a taxi down to Barney Gallant's. Peewee Byers has got the orchestra there now. Used to be with Whiteman's. Gee! How he can dance! I mean Roy."

" Your G. F.'s B. F.? "

" Yes, but I don't believe he's as crazy about her as she thinks he is. Anyway—but this is a secret—he took down the phone number of the hospital while Marian was out powdering her nose, and he said he'd give me a ring about noon. Gee! I'm sleepy! Roy Stewart! "

" Well," said Miss Lyons, " how's my patient? I'm twenty minutes late, but honest, it's a wonder I got up at all! Two nights in succession is too much for this child! "

" Barney Gallant's again? " asked the man in bed.

" No, but it was dancing, and pretty near as late. It'll be different tonight. I'm going to bed just the minute I get home. But I did have a dandy time. And I'm crazy about a certain somebody."

" Roy Stewart? "

" How'd you guess it? But honest, he's wonderful! And so different than most of the fellas I've met. He says the craziest things, just keeps you in hysterics. We were talking about books and reading, and he asked me if I liked poetry—only he called it ' poultry '—and I said I was wild about it and Edgar M. Guest was just about my favorite, and then I asked him if he liked Kipling and what do you think he said? He said he didn't know; he'd never kipled.

" He's a scream! We just sat there in the house till half past eleven and didn't do nothing but just talk and the time went like we was at a show. He's better than a show. But finally I noticed how late it was and I asked him didn't he think he better be going and he said he'd go if I'd go with him, so I asked him where could we go at that hour of night, and he said he knew a roadhouse just a little ways away, and I didn't want to go, but he said we wouldn't stay for only just one dance, so I went with him. To the Jericho Inn.

" I don't know what the woman thought of me where I stay, going out that time of night. But he *is* such a wonderful dancer and such a perfect gentleman! Of course we had more than one dance and it was after two o'clock before I knew it. We had some gin, too, but he just kissed me once and that was when we said good night."

" What about your G. F., Marian? Does she know? "

" About Roy and I? No. I always say that what a person don't know don't hurt them. Besides, there's nothing *for* her to know—yet. But listen. If there was a chance in the world for her, if I thought he cared anything about her, I'd be the last one in the world to accept his intentions. I hope I'm not that kind! But as far as anything serious between them is concerned, well, it's cold. I happen to *know* that! She's not the girl for him.

" In the first place, while she's pretty in a way, her complexion's bad and her hair's scraggy and her figure, well, it's like some woman in the funny pictures. And she's not peppy enough for Roy. She'd rather stay home than do anything. Stay home! It'll be time enough for that when you can't get anybody to take you out.

" She'd never make a wife for him. He'll be a rich man in another year; that is, if things go right for him in Wall Street like he expects. And a man as rich as he'll be wants a wife that can live up to it and entertain and step out once in a while. He don't want a wife that's a drag on him. And he's too good-looking for Marian. A fella as good-looking as him needs a pretty wife or the first thing you know some girl that is pretty will steal him off of you. But it's silly to talk about them marrying each other. He'd have to ask her first, and he's not going to. I know! So I don't feel at all like I'm trespassing.

" Anyway, you know the old saying, everthing goes in love. And I—— But I'm keeping you from reading your book. Oh, yes; I almost forgot a T. L. that Miss Halsey said about you. Do you know what a T. L. is? "

" Yes."

" Well, then, you give me one and I'll give you this one."

"But I haven't talked to anybody but the Doctor. I can give you one from myself. He asked me how I liked you and I said all right."

"Well, that's better than nothing. Here's what Miss Halsey said: She said if you were shaved and fixed up, you wouldn't be bad. And now I'm going out and see if there's any mail for me. Most of my mail goes to where I live, but some of it comes here sometimes. What I'm looking for is a letter from the state board telling me if I passed my state examination. They ask you the craziest questions. Like 'Is ice a disinfectant?' Who cares! Nobody's going to waste ice to kill germs when there's so much of it needed in high-balls. Do you like high-balls? Roy says it spoils whisky to mix it with water. He takes it straight. He's a terror! But maybe you want to read."

"Good morning," said Miss Lyons. "Did you sleep good?"

"Not so good," said the man in bed. "I——"

"I bet you got more sleep than I did," said Miss Lyons. "He's the most persistent somebody I ever knew! I asked him last night, I said, 'Don't you never get tired of dancing?' So he said, well, he did get tired of dancing with some people, but there was others who he never got tired of dancing with them. So I said, 'Yes, Mr. Jollier, but I wasn't born yesterday and I know apple sauce when I hear it and I bet you've told that to fifty girls.' I guess he really did mean it, though.

"Of course most anybody'd rather dance with slender girls than stout girls. I remember a B. F. I had one time in Washington. He said dancing with me was just like dancing with nothing. That sounds like he was insulting me, but it was really a compliment. He meant it wasn't any effort to dance with me like with some girls. You take Marian, for instance, and while I'm crazy about her, still that don't make her a good dancer and dancing with her must be a good deal like moving the piano or something.

"I'd die if I was fat! People are always making jokes about fat people. And there's the old saying, 'Nobody loves a fat man.' And it's even worse with a girl. Besides people making jokes about them and don't want to dance with them and so forth, besides that they're always trying to reduce and can't eat what they want to. I bet, though, if I was fat, I'd eat everything in sight. Though I guess not, either. Because I hardly eat anything as it is. But they do make jokes about them.

"I'll never forget one day last winter, I was on a case in Great

Neck and the man's wife was the fattest thing! So they had a
radio in the house and one day she saw in the paper where Bugs
Baer was going to talk on the radio and it would probably be
awfully funny because he writes so crazy. Do you ever read his
articles? But this woman, she was awfully sensitive about being
fat and I nearly died sitting there with her listening to Bugs
Baer, because his whole talk was all about some fat woman and
he said the craziest things, but I couldn't laugh on account of
she being there in the room with me. One thing he said was
that the woman, this woman he was talking about, he said she
was so fat that she wore a wrist watch on her thumb. Henry J.
Belden."

"Who is Henry J. Belden? Is that the name of Bugs Baer's
fat lady?"

"No, you crazy!" said Miss Lyons. "Mr. Belden was the case
I was on in Great Neck. He died."

"It seems to me a good many of your cases die."

"Isn't it a scream!" said Miss Lyons. "But it's true; that is,
it's been true lately. The last five cases I've been on has all died.
Of course it's just luck, but the girls have been kidding me about
it and calling me a jinx, and when Miss Halsey saw me here the
evening of the day you was operated, she said, 'God help him!'
That's the night floor nurse's name. But you're going to be mean
and live through it and spoil my record, aren't you? I'm just
kidding. Of course I want you to get all right.

"But it *is* queer, the way things have happened, and it's made
me feel kind of creepy. And besides, I'm not like some of the girls
and don't care. I get awfully fond of some of my cases and I hate
to see them die, especially if they're men and not very sick and
treat you half-way decent and don't yell for you the minute you
go out of the room. There's only one case I was ever on where I
didn't mind her dying and that was a woman. She had nephritis.
Mrs. Judson.

"Do you want some gum? I chew it just when I'm nervous.
And I always get nervous when I don't have enough sleep. You
can bet I'll stay home tonight, B. F. or no B. F. But anyway he's
got an engagement tonight, some directors' meeting or something.
He's the busiest somebody in the world. And I told him last
night, I said, 'I should think you'd need sleep, too, even more
than I do because you have to have all your wits about you in
your business or those big bankers would take advantage and rob
you. You can't afford to be sleepy,' I told him.

"So he said, 'No, but of course it's all right for you, because if you go to sleep on your job, there's no danger of you doing any damage except maybe give one of your patients a bichloride of mercury tablet instead of an alcohol rub.' He's terrible! But you can't help from laughing.

"There was four of us in the party last night. He brought along his B. F. and another girl. She was just blah, but the B. F. wasn't so bad, only he insisted on me helping him drink a half a bottle of Scotch, and on top of gin, too. I guess I was the life of the party; that is, at first. Afterwards I got sick and it wasn't so good.

"But at first I was certainly going strong. And I guess I made quite a hit with Roy's B. F. He knows Marian, too, but he won't say anything, and if he does, I don't care. If she don't want to lose her beaus, she ought to know better than to introduce them to all the pretty girls in the world. I don't mean that I'm any Norma Talmadge, but at least—well—but I sure was sick when I *was* sick!

"I must give Marian a ring this noon. I haven't talked to her since the night she introduced me to him. I've been kind of scared. But I've got to find out what she knows. Or if she's sore at me. Though I don't see how she can be, do you? But maybe you want to read."

"I called Marian up, but I didn't get her. She's out of town but she'll be back tonight. She's been out on a case. Hudson, New York, That's where she went. The message was waiting for her when she got home the other night, the night she introduced me to Roy."

"Good morning," said Miss Lyons.

"Good morning," said the man in bed. "Did you sleep enough?"

"Yes," said Miss Lyons. "I mean no, not enough."

"Your eyes look bad. They almost look as if you'd been crying."

"Who? Me? It'd take more than—I mean, I'm not a baby! But go on and read your book."

"Well, good morning," said Miss Lyons. "And how's my patient? And this is the last morning I can call you that, isn't it? I think you're mean to get well so quick and leave me out of a job.

I'm just kidding. I'm glad you're all right again, and I can use a little rest myself."

"Another big night?" asked the man in bed.

"Pretty big," said Miss Lyons. "And another one coming. But tomorrow I won't ever get up. Honest, I danced so much last night that I thought my feet would drop off. But he certainly is a dancing fool! And the nicest somebody to talk to that I've met since I came to this town. Not a smart Alex and not always trying to be funny like some people, but just nice. He understands. He seems to know just what you're thinking. George Morse."

"George Morse!" exclaimed the man in bed.

"Why yes," said Miss Lyons. "Do you know him?"

"No. But I thought you were talking about this Stewart, this Roy."

"Oh, him!" said Miss Lyons. "I should say not! He's private property; other people's property, not mine. He's engaged to my G. F. Marian. It happened day before yesterday, after she got home from Hudson. She was on a case up there. She told me about it night before last. I told her congratulations. Because I wouldn't hurt her feelings for the world! But heavens! what a mess she's going to be in, married to that dumb-bell. But of course some people can't be choosey. And I doubt if they ever get married unless some friend loans him the price of a license.

"He's got her believing he's in Wall Street, but I bet if he ever goes there at all, it's to sweep it. He's one of these kind of fellas that's got a great line for a little while, but you don't want to live with a clown. And I'd hate to marry a man that all he thinks about is to step out every night and dance and drink.

"I had a notion to tell her what I really thought. But that'd only of made her sore, or she'd of thought I was jealous or something. As if I couldn't of had him myself! Though even if he wasn't so awful, if I'd liked him instead of loathed him, I wouldn't of taken him from her on account of she being my G. F. And especially while she was out of town.

"He's the kind of a fella that'd marry a nurse in the hopes that some day he'd be an invalid. You know, that kind.

"But say—did you ever hear of J. P. Morgan and Company? That's where my B. F. works, and he don't claim to own it neither. George Morse.

"Haven't you finished that book yet?"

VII

MR. FRISBIE

I AM Mr. Allen Frisbie's chauffeur. Allen Frisbie is a name I made up because they tell me that if I used the real name of the man I am employed by that he might take offense and start trouble though I am sure he will never see what I am writing as he does not read anything except the American Golfer but of course some of his friends might call his attention to it. If you knew who the real name of the man is it would make more interesting reading as he is one of the 10 most wealthiest men in the United States and a man who everybody is interested in because he is so famous and the newspapers are always writing articles about him and sending high salary reporters to interview him but he is a very hard man to reproach or get an interview with and when they do he never tells them anything.

That is how I come to be writing this article because about two weeks ago a Mr. Kirk had an appointment to interview Mr. Frisbie for one of the newspapers and I drove him to the station after the interview was over and he said to me your boss is certainly a tough egg to interview and getting a word out of him is like pulling turnips.

"The public do not know anything about the man," said Mr. Kirk. "They know he is very rich and has got a wife and a son and a daughter and what their names are but as to his private life and his likes and dislikes he might just as well be a monk in a convent."

"The public knows he likes golf," I said.

"They do not know what kind of a game he plays."

"He plays pretty good," I said.

"How good?" said Mr. Kirk.

"About 88 or 90," I said.

"So is your grandmother," said Mr. Kirk.

He only meant the remark as a comparison but had either of my grandmothers lived they would both have been over 90. Mr. Kirk did not believe I was telling the truth about Mr. Frisbie's game and he was right though was I using real names I would not admit it as Mr. Frisbie is very sensitive in regards to his golf.

Mr. Kirk kept pumping at me but I am used to being pumped at and Mr. Kirk finally gave up pumping at me as he found me as closed mouth as Mr. Frisbie himself but he made the remark that he wished he was in my place for a few days and as close to the old man as I am and he would then be able to write the first real article which had ever been written about the old man. He called Mr. Frisbie the old man.

He said it was too bad I am not a writer so I could write up a few instance about Mr. Frisbie from the human side on account of being his caddy at golf and some paper or magazine would pay me big. He said if you would tell me a few instance I would write them up and split with you but I said no I could not think of anything which would make an article but after Mr. Kirk had gone I got to thinking it over and thought to myself maybe I could be a writer if I tried and at least there is no harm in trying so for the week after Mr. Kirk's visit I spent all my spare time writing down about Mr. Frisbie only at first I used his real name but when I showed the article they said for me not to use real names but the public would guess who it was anyway and that was just as good as using real names.

So I have gone over the writing again and changed the name to Allen Frisbie and other changes and here is the article using Allen Frisbie.

When I say I am Mr. Frisbie's chauffeur I mean I am his personal chauffeur. There are two other chauffeurs who drive for the rest of the family and run errands. Had I nothing else to do only drive I might well be turned a man of leisure as Mr. Frisbie seldom never goes in to the city more than twice a week and even less oftener than that does he pay social visits.

His golf links is right on the place an easy walk from the house to the first tee and here is where he spends a good part of each and every day playing alone with myself in the roll of caddy. So one would not be far from amiss to refer to me as Mr. Frisbie's caddy rather than his chauffeur but it was as a chauffeur that I was engaged and can flatter myself that there are very few men of my calling who would not gladly exchange their salary and position for mine.

Mr. Frisbie is a man just this side of 60 years of age. Almost 10 years ago he retired from active business with money enough to put him in a class with the richest men in the United States and since then his investments have increased their value to such an extent so that now he is in a class with the richest men in the United States.

It was soon after his retirement that he bought the Peter Vischer estate near Westbury, Long Island. On this estate there was a 9 hole golf course in good condition and considered one of the best private 9 hole golf courses in the United States but Mr. Frisbie would have had it plowed up and the land used for some other usage only for a stroke of chance which was when Mrs. Frisbie's brother came over from England for a visit.

It was during while this brother-in-law was visiting Mr. Frisbie that I entered the last named employee and was an onlooker when Mr. Frisbie's brother-in-law persuaded his brother-in-law to try the game of golf. As luck would have it Mr. Frisbie's first drive was so good that his brother-in-law would not believe he was a new beginner till he had seen Mr. Frisbie shoot again but that first perfect drive made Mr. Frisbie a slave of the game and without which there would be no such instance as I am about to relate.

I would better explain at this junction that I am not a golfer but I have learned quite a lot of knowledge about the game by cadding for Mr. Frisbie and also once or twice in company with my employer have picked up some knowledge of the game by witnessing players like Bobby Jones and Hagen and Sarazen and Smith in some of their matches. I have only tried it myself on a very few occasions when I was sure Mr. Frisbie could not observe me and will confide that in my own mind I am convinced that with a little practise that I would have little trouble defeating Mr. Frisbie but will never seek to prove same for reasons which I will leave it to the reader to guess the reasons.

One day shortly after Mr. Frisbie's brother-in-law had ended his visit I was cadding for Mr. Frisbie and as had become my custom keeping the score for him when a question arose as to whether he had taken 7 or 8 strokes on the last hole. A 7 would have given him a total of 63 for the 9 holes while a 8 would have made it 64. Mr. Frisbie tried to recall the different strokes but was not certain and asked me to help him.

As I remembered it he had sliced his 4th. wooden shot in to a trap but had recovered well and got on to the green and then had taken 3 putts which would make him a 8 but by some slip of the tongue when I started to say 8 I said 7 and before I could correct myself Mr. Frisbie said yes you are right it was a 7.

" That is even 7s," said Mr. Frisbie.

" Yes," I said.

On the way back to the house he asked me what was my salary which I told him and he said well I think you are worth more than that and from now on you will get $25.00 more per week.

On another occasion when 9 more holes had been added to the course and Mr. Frisbie was playing the 18 holes regular every day he came to the last hole needing a 5 to break 112 which was his best score.

The 18th. hole is only 120 yards with a big green but a brook in front and traps in back of it. Mr. Frisbie got across the brook with his second but the ball went over in to the trap and it looked like bad business because Mr. Frisbie is even worse with a niblick than almost any other club except maybe the No. 3 and 4 irons and the wood.

Well I happened to get to the ball ahead of him and it laid there burred in the deep sand about a foot from a straight up and down bank 8 foot high where it would have been impossible for any man alive to oust it in one stroke but as luck would have it I stumbled and gave the ball a little kick and by chance it struck the side of the bank and stuck in the grass and Mr. Frisbie got it up on the green in one stroke and was down in 2 putts for his 5.

" Well that is my record 111 or 3 over 6s," he said.

Now my brother had a couple of tickets for the polo at Meadowbrook the next afternoon and I am a great lover of horses flesh so I said to Mr. Frisbie can I go to the polo tomorrow afternoon and he said certainly any time you want a afternoon off do not hesitate to ask me but a little while later there was a friend of mine going to get married at Atlantic City and Mr. Frisbie had just shot a 128 and broke his spoon besides and when I mentioned about going to Atlantic City for my friend's wedding he snapped at me like a wolf and said what did I think it was the xmas holidays.

Personally I am a man of simple tastes and few wants and it is very seldom when I am not satisfied to take my life and work as they come and not seek fear or favor but of course there are times in every man's life when they desire something a little out of the ordinary in the way of a little vacation or perhaps a financial accommodation of some kind and in such cases I have found Mr. Frisbie a king amongst men provide it one uses discretion in choosing the moment of their reproach but a variable tyrant if one uses bad judgment in choosing the moment of their reproach.

You can count on him granting any reasonable request just after he has made a good score or even a good shot where as a person seeking a favor when he is off his game might just swell ask President Coolidge to do the split.

I wish to state that having learned my lesson along these lines I did not use my knowledge to benefit myself alone but have on the other hand utilized same mostly to the advantage of others especially the members of Mr. Frisbie's own family. Mr. Frisbie's wife and son and daughter all realized early in my employment that I could handle Mr. Frisbie better than anyone else and without me ever exactly divulging the secret of my methods they just naturally began to take it for granted that I could succeed with him where they failed and it became their habit when they sought something from their respective spouse and father to summons me as their adviser and advocate.

As an example of the above I will first sight an example in connection with Mrs. Frisbie. This occurred many years ago and was the instance which convinced her beyond all doubt that I was a expert on the subject of managing her husband.

Mrs. Frisbie is a great lover of music but unable to perform on any instrument herself. It was her hope that one of the children would be a pianiste and a great deal of money was spent on piano lessons for both Robert the son and Florence the daughter but all in vain as neither of the two showed any talent and their teachers one after another gave them up in despair.

Mrs. Frisbie at last became desirous of purchasing a player piano and of course would consider none but the best but when she brooched the subject to Mr. Frisbie he turned a deaf ear as he said pianos were made to be played by hand and people who could not learn same did not deserve music in the home.

I do not know how often Mr. and Mrs. Frisbie disgust the matter pro and con.

Personally they disgust it in my presence any number of times and finally being a great admirer of music myself and seeing no reason why a man of Mr. Frisbie's great wealth should deny his wife a harmless pleasure such as a player piano I suggested to the madam that possibly if she would leave matters to me the entire proposition might be put over. I can no more than fail I told her and I do not think I will fail so she instructed me to go ahead as I could not do worse than fail which she had already done herself.

I will relate the success of my plan as briefly as possible. Between the house and the golf course there was a summer house in which Mrs. Frisbie sat reading while Mr. Frisbie played golf. In this summer house she could sit so as to not be visible from the golf course. She was to sit there till she heard me whistle the strains of " Over There " where at she was to appear on the scene like she had come direct from the house and the fruits of our scheme would then be known.

For two days Mrs. Frisbie had to console herself with her book as Mr. Frisbie's golf was terrible and there was no moment when I felt like it would not be courting disaster to summons her on the scene but during the 3rd. afternoon his game suddenly improved and he had shot the 1st. 9 holes in 53 and started out on the 10th. with a pretty drive when I realized the time had come.

Mrs. Frisbie appeared promptly in answer to my whistling and walked rapidly up to Mr. Frisbie like she had hurried from the house and said there is a man at the house from that player piano company and he says he will take $50.00 off the regular price if I order today and please let me order one as I want one so much.

" Why certainly dear go ahead and get it dear," said Mr. Frisbie and that is the way Mrs. Frisbie got her way in regards to a player piano. Had I not whistled when I did but waited a little longer it would have spelt ruination to our schemes as Mr. Frisbie took a 12 on the 11th. hole and would have bashed his wife over the head with a No. 1 iron had she even asked him for a toy drum.

I have been of assistance to young Mr. Robert Frisbie the son with reference to several items of which I will only take time to touch on one item with reference to Mr. Robert wanting to drive a car. Before Mr. Robert was 16 years of age he was always after Mr. Frisbie to allow him to drive one of the cars and Mr. Frisbie always said him nay on the grounds that it is against the law for a person under 16 years of age to drive a car.

When Mr. Robert reached the age of 16 years old however this excuse no longer held good and yet Mr. Frisbie continued to say Mr. Robert nay in regards to driving a car. There is plenty of chauffeurs at your beckon call said Mr. Frisbie to drive you where ever and when ever you wish to go but of course Mr. Robert like all youngsters wanted to drive himself and personally I could see no harm in it as I personally could not drive for him and the other 2 chauffeurs in Mr. Frisbie's employee at the time were just as lightly to wreck a car as Mr. Robert so I promised Mr. Robert that I would do my best towards helping him towards obtaining permission to drive one of the cars.

" Leave it to me " was my bequest to Mr. Robert and sure enough my little strategy turned the trick though Mr. Robert did not have the patience like his mother to wait in the summer house till a favorable moment arrived so it was necessary for me to carry through the entire proposition by myself.

The 16th. hole on our course is perhaps the most difficult hole on our course at least it has always been a variable tartar for Mr. Frisbie.

It is about 350 yards long in lenth and it is what is called a blind hole as you can not see the green from the tee as you drive from the tee up over a hill with a direction flag as the only guide and down at the bottom of the hill there is a brook a little over 225 yards from the tee which is the same brook which you come to again on the last hole and in all the times Mr. Frisbie has played around the course he has seldom never made this 16th. hole in less than 7 strokes or more as his tee shot just barely skins the top of the hill giving him a down hill lie which upsets him so that he will miss the 2d. shot entirely or top it and go in to the brook.

Well I generally always stand up on top of the hill to watch where his tee shot goes and on the occasion referred to he got a pretty good tee shot which struck on top of the hill and rolled half way down and I hurried to the ball before he could see me and I picked it up and threw it across the brook and when he climbed to the top of the hill I pointed to where the ball laid the other side of the brook and shouted good shot Mr. Frisbie. He was overjoyed and beamed with joy and did not suspect anything out of the way though in realty he could not hit a ball more than 160 yards if it was teed on the summit of Pike's Peak.

Fate was on my side at this junction and Mr. Frisbie hit a perfect mashie shot on to the green and sunk his 2d. put for the only 4 of his career on this hole. He was almost delirious with joy and you may be sure I took advantage of the situation and before we were fairly off the green I said to him Mr. Frisbie if you do not need me tomorrow morning do you not think it would be a good time for me to learn Mr. Robert to drive a car.

"Why certainly he is old enough now to drive a car and it is time he learned."

I now come to the main instance of my article which is in regards to Miss Florence Frisbie who is now Mrs. Henry Craig and of course Craig is not the real name but you will soon see that what I was able to do for her was no such childs play like gaining consent for Mr. Robert to run a automobile or Mrs. Frisbie to purchase a player piano but this was a matter of the up most importance and I am sure the reader will not consider me a vain bragger when I claim that I handled it with some skill.

Miss Florence is a very pretty and handsome girl who has always had a host of suiters who paid court to her on account of being pretty as much as her great wealth and I believe there has been times when no less than half a dozen or more young men were paying court to her at one time. Well about 2 years ago she lost her heart to young Henry Craig and at the same time Mr. Frisbie told her in no uncertain turns that she must throw young Craig over board and marry his own choice young Junior Holt or he would cut her off without a dime.

Holt and Craig are not the real names of the two young men referred to though I am using their real first names namely Junior and Henry. Young Holt is a son of Mr. Frisbie's former partner in business and a young man who does not drink or smoke and has got plenty of money in his own rights and a young man who any father would feel safe in trusting their daughter in the bands of matrimony. Young Craig at that time had no money and no position and his parents had both died leaving nothing but debts.

"Craig is just a tramp and will never amount to anything," said Mr. Frisbie. "I have had inquirys made and I understand he drinks when anyone will furnish him the drinks. He has never worked and never will. Junior Holt is a model young man from all accounts and comes of good stock and is the only young man I know whose conduct and habits are such that I would consider him fit to marry my daughter."

Miss Florence said that Craig was not a tramp and she loved him and would not marry anyone else and as for Holt he was terrible but even if he was not terrible she would never consider undergoing the bands of matrimony with a man named Junior.

"I will elope with Henry if you do not give in," she said.

Mr. Frisbie was not alarmed by this threat as Miss Florence has a little common sense and would not be lightly to elope with a young man who could hardly finance a honeymoon trip on the subway. But neither was she showing any signs of yielding in regards to his wishes in regards to young Holt and things began to take on the appearance of a dead lock between father and daughter with neither side showing any signs of yielding.

Miss Florence grew pale and thin and spent most of her time in her room instead of seeking enjoyment amongst her friends as was her custom. As for Mr. Frisbie he was always a man of iron will and things began to take on the appearance of a dead lock with neither side showing any signs of yielding.

It was when it looked like Miss Florence was on the verge of a serious illness when Mrs. Frisbie came to me and said we all realize that you have more influence with Mr. Frisbie than anyone else and is there any way you can think of to get him to change his status towards Florence and these 2 young men because if something is not done right away I am afraid of what will happen. Miss Florence likes you and has a great deal of confidence in you said Mrs. Frisbie so will you see her and talk matters over with her and see if you can not think up some plan between you which will put a end to this situation before my poor little girl dies.

So I went to see Miss Florence in her bedroom and she was a sad sight with her eyes red from weeping and so pale and thin and yet her face lit up with a smile when I entered the room and she shook hands with me like I was a long lost friend.

" I asked my mother to send you," said Miss Florence. " This case looks hopeless but I know you are a great fixer as far as Father is concerned and you can fix it if anyone can. Now I have got a idea which I will tell you and if you like it it will be up to you to carry it out."

" What is your idea ? "

" Well," said Miss Florence, " I think that if Mr. Craig the man I love could do Father a favor why Father would not be so set against him."

" What kind of a favor ? "

" Well Mr. Craig plays a very good game of golf and he might give Father some pointers which would improve Father's game."

" Your father will not play golf with anyone and certainly not with a good player and besides that your father is not the kind of a man that wants anyone giving him pointers. Personally I would just as leaf go up and tickle him as tell him that his stance is wrong."

" Then I guess my idea is not so good."

" No," I said and then all of a sudden I had a idea of my own. " Listen Miss Florence does the other one play golf ? "

" Who ? "

" Young Junior Holt."

" Even better than Mr. Craig."

" Does your father know that ? "

" Father does not know anything about him or he would not like him so well."

Well I said I have got a scheme which may work or may not work but no harm to try and the first thing to be done is for you to spruce up and pretend like you do not feel so unkindly towards young Holt after all. The next thing is to tell your father that Mr. Holt never played golf and never even saw it played but would like to watch your father play so he can get the hang of the game.

And then after that you must get Mr. Holt to ask your father to let him follow him around the course and very secretly you must tip Mr. Holt off that your father wants his advice. When ever your father does anything wrong Mr. Holt is to correct him. Tell him your father is crazy to improve his golf but is shy in regards to asking for help.

There is a lot of things that may happen to this scheme but if it should go through why I will guarantee that at least half your troubles will be over.

Well as I said there was a lot of things that might have happened to spoil my scheme but nothing did happen and the very next afternoon Mr. Frisbie confided in me that Miss Florence seemed to feel much better and seemed to have changed her mind in regards to Mr. Holt and also said that the last named had expressed a desire to follow Mr. Frisbie around the golf course and learn something about the game.

Mr. Holt was a kind of a fat pudgy young man with a kind of a sneering smile and the first minute I saw him I wished him the worst.

For a second before Mr. Frisbie started to play I was certain we were lost as Mr. Frisbie remarked where have you been keeping yourself Junior that you never watched golf before. But luckily young Holt took the remark as a joke and made no reply. Right afterwards the storm clouds began to gather in the sky. Mr. Frisbie sliced his tee shot.

"Mr. Frisbie," said young Holt, "there was several things the matter with you then but the main trouble was that you stood too close to the ball and cut across it with your club head and besides that you swang back faster than Alex Smith and you were off your balance and you gripped too hard and you jerked instead of hitting with a smooth follow through."

Well, Mr. Frisbie gave him a queer look and then made up his mind that Junior was trying to be humorous and he frowned at him so as he would not try it again but when we located the ball in the rough and Mr. Frisbie asked me for his spoon young Holt said Oh take your mashie Mr. Frisbie never use a wooden club in a place like that and Mr. Frisbie scowled and mumbled under his breath and missed the ball with his spoon and missed it again and then took a midiron and just dribbled it on to the fairway and finally got on the green in 7 and took 3 putts.

I suppose you might say that this was one of the quickest golf matches on record as it ended on the 2d. tee. Mr. Frisbie tried to drive and sliced again. Then young Holt took a ball from my pocket and a club from the bag and said here let me show you the swing and drove the ball 250 yards straight down the middle of the course.

I looked at Mr. Frisbie's face and it was puffed out and a kind of a purple black color. Then he burst and I will only repeat a few of the more friendlier of his remarks.

" Get to hell and gone of my place. Do not never darken my doors again. Just show up around here one more time and I will blow out what you have got instead of brains. You lied to my girl and you tried to make a fool out of me. Get out before I sick my dogs on you and tear you to pieces."

Junior most lightly wanted to offer some word of explanation or to demand one on his own account but saw at a glance how useless same would be. I heard later that he saw Miss Florence and that she just laughed at him.

" I made a mistake about Junior Holt," said Mr. Frisbie that evening. " He is no good and must never come to this house again."

" Oh Father and just when I was beginning to like him," said Miss Florence.

Well like him or not like him she and the other young man Henry Craig were married soon afterwards which I suppose Mr. Frisbie permitted the bands in the hopes that same would rile Junior Holt.

Mr. Frisbie admitted he had made a mistake in regards to the last named but he certainly was not mistaken when he said that young Craig was a tramp and would never amount to anything.

Well I guess I have rambled on long enough about Mr. Frisbie.

VIII

HURRY KANE

IT says here: "Another great race may be expected in the American League, for Philadelphia and New York have evidently added enough strength to give them a fighting chance with the White Sox and Yankees. But if the fans are looking for as 'nervous' a finish as last year's, with a climax such as the Chicago and New York clubs staged on the memorable first day of October, they are doubtless in for a disappointment. That was a regular Webster 'thrill that comes once in a lifetime,' and no oftener."

"Thrill" is right, but they don't know the half of it. Nobody knows the whole of it only myself, not even the fella that told me. I mean the big sap, Kane, who you might call him, I suppose, the hero of the story, but he's too dumb to have realized all that went on, and besides, I got some of the angles from other sources and seen a few things with my own eyes.

If you wasn't the closest-mouthed bird I ever run acrost, I wouldn't spill this to you. But I know it won't go no further and I think it may give you a kick.

Well, the year before last, it didn't take no witch to figure out what was going to happen to our club if Dave couldn't land a pitcher or two to help out Carney and Olds. Jake Lewis hurt his arm and was never no good after that and the rest of the staff belonged in the Soldiers' Home. Their aim was perfect, but they were always shooting at the pressbox or somebody's bat. On hot days I often felt like leaving my mask and protector in the clubhouse; what those fellas were throwing up there was either eighty feet over my head or else the outfielders had to chase it. I could have caught naked except on the days when Olds and Carney worked.

In the fall—that's a year and a half ago—Dave pulled the trade with Boston and St. Louis that brought us Frank Miller and Lefty Glaze in exchange for Robinson, Bullard and Roy Smith. The three he gave away weren't worth a dime to us or to the clubs that got them, and that made it just an even thing, as Miller showed up in the spring with a waistline that was eight laps to the mile and kept getting bigger and bigger till it took half the Atlantic cable

87

to hold up his baseball pants, while Glaze wanted more money than Landis and didn't report till the middle of June, and then tried to condition himself on wood alcohol. When the deal was made, it looked like Dave had all the best of it, but as it turned out, him and the other two clubs might as well have exchanged photographs of their kids in Girl Scout uniforms.

But Dave never lost no sleep over Glaze or Miller. We hadn't been in Florida three days before him and everybody on the ball club was absolutely nuts about big Kane. Here was a twenty-year-old boy that had only pitched half a season in Waco and we had put in a draft for him on the recommendation of an old friend of Dave's, Billy Moore. Billy was just a fan and didn't know much baseball, but he had made some money for Dave in Texas oil leases and Dave took this tip on Kane more because he didn't want to hurt Billy's feelings than out of respect for his judgment. So when the big sapper showed up at Fort Gregg, he didn't get much of a welcome. What he did get was a laugh. You couldn't look at him and not laugh; anyway, not till you got kind of used to him.

You've probably seen lots of pictures of him in a uniform, but they can't give you no idear of the sight he was the first day he blew in the hotel, after that clean, restful little train ride all the way from Yuma. Standing six foot three in what was left of his stockings, he was wearing a suit of Arizona store clothes that would have been a fair fit for Singer's youngest Midget and looked like he had pressed it with a tractor that had been parked on a river bottom.

He had used up both the collars that he figured would see him through his first year in the big league. This left you a clear view of his Adam's apple, which would make half a dozen pies. You'd have thought from his shoes that he had just managed to grab hold of the rail on the back platform of his train and been dragged from Yuma to Jacksonville. But when you seen his shirt, you wondered if he hadn't rode in the cab and loaned it to the fireman for a wash-cloth. He had a brown paper suitcase held together by bandages. Some of them had slipped and the raw wounds was exposed. But if the whole thing had fell to pieces, he could have packed the contents in two of his vest pockets without bulging them much.

One of the funniest things about him was his walk and I'll never forget the first time we seen him go out to take his turn pitching to the batters. He acted like he was barefooted and afraid of stepping on burrs. He'd lift one dog and hold it in the air a minute till he could locate a safe place to put it down. Then he'd do the same thing with the other, and it would seem about a half-hour from the time he left the bench till he got to his position. Of course Dave soon had him pretty well cured of that, or that is, Dave didn't, but Kid Farrell did. For a whole week, the Kid followed him every step he took and if he wasn't going fast enough, he either got spiked in the heel or kicked in the calf of his hind leg. People think he walks slow yet, but he's a shooting star now compared with when he broke in.

Well, everybody was in hysterics watching him make that first trip and he looked so silly that we didn't expect him to be any good to us except as a kind of a show. But we were in for a big surprise.

Before he threw a ball, Dave said to him: " Now, go easy. Don't cut loose and take a chance till you're in shape."

" All right," says Kane.

And all of a sudden, without no warning, he whammed a fast ball acrost that old plate that blew Tierney's cap off and pretty near knocked me down. Tierney hollered murder and ran for the bench. All of us were pop-eyed and it was quite a while before Dave could speak. Then he said:

" Boy, your fast one *is* a fast one! But I just got through telling you not to cut loose. The other fellas ain't ready for it and neither are you. I don't want nobody killed this time of year."

So Kane said: " I didn't cut loose. I can send them through there twice as fast as that. I'm scared to yet, because I ain't sure of my control. I'll show you something in a couple more days."

Well when he said " twice as fast," he was making it a little strong. But his real fast one was faster than that first one he threw, and before the week was over we looked at speed that made it seem like Johnson had never pitched nothing but toy balloons. What had us all puzzled was why none of the other clubs had tried to grab him. I found out by asking him one night at supper. I asked him if he'd been just as good the year before as he was now.

" I had the same stuff," he said, " but I never showed it, except once."

I asked him why he hadn't showed it. He said:

" Because I was always scared they would be a big league scout in the stand and I didn't want to go ' up.' "

Then I said why not, and he told me he was stuck on a gal in Waco and wanted to be near her.

"Yes," I said, "but your home town, Yuma, is a long ways from Waco and you couldn't see much of her winters even if you stayed in the Texas League."

"I got a gal in Yuma for winters," he says. "This other gal was just for during the season."

"How about that one time you showed your stuff?" I asked him. "How did you happen to do it?"

"Well," he said, "the Dallas club was playing a series in Waco and I went to a picture show and seen the gal with Fred Kruger. He's Dallas's manager. So the next day I made a monkey out of his ball club. I struck out fifteen of them and give them one hit —a fly ball that Smitty could have caught in a hollow tooth if he hadn't drunk his lunch."

Of course that was the game Dave's friend seen him pitch and we were lucky he happened to be in Waco just then. And it was Kane's last game in that league. Him and his "during the season" gal had a brawl and he played sick and got himself sent home.

Well, everybody knows now what a whale of a pitcher he turned out to be. He had a good, fast-breaking curve and Carney learned him how to throw a slow ball. Old Kid Farrell worked like a horse with him and got him so he could move around and field his position. At first he seemed to think he was moored out there. And another cute habit that had to be cured was his full wind-up with men on bases. The Kid starved him out of this.

Maybe I didn't tell you what an eater he was. Before Dave caught on to it, he was ordering one breakfast in his room and having another downstairs, and besides pretty near choking himself to death at lunch and supper, he'd sneak out to some lunchroom before bedtime, put away a Hamburger steak and eggs and bring back three or four sandwiches to snap at during the night.

He was rooming at the start with Joe Bonham and Joe finally told on him, thinking it was funny. But it wasn't funny to Dave and he named the Kid and Johnny Abbott a committee of two to see that Kane didn't explode. The Kid watched over him at table and Johnny succeeded Bonham as his roommate. And the way the Kid got him to cut out his wind-up was by telling him, "Now if you forget yourself and use it with a man on, your supper's going to be two olives and a finger-bowl, but if you hold up those runners, you can eat the chef."

As I say, the whole world knows what he is now. But they don't know how hard we worked with him, they don't know how close we came to losing him altogether, and they don't know the real story of that final game last year, which I'll tell you in a little while.

First, about pretty near losing him: As soon as Dave seen his possibilities and his value to us, he warned the boys not to ride him or play too many jokes on him because he was simple enough to take everything in dead earnest, and if he ever found out we were laughing at him, he might either lay down and quit trying or blow us entirely. Dave's dope was good, but you can't no more prevent a bunch of ball players from kidding a goofer like Kane than you can stop the Century at Herkimer by hollering " Whoa ! " He was always saying things and doing things that left him wide open and the gang took full advantage, especially Bull Wade.

I remember one night everybody was sitting on the porch and Bull was on the railing, right in front of Kane's chair.

" What's your first name, Steve ? " Bull asked him.

" Well," says Kane, " it ain't Steve at all. It's Elmer."

" It would be ! " says Bull. " It fits you like your suit. And that reminds me, I was going to inquire where you got that suit."

" In Yuma," said Kane. " In a store."

" A store ! " says Bull.

" A clothing store," says Kane. " They sell all kinds of clothes."

" I see they do," said Bull.

" If you want a suit like it, I'll write and find out if they've got another one," says Kane.

" They couldn't be two of them," says Bull, " and if they was, I'll bet Ed Wynn's bought the other. But anyway, I've already got a suit, and what I wanted to ask you was what the boys out West call you. I mean, what's your nickname ? "

" ' Hurry,' " says the sap. " ' Hurry ' Kane. Lefty Condon named me that."

" He seen you on your way to the dining-room," said Bull.

Kane didn't get it.

" No," he said. " It ain't nothing to do with a dining-room. A hurricane is a kind of a storm. My last name is Kane, so Lefty called me ' Hurry ' Kane. It's a kind of a storm."

" A brainstorm," says Bull.

" No," said Kane. "A hurricane is a big wind-storm."

" Does it blow up all of a sudden ? " asked Bull.

" Yeah, that's it," says Kane.

" We had three or four of them on this club last year," said Bull. "All pitchers, too. Dave got rid of them and he must be figuring on you to take their place."

" Do you mean you had four pitchers named Kane? " says the big busher.

" No," said Bull. " I mean we had four pitchers that could blow up all of a sudden. It was their hobby. Dave used to work them in turn, the same afternoon; on days when Olds and Carney needed a rest. Each one of the four would pitch an innings and a half."

Kane thought quite a while and then said: " But if they was four of them, and they pitched an innings and a half apiece, that's only six innings. Who pitched the other three? "

" Nobody," says Bull. " It was always too dark. By the way, what innings is your favorite? I mean, to blow in? "

" I don't blow," says the sap.

" Then," said Bull, " why was it that fella called you ' Hurry ' Kane? "

" It was Lefty Condon called me ' Hurry,' " says the sap. " My last name is Kane, and a hurricane is a big wind."

" Don't a wind blow? " says Bull.

And so on. I swear they kept it up for two hours, Kane trying to explain his nickname and Bull leading him on, and Joe Bonham said that Kane asked him up in the room who that was he had been talking to, and when Joe told him it was Wade, one of the smartest ball players in the league, Hurry said: " Well, then, he must be either stewed or else this is a damn sight dumber league than the one I came from."

Bull and some of the rest of the boys pulled all the old gags on him that's been in baseball since the days when you couldn't get on a club unless you had a walrus mustache. And Kane never disappointed them.

They made him go to the club-house after the key to the batter's box; they wrote him mash notes with fake names signed to them and had him spending half his evenings on some corner, waiting to meet gals that never lived; when he held Florida University to two hits in five innings, they sent him telegrams of congratulation from Coolidge and Al Smith, and he showed the telegrams to everybody in the hotel; they had him report at the ball park at six-thirty one morning for a secret " pitchers' conference "; they told him the Ritz was where all the unmarried ball players on the club lived while we were home, and they got him to write and ask for a parlor, bedroom and bath for the whole season. They was nothing he wouldn't fall for till Dave finally tipped him off that he was being kidded, and even then he didn't half believe it.

Now I never could figure how a man can fool themself about their own looks, but this bird was certain that he and Tommy Meighan were practically twins. Of course the boys soon found this out and strung him along. They advised him to quit baseball and go into pictures. They sat around his room and had him strike different poses and fix his hair different ways to see how he could show off his beauty to the best advantage. Johnny Abbott told me, after he began rooming with him, that for an hour before he went to bed and when he got up, Kane would stand in front of the mirror staring at himself and practising smiles and scowls and all kinds of silly faces, while Johnny pretended he was asleep.

Well, it wasn't hard to kid a fella like that into believing the dames were mad about him and when Bull Wade said that Evelyn Corey had asked who he was, his chest broke right through his shirt.

I know more about Evelyn now, but I didn't know nothing than except that she was a beautiful gal who had been in Broadway shows a couple of seasons and didn't have to be in them no more. Her room was two doors down the hall from Johnny's and Kane's. She was in Florida all alone, probably because her man friend, whoever he was at that time, had had to go abroad or somewheres with the family. All the ball players were willing to meet her, but she wasn't thrilled over the idear of getting acquainted with a bunch of guys who hadn't had a pay day in four or five months. Bull got Kane to write her a note; then Bull stole the note and wrote an answer, asking him to call. Hurry went and knocked at her door. She opened it and slammed it in his face.

"It was kind of dark," he said to Johnny, "and I guess she failed to recognize me." But he didn't have the nerve to call again.

He showed Johnny a picture of his gal in Yuma, a gal named Minnie Olson, who looked like she patronized the same store where Kane had bought his suit. He said she was wild about him and would marry him the minute he said the word and probably she was crying her eyes out right now, wishing he was home. He asked if Johnny had a gal and Johnny loosened up and showed him the picture of the gal he was engaged to. (Johnny married her last November.) She's a peach, but all Kane would say was, "Kind of skinny, ain't she?" Johnny laughed and said most gals liked to be that way.

"Not if they want me," says Kane.

"Well," said Johnny, "I don't think this one does. But how

about your friend, that Miss Corey? You certainly can't call her plump, yet you're anxious to meet her."

" She's got class! " said Kane.

Johnny laughed that off, too. This gal of his, that he's married to now, she's so far ahead of Corey as far as class is concerned—well, they ain't no comparison. Johnny, you know, went to Cornell a couple of years and his wife is a college gal he met at a big house-party. If you put her and Evelyn beside of each other you wouldn't have no trouble telling which of them belonged on Park Avenue and which Broadway.

Kane kept on moaning more and more about his gal out West and acting glummer and glummer. Johnny did his best to cheer him up, as he seen what was liable to happen. But they wasn't no use. The big rube "lost" his fast ball and told Dave he had strained his arm and probably wouldn't be no good all season. Dave bawled him out and accused him of stalling. Kane stalled just the same. Then Dave soft-soaped him, told him how he'd burn up the league and how we were all depending on him to put us in the race and keep us there. But he might as well have been talking to a mounted policeman.

Finally, one day during the last week at Fort Gregg, Johnny Abbott got homesick himself and put in a long-distance call for his gal in New York. It was a rainy day and him and Kane had been just laying around the room. Before the call went through Johnny hinted that he would like to be alone while he talked. Kane paid no attention and began undressing to take a nap. So Johnny had to speak before an audience and not only that, but as soon as Kane heard him say "Darling" or "Sweetheart," or whatever he called her, he moved right over close to the phone where he wouldn't miss nothing. Johnny was kind of embarrassed and hung up before he was ready to; then he gave Kane a dirty look and went to the window and stared out at the rain, dreaming about the gal he'd just talked with.

Kane laid down on his bed, but he didn't go to sleep. In four or five minutes he was at the phone asking the operator to get Minnie Olson in Yuma. Then he laid down again and tossed a while, and then he sat up on the edge of the bed.

" Johnny," he says, " how far is it from here to New York? "

" About a thousand miles," said Johnny.

" And how far to Yuma? " said Kane.

" Oh," says Johnny, " that must be three thousand miles at least."

" How much did that New York call cost you? " asked Kane.

" I don't know yet," said Johnny. " I suppose it was around seven bucks."

Kane went to the writing table and done a little arithmetic. From there he went back to the phone.

" Listen, girlie," he said to the operator, " you can cancel that Yuma call. I just happened to remember that the party I wanted won't be home. She's taking her mandolin lesson, way the other side of town."

Johnny told me afterwards that he didn't know whether to laugh or cry. Before he had a chance to do either, Kane says to him:

" This is my last day on this ball club."

" What do you mean? " said Johnny.

" I mean I'm through; I'm going home," says Kane.

" Don't be a fool! " says Johnny. " Don't throw away the chance of a lifetime just because you're a little lonesome. If you stay in this league and pitch like you can pitch, you'll be getting the big money next year and you can marry that gal and bring her East with you. You may not have to wait till next year. You may pitch us into the world's series and grab a chunk of dough this fall."

" We won't be in no world's series," says Kane.

" What makes you think so? " said Johnny.

" I can't work every day," says Kane.

" You'll have help," says Johnny. " With you and Carney and Olds taking turns, we can be right up in that old fight. Without you, we can't even finish in the league. If you won't do it for yourself or for Dave, do it for me, your roomy. You just seen me spend seven or eight bucks on a phone call, but that's no sign I'm reeking with jack. I spent that money because I'd have died if I hadn't. I've got none to throw away and if we don't win the pennant, I can't marry this year and maybe not next year or the year after."

" I've got to look out for myself," says Kane. " I tell you I'm through and that's all there is to it. I'm going home where my gal is, where they ain't no smart Alecks kidding me all the while, and where I can eat without no assistant manager holding me down to a sprig of parsley, and a thimbleful of soup. For your sake, Johnny," he says, " I'd like to see this club finish on top, but I can't stick it out and I'm afraid your only hope is for the other seven clubs to all be riding on the same train and hit an open bridge."

Well, of course Johnny didn't lose no time getting to Dave with the bad news, and Dave and Kid Farrell rushed to the sapper's room. They threatened him and they coaxed him. They promised him he could eat all he wanted. They swore that anybody who tried to play jokes on him would either be fined or fired off the club. They reminded him that it cost a lot of money to go from Florida to Yuma, and he would have to pay his own way. They offered him a new contract with a five-hundred-dollar raise if he would stay. They argued and pleaded with him from four in the afternoon till midnight. When they finally quit, they were just where they'd been when they started. He was through.

"All right!" Dave hollered. "Be through and go to hell! If you ain't out of here by tomorrow noon, I'll have you chased out! And don't forget that you'll never pitch in organized baseball again!"

"That suits me," says Kane, and went to bed.

When Johnny Abbott woke up about seven the next morning, Hurry was putting his extra collar and comb in the leaky suitcase. He said:

"I'm going to grab the eleven-something train for Jacksonville. I got money enough to take me from here to New Orleans and I know a fella there that will see me the rest of the way—if I can find him and he ain't broke."

Well, Johnny couldn't stand for that and he got up and dressed and was starting out to borrow two hundred dollars from me to lend to Kane, when the phone rang loud and long. Kane took off the receiver, listened a second, and then said "Uh-huh" and hung up.

"Who was it?" asked Johnny.

"Nobody," says Kane. "Just one of Bull Wade's gags."

"What did he say?" Johnny asked him.

"It was a gal, probably the telephone operator," said Kane. "She said the hotel was on fire and not to get excited, but that we better move out."

"You fool!" yelled Johnny and run to the phone.

They was no gag about it. The hotel had really caught fire in the basement and everybody was being warned to take the air. Johnny tossed some of his stuff in a bag and started out, telling Kane to follow him quick. Hurry got out in the hall and then remembered that he had left his gal's picture on the dresser and went back after it. Just as he turned towards the door again, in dashed a dame with a kimono throwed over her nightgown. It was Evelyn Corey herself, almost in the flesh.

"Oh, please!" she said, or screamed. "Come and help me carry my things!"

Well, here was once that the name "Hurry" was on the square. He dropped his own suitcase and was in her room in nothing and no-fifths. He grabbed her four pieces of hand baggage and was staggering to the hall with them when a bellhop bounced in and told them the danger was over, the fire was out.

This seemed to be more of a disappointment than Evelyn could stand. Anyway, she fainted—onto a couch—and for a few minutes she was too unconscious to do anything but ask Kane to pour her a drink. He also poured himself one and settled down in the easy chair like he was there for the day. But by now she had come to and got a good look at him.

"I thank you very much," she said, "and I'm so exhausted with all this excitement that I think I'll go back to bed."

Kane took his hint and got up.

"But ain't I going to see you again?" he asked her.

"I'm afraid not," says Evelyn. "I'm leaving here this evening and I'll be getting ready from now till then."

"Where are you headed for?" Kane asked her.

"For home, New York," she said.

"Can't I have your address?" said Kane.

"Why, yes," said Evelyn without batting an eye. "I live at the Ritz."

"The Ritz!" says Kane. "That's where I'm going to live, if they ain't filled up."

"How wonderful!" said Evelyn. "Then we'll probably see each other every day."

Kane beat it down to the dining-room and straight to Dave's table.

"Boss," he said, "I've changed my mind."

"Your what!" says Dave.

"My mind," says Kane. "I've decided to stick."

It was all Dave could do not to kiss him. But he thought it was best to act calm.

"That's fine, Hurry!" he said. "And I'll see that you get that extra five hundred bucks."

"What five hundred bucks?" says Kane.

"The five hundred I promised you if you'd stay," says Dave.

" I hadn't heard about it," said Kane. " But as long as I ain't going home, I'm in no rush for money. Though I'm liable to need it," he says, " as soon as we hit New York."

And he smiled the silliest smile you ever seen.

I don't have to tell you that he didn't live at the Ritz. Or that Evelyn Corey didn't live there neither. He found out she hadn't never lived there, but he figured she'd intended to and had to give it up because they didn't have a suite good enough for her.

I got him a room in my boarding-house in the Bronx and for the first few days he spent all his spare time looking through city directories and different telephone directories and bothering the life out of Information, trying to locate his lost lady. It was when he had practically give up hope that he told me his secret and asked for help.

" She's all I came here for," he said, " and if I can't find her, I ain't going to stay."

Well, of course if you went at it the right way, you wouldn't have much trouble tracing her. Pretty near anybody in the theatrical business, or the people that run the big night clubs, or the head waiters at the hotels and restaurants—they could have put you on the right track. The thing was that it would be worse to get a hold of her than not to, because she'd have give him the air so strong that he would have caught his death of cold.

So I just said that they was no question but what she had gone away somewheres, maybe to Europe, and he would hear from her as soon as she got back. I had to repeat this over and over and make it strong or he'd have left us flatter than his own feet before he pitched two games. As it was, we held him till the end of May without being obliged to try any tricks, but you could see he was getting more impatient and restless all the while and the situation got desperate just as we were starting on our first trip West. He asked me when would we hit St. Louis and I told him the date and said:

" What do you want to know for? "

" Because," he says, " I'm going home from there."

I repeated this sweet news to Dave and Kid Farrell. We finally called in Bull Wade and it was him that saved the day. You remember Bull had faked up a note from Evelyn to Kane down at Fort Gregg; now he suggested that he write some more notes, say one every two or three weeks, sign her name to them, send them to Bull's brother in Montreal and have the brother mail them from there. It was a kind of a dirty, mean thing to do, but it worked. The notes all read about the same——

" Dear Mr. Kane :—I am keeping track of your wonderful pitching and looking forward to seeing you when I return to New York, which will be early in the fall. I hope you haven't forgotten me."

And so on, signed " Your friend and admirer, Evelyn Corey."

Hurry didn't answer only about half of them as it was a real chore for him to write. He addressed his answers in care of Mr. Harry Wade, such and such a street number, Montreal, and when Bull's brother got them, he forwarded them to Bull, so he'd know if they was anything special he ought to reply to.

The boys took turns entertaining Kane evenings, playing cards with him and staking him to picture shows. Johnny Abbott done more than his share. You see the pennant meant more to Johnny than to anybody else; it meant the world's series money and a fall wedding, instead of a couple of years' wait. And Johnny's gal, Helen Kerslake, worked, too. She had him to her house to supper— when her folks were out—and made him feel like he was even handsomer and more important than he thought. She went so far as to try and get some of her gal friends to play with him, but he always wanted to pet and that was a little too much.

Well, if Kane hadn't stuck with us and turned out to be the marvel he is, the White Sox would have been so far ahead by the Fourth of July that they could have sat in the stand the rest of the season and let the Bloomer Girls play in their place. But Hurry had their number from the first time he faced them till the finish. Out of eleven games he worked against them all last year, he won ten and the other was a nothing to nothing tie. And look at the rest of his record! As I recall it, he took part in fifty-eight games. He pitched forty-three full games, winning thirty-six, losing five and tying two. And God knows how many games he saved! He had that free, easy side-arm motion that didn't take much out of him and he could pitch every third day and be at his best.

But don't let me forget to credit myself with an assist. Late in August, Kane told me he couldn't stand it no longer to just get short notes from the Corey gal and never see her, and when we started on our September trip West, he was going to steal a week off and run up to Montreal; he would join us later, but he must see Evelyn. Well, for once in my life I had an idear hit me right between the eyes.

The Yuma gal, Minnie Olson, had been writing to him once a

week and though he hardly ever wrote to her and seemed to only
be thinking of Corey, still I noticed that he could hardly help from
crying when Minnie's letters came. So I suggested to Dave that
he telegraph Minnie to come East and visit with all her expenses
paid, wire her money for her transportation, tell her it would be
doing Kane a big favor as well as the rest of us, and ask her to
send Kane a telegram, saying when she would reach New York,
but to be sure and never mention that she wasn't doing it on her
own hook.

Two days after Dave's message was sent, Kane got a wire from
El Paso. She was on her way and would he meet her at the Pennsylvania Station on such and such a date. I never seen a man as
happy as Hurry was when he read that telegram.

"I knew she was stuck on me," he said, "but I didn't know it
was that strong. She must have worked in a store or something
since spring to save up money for this trip."

You would have thought he'd never heard of or seen a gal by the
name of Evelyn Corey.

Minnie arrived and was just what we expected: a plain, honest,
good-hearted, small-town gal, dressed for a masquerade. We had
supper with her and Kane her first night in town—I and Johnny
and Helen. She was trembling like a leaf, partly from excitement over being in New York and amongst strangers, but mostly
on account of seeing the big sap again. He wasn't no sap to her
and I wished they was some dame would look at me the way she
kept looking at Hurry.

The next morning Helen took her on a shopping tour and got
her fixed up so cute that you couldn't hardly recognize her. In
the afternoon she went to the ball game and seen Kane shut the
Detroit club out with two hits.

When Hurry got a glimpse of her in her Fifth Avenue clothes,
he was as proud as if he had bought them himself and it didn't
seem to occur to him that they must have cost more than she could
have paid.

Well, with Kane happy and no danger of him walking out on
us, all we had to worry about was that the White Sox still led us
by three games, with less than twenty left to play. And the schedule was different than usual—we had to wind up with a Western
trip and play our last thirteen games on the road. I and Johnny
and Dave was talking it over one day and the three of us agreed
that we would be suckers not to insist on Miss Olson going along.
But Dave wondered if she wouldn't feel funny, being the only girl.

" I'll make my gal go, too," said Johnny.

And that's the way it was fixed.

We opened in St. Louis and beat them two out of three. Olds was trimmed, but Carney and Kane both won. We didn't gain no ground, because the White Sox grabbed two out of three from Washington. We made a sweep of our four games in Detroit, while the Sox was winning three from Philadelphia. That moved us up to two and a half games from first place. We beat Cleveland three straight, Kane licking them 6 to 1 and holding Carney's one run lead through the eighth and ninth innings of another game. At the same time, Chicago took three from Boston.

So we finally struck old Chi, where the fans was already counting the pennant won, two and a half games behind and three to go—meaning we had to win all three or be sunk.

I told you how Kane had the Chicago club's number. But I didn't tell you how Eddie Brainard had been making a monkey of us. He had only worked against us six times and had beat us five. His other game was the nothing to nothing tie with Hurry. Eddie is one sweet pitcher and if he had been the horse for work that Kane was, that last series wouldn't have got us nowheres. But Eddie needs his full rest and it was a cinch he wouldn't be in there for more than one game and maybe part of another.

In Brainard's six games against us, he had give us a total of four runs, shutting us out three times and trimming us 3 to 2, 4 to 1 and 2 to 1. As the White Sox only needed one game, it was a cinch that they wouldn't start Eddie against Kane, who was so tough for them, but would save him for Carney or Olds, whichever one worked first. Carney hadn't been able to finish a game with Chicago and Olds' record wasn't much better.

Well, we was having breakfast in our hotel the morning we got in from Cleveland, and Kane sent for Dave to come to the table where him and Johnny Abbott and the two gals was eating.

" Boss," he says, " I'm thinking of getting married and so is Johnny here, but they ain't neither of us can do it, not now anyway, unless we grab some of that world's series jack. And we can't get into the series without we win these three games. So if I was managing this ball club, I'd figure on that and know just how to work my pitchers."

" Maybe I've thought about it a little myself," says Dave. " But I'd like to listen to your idears."

" All right," says Kane. " I'd start Kane today, and I'd start Kane tomorrow, and I'd start Kane the day after that."

" My plan is a little different," said Dave. " Of course you start today, and if you win, why, I want to play a joke on them tomorrow. I intend to start Olds so they'll start Brainard. And if the game is anywheres near close at the end of the third or fourth innings, you're going in. It will be too late for them to take Brainard out and expect him to be as good the third day. And if we win that second game, why, you won't have to beg me to pitch the last one."

You'll think I'm getting long-winded, but they ain't much more to tell. You probably heard the details of those first two games even if you was on the Other Side. Hurry beat them the first one, 7 to 1, and their one run was my fault. Claymore was on second base with two men out in the sixth innings. King hit a foul ball right straight up and I dropped it. And then he pulled a base-hit inside of Bull, and Claymore scored. Olds and Brainard started the second game and at the end of our half of the fourth innings, the score was one and one. Hurry had been warming up easy right along, but it certainly was a big surprise to the Chicago club and pretty near everybody else when Dave motioned him in to relieve Olds. The White Sox never came close to another run and we got to Brainard for one in the eighth, just enought to beat him.

Eddie had pitched his head off and it was a tough one for him to lose. But the best part of it was, he was through and out of the way.

Well, Johnny and Kane had their usual date with the two gals for supper. Johnny was in his bathroom, washing up, when the phone rang. Kane answered it, but he talked kind of low and Johnny didn't hear what he was saying. But when Hurry had hung up, he acted kind of nervous and Johnny asked him what was the matter.

" It's hard luck," said Kane. " They's a friend of mine from Yuma here, and he's in trouble and I've got to go over on the North Side and see him. Will you take both the gals to supper yourself? Because I may not be back till late. And don't tell Min who I'm going to see."

" How could I tell her when you ain't told me? " said Johnny.

" Well," said Kane, " just tell her I'm wore out from working so hard two days in a row and I went right to bed so I'd be all right for tomorrow."

Johnny was kind of worried and tried to coax him not to go. But Kane ducked out and didn't come in till midnight. Johnny tried to find out where he'd been and what had happened, but he said he was too sleepy to talk. Just the same, Johnny says, he tossed around and moaned all night like he was having a nightmare, and he usually slept like a corpse.

Kane got up early and went down to breakfast before Johnny was dressed. But Johnny was still worried, and hustled up and caught him before he was out of the dining-room. He was hoping Hurry would explain his getting in late and not sleeping. Kane wouldn't talk, though, and still acted nervous. So Johnny finally said :

" Hurry, you know what this game today means to me and you ought to know what it means to you. If we get trimmed, a lot of people besides ourselves will be disappointed, but they won't nobody be as disappointed as me. I wished you'd have had a good sleep last night and if you'll take my advice, you'll go up in the room and rest till it's time to go to the ball yard. If you're anywheres near yourself, this Chicago club is licked. And for heaven's sakes, be yourself, or your roomy is liable to walk out into Lake Michigan tonight so far that I can't get back ! "

" I'm myself," says Kane and got up and left the table, but not quick enough so that Johnny didn't see tears in his eyes.

That afternoon's crowd beat all records and I was tickled to death to see it, because Hurry had always done his best work in front of crowds that was pulling against him. He warmed up fine and they wasn't nobody on our club, nobody but Kane himself and two others, who didn't feel perfectly confident that we were " in."

The White Sox were starting Sam Bonner and while he had beat us three or four times, we'd always got runs off him, and they'd always been lucky to score at all against Kane.

Bonner went through the first innings without no trouble. And then we got the shock of our lives. The first ball Hurry pitched was high and outside and it felt funny when I caught it. I was used to that old " zip " and I could have caught this one in my bare hand. Claymore took a cut at the next one and hit it a mile to left center for three bases. King hit for two bases, Welsh was safe when Digman threw a ground ball into the seats, and Kramer slapped one out of the park for a homer. Four runs. The crowd was wild and we were wilder.

You ought to have heard us on that bench. " Yellow so-and-so " was the mildest name Hurry got called. Dave couldn't do nothing but just mumble and shake his fists at Kane. We was all raving and asking each other what in hell was going on. Hurry stood in front facing us, but he was looking up in the stand and he acted like he didn't hear one word of the sweet remarks meant for his ears.

Johnny Abbott pulled me aside.

"Listen," he says. "This kid ain't yellow and he ain't wore out. They's something wrong here."

By this time Dave had found his voice and he yelled at Kane: "You so-and-so so-and-so! You're going to stay right in there and pitch till this game is over! And if you don't pitch like you can pitch, I'll shoot you dead tonight just as sure as you're a yellow, quitting——!"

We'd forgot it was our turn to bat and Hildebrand was threatening to forfeit the game before he could get Bull Wade to go up there. Kane still stood in front of us, staring. But pretty soon Dave told young Topping to run out to the bull pen and warn Carney and Olds to both be ready. I seen Topping stop a minute alongside of Kane and look up in the stand where Kane was looking. I seen Topping say something to Kane and I heard Kane call him a liar. Then Topping said something more and Hurry turned white as a sheet and pretty near fell into the dugout. I noticed his hand shake as he took a drink of water. And then he went over to Dave and I heard him say:

"I'm sorry, Boss. I had a bad inning. But I'll be all right from now on."

"You'd better!" says Dave.

"Get me some runs is all I ask," says Kane.

And the words wasn't no sooner out of his mouth when Bull smacked one a mile over Claymore's head and came into the plate standing up. They was another tune on the bench now. We were yelling for blood, and we got it. Before they relieved Bonner, we'd got to him for three singles and a double—mine, if you must know—and the score was tied.

Say, if you think you ever seen pitching, you ought to have watched Kane cut them through there the rest of that day. Fourteen strike-outs in the last eight innings! And the only man to reach first base was Kramer, when Stout dropped an easy fly ball in the fifth.

Well, to shorten it up, Bull and Johnny Abbott and myself had some luck against Pierce in the seventh innings. Bull and Johnny scored and we licked them, 6 to 4.

In the club-house, Dave went to Hurry and said:

"Have you got anything to tell me, any explanation of the way you looked at the start of that game?"

"Boss," said Kane, "I didn't sleep good last night. Johnny will be a witness to that. I felt terrible in that first innings. I seemed to have lost my 'fast.' In the second innings it came back and I was all right."

And that's all he would say.

You know how we went ahead and took the big series, four games out of five, and how Hurry gave them one run in the three games he pitched. And now you're going to know what I promised to tell you when we first sat down, and I hope I ain't keeping you from a date with that gal from St. Joe.

The world's series ended in St. Louis and naturally I didn't come back East when it was over. Neither did Kane, because he was going home to Yuma, along with his Minnie. Well, they were leaving the next night, though most of the other boys had ducked out right after the final game. Hurry called me up at my house three or four hours before his train was due to leave and asked me would I come and see him and give him some advice. So I went to the hotel and he got me in his room and locked the door.

Here is what he had to say:

On the night before that last game in Chi, a gal called him up and it was nobody but our old friend Evelyn Corey. She asked him to come out to a certain hotel on the North Side and have supper with her. He went because he felt kind of sorry for her. But when he seen her, he lost his head and was just as nuts about her as he'd been at Fort Gregg. She encouraged him and strung him along till he forgot all about poor Minnie. Evelyn told him she knew he could have his pick of a hundred gals and she was brokenhearted because they was no chance for her. He asked her what made her think that, and she put her handkerchief to her eyes and pretended she was crying and that drove him wild and he said he wouldn't marry nobody but her.

Then she told him they had better forget it, that she was broke now, but had been used to luxury, and he promised he would work hard and save up till he had three or four thousand dollars and that would be enough for a start.

"Four thousand dollars!" she says. "Why, that wouldn't buy the runs in my stockings! I wouldn't think of marrying a man who had less than twenty thousand. I would want a honeymoon in Europe and we'd buy a car over there and tour the whole continent, and then come home and settle down in some nice suburb of New York. And so," she says, "I am going to get up and leave you right now because I see that my dream won't never come true."

She left him sitting in the restaurant and he was the only person there outside of the waiters. But after he'd sat a little while—he was waiting till the first shock of his disappointment had wore off—a black-haired bird with a waxed mustache came up to him and asked if he wasn't Hurry Kane, the great pitcher. Then he said: "I suppose you'll pitch again tomorrow," and Kane said yes.

"I haven't nothing against you," says the stranger, "but I hope you lose. It will cost me a lot of money if you win."

"How much?" said Kane.

"So much," says the stranger, "that I will give you twenty thousand dollars if you get beat."

"I can't throw my pals," said Kane.

"Well," said the stranger, "two of your pals has already agreed to throw you."

Kane asked him who he referred to, but he wouldn't tell. Kane don't know yet, but I do. It was Dignan and Stout, our short-stopper and first baseman, and you'll notice they ain't with our club no more.

Hurry held out as long as he could, but he thought of Evelyn and that honeymoon in Europe broke him down. He took five thousand dollars' advance and was to come to the same place and get the balance right after the game.

He said that after Johnny Abbott had give him that talk at the breakfast table, he went out and rode around in a taxi so he could cry without being seen.

Well, I've told you about that terrible first innings. And I've told you about young Topping talking to him before he went down to the bull pen to deliver Dave's message to Carney and Olds. Topping asked him what he was staring at and Hurry pointed Evelyn out to him and said she was his gal.

"Your gal's grandmother!" said Topping. "That's Evelyn Corey and she belongs to Sam Morris, the bookie. If I was you, I'd lay off. You needn't tell Dave, but I was in Ike Bloom's at one o'clock this morning, and Sam and she were there, too. And one of the waiters told me that Sam had bet twenty thousand dollars on the White Sox way last spring and had got six to one for his money."

Hurry quit talking and I started to bawl him out. But I couldn't stay mad at him, especially when I realized that they was a fifty-three-hundred-dollar check in my pocket which I'd never have had only for him. Besides, they ain't nothing crooked about him. He's just a bone-headed sap.

" I won't tell Dave on you," I said, and I got up to go.

" Wait a minute," says Kane. " I confessed so I could ask you a question. I've still got that five thousand which Morris paid me in advance. With that dough and the fifty-three hundred from the series, I and Min could buy ourself a nice little home in Yuma. But do you think I should ought to give it back to that crook? "

" No," said I. " What you ought to do is split it with young Topping. He was your good luck! "

I run acrost Topping right here in town not long ago. And the first thing he said was, " What do you think of that goofey Kane? I had a letter from him and a check. He said the check was what he owed me."

" Twenty-five hundred dollars? " I says.

" Two hundred," said Topping, " and if I ever lent him two hundred or two cents, I'll roll a hoop from here to Yuma."

IX

CHAMPION

MIDGE KELLY scored his first knockout when he was seventeen. The knockee was his brother Connie, three years his junior and a cripple. The purse was a half dollar given to the younger Kelly by a lady whose electric had just missed bumping his soul from his frail little body.

Connie did not know Midge was in the house, else he never would have risked laying the prize on the arm of the least comfortable chair in the room, the better to observe its shining beauty. As Midge entered from the kitchen, the crippled boy covered the coin with his hand, but the movement lacked the speed requisite to escape his brother's quick eye.

"Watcha got there?" demanded Midge.

"Nothin'," said Connie.

"You're a one legged liar!" said Midge.

He strode over to his brother's chair and grasped the hand that concealed the coin.

"Let loose!" he ordered.

Connie began to cry.

"Let loose and shut up your noise," said the elder, and jerked his brother's hand from the chair arm.

The coin fell onto the bare floor. Midge pounced on it. His weak mouth widened in a triumphant smile.

"Nothin', huh?" he said. "All right, if it's nothin' you don't want it."

"Give that back," sobbed the younger.

"I'll give you a red nose, you little sneak! Where'd you steal it?"

"I didn't steal it. It's mine. A lady give it to me after she pretty near hit me with a car."

"It's a crime she missed you," said Midge.

Midge started for the front door. The cripple picked up his crutch, rose from his chair with difficulty, and, still sobbing, came toward Midge. The latter heard him and stopped.

"You better stay where you're at," he said.

109

" I want my money," cried the boy.

" I know what you want," said Midge.

Doubling up the fist that held the half dollar, he landed with all his strength on his brother's mouth. Connie fell to the floor with a thud, the crutch tumbling on top of him. Midge stood beside the prostrate form.

" Is that enough? " he said. " Or do you want this, too? "

And he kicked him in the crippled leg.

" I guess that'll hold you," he said.

There was no response from the boy on the floor. Midge looked at him a moment, then at the coin in his hand, and then went out into the street, whistling.

An hour later, when Mrs. Kelly came home from her day's work at Faulkner's Steam Laundry, she found Connie on the floor, moaning. Dropping on her knees beside him, she called him by name a score of times. Then she got up and, pale as a ghost, dashed from the house. Dr. Ryan left the Kelly abode about dusk and walked toward Halsted Street. Mrs. Dorgan spied him as he passed her gate.

" Who's sick, Doctor? " she called.

" Poor little Connie," he replied. " He had a bad fall."

" How did it happen? "

" I can't say for sure, Margaret, but I'd almost bet he was knocked down."

" Knocked down! " exclaimed Mrs. Dorgan.

" Why, who——? "

" Have you seen the other one lately? "

" Michael? No, not since mornin'. You can't be thinkin'——"

" I wouldn't put it past him, Margaret," said the doctor gravely. " The lad's mouth is swollen and cut, and his poor, skinny little leg is bruised. He surely didn't do it to himself and I think Helen suspects the other one."

" Lord save us! " said Mrs. Dorgan. " I'll run over and see if I can help."

" That's a good woman," said Doctor Ryan, and went on down the street.

Near midnight, when Midge came home, his mother was sitting at Connie's bedside. She did not look up.

" Well," said Midge, " what's the matter? "

She remained silent. Midge repeated his question.

" Michael, you know what's the matter," she said at length.

" I don't know nothin'," said Midge.

" Don't lie to me, Michael. What did you do to your brother? "

" Nothin'."

" You hit him."

" Well, then, I hit him. What of it? It ain't the first time."

Her lips pressed tightly together, her face like chalk, Ellen Kelly rose from her chair and made straight for him. Midge backed against the door.

" Lay off'n me, Ma. I don't want to fight no woman."

Still she came on breathing heavily.

" Stop where you're at, Ma," he warned.

There was a brief struggle and Midge's mother lay on the floor before him.

" You ain't hurt, Ma. You're lucky I didn't land good. And I told you to lay off'n me."

" God forgive you, Michael! "

Midge found Hap Collins in the showdown game at the Royal.

" Come on out a minute," he said.

Hap followed him out on the walk.

" I'm leavin' town for a w'ile," said Midge.

" What for? "

" Well, we had a little run-in up to the house. The kid stole a half buck off'n me, and when I went after it he cracked me with his crutch. So I nailed him. And the old lady came at me with a chair and I took it off'n her and she fell down."

" How is Connie hurt? "

" Not bad."

" What are you runnin' away for? "

" Who the hell said I was runnin' away? I'm sick and tired o' gettin' picked on; that's all. So I'm leavin' for a w'ile and I want a piece o' money."

" I ain't only got six bits," said Happy.

" You're in bad shape, ain't you? Well, come through with it."

Happy came through.

" You oughtn't to hit the kid," he said.

" I ain't astin' you who can I hit," snarled Midge. " You try to put somethin' over on me and you'll get the same dose. I'm goin' now."

" Go as far as you like," said Happy, but not until he was sure that Kelly was out of hearing.

Early the following morning, Midge boarded a train for Milwaukee. He had no ticket, but no one knew the difference. The conductor remained in the caboose.

On a night six months later, Midge hurried out of the " stage door " of the Star Boxing Club and made for Duane's saloon, two blocks away. In his pocket were twelve dollars, his reward for having battered up one Demon Dempsey through the six rounds of the first preliminary.

It was Midge's first professional engagement in the manly art. Also it was the first time in weeks that he had earned twelve dollars.

On the way to Duane's he had to pass Niemann's. He pulled his cap over his eyes and increased his pace until he had gone by. Inside Niemann's stood a trusting bartender, who for ten days had staked Midge to drinks and allowed him to ravage the lunch on a promise to come in and settle the moment he was paid for the " prelim."

Midge strode into Duane's and aroused the napping bartender by slapping a silver dollar on the festive board.

" Gimme a shot," said Midge.

The shooting continued until the wind-up at the Star was over and part of the fight crowd joined Midge in front of Duane's bar. A youth in the early twenties, standing next to young Kelly, finally summoned sufficient courage to address him.

" Wasn't you in the first bout? " he ventured.

" Yeh," Midge replied.

" My name's Hersch," said the other.

Midge received the startling information in silence.

" I don't want to butt in," continued Mr. Hersch, " but I'd like to buy you a drink."

" All right," said Midge, " but don't overstrain yourself."

Mr. Hersch laughed uproariously and beckoned to the bartender.

" You certainly gave that wop a trimmin' tonight," said the buyer of the drink, when they had been served. " I thought you'd kill him."

" I would if I hadn't let up," Midge replied. " I'll kill 'em all."

" You got the wallop all right," the other said admiringly.

" Have I got the wallop? " said Midge. " Say, I can kick like a mule. Did you notice them muscles in my shoulders? "

" Notice 'em? I couldn't help from noticin' 'em," said Hersch. " I says to the fella settin' alongside o' me, I says: ' Look at them shoulders! No wonder he can hit,' I says to him."

" Just let me land and it's good-by, baby," said Midge. " I'll kill 'em all."

The oral manslaughter continued until Duane's closed for the night. At parting, Midge and his new friend shook hands and arranged for a meeting the following evening.

For nearly a week the two were together almost constantly. It was Hersch's pleasant rôle to listen to Midge's modest revelations concerning himself, and to buy every time Midge's glass was empty. But there came an evening when Hersch regretfully announced that he must go home to supper.

" I got a date for eight bells," he confided. " I could stick till then, only I must clean up and put on the Sunday clo'es, 'cause she's the prettiest little thing in Milwaukee."

" Can't you fix it for two? " asked Midge.

" I don't know who to get," Hersch replied. " Wait, though. I got a sister and if she ain't busy, it'll be O. K. She's no bum for looks herself."

So it came about that Midge and Emma Hersch and Emma's brother and the prettiest little thing in Milwaukee foregathered at Wall's and danced half the night away. And Midge and Emma danced every dance together, for though every little onestep seemed to induce a new thirst of its own, Lou Hersch stayed too sober to dance with his own sister.

The next day, penniless at last in spite of his phenomenal ability to make someone else settle, Midge Kelly sought out Doc Hammond, matchmaker for the Star, and asked to be booked for the next show.

" I could put you on with Tracy for the next bout," said Doc.

" What's they in it? " asked Midge.

" Twenty if you cop," Doc told him.

" Have a heart," protested Midge. " Didn't I look good the other night? "

" You looked all right. But you aren't Freddie Welsh yet by a consid'able margin."

" I ain't scared of Freddie Welsh or none of 'em," said Midge.

" Well, we don't pay our boxers by the size of their chests," Doc said. " I'm offerin' you this Tracy bout. Take it or leave it."

" All right ; I'm on," said Midge, and he passed a pleasant afternoon at Duane's on the strength of his booking.

Young Tracy's manager came to Midge the night before the show.

" How do you feel about this go? " he asked.

"Me?" said Midge, "I feel all right. What do you mean, how do I feel?"

"I mean," said Tracy's manager, "that we're mighty anxious to win, 'cause the boy's got a chanct in Philly if he cops this one."

"What's your proposition?" asked Midge.

"Fifty bucks," said Tracy's manager.

"What do you think I am, a crook? Me lay down for fifty bucks. Not me!"

"Seventy-five, then," said Tracy's manager.

The market closed on eighty and the details were agreed on in short order. And the next night Midge was stopped in the second round by a terrific slap on the forearm.

This time Midge passed up both Niemann's and Duane's, having a sizable account at each place, and sought his refreshment at Stein's farther down the street.

When the profits of his deal with Tracy were gone, he learned, by first-hand information from Doc Hammond and the matchmakers at the other "clubs," that he was no longer desired for even the cheapest of preliminaries. There was no danger of his starving or dying of thirst while Emma and Lou Hersch lived. But he made up his mind, four months after his defeat by Young Tracy, that Milwaukee was not the ideal place for him to live.

"I can lick the best of 'em," he reasoned, "but there ain't no more chanct for me here. I can maybe go east and get on somewheres. And besides——"

But just after Midge had purchased a ticket to Chicago with the money he had "borrowed" from Emma Hersch "to buy shoes," a heavy hand was laid on his shoulders and he turned to face two strangers.

"Where are you goin', Kelly?" inquired the owner of the heavy hand.

"Nowheres," said Midge. "What the hell do you care?"

The other stranger spoke:

"Kelly, I'm employed by Emma Hersch's mother to see that you do right by her. And we want you to stay here till you've done it."

"You won't get nothin' but the worst of it, monkeying with me," said Midge.

Nevertheless, he did not depart for Chicago that night. Two days later, Emma Hersch became Mrs. Kelly, and the gift of the groom, when once they were alone, was a crushing blow on the bride's pale cheek.

Next morning, Midge left Milwaukee as he had entered it—by fast freight.

" They's no use kiddin' ourself any more," said Tommy Haley. " He might get down to thirty-seven in a pinch, but if he done below that a mouse could stop him. He's a welter; that's what he is and he knows it as well as I do. He's growed like a weed in the last six mont's. I told him, I says, ' If you don't quit growin' they won't be nobody for you to box, only Willard and them.' He says, ' Well, I wouldn't run away from Willard if I weighed twenty pounds more.' "

" He must hate himself," said Tommy's brother.

" I never seen a good one that didn't," said Tommy. " And Midge is a good one; don't make no mistake about that. I wisht we could of got Welsh before the kid growed so big. But it's too late now. I won't make no holler, though, if we can match him up with the Dutchman."

" Who do you mean? "

" Young Goetz, the welter champ. We mightn't not get so much dough for the bout itself, but it'd roll in afterward. What a drawin' card we'd be, 'cause the people pays their money to see the fella with the wallop, and that's Midge. And we'd keep the title just as long as Midge could make the weight."

" Can't you land no match with Goetz? "

" Sure, 'cause he needs the money. But I've went careful with the kid so far and look at the results I got! So what's the use of takin' a chanct? The kid's comin' every minute and Goetz is goin' back faster'n big Johnson did. I think we could lick him now; I'd bet my life on it. But six mont's from now they won't be no risk. He'll of licked hisself before that time. Then all as we'll have to do is sign up with him and wait for the referee to stop it. But Midge is so crazy to get at him now that I can't hardly hold him back."

The brothers Haley were lunching in a Boston hotel. Dan had come down from Holyoke to visit with Tommy and to watch the latter's protégé go twelve rounds, or less, with Bud Cross. The bout promised little in the way of a contest, for Midge had twice stopped the Baltimore youth and Bud's reputation for gameness was all that had earned him the date. The fans were willing to pay the price to see Midge's hay-making left, but they wanted to see it used on an opponent who would not jump out of the ring the first time he felt its crushing force. But Cross was such an opponent, and his willingness to stop boxing-gloves with his eyes, ears, nose and throat had long enabled him to escape the horrors of honest labor. A game boy was Bud, and he showed it in his battered, swollen, discolored face.

" I should think," said Dan Haley, " that the kid'd do whatever you tell him after all you done for him."

" Well," said Tommy, " he's took my dope pretty straight so far, but he's so sure of hisself that he can't see no reason for waitin'. He'll do what I say, though; he'd be a sucker not to."

" You got a contrac' with him ? "

" No, I don't need no contrac'. He knows it was me that drug him out o' the gutter and he ain't goin' to turn me down now, when he's got the dough and bound to get more. Where'd he of been at if I hadn't listened to him when he first come to me? That's pretty near two years ago now, but it seems like last week. I was settin' in the s'loon acrost from the Pleasant Club in Philly, waitin' for McCann to count the dough and come over, when this little bum blowed in and tried to stand the house off for a drink. They told him nothin' doin' and to beat it out o' there, and then he seen me and come over to where I was settin' and ast me wasn't I a boxin' man and I told him who I was. Then he ast me for money to buy a shot and I told him to set down and I'd buy it for him.

" Then we got talkin' things over and he told me his name and told me about fightn' a couple o' prelims out to Milwaukee. So I says, ' Well, boy, I don't know how good or how rotten you are, but you won't never get nowheres trainin' on that stuff.' So he says he'd cut it out if he could get on in a bout and I says I would give him a chanct if he played square with me and didn't touch no more to drink. So we shook hands and I took him up to the hotel with me and give him a bath and the next day I bought him some clo'es. And I staked him to eats and sleeps for over six weeks. He had a hard time breakin' away from the polish, but finally I thought he was fit and I give him his chanct. He went on with Smiley Sayer and stopped him so quick that Smiley thought sure he was poisoned.

" Well, you know what he's did since. The only beatin' in his record was by Tracy in Milwaukee before I got hold of him, and he's licked Tracy three times in the last year.

" I've gave him all the best of it in a money way and he's got seven thousand bucks in cold storage. How's that for a kid that was in the gutter two years ago? And he'd have still more yet if he wasn't so nuts over clo'es and got to stop at the good hotels and so forth."

" Where's his home at ? "

" Well, he ain't really got no home. He came from Chicago and his mother canned him out o' the house for bein' no good. She give him a raw deal, I guess, and he says he won't have nothin' to do with her unlest she comes to him first. She's got a pile o' money, he says, so he ain't worryin' about her."

The gentleman under discussion entered the café and swaggered to Tommy's table, while the whole room turned to look.

Midge was the picture of health despite a slightly colored eye and an ear that seemed to have no opening. But perhaps it was not his healthiness that drew all eyes. His diamond horse-shoe tie pin, his purple cross-striped shirt, his orange shoes and his light blue suit fairly screamed for attention.

" Where you been? " he asked Tommy. " I been lookin' all over for you."

" Set down," said his manager.

" No time," said Midge. " I'm goin' down to the w'arf and see 'em unload the fish."

" Shake hands with my brother Dan," said Tommy.

Midge shook with the Holyoke Haley.

" If you're Tommy's brother, you're O. K. with me," said Midge, and the brothers beamed with pleasure.

Dan moistened his lips and murmured an embarrassed reply, but it was lost on the young gladiator.

" Leave me take twenty," Midge was saying. " I prob'ly won't need it, but I don't like to be caught short."

Tommy parted with a twenty dollar bill and recorded the trans-action in a small black book the insurance company had given him for Christmas.

" But," he said, " it won't cost you no twenty to look at them fish. Want me to go along? "

" No," said Midge hastily. " You and your brother here prob'ly got a lot to say to each other."

" Well," said Tommy, " don't take no bad money and don't get lost. And you better be back at four o'clock and lay down a w'ile."

" I don't need no rest to beat this guy," said Midge. " He'll do enough layin' down for the both of us."

And laughing even more than the jest called for, he strode out through the fire of admiring and startled glances.

The corner of Boylston and Tremont was the nearest Midge got to the wharf, but the lady awaiting him was doubtless a more daz-zling sight than the catch of the luckiest Massachusetts fisherman. She could talk, too—probably better than the fish.

" O you Kid ! " she said, flashing a few silver teeth among the
gold.   " O you fighting man ! "

Midge smiled up at her.

" We'll go somewheres and get a drink," he said.   " One won't
hurt."

In New Orleans, five months after he had rearranged the map
of Bud Cross for the third time, Midge finished training for his
championship bout with the Dutchman.

Back in his hotel after the final workout, Midge stopped to chat
with some of the boys from up north, who had made the long trip
to see a champion dethroned, for the result of this bout was so
nearly a foregone conclusion that even the experts had guessed it.

Tommy Haley secured the key and the mail and ascended to the
Kelly suite. He was bathing when Midge came in, half an hour
later.

" Any mail ? " asked Midge.

" There on the bed," replied Tommy from the tub.

Midge picked up the stack of letters and postcards and glanced
them over.   From the pile he sorted out three letters and laid them
on the table. The rest he tossed into the waste-basket. Then he
picked up the three and sat for a few moments holding them, while
his eyes gazed off into space. At length he looked again at the
three unopened letters in his hand ; then he put one in his pocket
and tossed the other two at the basket. They missed their target
and fell on the floor.

" Hell ! " said Midge, and stooping over picked them up.

He opened one postmarked Milwaukee and read :

Dear Husband :

I have wrote to you so manny times and got no anser and I dont
know if you ever got them, so I am writeing again in the hopes
you will get this letter and anser. I dont like to bother you with
my trubles and I would not only for the baby and I am not asking
you should write to me but only send a little money and I am not
asking for myself but the baby has not been well a day sence last
Aug. and the dr. told me she cant live much longer unless I give
her better food and thats impossible the way things are. Lou has
not been working for a year and what I make dont hardley pay for
the rent. I am not asking for you to give me any money, but only
you should send what I loaned when convenient and I think it

amts. to about $36.00. Please try and send that amt. and it will help me, but if you cant send the whole amt. try and send me something.

Your wife,

Emma.

Midge tore the letter into a hundred pieces and scattered them over the floor.

"Money, money, money!" he said. "They must think I'm made o' money. I s'pose the old woman's after it too."

He opened his mother's letter:

dear Michael Connie wonted me to rite and say you must beet the dutchman and he is sur you will and wonted me to say we wont you to rite and tell us about it, but I gess you havent no time to rite or we herd from you long beffore this but I wish you would rite jest a line or 2 boy becaus it wuld be better for Connie then a barl of medisin. It wuld help me to keep things going if you send me money now and then when you can spair it but if you cant send no money try and fine time to rite a letter onley a few lines and it will please Connie. jest think boy he hasent got out of bed in over 3 yrs. Connie says good luck.

Your Mother,

Ellen F. Kelly.

"I thought so," said Midge. "They're all alike."

The third letter was from New York. It read:

Hon:—This is the last letter you will get from me before your champ, but I will send you a telegram Saturday, but I can't say as much in a telegram as in a letter and I am writeing this to let you know I am thinking of you and praying for good luck.

Lick him good hon and don't wait no longer than you have to and don't forget to wire me as soon as its over. Give him that little old left of yours on the nose hon and don't be afraid of spoiling his good looks because he couldn't be no homlier than he is. But don't let him spoil my baby's pretty face. You won't will you hon.

Well hon I would give anything to be there and see it, but I guess you love Haley better than me or you wouldn't let him keep me away. But when your champ hon we can do as we please and tell Haley to go to the devil.

Well hon I will send you a telegram Saturday and I almost forgot to tell you I will need some more money, a couple hundred say and you will have to wire it to me as soon as you get this. You will won't you hon.

I will send you a telegram Saturday and remember hon I am pulling for you.

Well good-by sweetheart and good luck.

Grace.

"They're all alike," said Midge. "Money, money, money."

Tommy Haley, shining from his ablutions, came in from the adjoining room.

"Thought you'd be layin' down," he said.

"I'm goin' to," said Midge, unbuttoning his orange shoes.

"I'll call you at six and you can eat up here without no bugs to pester you. I got to go down and give them birds their tickets."

"Did you hear from Goldberg?" asked Midge.

"Didn't I tell you? Sure; fifteen weeks at five hundred, if we win. And we can get a guarantee o' twelve thousand, with privileges either in New York or Milwaukee."

"Who with?"

"Anybody that'll stand up in front of you. You don't care who it is, do you?"

"Not me. I'll make 'em all look like a monkey."

"Well you better lay down aw'ile."

"Oh, say, wire two hundred to Grace for me, will you? Right away; the New York address."

"Two hundred! You just sent her three hundred last Sunday."

"Well, what the hell do you care?"

"All right, all right. Don't get sore about it. Anything else?"

"That's all," said Midge, and dropped onto the bed.

"And I want the deed done before I come back," said Grace as she rose from the table. "You won't fall down on me, will you, hon?"

"Leave it to me," said Midge. "And don't spend no more than you have to."

Grace smiled a farewell and left the café. Midge continued to sip his coffee and read his paper.

They were in Chicago and they were in the middle of Midge's first week in vaudeville. He had come straight north to reap the rewards of his glorious victory over the broken down Dutchman. A fortnight had been spent in learning his act, which consisted of a gymnastic exhibition and a ten minutes' monologue on the various excellences of Midge Kelly. And now he was twice daily turning 'em away from the Madison Theater.

His breakfast over and his paper read, Midge sauntered into the lobby and asked for his key. He then beckoned to a bell-boy, who had been hoping for that very honor.

" Find Haley, Tommy Haley," said Midge. " Tell him to come up to my room."

" Yes, sir, Mr. Kelly," said the boy, and proceeded to break all his former records for diligence.

Midge was looking out of his seventh-story window when Tommy answered the summons.

" What'll it be? " inquired his manager.

There was a pause before Midge replied.

" Haley," he said, " twenty-five per cent's a whole lot o' money."

" I guess I got it comin', ain't I? " said Tommy.

" I don't see how you figger it. I don't see where you're worth it to me."

" Well," said Tommy, " I didn't expect nothin' like this. I thought you was satisfied with the bargain. I don't want to beat nobody out o' nothin', but I don't see where you could have got anybody else that would of did all I done for you."

" Sure, that's all right," said the champion. " You done a lot for me in Philly. And you got good money for it, didn't you? "

" I ain't makin' no holler. Still and all, the big money's still ahead of us yet. And if it hadn't of been for me, you wouldn't of never got within grabbin' distance."

" Oh, I guess I could of went along all right," said Midge. " Who was it that hung that left on the Dutchman's jaw, me or you? "

" Yes, but you wouldn't been in the ring with the Dutchman if it wasn't for how I handled you."

" Well, this won't get us nowheres. The idear is that you ain't worth no twenty-five per cent now and it don't make no diff'rence what come off a year or two ago."

" Don't it? " said Tommy. " I'd say it made a whole lot of difference."

" Well, I say it don't and I guess that settles it."

" Look here, Midge," Tommy said, " I thought I was fair with you, but if you don't think so, I'm willin' to hear what you think is fair. I don't want nobody callin' me a Sherlock. Let's go down to business and sign up a contrac'. What's your figger? "

" I ain't namin' no figger," Midge replied. " I'm sayin' that twenty-five's too much. Now what are you willin' to take? "

" How about twenty? "

" Twenty's too much," said Kelly.

" What ain't too much? " asked Tommy.

" Well, Haley, I might as well give it to you straight. They ain't nothin' that ain't too much."

" You mean you don't want me at no figger? "

" That's the idear."

There was a minute's silence. Then Tommy Haley walked toward the door.

" Midge," he said, in a choking voice, " you're makin' a big mistake, boy. You can't throw down your best friends and get away with it. That damn woman will ruin you."

Midge sprang from his seat.

" You shut your mouth! " he stormed. " Get out o' here before they have to carry you out. You been spongin' off o' me long enough. Say one more word about the girl or about anything else and you'll get what the Dutchman got. Now get out! "

And Tommy Haley, having a very vivid memory of the Dutchman's face as he fell, got out.

Grace came in later, dropped her numerous bundles on the lounge and perched herself on the arm of Midge's chair.

" Well? " she said.

" Well," said Midge, " I got rid of him."

" Good boy! " said Grace. " And now I think you might give me that twenty-five per cent."

" Besides the seventy-five you're already gettin'? " said Midge.

" Don't be no grouch, hon. You don't look pretty when you're grouchy."

" It ain't my business to look pretty," Midge replied.

" Wait till you see how I look with the stuff I bought this mornin'! "

Midge glanced at the bundles on the lounge.

" There's Haley's twenty-five per cent," he said, " and then some."

The champion did not remain long without a manager. Haley's successor was none other than Jerome Harris, who saw in Midge a better meal ticket than his popular-priced musical show had been.

The contract, giving Mr. Harris twenty-five per cent of Midge's earnings, was signed in Detroit the week after Tommy Haley had heard his dismissal read. It had taken Midge just six days to learn that a popular actor cannot get on without the ministrations of a man who thinks, talks and means business. At first Grace objected to the new member of the firm, but when Mr. Harris had demanded and secured from the vaudeville people a one-hundred dollar increase in Midge's weekly stipend, she was convinced that the champion had acted for the best.

" You and my missus will have some great old times," Harris told Grace. " I'd of wired her to join us here, only I seen the Kid's bookin' takes us to Milwaukee next week, and that's where she is."

But when they were introduced in the Milwaukee hotel, Grace admitted to herself that her feeling for Mrs. Harris could hardly be called love at first sight. Midge, on the contrary, gave his new manager's wife the many times over and seemed loath to end the feast of his eyes.

" Some doll," he said to Grace when they were alone.

" Doll is right," the lady replied, " and sawdust where her brains ought to be."

" I'm li'ble to steal that baby," said Midge, and he smiled as he noted the effect of his words on his audience's face.

On Tuesday of the Milwaukee week the champion successfully defended his title in a bout that the newspapers never reported. Midge was alone in his room that morning when a visitor entered without knocking. The visitor was Lou Hersch.

Midge turned white at sight of him.

" What do you want? " he demanded.

" I guess you know," said Lou Hersch. " Your wife's starvin' to death and your baby's starvin' to death and I'm starvin' to death. And you're dirty with money."

" Listen," said Midge, " if it wasn't for you, I wouldn't never saw your sister. And, if you ain't man enough to hold a job, what's that to me? The best thing you can do is keep away from me."

" You give me a piece o' money and I'll go."

Midge's reply to the ultimatum was a straight right to his brother-in-law's narrow chest.

" Take that home to your sister."

And after Lou Hersch had picked himself up and slunk away, Midge thought: " It's lucky I didn't give him my left or I'd of croaked him. And if I'd hit him in the stomach, I'd of broke his spine."

There was a party after each evening performance during the

Milwaukee engagement. The wine flowed freely and Midge had more of it than Tommy Haley ever would have permitted him. Mr. Harris offered no objection, which was possibly just as well for his own physical comfort.

In the dancing between drinks, Midge had his new manager's wife for a partner as often as Grace. The latter's face as she floundered round in the arms of the portly Harris, belied her frequent protestations that she was having the time of her life.

Several times that week, Midge thought Grace was on the point of starting the quarrel he hoped to have. But it was not until Friday night that she accommodated. He and Mrs. Harris had disappeared after the matinee and when Grace saw him again at the close of the night show, she came to the point at once.

" What are you tryin' to pull off? " she demanded.

" It's none o' your business, is it? " said Midge.

" You bet it's my business; mine and Harris's. You cut it short or you'll find out."

"Listen," said Midge, " have you got a mortgage on me or somethin'? You talk like we was married."

" We're goin' to be, too. And to-morrow's as good a time as any."

" Just about," Midge said. " You got as much chanct o' marryin' me to-morrow as the next day or next year and that ain't no chanct at all."

" We'll find out," said Grace.

" You're the one that's got somethin' to find out."

" What do you mean? "

" I mean I'm married already."

" You lie! "

" You think so, do you? Well, s'pose you go to this here address and get acquainted with my missus."

Midge scrawled a number on a piece of paper and handed it to her. She stared at it unseeingly.

" Well," said Midge, " I ain't kiddin' you. You go there and ask for Mrs. Michael Kelly, and if you don't find her, I'll marry you to-morrow before breakfast."

Still Grace stared at the scrap of paper. To Midge it seemed an age before she spoke again.

" You lied to me all this w'ile."

" You never ast me was I married. What's more, what the hell diff'rence did it make to you? You got a split, didn't you? Better'n fifty-fifty."

He started away.

" Where you goin'? "

" I'm goin' to meet Harris and his wife."

" I'm goin' with you. You're not goin' to shake me now."

" Yes, I am, too," said Midge quietly. " When I leave town to-morrow night, you're going to stay here. And if I see where you're goin' to make a fuss, I'll put you in a hospital where they'll keep you quiet. You can get your stuff to-morrow mornin' and I'll slip you a hundred bucks. And then I don't want to see no more o' you. And don't try and tag along now or I'll have to add another K. O. to the old record."

When Grace returned to the hotel that night, she discovered that Midge and the Harrises had moved to another. And when Midge left town the following night, he was again without a manager, and Mr. Harris was without a wife.

Three days prior to Midge Kelly's ten-round bout with Young Milton in New York City, the sporting editor of *The News* assigned Joe Morgan to write two or three thousand words about the champion to run with a picture lay-out for Sunday.

Joe Morgan dropped in at Midge's training quarters Friday afternoon. Midge, he learned, was doing road work, but Midge's manager, Wallie Adams, stood ready and willing to supply reams of dope about the greatest fighter of the age.

" Let's hear what you've got," said Joe, " and then I'll try to fix up something."

So Wallie stepped on the accelerator of his imagination and shot away.

" Just a kid; that's all he is; a regular boy. Get what I mean? Don't know the meanin' o' bad habits. Never tasted liquor in his life and would prob'bly get sick if he smelled it. Clean livin' put him up where he's at. Get what I mean? And modest and unassumin' as a school girl. He's so quiet you wouldn't never know he was round. And he'd go to jail before he'd talk about himself.

"No job at all to get him in shape, 'cause he's always that way. The only trouble we have with him is gettin' him to light into these poor bums they match him up with. He's scared he'll hurt somebody. Get what I mean? He's tickled to death over this match with Milton, 'cause everybody says Milton can stand the gaff. Midge'll maybe be able to cut loose a little this time. But the last two bouts he had, the guys hadn't no business in the ring with him, and he was holdin' back all the w'ile for the fear he'd kill somebody. Get what I mean? "

" Is he married ? " inquired Joe.

" Say, you'd think he was married to hear him rave about them kiddies he's got. His fam'ly's up in Canada to their summer home and Midge is wild to get up there with 'em. He thinks more o' that wife and them kiddies than all the money in the world. Get what I mean ? "

" How many children has he ? "

" I don't know, four or five, I guess. All boys and every one of 'em a dead ringer for their dad."

" Is his father living ? "

" No, the old man died when he was a kid. But he's got a grand old mother and a kid brother out in Chi. They're the first ones he thinks about after a match, them and his wife and kiddies. And he don't forget to send the old woman a thousand bucks after every bout. He's goin' to buy her a new home as soon as they pay him off for this match."

" How about his brother ? Is he going to tackle the game ? "

" Sure, and Midge says he'll be a champion before he's twenty years old. They're a fightin' fam'ly and all of 'em honest and straight as a die. Get what I mean ? A fella that I can't tell you his name come to Midge in Milwaukee onct and wanted him to throw a fight and Midge give him such a trimmin' in the street that he couldn't go on that night. That's the kind he is. Get what I mean ? "

Joe Morgan hung around the camp until Midge and his trainers returned.

" One o' the boys from *The News*," said Wallie by way of introduction. " I been givin' him your fam'ly hist'ry."

" Did he give you good dope ? " he inquired.

" He's some historian," said Joe.

" Don't call me no names," said Wallie smiling. " Call us up if they's anything more you want. And keep your eyes on us Monday night. Get what I mean ? "

The story in Sunday's *News* was read by thousands of lovers of the manly art. It was well written and full of human interest. Its slight inaccuracies went unchallenged, though three readers, besides Wallie Adams and Midge Kelly, saw and recognized them. The three were Grace, Tommy Haley and Jerome Harris and the comments they made were not for publication.

Neither the Mrs. Kelly in Chicago nor the Mrs. Kelly in Milwaukee knew that there was such a paper as the New York *News*. And even if they had known of it and that it contained two columns of reading matter about Midge, neither mother nor wife could have bought it.   For *The News* on Sunday is a nickel a copy.

Joe Morgan could have written more accurately, no doubt, if instead of Wallie Adams, he had interviewed Ellen Kelly and Connie Kelly and Emma Kelly and Lou Hersch and Grace and Jerome Harris and Tommy Haley and Hap Collins and two or three Milwaukee bartenders.

But a story built on their evidence would never have passed the sporting editor.

" Suppose you can prove it," that gentleman would have said, " It wouldn't get us anything but abuse to print it. The people don't want to see him knocked.   He's champion."

X

CONTRACT

WHEN the Sheltons were settled in their new home in the pretty little suburb of Linden, Mrs. Shelton was afraid nobody would call on them. Her husband was afraid somebody would. For ages Mrs. Shelton had bravely pretended to share her husband's aversion to a social life; he hated parties that numbered more than four people and she had convincingly, so she thought, played the rôle of indifference while declining invitations she would have given her right eye to accept. Shelton had not been fooled much, but his dislike of " crowds " was so great that he seldom sought to relieve her martyrdom by insisting that they " go " somewhere.

This was during the first six years of their connubial existence, while it was necessary to live, rather economically, in town. Recently, however, Shelton's magazine had advanced him to a position as associate editor and he was able, with the assistance of a benignant bond and mortgage company, to move into a house in Linden. Mrs. Shelton was sure suburbanites would be less tedious and unattractive than people they had known in the city and that it would not be fatal to her spouse to get acquainted and play around a little; anyway she could make friends with other wives, if they were willing, and perhaps enjoy afternoons of contract bridge, a game she had learned to love in three lessons. At the same time Shelton resolved to turn over a new leaf for his wife's sake and give her to understand that he was open for engagements, secretly hoping, as I have hinted, that Linden's denizens would treat them as if they were quarantined.

Mrs. Shelton's fears were banished, and Shelton's resolution put to a test, on an evening of their second week in the new house. They were dropped in on by Mr. and Mrs. Robert French who lived three blocks away. Mrs. French was pretty and Shelton felt inclined to like her until she remarked how fascinating it must be to edit a magazine and meet Michael Arlen. French had little to say, being occupied most of the while in a petting party with his mustache.

Mrs. Shelton showed Mrs. French her seven hooked rugs. Mrs. French said, " Perfectly darling! " seven times, inquired where

129

each of the seven had been procured and did not listen to the answers. Shelton served highballs of eighty dollar Scotch he had bought from a Linden bootlegger. French commented favorably on the Scotch. Shelton thought it was terrible himself and that French was a poor judge, or was being polite, or was deceived by some flavor lurking in the mustache. Mrs. Shelton ran out of hooked rugs and Mrs. French asked whether they played contract. Mrs. Shelton hesitated from habit. Shelton swallowed hard and replied that they did, and liked it very much.

"That's wonderful!" said Mrs. French. "Because the Wilsons have moved to Chicago. They were crazy about contract and we used to have a party every Wednesday night; two tables—the Wilsons, ourselves, and the Dittmars and Camerons. It would be just grand if you two would take the Wilsons' place. We have dinner at somebody's house and next Wednesday is our turn. Could you come?"

Mrs. Shelton again hesitated and Shelton (to quote O. O. McIntyre) once more took the bull by the horns.

"It sounds fine!" he said. "We haven't anything else on for that night, have we, dear?"

His wife uttered an astonished no and the Frenches left.

"What in the world has happened to you?" demanded Mrs. Shelton.

"Nothing at all. They seem like nice people and we've got to make friends here. Besides, it won't be bad playing cards."

"I don't know about contract," said Mrs. Shelton doubtfully. "You've got good card sense, and the only time you played it, you were all right. But I'm afraid I'll make hideous mistakes."

"Why should you? And even if you do, what of it?"

"These people are probably whizzes."

"I don't care if they're Lenz's mother-in-law."

"But you'll care if they criticise you."

"Of course I will. People, and especially strangers, have no more right to criticise your bridge playing than your clothes or your complexion."

"You know that's silly. Bridge is a game."

"Tennis is a game, too. But how often do you hear one tennis player say to another, 'You played that like an old fool!'?"

"You're not partners in tennis."

"You are in doubles. However, criticism in bridge is not confined to partners. I've made bonehead plays in bridge (I'll admit it), and been laughed at and scolded for them by opponents who ought to have kissed me. It's a conviction of most bridge players, and some golf players, that God sent them into the world to teach. At that, what they tell you isn't intended for your edification and future good. It's just a way of announcing ' I'm smart and you're a lunkhead.' And to my mind it's a revelation of bad manners and bad sportsmanship. If I ask somebody what I did wrong, that's different. But when they volunteer——"

It was an old argument and Mrs. Shelton did not care to continue it. She knew she couldn't win and she was sleepy. Moreover, she was so glad they were " going out " on her husband's own insistence that she felt quite kindly toward him. She did hope, though, that their new acquaintances would suppress their educational complex if any.

On Wednesday night this hope was knocked for a double row of early June peas. Mrs. Shelton was elected to play with French, Mrs. Cameron and Mr. Dittmar. Mrs. Cameron was what is referred to as a statuesque blonde, but until you were used to her you could think of nothing but her nostrils, where she might easily have carried two after dinner mints. Mr. Dittmar appeared to be continuing to enjoy his meal long after it was over. And French had to deal one-handed to be sure his mustache remained loyal. These details distracted Mrs. Shelton's mind to such an extent that she made a few errors and was called for them. But she didn't mind that and her greatest distraction was caused by words and phrases that came from the other table, where her husband was engaged with Mr. Cameron, Mrs. Dittmar and the hostess.

The French cocktails had been poured from an eye-dropper and Shelton maintained perfect control of his temper and tongue. His polite reception of each criticism was taken as a confession of ignorance and a willingness to learn, and his three table-mates were quick to assume the rôle of faculty, with him as the entire student-body. He was stepped on even when he was dummy, his partner at the time, Mrs. Dittmar, attributing the loss of a trick to the manner in which he had laid out his cards, the light striking the nine of diamonds in such a way as to make her think it was an honor.

Mrs. Dittmar had married a man much younger than herself and was trying to disguise that fact by acting much younger than he. An eight-year-old child who is kind of backward hardly ever plays contract bridge; otherwise, if you didn't look at Mrs. Dittmar and judged only by her antics and manner of speech, you would have thought Dittmar had spent the final hours of his courtship waiting outside the sub-primary to take her home. Mrs. French, when she was not picking flaws in Shelton's play, sought to make him feel at home by asking intelligent questions about his work—" Do the people who draw the illustrations read the stories first? " " Does H. C. Witwer talk Negro dialect all the time? " And " How old is Peter B. Kinney? " Cameron, from whom Work, Lenz, Whitehead and Shepard had plagiarized the game, was frankly uninterested in anything not connected with it. The stake was half a cent a point and the pains he took to see that his side's score was correct or better proved all the rumors about the two Scotchmen.

Mrs. Shelton was well aware that her husband was the politest man in the world when sober; yet he truly amazed her that evening by his smiling acquiescence to all that was said. From tho snatches she overheard, she knew he must be afire inside and it was really wonderful of him not to show it.

There was a time when Mrs. Dittmar passed and he passed and Cameron bid two spades. Mrs. French Passed and Mrs. Dittmar bid three hearts, a denial of her partner's spades if Shelton ever heard one. Shelton passed and Cameron went three hearts, which stood. Shelton held four spades to the nine, four diamonds to the king, two small hearts and the eight, six and five of clubs. He led the trey of diamonds. I am not broadcasting the battle play by play, but when it was over, " Oh, partner! Any other opening and we could have set them," said Mrs. French.

" My! My! My! My! Leading away from a king! " gurgled the child-wife.

" That lead was all that saved us," said Cameron.

They waited for Shelton to apologize and explain, all prepared to scrunch him if he did either.

" I guess I made a mistake," he said.

" Haven't you played much bridge? " asked Mrs. French.

" Evidently not enough," he replied.

" It's a game you can't learn in a minute," said Cameron.

" Never you mind! " said Mrs. Dittmar. " I've played contract ever since it came out, and Daddy still scolds me terribly for some of the things I do."

Shelton presumed that Daddy was her husband. Her father must be dead or at least too feeble to scold.

There was a time when a hand was passed around.

" Oh! A goulash! " crowed Mrs. Dittmar.

" Do you play them, Mr. Shelton? " asked his hostess.

"Yes," said Shelton.

"Mrs. Shelton," called Mrs. Dittmar to the other table, "does your big man play goulashes?"

"Oh, yes," said Mrs. Shelton.

"You're sure you know what they are," said Cameron to Shelton.

"I've played them often," said the latter.

"A goulash," said the hostess, "is where the hand is passed and then we all put our hands together like this and cut them and the dealer deals five around twice and then three. It makes crazy hands, but it's thrilling."

"And the bidding is different," said Mrs. Dittmar, his partner at this stage. "Big mans musn't get too wild."

Shelton, who had dealt, looked at his hand and saw no temptation to get wild; at least, not any wilder than he was. He had the king, queen and jack of spades, four silly hearts, four very young clubs and two diamonds of no standing. He passed. Cameron bid three clubs and Mrs. Dittmar four diamonds. That was enough to make game (they already had thirty), and when Mrs. French went by, Shelton unhesitatingly did the same. So did Cameron. It developed that Mrs. Dittmar had the ace, king, jack, ten and another diamond. Cameron had none and Mrs. French reeked with them. The bidder was set two. Her honors counted one hundred and the opponents' net profit was two hundred, Mrs. Dittmar being vulnerable, or "venerable," as Mrs. French laughingly, but not very tactfully, called it.

Cameron lighted into Mrs. French for not doubling Mrs. Dittmar and Mrs. French observed that she guessed she knew what she was doing. Shelton hoped this would develop into a brawl, but it was forgotten when Mrs. Dittmar asked him querulously why he had not shown her his spades, a suit of which she had held the ace, ten to five.

"We're lucky, partner," said Mrs. French to Cameron. "They could have made four spades like a breeze."

"I'd have lost only the ace of hearts and queen of diamonds," said Mrs. Dittmar, doubtless figuring that the maid would have disposed of her two losing clubs when she swept next morning.

"In this game, everything depends on the bidding," said Mrs. French to Shelton. "You *must* give your partner all the information you can."

"Don't coach him!" said Cameron with an exasperating laugh. "He's treating us pretty good."

"Maybe," said Mrs. French to Mrs. Dittmar, "he would have shown you his spades if you had bid three diamonds instead of four."

"But you see," said Mrs. Dittmar, "we needed four for game and I didn't know if he'd think of that."

And there was a time when Shelton bid a fair no trump and was raised to three by his partner, Cameron, who held king, queen, ten to five hearts and the ace of clubs for a re-entry. The outstanding hearts were bunched in Mrs. French's hand, Shelton himself having the lone ace. After he had taken a spade trick, led his ace of hearts and then a low club to make all of dummy's hearts good (which turned out to be impossible), he put over two deep sea finesses of the eight and nine of diamonds from the dummy hand, made four odd and heard Cameron murmur, "A fool for luck!"

"My! What a waste of good hearts!" said Mrs. Dittmar, ignoring the facts that they weren't good hearts, that if he had continued with them, Mrs. French would have taken the jack and led to her (Mrs. Dittmar's) four good spade tricks, and that with the ace of clubs gone, Shelton couldn't have got back in the dummy's hands with a pass from Judge Landis.

At the close of a perfect evening, the Sheltons were six dollars ahead and invited to the Dittmars' the following Wednesday. Mrs. Shelton expected an explosion on the way home, but was agreeably disappointed. Shelton seemed quite cheerful. He had a few jocose remarks to make about their new pals, but gave the impression that he had enjoyed himself. Knowing him as she did, she might have suspected that a plot was hatching in his mind. However, his behavior was disarming and she thought he had at last found a "crowd" he didn't object to, that they would now be neighborly and gregarious for the first time in their married life.

On the train from the city Friday afternoon, Shelton encountered Gale Bartlett, the writer, just returned from abroad. Bartlett was one of the star contributors to Shelton's magazine and it was he who had first suggested Linden when Shelton was considering a suburban home. He had a place there himself though most of his time was spent in Paris and he was back now for only a brief stay.

"How do you like it?" he asked.

"Fine," said Shelton.

"Whom have you met?"

"Three married couples, the Camerons, the Frenches and the Dittmars."

"Good Lord!" said Bartlett. "I don't know the Dittmars but otherwise you're slumming. Cameron and French are new rich who probably made their money in a hotel washroom. I think they met their wives on an excursion to Far Rockaway. How did you happen to get acquainted?"

"The Frenches called on us, and Wednesday night we went to their house for dinner and bridge."

"Bridge!"

"Contract bridge at that."

"Well, maybe Dittmar's a contractor. But from what I've seen of the Frenches and Camerons, they couldn't even cut the cards without smearing them with shoe polish. You break loose from them before they forget themselves and hand you a towel."

"We're going to the Dittmars' next Wednesday night."

"Either call it off or keep it under your hat. I'll introduce you to people that are people! I happen to know them because my wife went to their sisters' boarding school. I'll see that you get the entree and then you can play bridge with bridge players."

Shelton brightened at the prospect. He knew his wife was too kind-hearted to wound the Camerons et al. by quitting them cold and it was part of his scheme, all of it in fact, to make them do the quitting. With the conviction that she would be more than compensated by the promised acquaintance of people they both could really like, he lost what few scruples he had against separating her from people who sooner or later would drive him to the electric chair. The thing must be done at the first opportunity, next Wednesday at the Dittmars'. It would be kind of fun, but unpleasant, too, the unpleasant part consisting in the mental anguish it would cause her and the subsequent days, not many he hoped, when she wouldn't be speaking to him at all.

Fate, in the form of one of Mrs. Shelton's two-day headaches, brought about the elimination of the unpleasant part. The ache began Wednesday afternoon and from past experience, she knew she would not be able to sit through a dinner or play cards that night. She telephoned her husband.

"Say we can't come," was his advice.

"But I hate to do that. They'll think we don't want to and they won't ask us again. I wish you'd go, and maybe they could ask somebody in to take my place. I don't suppose you'd consider that, would you?"

Shelton thought it over a moment and said yes, he would.

Before retiring to her darkened room and her bed, Mrs. Shelton called up Mrs. Dittmar. Mrs. Dittmar expressed her sympathy in baby talk and said it was all right for Mr. Shelton to come alone; it was more than all right, Mrs. Shelton gathered, because Mrs. Dittmar's brother was visiting her and they would be just eight.

Shelton, who had learned long ago that his wife did not want him around when her head was threatening to burst open, stayed in town until six o'clock, preparing himself for the evening's task with liberal doses of the business manager's week-old rye. He was not going to be tortured by any drought such as he had endured at the Frenches'. He arrived at the party in grand shape and, to his surprise, was plied with cocktails potent enough to keep him on edge.

Mrs. Dittmar's brother (she called him her dreat, big B'udder) was an amateur jazz pianist. Or rather, peeanist. He was proving his amateur standing when Shelton got there and something in the way he treated " Rhapsody in Blue " made Shelton resolve to open fire at once. His eagerness was increased when, on the way to the dining room, Mrs. Dittmar observed that her b'udder had not played much contract " either " and she must be sure and not put them (Shelton and B'udder) at the same table, for they might draw each other as partners and that would hardly be fair.

Dinner began and so did Shelton.

" A week ago," he said, " you folks criticised my bridge playing." The Camerons, Dittmars and Frenches looked queer.

" You didn't mind it, I hope," said Mrs. Dittmar. " We were just trying to teach you."

" I didn't mind it much," said Shelton. " But I was just wondering whether it was good manners for one person to point out another person's mistakes when the other person didn't ask to have them pointed out."

" Why," said Cameron, " when one person don't know as much about a thing as other people, it's their duty to correct him."

" You mean just in bridge," said Shelton.

" I mean in everything," said Cameron.

" And the person criticised or corrected has no right to resent it? " said Shelton.

" Certainly not ! "

" Does everybody here agree with that? "

" Yes," " Of course," " Sure," came from the others.

" Well, then," said Shelton, " I think it's my duty to tell you, Mr. Cameron, that soup should be dipped away from you and not toward you."

There was a puzzled silence, then a laugh, to which Cameron contributed feebly.

"If that's right I'm glad to know it, and I certainly don't resent your telling me," he said.

"It looks like Mr. Shelton was out for revenge," said Mrs. Cameron.

"And I must inform you, Mrs. Cameron," said Shelton, "that 'like' is not a conjunction. 'It looks as if Mr. Shelton were out for revenge' would be the correct phrasing."

A smothered laugh at the expense of Mrs. Cameron, whose embarrassment showed itself in a terrifying distension of the nostrils. Shelton decided not to pick on her again.

"Let's change the subject," said Mrs. Dittmar. "Mr. Shelton's a mean, bad man and he'll make us cwy."

"That verb," said Shelton, "is cry, not cwy. It is spelled c-r-y."

"Tell a story, Bob," said Mrs. French to her husband.

"Well, let's see," said French. "I'll tell the one about the Scotchman and the Jew playing golf. Stop me if anybody's heard it."

"I have, for one," said Shelton.

"Maybe the others haven't," said French.

"They must have been unconscious for years," said Shelton. "But go ahead and tell it. I knew I couldn't stop you."

French went ahead and told it, and the others laughed as a rebuke to Shelton.

Cameron wanted things understood.

"You see," he said, "the reason we made a few little criticisms of your bridge game was because we judged you were a new beginner."

"I think 'beginner' is enough, without the 'new,'" said Shelton. "I don't know any old beginners excepting, perhaps, people old in years who are doing something or taking up something for the first time. But probably you judged I was a beginner at bridge because of mistakes I made, and you considered my apparent inexperience justified you in criticising me."

"Yes," said Cameron.

"Well," said Shelton, "I judge from observing Mrs. French eat her fish that she is a new beginner at eating and I take the liberty of stating that the fork ought never to be conveyed to the mouth with the left hand, even by a left-handed eater. To be sure, these forks are salad forks, not fish forks, as Mrs. Dittmar may believe. But even salad forks, substituting for fish forks, must not be carried mouthward by the left hand."

A storm was gathering and Mrs. Cameron sought to ward it off. She asked Mrs. Dittmar what had become of Peterson, a butler.

"He just up and left me last week," said Mrs. Dittmar. "He was getting too impudent, though, and you can bet I didn't object to him going."

"'*His* going,'" said Shelton. "A participle used as a substantive is modified in the possessive."

Everyone pretended not to hear him.

"This new one is grand!" said Mrs. Dittmar. "I didn't get up till nearly eleven o'clock this morning——"

"Eleven!" exclaimed Mrs. French.

"Yes. Imagine!" said Mrs. Dittmar. "The itta girl just overslept herself, that's all."

"Mrs. Dittmar," said Shelton, "I have no idea who the itta girl is, but I am interested in your statement that she overslept herself. Would it be possible for her, or any other itta girl, to oversleep somebody else? If it were a sleeping contest, I should think 'outsleep' would be preferable, but even so I can't understand how a girl of any size outsleeps herself."

The storm broke. Dittmar sprang to his feet.

"That's enough, Shelton!" he bellowed. "We've had enough of this nonsense! More than enough!"

"I think," said Shelton, "that the use of the word 'enough' three times in one short speech is more than enough. It grates on me to hear or read a word reiterated like that. I suggest as synonyms 'plenty,' 'a sufficiency,' 'an abundance,' 'a plethora.'"

"Shut your smart aleck mouth and get out!"

"Carl! Carl! Mustn't lose temper!" said Mrs. Dittmar. "Lose temper and can't digest food. Daddy mustn't lose temper and be sick all nighty night."

"Shelton just thinks he's funny," said Cameron.

"He's drunk and he'll leave my house at once!" said Dittmar.

"If that's the way you feel about it," said Shelton.

He stopped on the way out to bid Mrs. Dittmar's brother good-night.

"Good-night, B'udder old boy," he said. "I'm glad to have met you, but sorry to learn you're deaf."

"Deaf! What makes you think I'm deaf?"

"I understood your sister to say you played the piano by ear."

Knowing his wife would have taken something to make her

sleep, and therefore not afraid of disturbing her, Shelton went home, got out a bottle of Linden Scotch and put the finishing touches on his bender. In the morning Mrs. Shelton was a little better and came to the breakfast table where he was fighting an egg.

"Well, what kind of time did you have?"

"Glorious! Much more exciting than at the Frenches'. Mrs. Dittmar's brother is a piano playing fool."

"Oh, wasn't there any bridge then?"

"No. Just music and banter."

"Maybe the brother can't play contract and I spoiled the party by not going."

"Oh, no. *You* didn't spoil the party!"

"And do we go to the Camerons' next Wednesday?"

"I don't believe so. Nothing was said."

They did go next Wednesday night to the palatial home of E. M. Pardee, a friend of Gale Bartlett's and one of the real aristocrats of Linden. After dinner, Mrs. Pardee asked the Sheltons whether they played contract, and they said they did. The Pardees, not wishing to impoverish the young immigrants, refused to play "families." They insisted on cutting and Shelton cut Mrs. Pardee.

"Oh, Mr. Shevlin," she said at the end of the first hand, "why *didn't* you lead me a club? You *must* watch the discards!"

Author's Postscript: This story won't get me anything but the money I am paid for it. Even if it be read by those with whom I usually play—Mr. C., Mrs. W., Mr. T., Mrs. R. and the rest—they will think I mean two other fellows and tear into me like wolves next time I bid a slam and make one odd.

XI

DINNER

HARRY BARTON was thirty-three years old, unmarried and good-looking. Young matrons liked him as a filler-in at dinner parties, but he hated dinner parties unless they promised an evening of contract. So it was with a heavy heart that he heard Grace Halpern's voice on the telephone.

"You've just got to do this for me! I know you'll hate it. There won't be any bridge. But Frank backed out at the last minute and I can't get anybody else. I honestly tried. I tried Bill; I even tried Lester Graham, but neither of them can come. And I must have two bachelors because there are going to be two girls from out of town, girls who were in my class in boarding school. They really are peaches and I can't disappoint them. Please say——"

Harry was a bad liar and, besides, he liked Grace. He had had lots of good times at her house. He said yes and wished all the rest of the day that he hadn't.

He arrived late at the Halperns', too late to get half enough cocktails. He knew everybody there excepting the two peaches, a Miss Coakley and a Miss Rell. They were strikingly pretty, Miss Coakley a pony brunette and Miss Rell a rather tall, slender blonde. Harry thought maybe it wouldn't be so bad after all.

His hostess drew him aside before dinner was announced.

"I'm going to reward you for this. I'm going to let you sit between them at dinner. And remember, they're both free."

"What do you mean, free?"

"Not engaged or anything. And I think it's about time you were settling down."

The other bachelor, Dave Wallace, sat on Miss Coakley's left, with Harry, as Grace had promised, between Miss Coakley and Miss Rell.

"Grace tells me you're a great bridge player," Miss Rell said.

"No, but I like——"

"Which do you consider the greatest authority, Lenz or Works or Whitehall? I don't know anything about it myself, but I hear

141

people arguing about it at home, I mean I live in Chicago. I belong to a bridge club there and I was just getting so the others
didn't laugh at me when somebody introduced this horrible contract and I simply gave up. That's the game, you know, where you
don't bid anything but slams and I just haven't the nerve, I mean
in bridge. I don't want you to think I'm a coward in everything."

" I——"

" Because I'm not. I made a flight with Lindbergh in Washington. It was arranged through Congressman Burleigh. He's
a great friend of my father's. You know, Burleigh the paint people in South Chicago. Oh, it was too thrilling for words! But I
felt just as safe as if I'd been in a car, safer because once I was in
a terrible smash-up out in Lake Forest and the doctor said I was
lucky to escape without at least a few broken ribs.

" I was a little bit scared when we first started, but then I
thought to myself this is the man who flew from Detroit to Paris
and why should anybody be frightened just flying twenty minutes
over Washington with him at the wheel. Have you ever been up ? "

" Yes, I——"

" Then you don't know what a real thrill is. Honestly, it just
makes you gasp, like the first time you dive in Lake Michigan. I
really dive and I swim awfully well and some of the men say I
swim awfully well for a girl. There's one man in Chicago, Lee
Roberts—he and his wife are our best friends, I mean my brother's
and mine—Lee calls me Gertrude Ederle ; you know she's the girl
who swam across the English Channel and back.

" Of course he says it just joking because naturally I'm not in
her class. She's quite fat, isn't she? Or haven't you ever seen
her ? She looks fat in her pictures. But then you can't always tell
from pictures. There was a picture of me in the rotogravure section that made me look simply hideous."

Mr. Halpern, on Miss Rell's right, spoke to her and Harry
found himself attacked by Miss Coakley.

" Mr. Burton, I was just telling Mr. Walters about—— I don't
know whether you'd be interested or not—maybe you don't—but
still everybody I've told, they think—it's probably——"

" I'm sure I'd like to hear it," said Harry.

" I hate to bore people with—you know how it is—you'd be too
polite to—and this is so awfully—well, it isn't a thing that—it's
just interesting if you happen—people in Baltimore—though
we've only lived there a few——"

" If," said Harry to himself, " she doesn't complete a sentence in the next two minutes, I'm going to ask Grace for a high-ball."

"——it was some people who lived—well, our apartment was just two buildings—they were people you wouldn't want—but it was in a kind of secluded—not many apartments—it's a neighborhood that's just—and my sister's little boy goes to the same school as——"

"Grace," said Harry, "am I an old enough customer here to ask for a drink?"

"Whatever you like," said his hostess.

"I'd like a high-ball. I had a pretty tough day."

Miss Rell turned on him.

"Oh, are you in the Street? That's what they call Wall Street, isn't it? I should think it would be just thrilling! But I suppose it is hard work, too. You stand there all day and shout at other men, don't you, and they shout back at you? It must ruin your voice. Why, I know we went to the Illinois-Chicago game last fall and I got excited and yelled so for Illinois that I couldn't talk for a week."

"That must have——"

"Do you have football here in the East? Oh, certainly you do! I'd forgotten—Yale and Harvard. And which are the Giants? I never can keep them straight. My father and Lou—that's my brother; we're great pals—he and Father read the sporting page religiously every day. I tease them about it and they tease me about reading the society news and the movies. We have great tiffs over it, all in fun of course.

"Father is a great golfer, I mean really. He's fifty-four years old and he plays the Onwentsia course in sixty, or maybe it's a hundred and sixty. Which would be right? He wanted me to take it up and begged and begged till finally one day I went out and played nine holes with him.

"I made some wonderful shots, I mean I really did, and he said I had a perfect natural swing and if I would take lessons from the professor it wouldn't be long before I could be playing in tournaments, just for women I mean. Wouldn't that be exciting! But I just couldn't do it; I'd die!

"And besides, it seems to me that girls who win things in sports are always queer looking, at least most of them, and what chance would—I mean it would be almost unheard of if—— Well, I just don't believe I could ever be a champion of anything. Do you play golf?"

"Yes."

" You ought to try it. It's lots of fun, especially for a man. I mean men seem to have such good times playing together, the nineteenth hole and all that. And I should think it would be such wonderful relaxation for you over the weekend after that Wall Street grind."

" I'm not in Wall Street."

" Oh, now I've got an expert here, I wish you'd tell me what are bulls and what are bears? Father's tried to explain it to me, but I can't get it straight."

" Well, a bull is——"

" Have you ever been to bull-fights, I mean in Spain or Mexico? They say they are terribly thrilling, but terribly cruel. I mean about the horses. You know what they do, don't you? "

" No. I never heard of them."

" Well, they bring out three or four old horses into the ring and men with spears spear the bull and get him mad at the horses and he goes after them and kills them and the blood makes him mad at everybody and then the man comes out and kills him. They call them toreadors."

" Who? "

" The man that fights the bull. Haven't you ever heard ' Carmen,' I mean the opera? There's a toreador in that. He sings a song; it goes, 'Toreador, en garde.' That's the French. It's a French opera. Carmen is the girl; she works in a cigaret factory. First she falls in love with a soldier and then this toreador wins her away from him, but the soldier kills himself and her.

" I haven't heard it for years; I like to go to ones I haven't heard so much. We've got a simply gorgeous opera company in Chicago. Everybody says it's better than the Metropolitan. And Rosa Raisa is the greatest dramatic soprano I ever heard. She's Ruffo's wife. No, I guess she's Rimini's. Anyway, they're both barytones."

Again Mr. Halpern intervened and Harry took on Miss Coakley for another round.

" Mr. Walters and I were just—— Don't you like Nassau better than—I mean for climate—and the different colors of the water—and it's ideal bathing, hardly any surf—of course lots of people prefer heavy surf—but for people like me who can't—and I think the crowd that goes there—and the tennis. Then there's that lovely garden, with the orchestra.

" Three of us girls—I think it was four winters—it was three winters ago. One night we went—it's the Holy Rollers—honestly they do the craziest—a man told us they were just—but I couldn't believe it, they were so—I think—— Have you ever been there, Mr. Burton?"

"No."

"We went by land to—and then from Miami—when you wake up—it's the most beautiful—with the sun just rising over the islands—it's simply heavenly—it's just—— Well, you have no idea!"

"Yes, I have," said Harry to himself, and aloud: "Grace, I'd like a high-ball. I had a tough day."

"The days are getting shorter," said his hostess.

"I imagine every day must be pretty hard for you men in the Street," said Miss Rell.

"I'm not in any street," said Harry. "Not even a path."

"I know how secretive you Wall Street men are," said Miss Rell, "but I wonder if you would do me a favor. Just before I left home, I heard Father talking about some stock that I think he said he had a tip on—he's got a lot of influential friends that tell him things like that, but of course nobody like you who is right in Wall Street. Now it would be perfectly wonderful if you would tell me whether this stock is any good or not and then when I go home, I can tell Father what you said and who you are and he'll think his child isn't so dumb after all. Will you?"

"What's the stock?"

"Isn't it marvelous that I remember the name of it? It's General Motors."

"General Motors! Well, listen, if you'll keep this under your hat——"

"Oh, that reminds me, I saw your Mayor Jimmy Walker in the parade today and I told Grace I thought he was the only man in the world who could wear a high hat without looking silly. Do you know him? I'll bet he's fascinating to know. He's cute! I wish we had a cute mayor. I suppose you New Yorkers must think our town is a regular wild West show. It really isn't as bad as all that.

"Lou—that's my brother—he said the funniest thing the night before I came away. No, it was Wednesday night he said it and I didn't leave till Friday noon on the Century. What was I saying? Oh, yes, Father and Lou and I were waiting for dinner— you know we live on the North Side, just a block south of the park —and anyway there were some noises out on the street that sounded just like pistol-shots and Father hurried to the window and looked out and announced that it was just back-fire from a truck.

"Then Lou said, 'Well, I'm glad they're beginning to defend themselves.' He meant the trucks were firing back at whoever was shooting at them. Or would it be whomever? I never can get who and whom straight. But Lou is awfully witty; I mean he really is. He has had two or three things in 'College Humor.' What was your college?"

"The Electoral College."

"Oh, you're an engineer! And what are you doing on Wall Street? I suppose you gave up your profession 'for gold.' You ought to be ashamed of yourself! You might be accomplishing big things like building bridges. Which reminds me, do you play bridge?"

"Yes."

"You ought to, honestly. I'm not very good, but it's lots of fun. I belong to a club and we just have a circus. The other girls used to laugh at me, I was so dumb, but this last winter I got good; I mean really not bad at all. And then, just when I was doing so well, they decided to play this contract and I can't get it at all. You don't bid anything but slams and I just can't do that. I simply haven't the nerve."

"Have you ever been up with Lindbergh?" asked Harry.

"Yes. I'm not joking. I really mean it. It was while he was in Washington. My father arranged it through Congressman Burleigh. That's the Burleigh Paint Company in South Chicago. Mr. Burleigh is a congressman and one of Father's closest friends. It was the most thrilling experience I ever had in my life. And I wasn't frightened at all, only a little bit, like when you go in swimming and dive for the first time."

"Can you dive?"

"You ought to see me! Honestly, not boasting, I'm a regular Gertrude Ederle; you know, the girl that swam across the English Channel so many times. I wouldn't want to swim that Channel, though. It's bad enough in a boat. I'm a pretty good sailor, but the last time my brother and I crossed from Calais to Dover, well, 'it happens in the best of families,' as Briggs says, or is it Mutt and Jeff?

"Do you read the funny pages? I suppose I oughtn't to confess it, but I read them religiously. Father often jokes me about it and pretends the money he spent sending me to college was all wasted because all I got out of it was a taste for 'the funnies.' I answer him back by saying he went to college, too, and all he cares anything about now is golf. It's all joking of course. Father and I are the best friends and chums! What was your college?"

"The War College."

"Oh, West Point! I'd just love to go up there and watch them drill sometime! I've seen it across the river going by on the train and it looks lovely. And fall before last, Father and Lou and I went to the big football game between West Point and the Annapolis Navy. You know they had it in Chicago, at Soldiers' Field, in Grant Park. It's an enormous place and lots of people couldn't see the game at all, but our seats were grand. Father got them through Congressman Burleigh."

"Is that," asked Harry, "the Burleigh who's in the paint business in South Chicago?"

"Do you know him?"

"I bought a can of paint from him once when I was redecorating my garage."

"Why, he's one of Father's best friends. He's in Congress. How funny that you should really know him!"

"You can meet congressmen if you go at it the right way."

Miss Coakley was talking.

"Oh, Mr. Buckley, will you——? Mr. Walsh and I—— Just what was it you said, Mr.——?"

"I don't remember saying anything," replied Dave Wallace on her left.

"Why, you—— He did, too, Mr.—— He said the Mauretania was the—— And I said the Paris or the Majestic, or the Berengaria—— Now we want you to give us your honest——"

"I never crossed on anything but the Santa Maria," said Harry.

"Oh, Italy, how I love it! I could simply—— There's no other country—it just seems as if—— If it weren't for my sister in Baltimore—maybe some day—— But a girl is foolish——"

"Grace," said Harry, "how's the Scotch holding out?"

"The whole week must have been tough," said Grace.

"I don't see how you men live through it," said Miss Rell, "standing there on the floor of the Exchange all day, shouting at each other. Why, it simply kills me just to stand and wait five minutes in a shop! To have to do it all day, I'd perish! How do you endure it?"

"Well, you know those little stools that golf fans carry around with them. I never go on the floor without one," said Harry.

"My father is the greatest golf fan in the world; I mean I really

believe he is, without exception. He never plays less than four
times a week and he's a fine player, I mean for a man his age.
He's fifty-four years old and he goes around Onwentsia in a hundred and twenty. Can that be right?"

" Easily."

Dinner was over and they went into the living-room. Harry
and Dave Wallace were together a moment.

" I notice you didn't talk much," remarked Dave.

" But what I said made a big impression."

" I'd have traded you Coakley for your dame. Your gal just
goes along as if she were speaking into a mike, but Miss Coakley
is a perpetual missing-word contest and it's impossible to keep out
of it—every little while you feel as if you just had to guess what's
left out."

" She called me Burton and Buckley."

" She called me everything from Welling to Wolheim."

Harry tried to hide behind the piano, but Miss Rell soon found
him.

" If we could get two more, don't you think Grace would let
us play bridge?"

" I don't know the game," said Harry.

" But I'd just love to teach you. I can teach you regular auction, but not this new contract, where you just bid and bid till
you're dizzy."

" I haven't any card sense and besides, I think that liquor Grace
gave me was bad."

" Oh, truly?"

" I'm going to ask her where she got it."

" I know a man, or at least my father does, who gets the real
thing straight from Canada. Only he's out in Chicago."

Harry peremptorily summoned Grace into the hall.

" Grace, that's terrible Scotch you've got. It's given me the first
headache I've had in years."

" I understand, and I'll tell them you were sick and had to go
home. You were a darling to come and I'll never forget it."

" Neither will I."

At the door he said:

" Remember, old girl, I've left your schoolmates just as I found
them. They're still free."

XII

WOMEN

YOUNG JAKE uttered a few words which it would pain me to repeat.

"And what are *you* crabbin' about?" asked Mike Healy from his corner of the bench.

"Oh, nothin'!" said Jake. "Nothin' except that I'm sick of it!"

"Sick of what?" demanded Healy.

"Of settin' here!" Jake replied.

"You!" said Mike Healy, with a short laugh. "You've got a fine license to squawk! Why, let's see: what is it? The third of June, and your first June in the league. You ain't even *begin* to sit! Look at me! Been on this bench since catchers started wearin' a mast, or anyway it seems that long. And you never hear me crab, do you, Lefty?"

"Only when you talk," answered the athlete addressed. "And that's only at table or between meals."

"But if this kid's hollerin' already," said Mike, "what'll he be doin' along in August or September, to say nothin' about next August and the August after that?"

"Don't worry!" said Young Jake. "I'll either be a regular by the end of this season or I won't be on this ball club at all!"

"That-a-boy!" said Healy. "Threaten 'em!"

"I mean what I say!" retorted Jake. "I ain't goin' to spend my life on no bench! I come here to play baseball!"

"Oh, you did!" said Healy. "And what do you think I come here for, to fish?"

"I ain't talkin' about you," said Young Jake. "I'm talkin' about myself."

"That's a novelty in a ball player," remarked Lefty.

"And what I'm sayin'," Jake went on, "is that I'm sick of settin' on this bench."

"This ain't a bad bench," said Healy. "They's a hell of a lot worse places you might sit."

"And a hell of a lot better places!" said Jake. "I can think of one right now. I'm lookin' right at it."

" Where at? "

" Right up in the old stand; the third—no, the fourth row, next to the aisle, the first aisle beyond where the screen leaves off."

" I noticed her myself! " put in Lefty. " Damn cute! Too damn cute for a busher like you to get smoked up over."

" Oh, I don't know! " said Young Jake. " I didn't get along so bad with them dames down South."

" Down South ain't here! " replied Lefty. " Those dames in some of those swamps, they lose their head when they see a man with shoes on. But up here you've got to have something. If you pulled that Calhoun County stuff of yours on a gal like that gal in the stand she'd yell for the dog catcher. She'd——"

" They're all alike! " interrupted Mike Healy. " South, or here, or anywheres, they're all the same, and all poison! "

" What's poison? " asked Jake.

" Women! " said Healy. "And the more you have to do with 'em the better chance you've got of spendin' your life on this bench. Why—— That's pitchin', Joe! " he shouted when the third of the enemy batters had popped out and left a runner stranded at second base. " You look good in there today," he added to Joe as the big pitcher approached the dugout.

" I'm all right, I guess," said Joe, pulling on his sweater and moving toward the water bottle. " I wished that wind'd die down."

The manager had come in.

" All right! Let's get at 'em! " he said. " Nice work, Joe. Was that a fast one Meusel hit? "

" No," said Joe. "A hook, but it didn't break."

" A couple of runs will beat 'em the way you're going," said the manager, stooping over to select his bat. " Make this fella pitch, boys," he added. " He was hog wild in Philly the other day."

The half inning wore on to its close, and the noncombatants were again left in possession of the bench. Young Jake addressed Healy.

" What's women done to you, Mike? "

" Only broke me. That's all! " said Healy.

" What do you mean, broke you! The boys tells me you ain't spent nothin' but the summer since you been in the league."

" Oh, I've got a little money," said Healy. " I don't throw it away. I don't go around payin' ten smackers a quart for liquid catnip. But they's more kinds of broke than money broke, a damn sight worse kinds, too. And when I say women has broke me, I mean they've made a bum out of my life; they've wrecked my—what-do-you-call-it?"

"Your career," supplied Lefty.

"Yes, sir," said Healy. "And I ain't kiddin', neither. Why say, listen: Do you know where I'd be if it wasn't for a woman? Right out there in that infield, playin' that old third sack."

"What about Smitty?" asked Young Jake.

"He'd be where I am—on this bench."

"Aw, come on, Mike! Be yourself! You don't claim you're as good as him!" Jake remonstrated.

"I do claim it, but it don't make no difference if I am or I ain't. He shouldn't never ought to of had a chance, not on this club, anyway. You'd say the same if you knowed the facts."

"Well, let's hear 'em."

"It's a long story, and these boys has heard it before."

"That's all right, Mike," said Gephart, a spare catcher. "We ain't listened the last twelve times."

"Well, it was the year I come in this league, four years ago this spring. I'd been with the Toledo club a couple of years. I was the best hitter on the Toledo club. I hit .332 the first year and .354 the next year. And I led the third basemen in fieldin'."

"It would be hard not to," interposed Lefty. "Anything a third baseman don't get they call it a base hit. A third baseman ought to pay to get in the park."

Healy glanced coldly at the speaker, and resumed:

"This club had Johnnie Lambert. He was still about the best third baseman in this league, but he was thirty-five years old and had a bad knee. It had slipped out on him and cost this club the pennant. They didn't have no other third baseman. They lose sixteen out of twenty games. So that learned 'em a lesson, and they bought me. Their idear was to start Johnnie in the spring, but they didn't expect his knee to hold up. And then it was goin' to be my turn.

"But durin' the winter Johnnie got a hold of some specialist somewheres that fixed his knee, and he come South with a new least of life. He hit good and was as fast as ever on the bases. Meanw'ile I had been on a huntin' trip up in Michigan that winter and froze my dogs, and they ailed me so that I couldn't do myself justice all spring."

"I suppose it was some woman made you go huntin'," said Gephart, but Healy continued without replying:

"They was a gal from a town named Ligonier, Indiana, that

had visited in Toledo the second year I played ball there. The people where she was visitin' was great baseball fans, and they brought her out to the game with them, and she got stuck on me."

"Ligonier can't be a town! It must be an asylum!" said Lefty.

"She got stuck on me," Healy repeated, "and the people where she was stayin' asked me to their house to supper. After supper the man and his wife said how about goin' to the picture show, and the gal said she was tired and rather stay home. So the man and woman excused themselves. They said it was a picture they wanted to see and would I excuse them runnin' off and leavin' we two together. They were clubbin' on me, see?

"Well, I thought to myself, I'll give this dame an unpleasant surprise, so I didn't even hold her hand all evenin'. When I got up to go she says she supposed it would be the last time she seen me as she expected to go back to Ligonier the next day. She didn't have no more intentions of goin' back the next day than crossin' Lake Erie in a hollow tooth. But she knowed if I thought it was good-by I'd kiss her. Well, I knowed it wasn't good-by, but what the hell! So that's how it started, and I went to Ligonier that fall to see her, and we got engaged to be married. At least she seemed to think so."

"Look at that!" interrupted Young Jake, his eyes on the field of action. "What could Sam of been thinkin'!"

"Thinkin'!" said Gephart. "Him!"

"What would Sam do," wondered Lefty, "if they played baseball with only one base? He wouldn't enjoy the game if he couldn't throw to the wrong one."

"That play's liable to cost us somethin'," said Gephart.

"I went up in Michigan on a huntin' trip with some friends of mine," Healy continued. "I froze my feet and was laid up all through January and February and shouldn't of never went South. It was all as I could do to wear shoes, let alone play baseball. I wasn't really myself till along the first of May. But, as I say, Johnnie Lambert had a new least of life and was lookin' better than he'd looked for years. His knee wasn't troublin' him at all.

"Well, that's how things went till around the last part of June. I didn't get no action except five or six times goin' up to hit for somebody. And I was like a young colt, crazy to be let loose. I knowed that if I once got in there and showed what I could do Judge Landis himself couldn't keep me on the bench. I used to kneel down every night and pray to God to get to work on Lambert's knee.

"The gal kept writin' me letters and I answered 'em once in a w'ile, but we hadn't saw each other since before Christmas. She hinted once or twice about when was we goin' to get married, but I told her I didn't want to even disgust the subject till I was somethin' besides a bench warmer.

"We had a serious in Chi the tail-end of June, and the first night we was there I got a long-distance call from Ligonier. It was the gal's sister, sayin' the gal was sick. She was delirious part of the time and hollerin' for me, and the doctor said if she could see me, it'd probably do her more good than medicine.

"So I said that's all right, but they ain't no off days in the schedule right now and I can't get away. But they had looked up the time table and seen where I could leave Chi after the ball game, spend the night in Ligonier and get back for the game the next day.

"So I took a train from Englewood in the evenin' and when I got off at Ligonier, there was my gal to meet me. She was the picture of health and no more delirious than usual. They said she had been just about ready to pass out when she learned I was comin' and it cured her. They didn't tell me what disease she'd had, but I suppose it was a grasshopper bite or somethin'.

"When I left next mornin', the weddin' date was set for that fall.

"Somewheres between South Bend and Laporte, the train stopped and liked it so well that we stayed there over three hours. We hit Englewood after four o'clock and I got to the park just in time to see them loadin' Lambert into a machine to take him away. His knee had broke down on him in the first innin's. He ain't never played ball since. And Smitty, who's always been a natural second baseman, he had my job."

"He's filled it pretty good," said Lefty.

"That's either here or there," retorted Healy. "If I'd been around, nobody'd ever knowed if he could play third base or not. And the worst of him is," he added, "that he never gets hurt."

"Maybe you ain't prayed for him like you done for Lambert," said Young Jake. "What happened to the gal? Did you give her the air?"

"No, I didn't," said Healy. "When I give my word, I keep it. I simply wrote and told her that I'd agreed to marry her and I wouldn't go back on it. But that my feelin's towards her was the same as if she was an advanced case of spinal meningitis. She never answered the letter, so I don't know if we're still engaged or not."

The inning was over and the boys were coming in.

" Joe was lucky to get out of that with only two runs," remarked Lefty. " But of course it was Sam that put him in bad."

" I'm goin' to see if he'll leave me get up on the lines," said Young Jake, " so I can get a better look at that dame."

The manager waited for Sam to catch up.

" What the hell was the matter with you, Sam? " he demanded.
Sam looked silly.

" I thought——"

" That's where you make your mistake! " the manager broke in. " Tough luck, Joe! But two runs are nothing. We'll get 'em back."

" Shall I go up on the lines? " asked Young Jake, hopefully.

" You? No! " said the manager. " You, Mike," turning to Healy, " go over and coach at third base. You brought us luck yesterday."

So it was Mike who was held partly responsible a few moments later when Smitty, who had tripled, was caught napping off the bag.

" Nice coachin', Mike! " said Lefty, as Healy came back to the bench.

" Why don't he watch hisself! " growled Mike. "And besides, I did yell at him! "

" You're a liar! " said Lefty. " Your back was to the ball game. You were lookin' up in the stand."

" Why would I be lookin' at the stand! " demanded Healy.

But nobody answered him. There was silence for a time. The boys were depressed; in their own language, their dauber was down. Finally Young Jake spoke.

" She's starin' right over this way! " he said.

" Who? " asked Gephart.

" That dame I pointed out. In the tan suit. 'Way over behind third base, the other side of the screen, in the fourth row."

" I see her. Not bad! "

" I'll say she's not bad! " said Jake.

" Women! " said Healy. " You better get your mind on baseball or you'll be back in that silo league, jumpin' from town to town in a w'eelbarrow."

" I don't see why you should be off all women just because one of them brought you a little hard luck."

" She wasn't the only one! Why, say, if it wasn't for women I'd be playin' regular third base for McGraw right now and cuttin' in on the big money every fall."

" I didn't know you was ever with McGraw."

" I wasn't," said Healy, " but I ought to been, and would of been only for a woman. It was when I was playin' with the Dayton club; my first year in baseball. Boy, I was fast as a streak! I was peggin' bunts to first base before the guy could drop his bat. I covered so much ground to my left that I was always knockin' the shortstop down and bumpin' heads with the right fielder. Everybody was marvelin' at me. Some of the old timers said I reminded them of Bill Bradley at his best, only that I made Bradley look like he was out of the game for a few days.

" Baldy Pierce was umpirin' in our league that year. He wasn't a bad umps, but he never left business interfere with pleasure. Many's the time he called the last fella out in the last innin's when the fella was safer than a hot chocolate at the Elks' convention—just because Baldy was hungry for supper.

" He was so homely that dogs wouldn't live in the same town, and his friends used to try and make him wear his mask off the field as well as on. And yet he grabbed some of the prettiest gals you ever see. He said to me once, he said, ' Mike,' he said, ' you tell me I'm homelier than Railroad Street, but I can cop more pips than you can with all your good looks! ' "

At this point there were unprintable comments by Lefty, Gephart, and other occupants of the bench.

" One of these gals of his," Healy went on, " was a gal named Helen Buck from Hamilton, Ohio. She was visitin' in Dayton and come out to the ball game. The first day she was there a lot of the boys was hit in the face by thrown balls, and every time a foul went to the stand the whole infield run in to shag it. But she wouldn't look at nobody but Pierce.

" Well, McGraw had heard about me, and he sent a fella named McDonald, that was scoutin' for him, to look me over. It was in September and we was just about through. How the games come out didn't make no difference, but I knowed this McDonald was there and what he was there for, so I wanted to make a showin'. He had came intendin' to stay two days, but he'd overlooked a skip in the schedule that left us without no game the second day, so he said one game would have to be enough, as he had to go somewheres else.

" We was playin' the Springfield club. I had a good day in the field, but Bill Hutton, who started pitchin' for them, he was hog wild and walked me the first two times up. The third time they was a man on third and I had to follow orders and squeeze him home. So I hadn't had no chance to really show what I could do up there at the plate.

"Well, we come into the ninth innin's with the score tied and it was gettin' pretty dark. We got two of them out, and then their first baseman, Jansen, he got a base on balls. Bill Boone caught a hold of one just right and cracked it to the fence and it looked like Jansen would score, but he was a slow runner. Davy Shaw, our shortstop, thought he must of scored and when the ball was thrown to him he throwed it to me to get Boone, who was tryin' for three bases.

"Well, I had took in the situation at a glance; I seen that Jansen hadn't scored and if I put the ball on Boone quick enough, why the run wouldn't count. So I lunged at Boone and tagged him before Jansen had crossed the plate. But Pierce said the score counted and that Boone wasn't out because I'd missed him. Missed him! Say, I bet that where I tagged him they had to take stitches!

"Anyway, that give 'em a one run lead, and when the first two fellas got out in our half everybody thought it was over. But Davy Shaw hit one to right center that a man like I could of ran around twice on it, but they held Davy at third base. And it was up to me to bring him in.

"By this time Jim Preston was pitchin' for Springfield, and Jim was always a mark for me. I left the first one go by, as it was outside, but Pierce called it a strike. Then they was a couple of balls that he couldn't call strikes. I cracked the next one over the leftfield fence, but it was a few inches foul. That made it two and two, and the next ball he throwed, well, if I hadn't ducked my head just when I did they'd of been brains scattered all over Montgomery County. And what does Pierce do but yell ' Batter out!' and run for the clubhouse!

"Well, I run after him and asked him what the hell, and here is what he said. He said, ' Mike,' he said, ' these games don't mean nothin', but if this here game had of wound up a tie it would of meant a game tomorrow, when we got a off day. And I made a date for tomorrow to go on a picnic with my little gal in Hamilton. You wouldn't want me to miss that, would you?'"

"Why," inquired Young Jake, " didn't you break his nose or bust him in the chin?"

"His nose was already broke," said Healy, " and he didn't have no chin. I tried to get a hold of McDonald, the fella that was there scoutin' me. I was goin' to explain the thing to him. But he'd left town before I could catch him. It seems, though, that he'd set over to the side where he couldn't see what a lousy strike it was and he told a friend of mine that he couldn't recommend a man that would take a third strike when a base hit would of tied up the game; that on top of me ' missin' ' Boone at third——"

Another half inning was over and Healy started for the third-base coaching line without waiting for the manager to reach the bench. His teammates were not in a position to see the glance he threw at a certain spot in the stand as he walked to his " work." When the side was retired scoreless and he had returned to his corner of the dugout he looked more desolate than ever.

" Women ! " he said. " Why, if it wasn't for women I'd be playin' third base for Huggins; I'd have Joe Dugan's job; I'd be livin' right here in the capital of the world."

" How do you make that out? " asked Young Jake.

" It's a long story," said Healy, " but I can tell you in a few words. We was playin' the New York Club out home. Frank Baker had began to slip and Huggins was lookin' for a good young fella to take his place. He was crazy to get me, but he had heard that I didn't want to play in New York. This had came from me kiddin' with some of the boys on the New York Club, tellin' 'em I wouldn't play here if they give me the town. So Huggins wanted to make sure before he started a trade. And he didn't want no one to see him talkin' to me. So he came around one night to the hotel where I was livin' at the time. I was up in my room waitin' for the phone gal to be off duty. She was stuck on me and I had a date to take her for a drive. So when Huggins come to see me she said I was out. She was afraid her date was goin' to be interfered with. So Huggins went away and his club left town that night."

" What did you do to her? " asked Jake.

" Oh, I couldn't do nothin' to her," said Healy. " She claimed she didn't know who it was."

" Didn't he give his name? "

" No."

" Then how do you know it was Huggins? "

" She said it was a little fella."

" He ain't the only little fella."

" He's the littlest fella I know," said Healy.

" But you ain't sure what he wanted to see you for."

" What *would* Huggins want to see me for—to scratch my

back? But as I say, she didn't know who it was, so I couldn't do nothin' to her except ignore her from then on, and they couldn't of been no worse punishment as far as she was concerned."

"All and all," summed up Lefty, "if it wasn't for women, you'd of been playin' third base for McGraw and Huggins and this club, all at the same time."

"Yes," said Healy, "and with Washin'ton, too. Why——"

"Mike Healy!" interrupted the voice of Dick Trude, veteran usher. "Here's a mash note and it wants an answer."

Healy read the note and crumpled it in his hand.

"Who is she?" he asked.

"Look where I point," said Trude. "It's that good-lookin' dame in the tan suit, in the fourth row, back of third base. There! She asked me who you was when you was out there coachin'. So I told her, and she give me that note. She said you could answer yes or no."

"Make it 'yes,'" said Healy, and Trude went away.

Healy threw the crumpled note under the water bottle and addressed Young Jake.

"What I want you to get through your head, boy——"

"Oh, for God's sakes, shut up!" said Young Jake.

XIII

A DAY WITH CONRAD GREEN

CONRAD GREEN woke up depressed and, for a moment, could not think why. Then he remembered. Herman Plant was dead; Herman Plant, who had been his confidential secretary ever since he had begun producing; who had been much more than a secretary —his champion, votary, shield, bodyguard, tool, occasional lackey, and the butt of his heavy jokes and nasty temper. For forty-five dollars a week.

Herman Plant was dead, and this Lewis, recommended by Ezra Peebles, a fellow entrepreneur, had not, yesterday, made a good first impression. Lewis was apparently impervious to hints. You had to tell him things right out, and when he did understand he looked at you as if you were a boob. And insisted on a salary of sixty dollars right at the start. Perhaps Peebles, who, Green knew, hated him almost enough to make it fifty-fifty, was doing him another dirty trick dressed up as a favor.

After ten o'clock, and still Green had not had enough sleep. It had been nearly three when his young wife and he had left the Bryant-Walkers'. Mrs. Green, the former Marjorie Manning of the Vanities chorus, had driven home to Long Island, while he had stayed in the rooms he always kept at the Ambassador.

Majorie had wanted to leave a good deal earlier; through no lack of effort on her part she had been almost entirely ignored by her aristocratic host and hostess and most of the guests. She had confided to her husband more than once that she was sick of the whole such-and-such bunch of so-and-so's. As far as she was concerned, they could all go to hell and stay there! But Green had been rushed by the pretty and stage-struck Joyce Brainard, wife of the international polo star, and had successfully combated his own wife's importunities till the Brainards themselves had gone.

Yes, he could have used a little more sleep, but the memory of the party cheered him. Mrs. Brainard, excited by his theatrical aura and several highballs, had been almost affectionate. She had promised to come to his office some time and talk over a stage career which both knew was impossible so long as Brainard lived. But, best of all, Mr. and Mrs. Green would be listed in the papers

as among those present at the Bryant-Walkers', along with the
Vanderbecks, the Suttons, and the Schuylers, and that would just
about be the death of Peebles and other social sycophants of " show
business." He would order all the papers now and look for his
name. No; he was late and must get to his office. No telling
what a mess things were in without Herman Plant. And, by the
way, he mustn't forget Plant's funeral this afternoon.

He bathed, telephoned for his breakfast, and his favorite barber,
dressed in a symphony of purple and gray, and set out for Broadway, pretending not to hear the " There's Conrad Green ! " spoken
in awed tones by two flappers and a Westchester realtor whom he
passed en route.

Green let himself into his private office, an office of luxurious,
exotic furnishings, its walls adorned with expensive landscapes
and a Zuloaga portrait of his wife. He took off his twenty-five
dollar velour hat, approved of himself in the large mirror, sat
down at his desk, and rang for Miss Jackson.

"All the morning papers," he ordered, "and tell Lewis to
come in."

"I'll have to send out for the papers," said Miss Jackson, a
tired-looking woman of forty-five or fifty.

"What do you mean, send out? I thought we had an arrangement with that boy to leave them every morning."

"We did. But the boy says he can't leave them any more till
we've paid up to date."

"What do we owe?"

"Sixty-five dollars."

"Sixty-five dollars! He's crazy! Haven't you been paying
him by the week?"

"No. You told me not to."

"I told you nothing of the kind! Sixty-five dollars! He's trying to rob us!"

"I don't believe so, Mr. Green," said Miss Jackson. "He
showed me his book. It's more than thirty weeks since he began,
and you know we've never paid him."

"But hell! There isn't sixty-five dollars' worth of newspapers
ever been printed! Tell him to sue us! And now send out for the
papers and do it quick! After this we'll get them down at the corner every morning and pay for them. Tell Lewis to bring me the
mail."

Miss Jackson left him, and presently the new secretary came in.
He was a man under thirty, whom one would have taken for a

high school teacher rather than a theatrical general's aide-de-camp.

"Good-morning, Mr. Green," he said.

His employer disregarded the greeting.

"Anything in the mail?" he asked.

"Not much of importance. I've already answered most of it. Here are a few things from your clipping bureau and a sort of dunning letter from some jeweler in Philadelphia."

"What did you open that for?" demanded Green, crossly. "Wasn't it marked personal?"

"Look here, Mr. Green," said Lewis quietly: "I was told you had a habit of being rough with your employees. I want to warn you that I am not used to that sort of treatment and don't intend to get used to it. If you are decent with me, I'll work for you. Otherwise I'll resign."

"I don't know what you're talking about, Lewis. I didn't mean to be rough. It's just my way of speaking. Let's forget it and I'll try not to give you any more cause to complain."

"All right, Mr. Green. You told me to open all your mail except the letters with that one little mark on them——"

"Yes, I know. Now let's have the clippings."

Lewis laid them on the desk.

"I threw away about ten of them that were all the same—the announcement that you had signed Bonnie Blue for next season. There's one there that speaks of a possible partnership between you and Sam Stein——"

"What a nerve he's got, giving out a statement like that. Fine chance of me mixing myself up with a crook like Stein! Peebles says he's a full stepbrother to the James boys. So is Peebles himself, for that matter. What's this long one about?"

"It's about that young composer, Casper Ettelson. It's by Deems Taylor of the *World*. There's just a mention of you down at the bottom."

"Read it to me, will you? I've overstrained my eyes lately."

The dead Herman Plant had first heard of that recent eye strain twenty years ago. It amounted to almost total blindness where words of over two syllables were concerned.

"So far," Lewis read, "Ettelson has not had a book worthy of his imaginative, whimsical music. How we would revel in an Ettelson score with a Barrie libretto and a Conrad Green production."

"Who is this Barrie?" asked Green.

" I suppose it's James M. Barrie," replied Lewis, " the man who wrote Peter Pan."

" I thought that was written by a fella over in England," said Green.

" I guess he does live in England. He was born in Scotland. I don't know where he is now."

" Well, find out if he's in New York, and, if he is, get a hold of him. Maybe he'll do a couple of scenes for our next show. Come in, Miss Jackson. Oh, the papers! "

Miss Jackson handed them to him and went out. Green turned first to the society page of the *Herald Tribune*. His eye trouble was not so severe as to prevent his finding that page. And he could read his name when it was there to be read.

Three paragraphs were devoted to the Bryant-Walker affair, two of them being lists of names. And Mr. and Mrs. Conrad Green were left out.

"——! " commented Green, and grabbed the other papers. The *World* and *Times* were searched with the same hideous result. And the others did not mention the party at all.

"——! " repeated Green. " I'll get somebody for this! " Then, to Lewis: " Here! Take this telegram. Send it to the managing editors of all the morning papers; you'll find their names pasted on Plant's desk. Now: 'Ask your society editor why my name was not on list of guests at Bryant-Walker dinner Wednesday night. Makes no difference to me, as am not seeking and do not need publicity, but it looks like conspiracy, and thought you ought to be informed, as have always been good friend of your paper, as well as steady advertiser.' I guess that's enough."

" If you'll pardon a suggestion," said Lewis, " I'm afraid a telegram like this would just be laughed at."

" You send the telegram; I'm not going to have a bunch of cheap reporters make a fool of me! "

" I don't believe you can blame the reporters. There probably weren't reporters there. The list of guests is generally given out by the people who give the party."

" But listen——" Green paused and thought. "All right. Don't send the telegram. But if the Bryant-Walkers are ashamed of me, why the hell did they invite me? I certainly didn't want to go and they weren't under obligations to me. I never——"

As if it had been waiting for its cue, the telephone rang at this instant, and Kate, the switchboard girl, announced that the Bryant-Walkers' secretary was on the wire.

"I am speaking for Mrs. Bryant-Walker," said a female voice. "She is chairman of the committee on entertainment for the Women's Progress Bazaar. The bazaar is to open on the third of next month and wind up on the evening of the fifth with a sort of vaudeville entertainment. She wanted me to ask you——"

Green hung up with an oath.

"That's the answer!" he said. "The damn grafters!"

Miss Jackson came in again.

"Mr. Robert Blair is waiting to see you."

"Who is he?"

"You know. He tried to write some things for one of the shows last year."

"Oh, yes. Say, did you send flowers to Plant's house?"

"I did," replied Miss Jackson. "I sent some beautiful roses."

"How much?"

"Forty-five dollars," said Miss Jackson.

"Forty-five dollars for roses! And the man hated flowers even when he was alive! Well, send in this Blair."

Robert Blair was an ambitious young free lance who had long been trying to write for the stage, but with little success.

"Sit down, Blair," said Green. "What's on your mind?"

"Well, Mr. Green, my stuff didn't seem to suit you last year, but this time I think I've got a scene that can't miss."

"All right. If you want to leave it here, I'll read it over."

"I haven't written it out. I thought I'd tell you the idea first."

"Well, go ahead, but cut it short; I've got a lot of things to do today. Got to go to old Plant's funeral for one thing."

"I bet you miss him, don't you?" said Blair, sympathetically.

"Miss him! I should say I do! A lovable character and "— with a glance at Lewis—" the best secretary I'll ever have. But let's hear your scene."

"Well," said Blair, "it may not sound like much the way I tell it, but I think it'll work out great. Well, the police get a report that a woman has been murdered in her home, and they go there and find her husband, who is acting very nervous. They give him the third degree, and he finally breaks down and admits he killed her. They ask him why, and he tells them he is very fond of beans, and on the preceding evening he came home to dinner and asked her what there was to eat, and she told him she had lamb chops, mashed potatoes, spinach, and apple pie. So he says, 'No beans?' and she says, 'No beans.' So he shoots her dead. Of course, the scene between the husband and wife is acted out on the stage. Then——"

" It's no good!" said Conrad Green. " In the first place, it takes too many people, all those policemen and everybody."

" Why, all you need is two policemen and the man and his wife. And wait till I tell you the rest of it."

" I don't like it; it's no good. Come back again when you've got something."

When Blair had gone Green turned to Lewis.

" That's all for just now," he said, " but on your way out tell Miss Jackson to get a hold of Martin and say I want him to drop in here as soon as he can."

" What Martin?" asked Lewis.

" She'll know—Joe Martin, the man that writes most of our librettos."

Alone, Conrad Green crossed the room to his safe, opened it, and took out a box on which was inscribed the name of a Philadelphia jeweler. From the box he removed a beautiful rope of matched pearls and was gazing at them in admiration when Miss Jackson came in; whereupon he hastily replaced them in their case and closed the safe.

" That man is here again," said Miss Jackson, " That man Hawley from *Gay New York.*"

" Tell him I'm not in."

" I did, but he says he saw you come in and he's going to wait till you'll talk to him. Really, Mr. Green, I think it would be best in the long run to see him. He's awfully persistent."

" All right; send him in," said Green, impatiently, " though I have no idea what he can possibly want of me."

Mr. Hawley, dapper and eternally smiling, insisted on shaking hands with his unwilling host, who had again sat down at his desk.

" I think," he said, " we've met before."

" Not that I know of," Green replied shortly.

" Well, it makes no difference, but I'm sure you've read our little paper, *Gay New York.*"

" No," said Green. "All I have time to read is manuscripts."

" You don't know what you're missing," said Hawley. " It's really a growing paper, with a big New York circulation, and a circulation that is important from your standpoint."

" Are you soliciting subscriptions?" asked Green.

" No. Advertising."

" Well, frankly, Mr. Hawley, I don't believe I need any advertising. I believe that even the advertising I put in the regular daily papers is a waste of money."

"Just the same," said Hawley, "I think you'd be making a mistake not to take a page in *Gay New York*. It's only a matter of fifteen hundred dollars."

"Fifteen hundred dollars! That's a joke! Nobody's going to hold *me* up!"

"Nobody's trying to, Mr. Green. But I might as well tell you that one of our reporters came in with a story the other day—well, it was about a little gambling affair in which some of the losers sort of forgot to settle, and—well, my partner was all for printing it, but I said I had always felt friendly toward you and why not give you a chance to state your side of it?"

"I don't know what you're talking about. If your reporter has got my name mixed up in a gambling story he's crazy."

"No. He's perfectly sane and very, very careful. We make a specialty of careful reporters and we're always sure of our facts."

Conrad Green was silent for a long, long time. Then he said:

"I tell you, I don't know what gambling business you refer to, and, furthermore, fifteen hundred dollars is a hell of a price for a page in a paper like yours. But still, as you say, you've got the kind of circulation that might do me good. So if you'll cut down the price——"

"I'm sorry, Mr. Green, but we never do that."

"Well, then, of course you'll have to give me a few days to get my ad fixed up. Say you come back here next Monday afternoon."

"That's perfectly satisfactory, Mr. Green," said Hawley, "and I assure you that you're not making a mistake. And now I won't keep you any longer from your work."

He extended his hand, but it was ignored, and he went out, his smile a little broader than when he had come in. Green remained at his desk, staring straight ahead of him and making semi-audible references to certain kinds of dogs as well as personages referred to in the Old and New Testaments. He was interrupted by the entrance of Lewis.

"Mr. Green," said the new secretary, "I have found a check for forty-five dollars, made out to Herman Plant. I imagine it is for his final week's pay. Would you like to have me change it and make it out to his widow?"

"Yes," said Green. "But no; wait a minute. Tear it up and I'll make out my personal check to her and add something to it."

" All right," said Lewis, and left.

" Forty-five dollars' worth of flowers," said Green to himself, and smiled for the first time that morning.

He looked at his watch and got up and put on his beautiful hat.

" I'm going to lunch," he told Miss Jackson on his way through the outer office. " If Peebles or anybody important calls up, tell them I'll be here all afternoon."

" You're not forgetting Mr. Plant's funeral ? "

" Oh, that's right. Well, I'll be here from one-thirty to about three."

A head waiter at the Astor bowed to him obsequiously and escorted him to a table near a window, while the occupants of several other tables gazed at him spellbound and whispered, " Conrad Green."

A luncheon of clams, sweetbreads, spinach, strawberry ice cream, and small coffee seemed to satisfy him. He signed his check and then tipped his own waiter and the head waiter a dollar apiece, the two tips falling just short of the cost of the meal.

Joe Martin, his chief librettist, was waiting when he got back to his office.

" Oh, hello, Joe ! " he said, cordially. " Come right inside. I think I've got something for you."

Martin followed him in and sat down without waiting for an invitation. Green seated himself at his desk and drew out his cigarette case.

" Have one, Joe ? "

" Not that kind ! " said Martin, lighting one of his own. " You've got rotten taste in everything but gals."

" And librettists," replied Green, smiling.

" But here's what I wanted to talk about. I couldn't sleep last night, and I just laid there and an idea came to me for a comedy scene. I'll give you the bare idea and you can work it out. It'll take a girl and one of the comics, maybe Fraser, and a couple of other men that can play.

" Well, the idea is that the comic is married to the girl. In the first place, I'd better mention that the comic is crazy about beans. Well, one night the comic—no, wait a minute. The police get word that the comic's wife has been murdered and two policemen come to the comic's apartment to investigate. They examine the corpse and find out she's been shot through the head. They ask the comic if he knows who did it and he says no, but they keep after him, and finally he breaks down and admits that he did it himself.

"But he says, 'Gentlemen, if you'll let me explain the circumstances, I don't believe you'll arrest me.' So they tell him to explain, and he says that he came home from work and he was very hungry and he asked his wife what they were going to have for dinner. So she tells him—clams and sweetbreads and spinach and strawberry ice cream and coffee. So he asks her if she isn't going to have any beans and she says no, and he shoots her. What do you think you could do with that idea?"

"Listen, Connie," said Martin: "You've only got half the scene, and you've got that half wrong. In the second place, it was played a whole season in the Music Box and it was written by Bert Kalmar and Harry Ruby. Otherwise I can do a whole lot with it."

"Are you sure you're right?"

"I certainly am!"

"Why, that damn little thief! He told me it was his!"

"Who?" asked Martin.

"Why, that Blair, that tried to butt in here last year. I'll fix him!"

"I thought you said it was your own idea."

"Hell, no! Do you think I'd be stealing stuff, especially if it was a year old?"

"Well," said Martin, "when you get another inspiration like this, give me a ring and I'll come around. Now I've got to hurry up to the old Stadium and see what the old Babe does in the first inning."

"I'm sorry, Joe. I thought it was perfectly all right."

"Never mind! You didn't waste much of my time. But after this you'd better leave the ideas to me. So long!"

"Good-by, Joe; and thanks for coming in."

Martin went and Green pressed the button for Miss Jackson.

"Miss Jackson, don't ever let that young Blair in here again. He's a faker!"

"All right, Mr. Green. But don't you think it's about time you were starting for the funeral? It's twenty minutes of three."

"Yes. But let's see: where is Plant's house?"

"It's up on One Hundred and Sixtieth street, just off Broadway."

"My God! Imagine living there! Wait a minute, Miss Jackson. Send Lewis here."

"Lewis," he said, when the new secretary appeared, "I ate something this noon that disagreed with me. I wanted to go up to Plant's funeral, but I really think it would be dangerous to try it. Will you go up there, let them know who you are, and kind of represent me? Miss Jackson will give you the address."

"Yes, sir," said Lewis, and went out.

Almost immediately the sanctum door opened again and the beautiful Marjorie Green, née Manning, entered unannounced. Green's face registered not altogether pleasant surprise.

"Why, hello, dear!" he said. "I didn't know you were coming to town today.

"I never told you I wasn't," his wife replied.

They exchanged the usual connubial salutations.

"I supposed you noticed," said Mrs. Green, "that our names were not on the list of guests at the party."

"No; I haven't had time to look at the papers. But what's the difference?"

"No difference at all, of course. But do you know what I think? I think we were invited just because those people want to get something out of you, for some benefit or something."

"A fine chance! I hope they try it!"

"However, that's not what I came to talk about."

"Well, dear, what is it?"

"I thought maybe you'd remember something."

"What, honey?"

"Why—oh, well, there's no use talking about it if you've forgotten."

Green's forehead wrinkled in deep thought; then suddenly his face brightened.

"Of course I haven't forgotten! It's your birthday!"

"You just thought of it now!"

"No such a thing! I've been thinking of it for weeks!"

"I don't believe you! If you had been, you'd have said something, and "—his wife was on the verge of tears—"you'd have given me some little thing, just any little thing."

Once more Green frowned, and once more brightened up.

"I'll prove it to you," he said, and walked rapidly to the safe.

In a moment he had placed in her hands the jewel box from Philadelphia. In another moment she had opened it, gasped at the beauty of its contents, and thrown her arms around his neck.

"Oh, dearest!" she cried. "Can you ever forgive me for doubting you?"

She put the pearls to her mouth as if she would eat them.

"But haven't you been terribly extravagant?"

"I don't consider anything too extravagant for you."

" You're the best husband a girl ever had ! "

" I'm glad you're pleased," said Green.

" Pleased ! I'm overwhelmed. And to think I imagined you'd forgotten ! But I'm not going to break up your whole day. I know you want to get out to poor old Plant's funeral. So I'll run along. And maybe you'll take me to dinner somewhere tonight."

" I certainly will ! You be at the Ambassador about six-thirty and we'll have a little birthday party. But don't you want to leave the pearls here now ? "

" I should say not ! They're going to stay with me forever ! Anyone that tries to take them will do it over my dead body ! "

" Well, good-by, then, dear."

" Till half past six."

Green, alone again, kicked shut the door of his safe and returned to his desk, saying in loud tones things which are not ordinarily considered appropriate to the birthday of a loved one. The hubbub must have been audible to Miss Jackson ouside, but perhaps she was accustomed to it. It ceased at another unannounced entrance, that of a girl even more beautiful than the one who had just gone out. She looked at Green and laughed.

" My God ! You look happy ! " she said.

" Rose ! "

" Yes, it's Rose. But what's the matter with you ? "

" I've had a bad day."

" But isn't it better now ? "

" I didn't think you were coming till to-morrow."

" But aren't you glad I came today ? "

" You bet I am ! " said Green. " And if you'll come here and kiss me I'll be all the gladder."

" No. Let's get our business transacted first."

" What business ? "

" You know perfectly well ! Last time I saw you you insisted that I must give up everybody else but you. And I promised you it would be all off between Harry and I if—— Well, you know. There was a little matter of some pearls."

" I meant everything I said."

" Well, where are they ? "

" They're all bought and all ready for you. But I bought them in Philadelphia and for some damn reason they haven't got here yet."

" Got here yet ! Were they so heavy you couldn't bring them with you ? "

' Honest, dear, they'll be here day after tomorrow at the latest."

" ' Honest ' is a good word for you to use! Do you think I'm dumb? Or is it that you're so used to lying that you can't help it? "

" If you'll let me explain——"

" Explain hell! We made a bargain and you haven't kept your end of it. And now——"

" But listen——"

" I'll listen to nothing! You know where to reach me and when you've kept your promise you can call me up. Till then— Well, Harry isn't such bad company."

" Wait a minute, Rose! "

" You've heard all I've got to say. Good-by! "

And she was gone before he could intercept her.

Conrad Green sat as if stunned. For fifteen minutes he was so silent and motionless that one might have thought him dead. Then he shivered as if with cold and said aloud:

" I'm not going to worry about them any more. To hell with all of them! "

He drew the telephone to him and took off the receiver.

" Get me Mrs. Bryant-Walker."

And after a pause:

" Is this Mrs. Bryant-Walker? No, I want to speak to her personally. This is Conrad Green. Oh, hello, Mrs. Walker. Your secretary called me up this morning, but we were cut off. She was saying something about a benefit. Why, yes, certainly, I'll be glad to. As many of them as you want. If you'll just leave it all in my hands I'll guarantee you a pretty good entertainment. It's no bother at all. It's a pleasure. Thank you. Good-by."

Lewis came in.

" Well, Lewis, did you get to the funeral? "

" Yes, Mr. Green, and I saw Mrs. Plant and explained the circumstances to her. She said you had always been very kind to her husband. She said that during the week of his illness he talked of you nearly all the time and expressed confidence that if he died you would attend his funeral. So she wished you had been there."

" Good God! So do I! " said Conrad Green.

XIV

OLD FOLKS' CHRISTMAS

Tom and Grace Carter sat in their living-room on Christmas Eve, sometimes talking, sometimes pretending to read and all the time thinking things they didn't want to think. Their two children, Junior, aged nineteen, and Grace, two years younger, had come home that day from their schools for the Christmas vacation. Junior was in his first year at the university and Grace attending a boarding-school that would fit her for college.

I won't call them Grace and Junior any more, though that is the way they had been christened. Junior had changed his name to Ted and Grace was now Caroline, and thus they insisted on being addressed, even by their parents. This was one of the things Tom and Grace the elder were thinking of as they sat in their living-room Christmas Eve.

Other university freshmen who had lived here had returned on the twenty-first, the day when the vacation was supposed to begin. Ted had telegraphed that he would be three days late owing to a special examination which, if he passed it, would lighten the terrific burden of the next term. He had arrived at home looking so pale, heavy-eyed and shaky that his mother doubted the wisdom of the concentrated mental effort, while his father secretly hoped the stuff had been non-poisonous and would not have lasting effects. Caroline, too, had been behind schedule, explaining that her laundry had gone astray and she had not dared trust others to trace it for her.

Grace and Tom had attempted, with fair success, to conceal their disappointment over this delayed home-coming and had continued with their preparations for a Christmas that would thrill their children and consequently themselves. They had bought an imposing lot of presents, costing twice or three times as much as had been Tom's father's annual income when Tom was Ted's age, or Tom's own income a year ago, before General Motors' acceptance of his new weather-proof paint had enabled him to buy this suburban home and luxuries such as his own parents and Grace's had never dreamed of, and to give Ted and Caroline advantages that he and Grace had perforce gone without.

171

Behind the closed door of the music-room was the elaborately decked tree. The piano and piano bench and the floor around the tree were covered with beribboned packages of all sizes, shapes and weights, one of them addressed to Tom, another to Grace, a few to the servants and the rest to Ted and Caroline. A huge box contained a sealskin coat for Caroline, a coat that had cost as much as the Carters had formerly paid a year for rent. Even more expensive was a "set" of jewelry consisting of an opal brooch, a bracelet of opals and gold filigree, and an opal ring surrounded by diamonds.

Grace always had preferred opals to any other stone, but now that she could afford them, some inhibition prevented her from buying them for herself; she could enjoy them much more adorning her pretty daughter. There were boxes of silk stockings, lingerie, gloves and handkerchiefs. And for Ted, a three hundred-dollar watch, a de-luxe edition of Balzac, an expensive bag of shiny, new steel-shafted golf-clubs and the last word in portable phonographs.

But the big surprise for the boy was locked in the garage, a black Gorham sedan, a model more up to date and better-looking than Tom's own year-old car that stood beside it. Ted could use it during the vacation if the mild weather continued and could look forward to driving it around home next spring and summer, there being a rule at the university forbidding undergraduates the possession or use of private automobiles.

Every year for sixteen years, since Ted was three and Caroline one, it had been the Christmas Eve custom of the Carter's to hang up their children's stockings and fill them with inexpensive toys. Tom and Grace had thought it would be fun to continue the custom this year; the contents of the stockings—a mechanical negro dancing doll, music-boxes, a kitten that meowed when you pressed a spot on her back, et cetera—would make the "kids" laugh. And one of Grace's first pronouncements to her returned offspring was that they must go to bed early so Santa Claus would not be frightened away.

But it seemed they couldn't promise to make it so terribly early. They both had long-standing dates in town. Caroline was going to dinner and a play with Beatrice Murdock and Beatrice's nineteen-year-old brother Paul. The latter would call for her in his car at half past six. Ted had accepted an invitation to see the hockey match with two classmates, Herb Castle and Bernard King. He wanted to take his father's Gorham, but Tom told him untruthfully that the foot-brake was not working; Ted must be kept out of the garage till tomorrow morning.

Ted and Caroline had taken naps in the afternoon and gone off together in Paul Murdock's stylish roadster, giving their word that they would be back by midnight or a little later and that tomorrow night they would stay home.

And now their mother and father were sitting up for them, because the stockings could not be filled and hung till they were safely in bed, and also because trying to go to sleep is a painful and hopeless business when you are kind of jumpy.

"What time is it?" asked Grace, looking up from the third page of a book that she had begun to "read" soon after dinner.

"Half past two," said her husband. (He had answered the same question every fifteen or twenty minutes since midnight.)

"You don't suppose anything could have happened?" said Grace.

"We'd have heard if there had," said Tom.

"It isn't likely, of course," said Grace, "but they might have had an accident some place where nobody was there to report it or telephone or anything. We don't know what kind of a driver the Murdock boy is."

"He's Ted's age. Boys that age may be inclined to drive too fast, but they drive pretty well."

"How do you know?"

"Well, I've watched some of them drive."

"Yes, but not all of them."

"I doubt whether anybody in the world has seen every nineteen-year-old boy drive."

"Boys these days seem so kind of irresponsible."

"Oh, don't worry! They probably met some of their young friends and stopped for a bite to eat or something." Tom got up and walked to the window with studied carelessness. "It's a pretty night," he said. "You can see every star in the sky."

But he wasn't looking at the stars. He was looking down the road for headlights. There were none in sight and after a few moments he returned to his chair.

"What time is it?" asked Grace.

"Twenty-two of," he said.

"Of what?"

"Of three."

"Your watch must have stopped. Nearly an hour ago you told me it was half past two."

"My watch is all right. You probably dozed off."

"I haven't closed my eyes."

"Well, it's time you did. Why don't you go to bed?"

"Why don't *you*?"

"I'm not sleepy."

"Neither am I. But honestly, Tom, it's silly for you to stay up. I'm just doing it so I can fix the stockings, and because I feel so wakeful. But there's no use of your losing your sleep."

"I couldn't sleep a wink till they're home."

"That's foolishness! There's nothing to worry about. They're just having a good time. You were young once yourself."

"That's just it! When I was young, I was young." He picked up his paper and tried to get interested in the shipping news.

"What time is it?" asked Grace.

"Five minutes of three."

"Maybe they're staying at the Murdocks' all night."

"They'd have let us know."

"They were afraid to wake us up, telephoning."

At three-twenty a car stopped at the front gate.

"There they are!"

"I told you there was nothing to worry about."

Tom went to the window. He could just discern the outlines of the Murdock boy's roadster, whose lighting system seemed to have broken down.

"He hasn't any lights," said Tom. "Maybe I'd better go out and see if I can fix them."

"No, don't!" said Grace sharply. "He can fix them himself. He's just saving them while he stands still."

"Why don't they come in?"

"They're probably making plans."

"They can make them in here. I'll go out and tell them we're still up."

"No, don't!" said Grace as before, and Tom obediently remained at the window.

It was nearly four when the car lights flashed on and the car drove away. Caroline walked into the house and stared dazedly at her parents.

"Heavens! What are you doing up?"

Tom was about to say something, but Grace forestalled him.

"We were talking over old Christmases," she said. "Is it very late?"

"I haven't any idea," said Caroline.

" Where is Ted? "

" Isn't he home? I haven't seen him since we dropped him at the hockey place."

" Well, you go right to bed," said her mother. " You must be worn out."

" I am, kind of. We danced after the play. What time is breakfast? "

" Eight o'clock."

" Oh, Mother, can't you make it nine? "

" I guess so. You used to want to get up early on Christmas."

" I know, but——"

" Who brought you home? " asked Tom.

" Why, Paul Murdock—and Beatrice."

" You look rumpled."

" They made me sit in the ' rumple ' seat."

She laughed at her joke, said good night and went upstairs. She had not come even within hand-shaking distance of her father and mother.

" The Murdocks," said Tom, " must have great manners, making their guest ride in that uncomfortable seat."

Grace was silent.

" You go to bed, too," said Tom. " I'll wait for Ted."

" You couldn't fix the stockings."

" I won't try. We'll have time for that in the morning; I mean, later in the morning."

" I'm not going to bed till you do," said Grace.

" All right, we'll both go. Ted ought not to be long now. I suppose his friends will bring him home. We'll hear him when he comes in."

There was no chance not to hear him when, at ten minutes before six, he came in. He had done his Christmas shopping late and brought home a package.

Grace was downstairs again at half past seven, telling the servants breakfast would be postponed till nine. She nailed the stockings beside the fireplace, went into the music-room to see that nothing had been disturbed and removed Ted's hat and overcoat from where he had carefully hung them on the hall floor.

Tom appeared a little before nine and suggested that the children ought to be awakened.

" I'll wake them," said Grace, and went upstairs. She opened Ted's door, looked, and softly closed it again. She entered her daughter's room and found Caroline semiconscious.

" Do I have to get up now? Honestly I can't eat anything. If you could just have Molla bring me some coffee. Ted and I are both invited to the Murdock's for breakfast at half past twelve, and I could sleep for another hour or two."

" But dearie, don't you know we have Christmas dinner at one? "

" It's a shame, Mother, but I thought of course our dinner would be at night."

" Don't you want to see your presents? "

" Certainly I do, but can't they wait? "

Grace was about to go to the kitchen to tell the cook that dinner would be at seven instead of one, but she remembered having promised Signe the afternoon and evening off, as a cold, light supper would be all anyone wanted after the heavy midday meal.

Tom and Grace breakfasted alone and once more sat in the living-room, talking, thinking and pretending to read.

" You ought to speak to Caroline," said Tom.

" I will, but not today. It's Christmas."

" And I intend to say a few words to Ted."

" Yes, dear, you must. But not today."

" I suppose they'll be out again tonight."

" No, they promised to stay home. We'll have a nice cozy evening."

" Don't bet too much on that," said Tom.

At noon the " children " made their entrance and responded to their parents' salutations with almost the proper warmth. Ted declined a cup of coffee and he and Caroline apologized for making a " breakfast " date at the Murdocks'.

" Sis and I both thought you'd be having dinner at seven, as usual."

" We've always had it at one o'clock on Christmas," said Tom.

" I'd forgotten it was Christmas," said Ted.

" Well, those stockings ought to remind you."

Ted and Caroline looked at the bulging stockings.

" Isn't there a tree? " asked Caroline.

" Of course," said her mother. " But the stockings come first."

" We've only a little time," said Caroline. " We'll be terribly late as it is. So can't we see the tree now? "

" I guess so," said Grace, and led the way into the music-room. The servants were summoned and the tree stared at and admired.

" You must open your presents," said Grace to her daughter.

" I can't open them all now," said Caroline. " Tell me which is special."

The cover was removed from the huge box and Grace held up the coat.

"Oh, Mother!" said Caroline. "A sealskin coat!"

"Put it on," said her father.

"Not now. We haven't time."

"Then look at this!" said Grace, and opened the case of jewels.

"Oh, Mother! Opals!" said Caroline.

"They're my favorite stone," said Grace quietly.

"If nobody minds," said Ted, "I'll postpone my personal investigation till we get back. I know I'll like everything you've given me. But if we have no car in working order, I've got to call a taxi and catch a train."

"You can drive in," said his father.

"Did you fix the brake?"

"I think it's all right. Come up to the garage and we'll see."

Ted got his hat and coat and kissed his mother good-by.

"Mother," he said, "I know you'll forgive me for not having any presents for you and Dad. I was so rushed the last three days at school. And I thought I'd have time to shop a little when we got in yesterday, but I was in too much of a hurry to be home. Last night, everything was closed."

"Don't worry," said Grace. "Christmas is for young people. Dad and I have everything we want."

The servants had found their gifts and disappeared, expressing effusive Scandinavian thanks.

Caroline and her mother were left alone.

"Mother, where did the coat come from?"

"Lloyd and Henry's."

"They keep all kinds of furs, don't they?"

"Yes."

"Would you mind horribly if I exchanged this?"

"Certainly not, dear. You pick out anything you like, and if it's a little more expensive, it won't make any difference. We can go in town tomorrow or next day. But don't you want to wear your opals to the Murdocks'?"

"I don't believe so. They might get lost or something. And I'm not—well, I'm not so crazy about——"

"I think they can be exchanged, too," said Grace. "You run along now and get ready to start."

Caroline obeyed with alacrity, and Grace spent a welcome moment by herself.

Tom opened the garage door.

" Why, you've got two cars ! " said Ted.

" The new one isn't mine," said Tom.

" Whose is it ? "

" Yours. It's the new model."

" Dad, that's wonderful ! But it looks just like the old one."

" Well, the old one's pretty good. Just the same, yours is better. You'll find that out when you drive it. Hop in and get started. I had her filled with gas."

" I think I'd rather drive the old one."

" Why ? "

" Well, what I really wanted, Dad, was a Barnes sport roadster, something like Paul Murdock's, only a different color scheme. And if I don't drive this Gorham at all, maybe you could get them to take it back or make some kind of a deal with the Barnes people."

Tom didn't speak till he was sure of his voice. Then: "All right, son. Take my car and I'll see what can be done about yours."

Caroline, waiting for Ted, remembered something and called to her mother. " Here's what I got for you and Dad," she said. " It's two tickets to ' Jolly Jane,' the play I saw last night. You'll love it ! "

" When are they for ? " asked Grace.

" Tonight," said Caroline.

" But dearie," said her mother, " we don't want to go out tonight, when you promised to stay home."

" We'll keep our promise," said Caroline, " but the Murdocks may drop in and bring some friends and we'll dance and there'll be music. And Ted and I both thought you'd rather be away somewhere so our noise wouldn't disturb you."

" It was sweet of you to do this," said her mother, " but your father and I don't mind noise as long as you're enjoying yourselves."

" It's time anyway that you and Dad had a treat."

" The real treat," said Grace, " would be to spend a quiet evening here with just you two."

" The Murdocks practically invited themselves and I couldn't say no after they'd been so nice to me. And honestly, Mother, you'll love this play ! "

" Will you be home for supper ? "

" I'm pretty sure we will, but if we're a little late, don't you and Dad wait for us. Take the seven-twenty so you won't miss anything. The first act is really the best. We probably won't be hungry, but have Signe leave something out for us in case we are."

Tom and Grace sat down to the elaborate Christmas dinner and didn't make much impression on it. Even if they had had any appetite, the sixteen-pound turkey would have looked almost like new when they had eaten their fill. Conversation was intermittent and related chiefly to Signe's excellence as a cook and the mildness of the weather. Children and Christmas were barely touched on.

Tom merely suggested that on account of its being a holiday and their having theatre tickets, they ought to take the six-ten and eat supper at the Metropole. His wife said no; Ted and Caroline might come home and be disappointed at not finding them. Tom seemed about to make some remark, but changed his mind.

The afternoon was the longest Grace had ever known. The children were still absent at seven and she and Tom taxied to the train. Neither talked much on the way to town. As for the play, which Grace was sure to love, it turned out to be a rehash of "Cradle Snatchers" and "Sex," retaining the worst features of each.

When it was over, Tom said: "Now I'm inviting you to the Cove Club. You didn't eat any breakfast or dinner or supper and I can't have you starving to death on a feast-day. Besides, I'm thirsty as well as hungry."

They ordered the special *table d'hôte* and struggled hard to get away with it. Tom drank six high-balls, but they failed to produce the usual effect of making him jovial. Grace had one high-ball and some kind of cordial that gave her a warm, contented feeling for a moment. But the warmth and contentment left her before the train was half way home.

The living-room looked as if Von Kluck's army had just passed through. Ted and Caroline had kept their promise up to a certain point. They had spent part of the evening at home, and the Murdocks must have brought all their own friends and everybody else's, judging from the results. The tables and floors were strewn with empty glasses, ashes and cigaret stubs. The stockings had been torn off their nails and the wrecked contents were all over the place. Two sizable holes had been burnt in Grace's favorite rug.

Tom took his wife by the arm and led her into the music-room.

"You never took the trouble to open your own present," he said.

"And I think there's one for you, too," said Grace. "They didn't come in here," she added, "so I guess there wasn't much dancing or music."

Tom found his gift from Grace, a set of diamond studs and cuff buttons for festive wear. Grace's present from him was an opal ring.

" Oh, Tom ! " she said.

" We'll have to go out somewhere tomorrow night, so I can break these in," said Tom.

"Well, if we do that, we'd better get a good night's rest."

" I'll beat you upstairs," said Tom.

XV

HARMONY

EVEN a baseball writer must sometimes work. Regretfully I yielded my seat in the P. G., walked past the section where Art Graham, Bill Cole, Lefty Parks and young Waldron were giving expert tonsorial treatment to " Sweet Adeline," and flopped down beside Ryan, the manager.

" Well, Cap," I said, " we're due in Springfield in a little over an hour and I haven't written a line."

" Don't let me stop you," said Ryan.

" I want you to start me," I said.

" Lord ! " said Ryan. " You oughtn't to have any trouble grinding out stuff these days, with the club in first place and young Waldron gone crazy. He's worth a story any day."

" That's the trouble," said I. " He's been worked so much that there's nothing more to say about him. Everybody in the country knows that he's hitting .420, that he's made nine home runs, twelve triples and twenty-some doubles, that he's stolen twenty-five bases, and that he can play the piano and sing like Car*us*'. They've run his picture oftener than Billy Sunday and Mary Pickford put together. Of course, you might come through with how you got him."

" Oh, that's the mystery," said Ryan.

" So I've heard you say," I retorted. " But it wouldn't be a mystery if you'd let me print it."

" Well," said Ryan, " if you're really hard up I suppose I might as well come through. Only there's really no mystery at all about it ; it's just what I consider the most remarkable piece of scouting ever done. I've been making a mystery of it just to have a little fun with Dick Hodges. You know he's got the Jackson club and he's still so sore about my stealing Waldron he'll hardly speak to me.

" I'll give you the dope if you want it, though it's a boost for Art Graham, not me. There's lots of people think the reason I've kept the thing a secret is because I'm modest.

" They give me credit for having found Waldron myself. But Graham is the bird that deserves the credit and I'll admit that he almost had to get down on his knees to make me take his tip. Yes, sir, Art Graham was the scout, and now he's sitting on the bench and the boy he recommended has got his place."

"That sounds pretty good," I said. "And how did Graham get wise?"

"I'm going to tell you. You're in a hurry; so I'll make it snappy.

"You weren't with us last fall, were you? Well, we had a day off in Detroit, along late in the season. Graham's got relatives in Jackson; so he asked me if he could spend the day there. I told him he could and asked him to keep his eyes peeled for good young pitchers, if he happened to go to the ball game. So he went to Jackson and the next morning he came back all excited. I asked him if he'd found me a pitcher and he said he hadn't, but he'd seen the best natural hitter he'd ever looked at—a kid named Waldron.

" ' Well,' I said, ' you're the last one that ought to be recommending outfielders. If there's one good enough to hold a regular job, it might be your job he'd get.'

"But Art said that didn't make any difference to him—he was looking out for the good of the club. Well, I didn't see my way clear to asking the old man to dig up good money for an outfielder nobody'd ever heard of, when we were pretty well stocked with them, so I tried to stall Art; but he kept after me and kept after me till I agreed to stick in a draft for the kid just to keep Art quiet. So the draft went in and we got him. Then, as you know, Hodges tried to get him back, and that made me suspicious enough to hold on to him. Hodges finally came over to see me and wanted to know who'd tipped me to Waldron. That's where the mystery stuff started, because I saw that Hodges was all heated up and wanted to kid him along. So I told him we had some mighty good scouts working for us, and he said he knew our regular scouts and they couldn't tell a ball-player from a torn ligament. Then he offered me fifty bucks if I'd tell him the truth and I just laughed at him. I said: 'A fella happened to be in Jackson one day and saw him work. But I won't tell you who the fella was, because you're too anxious to know.' Then he insisted on knowing what day the scout had been in Jackson. I said I'd tell him that if he'd tell me why he was so blame curious. So he gave me his end of it.

"It seems his brother, up in Ludington, had seen this kid play ball on the lots and had signed him right up for Hodges and taken him to Jackson, and of course, Hodges knew he had a world beater the minute he saw him. But he also knew he wasn't going to be able to keep him in Jackson, and, naturally he began to figure how he could get the most money for him. It was already August when the boy landed in Jackson; so there wasn't much chance of getting a big price last season. He decided to teach the kid what he didn't know about baseball and to keep him under cover till this year. Then everybody would be touting him and there'd be plenty of competition. Hodges could sell to the highest bidder.

"He had Waldron out practising every day, but wouldn't let him play in a game, and every player on the Jackson club had promised to keep the secret till this year. So Hodges wanted to find out from me which one of his players had broken the promise.

"Then I asked him if he was perfectly sure that Waldron hadn't played in a game, and he said he had gone in to hit for somebody just once. I asked him what date that was and he told me. It was the day Art had been in Jackson. So I said:

"'There's your mystery solved. That's the day my scout saw him, and you'll have to give the scout a little credit for picking a star after seeing him make one base hit.'

"Then Hodges said:

"'That makes it all the more a mystery. Because, in the first place, he batted under a fake name. And, in the second place, he didn't make a base hit. He popped out.'

"That's about all there is to it. You can ask Art how he picked the kid out for a star from seeing him pop out once. I've asked him myself, and he's told me that he liked the way Waldron swung. Personally, I believe one of those Jackson boys got too gabby. But Art swears not."

"That is a story," I said gratefully. "An old outfielder who must know he's slipping recommends a busher after seeing him pop out once. And the busher jumps right in and gets his job."

I looked down the aisle toward the song birds. Art Graham, now a bench warmer, and young Waldron, whom he had touted and who was the cause of his being sent to the bench, were harmonizing at the tops of their strong and not too pleasant voices.

"And probably the strangest part of the story," I added, "is that Art doesn't seem to regret it. He and the kid appear to be the best of friends."

"Anybody who can sing is Art's friend," said Ryan.

I left him and went back to my seat to tear off my seven hundred words before we reached Springfield. I considered for a moment the advisability of asking Graham for an explanation of his wonderful bit of scouting, but decided to save that part of it for another day. I was in a hurry and, besides, Waldron was just teaching them a new " wallop," and it would have been folly for me to interrupt.

" It's on the word ' you,' " Waldron was saying. " I come down a tone; Lefty goes up a half tone, and Bill comes up two tones. Art just sings it like always. Now try her again," I heard him direct the song birds. They tried her again, making a worse noise than ever:

"I only know I love you;
Love me, and the world (the world) is mine (the world is mine)."

" No," said Waldron. " Lefty missed it. If you fellas knew music, I could teach it to you with the piano when we get to Boston. On the word ' love,' in the next to the last line, we hit a regular F chord. Bill's singing the low F in the bass and Lefty's hitting middle C in the baritone, and Art's on high F and I'm up to A. Then, on the word ' you,' I come down to G, and Art hits E, and Lefty goes up half a tone to C sharp, and Cole comes up from F to A in the bass. That makes a good wallop. It's a change from the F chord to the A chord. Now let's try her again," Waldron urged.

They tried her again:

"I only know I love you——"

" No, no ! " said young Waldron. "Art and I were all right ; but Bill came up too far, and Lefty never moved off that C. Half a tone up, Lefty. Now try her again."

We were an hour late into Springfield, and it was past six o'clock when we pulled out. I had filed my stuff, and when I came back in the car the concert was over for the time, and Art Graham was sitting alone.

" Where are your pals ? " I asked.

" Gone to the diner," he replied.

" Aren't you going to eat ? "

" No," he said, " I'm savin' up for the steamed clams." I took the seat beside him.

" I sent in a story about you," I said.

" Am I fired ? " he asked.

" No, nothing like that."

" Well," he said, " you must be hard up when you can't find nothin' better to write about than a old has-been."

"Cap just told me who it was that found Waldron," said I.

"Oh, that," said Art. "I don't see no story in that."

"I thought it was quite a stunt," I said. "It isn't everybody that can pick out a second Cobb by just seeing him hit a fly ball."

Graham smiled.

"No," he replied, "they's few as smart as that."

"If you ever get through playing ball," I went on, "you oughtn't to have any trouble landing a job. Good scouts don't grow on trees."

"It looks like I'm pretty near through now," said Art, still smiling. "But you won't never catch me scoutin' for nobody. It's too lonesome a job."

I had passed up lunch to retain my seat in the card game; so I was hungry. Moreover, it was evident that Graham was not going to wax garrulous on the subject of his scouting ability. I left him and sought the diner. I found a vacant chair opposite Bill Cole.

"Try the minced ham," he advised, "but lay off'n the sparrow-grass. It's tougher'n a double-header in St. Louis."

"We're over an hour late," I said.

"You'll have to do a hurry-up on your story, won't you?" asked Bill. "Or did you write it already?"

"All written and on the way."

"Well, what did you tell 'em?" he inquired. "Did you tell 'em we had a pleasant trip, and Lenke lost his shirt in the poker game, and I'm goin' to pitch to-morrow, and the Boston club's heard about it and hope it'll rain?"

"No," I said. "I gave them a regular story to-night—about how Graham picked Waldron."

"Who give it to you?"

"Ryan," I told him.

"Then you didn't get the real story," said Cole, "Ryan himself don't know the best part of it, and he ain't goin' to know it for a w'ile. He'll maybe find it out after Art's got the can, but not before. And I hope nothin' like that'll happen for twenty years. When it does happen, I want to be sent along with Art, 'cause I and him's been roomies now since 1911, and I wouldn't hardly know how to act with him off'n the club. He's a nut all right on the singin' stuff, and if he was gone I might get a chanct to give my voice a rest. But he's a pretty good guy, even if he is crazy."

"I'd like to hear the real story," I said.

"Sure you would," he answered, "and I'd like to tell it to you. I will tell it to you if you'll give me your promise not to spill it till

Art's gone. Art told it to I and Lefty in the club-house at Cleveland pretty near a month ago, and the three of us and Waldron is the only ones that knows it. I figure I've did pretty well to keep it to myself this long, but it seems like I got to tell somebody."

" You can depend on me," I assured him, " not to say a word about it till Art's in Minneapolis, or wherever they're going to send him."

" I guess I can trust you," said Cole. " But if you cross me, I'll shoot my fast one up there in the press coop some day and knock your teeth loose."

" Shoot," said I.

" Well," said Cole, " I s'pose Ryan told you that Art fell for the kid after just seein' him pop out."

" Yes, and Ryan said he considered it a remarkable piece of scouting."

" It was all o' that. It'd of been remarkable enough if Art'd saw the bird pop out and then recommended him. But he didn't even see him pop out."

" What are you giving me? "

" The fac's," said Bill Cole. "Art not only didn't see him pop out, but he didn't even see him with a ball suit on. He wasn't never inside the Jackson ball park in his life."

" Waldron? "

" No. Art I'm talkin' about."

" Then somebody tipped him off," I said, quickly.

" No, sir. Nobody tipped him off, neither. He went to Jackson and spent the ev'nin' at his uncle's house, and Waldron was there. Him and Art was together the whole ev'nin'. But Art didn't even ask him if he could slide feet first. And then he come back to Detroit and got Ryan to draft him. But to give you the whole story, I'll have to go back a ways. We ain't nowheres near Worcester yet, so they's no hurry, except that Art'll prob'ly be sendin' for me pretty quick to come in and learn Waldron's lost chord.

" You wasn't with this club when we had Mike McCann. But you must of heard of him; outside his pitchin', I mean. He was on the stage a couple o' winters, and he had the swellest tenor voice I ever heard. I never seen no grand opera, but I'll bet this here C'ruso or McCormack or Gadski or none o' them had nothin' on him for a pure tenor. Every note as clear as a bell. You couldn't hardly keep your eyes dry when he'd tear off ' Silver Threads ' or ' The River Shannon.'

" Well, when Art was still with the Washin'ton club yet, I and Lefty and Mike used to pal round together and onct or twict we'd hit up some harmony. I couldn't support a fam'ly o' Mormons with my voice, but it was better in them days than it is now. I used to carry the lead, and Lefty'd hit the baritone and Mike the tenor. We didn't have no bass. But most o' the time we let Mike do the singin' alone, 'cause he had us outclassed, and the other boys kept tellin' us to shut up and give 'em a treat. First it'd be ' Silver Threads ' and then ' Jerusalem ' and then ' My Wild Irish Rose ' and this and that, whatever the boys ast him for. Jake Martin used to say he couldn't help a short pair if Mike wasn't singin'.

" Finally Ryan pulled off the trade with Griffith, and Graham come on our club. Then they wasn't no more solo work. They made a bass out o' me, and Art sung the lead, and Mike and Lefty took care o' the tenor and baritone. Art didn't care what the other boys wanted to hear. They could holler their heads off for Mike to sing a solo, but no sooner'd Mike start singin' than Art'd chime in with him and pretty soon we'd all four be goin' it. Art's a nut on singin', but he don't care nothin' about list'nin', not even to a canary. He'd rather harmonize than hit one past the outfielders with two on.

" At first we done all our serenadin' on the train. Art'd get us out o' bed early so's we could be through breakfast and back in the car in time to tear off a few before we got to wherever we was goin'.

" It got so's Art wouldn't leave us alone in the different towns we played at. We couldn't go to no show or nothin'. We had to stick in the hotel and sing, up in our room or Mike's. And then he went so nuts over it that he got Mike to come and room in the same house with him at home, and I and Lefty was supposed to help keep the neighbors awake every night. O' course we had mornin' practice w'ile we was home, and Art used to have us come to the park early and get in a little harmony before we went on the field. But Ryan finally nailed that. He says that when he ordered mornin' practice he meant baseball and not no minstrel show.

" Then Lefty, who wasn't married, goes and gets himself a girl. I met her a couple o' times, and she looked all right. Lefty might of married her if Art'd of left him alone. But nothin' doin'. We was home all through June onct, and instead o' comin' round nights to sing with us, Lefty'd take this here doll to one o' the parks or somewheres. Well, sir, Art was pretty near wild. He scouted round till he'd found out why Lefty'd quit us and then he

tried pretty near everybody else on the club to see if they wasn't
some one who could hit the baritone. They wasn't nobody. So the
next time we went on the road, Art give Lefty a earful about what
a sucker a man was to get married, and looks wasn't everything
and the girl was prob'ly after Lefty's money and he wasn't bein' a
good fella to break up the quartette and spoil our good times, and
so on, and kept pesterin' and teasin' Lefty till he give the girl up.
I'd of saw Art in the Texas League before I'd of shook a girl to
please him, but you know these left-handers.

"Art had it all framed that we was goin' on the stage, the four
of us, and he seen a vaudeville man in New York and got us booked
for eight hundred a week—I don't know if it was one week or two.
But he sprung it on me in September and says we could get solid
bookin' from October to March; so I ast him what he thought my
Missus would say when I told her I couldn't get enough o' bein'
away from home from March to October, so I was figurin' on
travelin' the vaudeville circuit the other four or five months and
makin' it unanimous? Art says I was tied to a woman's apron and
all that stuff, but I give him the cold stare and he had to pass up
that dandy little scheme.

"At that, I guess we could of got by on the stage all right.
Mike was better than this here Waldron and I hadn't wore my
voice out yet on the coachin' line, tellin' the boys to touch all the
bases.

"They was about five or six songs that we could kill. 'Adeline'
was our star piece. Remember where it comes in, ' Your fair face
beams'? Mike used to go away up on ' fair.' Then they was ' The
Old Millstream ' and ' Put on Your Old Gray Bonnet.' I done
some fancy work in that one. Then they was ' Down in Jungle
Town ' that we had pretty good. And then they was one that
maybe you never heard. I don't know the name of it. It run
somethin' like this."

Bill sottoed his voice so that I alone could hear the beautiful
refrain:

> " 'Years, years, I've waited years
>   Only to see you, just to call you 'dear.'
>   Come, come, I love but thee,
>   Come to your sweetheart's arms; come back to me.'

"That one had a lot o' wallops in it, and we didn't overlook
none o' them. The boys used to make us sing it six or seven times
a night. But ' Down in the Cornfield ' was Art's favor-ight.

They was a part in that where I sung the lead down low and the other three done a banjo stunt. Then they was 'Castle on the Nile' and 'Come Back to Erin' and a whole lot more.

"Well, the four of us wasn't hardly ever separated for three years. We was practisin' all the w'ile like as if we was goin' to play the big time, and we never made a nickel off'n it. The only audience we had was the ball players or the people travelin' on the same trains or stoppin' at the same hotels, and they got it all for nothin'. But we had a good time, 'specially Art.

"You know what a pitcher Mike was. He could go in there stone cold and stick ten out o' twelve over that old plate with somethin' on 'em. And he was the willin'est guy in the world. He pitched his own game every third or fourth day, and between them games he was warmin' up all the time to go in for somebody else. In 1911, when we was up in the race for aw'ile, he pitched eight games out o' twenty, along in September, and win seven o' them, and besides that, he finished up five o' the twelve he didn't start. We didn't win the pennant, and I've always figured that them three weeks killed Mike.

"Anyway, he wasn't worth nothin' to the club the next year; but they carried him along, hopin' he'd come back and show somethin'. But he was pretty near through, and he knowed it. I knowed it, too, and so did everybody else on the club, only Graham. Art never got wise till the trainin' trip two years ago this last spring. Then he come to me one day.

"'Bill,' he says, 'I don't believe Mike's comin' back.'

"'Well,' I says, 'you're gettin's so's they can't nobody hide nothin' from you. Next thing you'll be findin' out that Sam Crawford can hit.'

"'Never mind the comical stuff,' he says. 'They ain't no joke about this!'

"'No,' I says, 'and I never said they was. They'll look a long w'ile before they find another pitcher like Mike.'

"'Pitcher my foot!' says Art. 'I don't care if they have to pitch the bat boy. But when Mike goes, where'll our quartette be?'

"'Well,' I says, 'do you get paid every first and fifteenth for singin' or for crownin' that old pill?'

"'If you couldn't talk about money, you'd be deaf and dumb,' says Art.

"'But you ain't playin' ball because it's fun, are you?'

"'No,' he says, 'they ain't no fun for me in playin' ball. They's no fun doin' nothin' but harmonizin', and if Mike goes, I won't even have that.'

" ' I and you and Lefty can harmonize,' I says.

" ' It'd be swell stuff harmonizin' without no tenor,' says Art. ' It'd be like swingin' without no bat.'

" Well, he ast me did I think the club'd carry Mike through another season, and I told him they'd already carried him a year without him bein' no good to them, and I figured if he didn't show somethin' his first time out, they'd ask for waivers. Art kept broodin' and broodin' about it till they wasn't hardly no livin' with him. If he ast me onct he ast me a thousand times if I didn't think they might maybe hold onto Mike another season on account of all he'd did for 'em. I kept tellin' him I didn't think so; but that didn't satisfy him and he finally went to Ryan and ast him point blank.

" ' Are you goin' to keep McCann? ' Art ast him.

" ' If he's goin' to do us any good, I am,' says Ryan. " If he ain't, he'll have to look for another job.'

" After that, all through the trainin' trip, he was right on Mike's heels.

" ' How does the old souper feel? ' he'd ask him.

" ' Great! ' Mike'd say.

" Then Art'd watch him warm up, to see if he had anything on the ball.

" ' He's comin' fine,' he'd tell me. ' His curve broke to-day just as good as I ever seen it.'

" But that didn't fool me, or it didn't fool Mike neither. He could throw about four hooks and then he was through. And he could of hit you in the head with his fast one and you'd of thought you had a rash.

" One night, just before the season opened up, we was singin' on the train, and when we got through, Mike says:

" ' Well, boys, you better be lookin' for another C'ruso.'

" ' What are you talkin' about? ' says Art.

" ' I'm talkin' about myself,' says Mike. ' I'll be up there in Minneapolis this summer, pitchin' onct a week and swappin' stories about the Civil War with Joe Cantillon.'

" ' You're crazy,' says Art. ' Your arm's as good as I ever seen it.'

" ' Then,' says Mike, ' you must of been playin' blindfolded all these years. This is just between us, 'cause Ryan'll find it out for himself; my arm's rotten, and I can't do nothin' to help it.'

" Then Art got sore as a boil.

" ' You're a yellow, quittin' dog,' he says. ' Just because you come round a little slow, you talk about Minneapolis. Why don't you resign off'n the club? '

" ' I might just as well,' Mike says, and left us.

" You'd of thought that Art would of gave up then, 'cause when a ball player admits he's slippin', you can bet your last nickel that he's through. Most o' them stalls along and tries to kid themself and everybody else long after they know they're gone. But Art kept talkin' like they was still some hope o' Mike comin' round, and when Ryan told us one night in St. Louis that he was goin' to give Mike his chanct, the next day, Art was as nervous as a bride goin' to get married. I wasn't nervous. I just felt sorry, 'cause I knowed the old boy was hopeless.

" Ryan had told him he was goin' to work if the weather suited him. Well, the day was perfect. So Mike went out to the park along about noon and took Jake with him to warm up. Jake told me afterwards that Mike was throwin', just easy like, from half-past twelve till the rest of us got there. He was tryin' to heat up the old souper and he couldn't of ast for a better break in the weather, but they wasn't enough sunshine in the world to make that old whip crack.

" Well, sir, you'd of thought to see Art that Mike was his son or his brother or somebody and just breakin' into the league. Art wasn't in the outfield practisin' more than two minutes. He come in and stood behind Mike w'ile he was warmin' up and kept tellin' how good he looked, but the only guy he was kiddin' was himself.

" Then the game starts and our club goes in and gets three runs.

" ' Pretty soft for you now, Mike,' says Art, on the bench. ' They can't score three off'n you in three years.'

" Say, it's lucky he ever got the side out in the first innin'. Everybody that come up hit one on the pick, but our infield pulled two o' the greatest plays I ever seen and they didn't score. In the second, we got three more, and I thought maybe the old bird was goin' to be lucky enough to scrape through.

" For four or five innin's, he got the grandest support that was ever gave a pitcher; but I'll swear that what he throwed up there didn't have no more on it than September Morning. Every time Art come to the bench, he says to Mike, ' Keep it up, old boy. You got more than you ever had.'

" Well, in the seventh, Mike still had 'em shut out, and we was six runs to the good. Then a couple o' the St. Louis boys hit 'em where they couldn't nobody reach 'em and they was two on and two out. Then somebody got a hold o' one and sent it on a line to the left o' second base. I forgot who it was now; but whoever it was, he was supposed to be a right field hitter, and Art was layin' over the other way for him. Art started with the crack o' the bat, and I never seen a man make a better try for a ball. He had it judged perfect; but Cobb or Speaker or none o' them couldn't of catched it. Art just managed to touch it by stretchin' to the limit. It went on to the fence and everybody come in. They didn't score no more in that innin'.

" Then Art come in from the field and what do you think he tried to pull?

" ' I don't know what was the matter with me on that fly ball,' he says. ' I ought to caught it in my pants pocket. But I didn't get started till it was right on top o' me.'

" ' You misjudged it, didn't you? ' says Ryan.

" ' I certainly did,' says Art without crackin'.

" ' Well,' says Ryan, ' I wisht you'd misjudge all o' them that way. I never seen a better play on a ball.'

" So then Art knowed they wasn't no more use trying to alibi the old boy.

" Mike had a turn at bat and when he come back, Ryan ast him how he felt.

" ' I guess I can get six more o' them out,' he says.

" Well, they didn't score in the eighth, and when the ninth come Ryan sent I and Lefty out to warm up. We throwed a few w'ile our club was battin'; but when it come St. Louis' last chanct, we was too much interested in the ball game to know if we was throwin' or bakin' biscuits.

" The first guy hits a line drive, and somebody jumps a mile in the air and stabs it. The next fella fouled out, and they was only one more to get. And then what do you think come off? Whoever it was hittin' lifted a fly ball to centre field. Art didn't have to move out of his tracks. I've saw him catch a hundred just like it behind his back. But you know what he was thinkin'. He was sayin' to himself, ' If I nail this one, we're li'ble to keep our tenor singer a w'ile longer.' And he dropped it.

" Then they was five base hits that sounded like the fourth o' July, and they come so fast that Ryan didn't have time to send for

I or Lefty. Anyway, I guess he thought he might as well leave
Mike in there and take it.

"They wasn't no singin' in the clubhouse after that game. I
and Lefty always let the others start it. Mike, o' course, didn't
feel like no jubilee, and Art was so busy tryin' not to let nobody
see him cry that he kept his head clear down in his socks. Finally
he beat it for town all alone, and we didn't see nothin' of him till
after supper. Then he got us together and we all went up to
Mike's room.

"'I want to try this here "Old Girl o' Mine,"' he says.

"'Better sing our old stuff,' says Mike. 'This looks like the
last time.'

"Then Art choked up and it was ten minutes before he could
get goin'. We sung everything we knowed, and it was two o'clock
in the mornin' before Art had enough. Ryan come in after midnight and set a w'ile listenin', but he didn't chase us to bed. He
knowed better'n any of us that it was a farewell. When I and Art
was startin' for our room, Art turned to Mike and says:

"'Old boy, I'd of gave every nickel I ever owned to of caught
that fly ball.'

"'I know you would,' Mike says, 'and I know what made you
drop it. But don't worry about it, 'cause it was just a question o'
time, and if I'd of got away with that game, they'd of murdered
some o' the infielders next time I started.'

"Mike was sent home the next day, and we didn't see him again.
He was shipped to Minneapolis before we got back. And the rest
o' the season I might as well of lived in a cemetery w'ile we was
on the road. Art was so bad that I thought onct or twict I'd have
to change roomies. Onct in a w'ile he'd start hummin' and then
he'd break off short and growl at me. He tried out two or three
o' the other boys on the club to see if he couldn't find a new tenor
singer, but nothin' doin'. One night he made Lefty try the tenor.
Well, Lefty's voice is bad enough down low. When he gets up
about so high, you think you're in the stockyards.

"And Art had a rotten year in baseball, too. The old boy's still
pretty near as good on a fly ball as anybody in the league; but you
ought to saw him before his legs begin to give out. He could cover
as much ground as Speaker and he was just as sure. But the year
Mike left us, he missed pretty near half as many as he got. He
told me one night, he says:

"'Do you know, Bill, I stand out there and pray that nobody'll hit one to me. Every time I see one comin' I think o' that one I dropped for Mike in St. Louis, and then I'm just as li'ble to have it come down on my bean as in my glove.'

" 'You're crazy,' I says, ' to let a thing like that make a bum out o' you.'

" But he kept on droppin' fly balls till Ryan was talkin' about settin' him on the bench where it wouldn't hurt nothin' if his nerve give out. But Ryan didn't have nobody else to play out there, so Art held on.

" He come back the next spring—-that's a year ago—feelin' more cheerful and like himself than I'd saw him for a long w'ile. And they was a kid named Burton tryin' out for second base that could sing pretty near as good as Mike. It didn't take Art more'n a day to find this out, and every mornin' and night for a few days the four of us would be together, hittin' her up. But the kid didn't have no more idea o' how to play the bag than Charley Chaplin. Art seen in a minute that he couldn't never beat Cragin out of his job, so what does he do but take him out and try and learn him to play the outfield. He wasn't no worse there than at second base; he couldn't of been. But before he'd practised out there three days they was bruises all over his head and shoulders where fly balls had hit him. Well, the kid wasn't with us long enough to see the first exhibition game, and after he'd went, Art was Old Man Grump again.

" 'What's the matter with you?' I says to him. ' You was all smiles the day we reported and now you could easy pass for a undertaker.'

" 'Well,' he says, ' I had a great winter, singin' all the w'ile. We got a good quartette down home and I never enjoyed myself as much in my life. And I kind o' had a hunch that I was goin' to be lucky and find somebody amongst the bushers that could hit up the old tenor.'

" 'Your hunch was right,' I says. ' That Burton kid was as good a tenor as you'd want.'

" 'Yes,' he says, ' and my hunch could of played ball just as good as him.'

" Well, sir, if you didn't never room with a corpse, you don't know what a whale of a time I had all last season. About the middle of August he was at his worst.

" 'Bill,' he says, ' I'm goin' to leave this old baseball flat on its back if somethin' don't happen. I can't stand these here lonesome

nights. I ain't like the rest o' the boys that can go and set all
ev'nin' at a pitcher show or hang round them Dutch gardens. I
got to be singin' or I am mis'rable.'

"'Go ahead and sing,' says I. 'I'll try and keep the cops
back.'

"'No,' he says, 'I don't want to sing alone. I want to harmonize and we can't do that 'cause we ain't got no tenor.'

"I don't know if you'll believe me or not, but sure as we're
settin' here he went to Ryan one day in Philly and tried to get
him to make a trade for Harper.

"'What do I want him for?' says Ryan.

"'I hear he ain't satisfied,' says Art.

"'I ain't runnin' no ball players' benefit association,' says
Ryan, and Art had to give it up. But he didn't want Harper on
the club for no other reason than because he's a tenor singer!

"And then come that Dee-troit trip, and Art got permission to
go to Jackson. He says he intended to drop in at the ball park, but
his uncle wanted to borry some money off'n him on a farm, so Art
had to drive out and see the farm. Then, that night, this here
Waldron was up to call on Art's cousin—a swell doll, Art tells me.
And Waldron set down to the py-ana and begin to sing and play.
Then it was all off; they wasn't no spoonin' in the parlor that
night. Art wouldn't leave the kid get off'n the py-ana stool long
enough to even find out if the girl was a blonde or a brunette.

"O' course Art knowed the boy was with the Jackson club as
soon as they was interduced, 'cause Art's uncle says somethin'
about the both o' them bein' ball players, and so on. But Art
swears he never thought o' recommendin' him till the kid got up
to go home. Then he ast him what position did he play and found
out all about him, only o' course Waldron didn't tell him how good
he was 'cause he didn't know himself.

"So Art ast him would he like a trial in the big show, and the
kid says he would. Then Art says maybe the kid would hear from
him, and then Waldron left and Art went to bed, and he says he
stayed awake all night plannin' the thing out and wonderin' would
he have the nerve to pull it off. You see he thought that if Ryan
fell for it, Waldron'd join us as soon as his season was over and
then Ryan'd see he wasn't no good; but he'd prob'ly keep him till
we was through for the year, and Art could alibi himself some way,
say he'd got the wrong name or somethin'. All he wanted, he says,

was to have the kid along the last month or six weeks, so's we could harmonize. A nut? I guess not.

"Well, as you know, Waldron got sick and didn't report, and when Art seen him on the train this spring he couldn't hardly believe his eyes. He thought surely the kid would of been canned durin' the winter without no trial.

"Here's another hot one. When we went out the first day for practice, Art takes the kid off in a corner and tries to learn him enough baseball so's he won't show himself up and get sent away somewheres before we had a little benefit from his singin'. Can you imagine that? Tryin' to learn this kid baseball, when he was born with a slidin' pad on.

"You know the rest of it. They wasn't never no question about Waldron makin' good. It's just like everybody says—he's the best natural ball player that's broke in since Cobb. They ain't nothin' he can't do. But it *is* a funny thing that Art's job should be the one he'd get. I spoke about that to Art when he give me the story.

"'Well,' he says, 'I can't expect everything to break right. I figure I'm lucky to of picked a guy that's good enough to hang on. I'm in stronger with Ryan right now, and with the old man, too, than when I was out there playin' every day. Besides, the bench is a pretty good place to watch the game from. And this club won't be shy a tenor singer for nine years.'

"'No,' I says, 'but they'll be shy a lead and a baritone and a bass before I and you and Lefty is much older.'

"'What of it?' he says. 'We'll look up old Mike and all go somewheres and live together.'"

We were nearing Worcester. Bill Cole and I arose from our table and started back toward our car. In the first vestibule we encountered Buck, the trainer.

"Mr. Graham's been lookin' all over for you, Mr. Cole," he said.

"I've been rehearsin' my part," said Bill.

We found Art Graham, Lefty, and young Waldron in Art's seat. The kid was talking.

"Lefty missed it again. If you fellas knew music, I could teach it to you on the piano when we get to Boston. Lefty, on the word 'love,' in the next to the last line, you're on middle C. Then, on the word 'you,' you slide up half a tone. That'd ought to be a snap, but you don't get it. I'm on high A and come down to G and Bill's on low F and comes up to A. Art just sings the regular two notes, F and E. It's a change from the F chord to the A chord. It makes a dandy wallop and it ought to be a——"

"Here's Bill now," interrupted Lefty, as he caught sight of Cole.

Art Graham treated his roommate to a cold stare.

"Where the h——l have you been?" he said angrily.

"Lookin' for the lost chord," said Bill.

"Set down here and learn this," growled Art. "We won't never get it if we don't work."

"Yes, let's tackle her again," said Waldron. "Bill comes up two full tones, from F to A. Lefty goes up half a tone, Art sings just like always, and I come down a tone. Now try her again."

Two years ago it was that Bill Cole told me that story. Two weeks ago Art Graham boarded the evening train on one of the many roads that lead to Minneapolis.

The day Art was let out, I cornered Ryan in the club-house after the others had dressed and gone home.

"Did you ever know," I asked, "that Art recommended Waldron without having seen him in a ball suit?"

"I told you long ago how Art picked Waldron," he said.

"Yes," said I, "but you didn't have the right story."

So I gave it to him.

"You newspaper fellas," he said when I had done, "are the biggest suckers in the world. Now I've never given you a bad steer in my life. But you don't believe what I tell you and you go and fall for one of Bill Cole's hop dreams. Don't you know that he was the biggest liar in baseball? He'd tell you that Walter Johnson was Jack's father if he thought he could get away with it. And that bunk he gave you about Waldron. Does it sound reasonable?"

"Just as reasonable," I replied, "as the stuff about Art's grabbing him after seeing him pop out."

"I don't claim he did," said Ryan. "That's what Art told me. One of those Jackson ball players could give you the real truth, only of course he wouldn't, because if Hodges ever found it out he'd shoot him full of holes. Art Graham's no fool. He isn't touting ball players because they can sing tenor or alto or anything else."

Nevertheless, I believe Bill Cole; else I wouldn't print the story. And Ryan would believe, too, if he weren't in such a mood these days that he disagrees with everybody. For in spite of Waldron's wonderful work, and he is at his best right now, the club hasn't done nearly as well as when Art and Bill and Lefty were still with us.

There seems to be a lack of harmony.

XVI

THE LOVE NEST

"I'll tell you what I'm going to do with you, Mr. Bartlett," said the great man. " I'm going to take you right out to my home and have you meet the wife and family; stay to dinner and all night. We've got plenty of room and extra pajamas, if you don't mind them silk. I mean that'll give you a chance to see us just as we are. I mean you can get more that way than if you sat here a whole week, asking me questions."

" But I don't want to put you to a lot of trouble," said Bartlett.

" Trouble!" The great man laughed. " There's no trouble about it. I've got a house that's like a hotel. I mean a big house with lots of servants. But anyway I'm always glad to do anything I can for a writing man, especially a man that works for Ralph Doane. I'm very fond of Ralph. I mean I like him personally besides being a great editor. I mean I've known him for years and when there's anything I can do for him, I'm glad to do it. I mean it'll be a pleasure to have you. So if you want to notify your family——"

" I haven't any family," said Bartlett.

" Well, I'm sorry for you! And I bet when you see mine, you'll wish you had one of your own. But I'm glad you can come and we'll start now so as to get there before the kiddies are put away for the night. I mean I want you to be sure and see the kiddies. I've got three."

" I've seen their pictures," said Bartlett. " You must be very proud of them. They're all girls, aren't they?"

" Yes, sir; three girls. I wouldn't have a boy. I mean I always wanted girls. I mean girls have got a lot more zip to them. I mean they're a lot zippier. But let's go! The Rolls is downstairs and if we start now we'll get there before dark. I mean I want you to see the place while it's still daylight."

The great man—Lou Gregg, president of Modern Pictures, Inc. —escorted his visitor from the magnificent office by a private door and down a private stairway to the avenue, where the glittering car with its glittering chauffeur waited.

" My wife was in town today," said Gregg as they glided northward, " and I hoped we could ride out together, but she called up about two and asked would I mind if she went on home in the Pierce. She was through with her shopping and she hates to be away from the house and the kiddies any longer than she can help. Celia's a great home girl. You'd never know she was the same girl now as the girl I married seven years ago. I mean she's different. I mean she's not the same. I mean her marriage and being a mother has developed her. Did you ever see her? I mean in pictures? "

" I think I did once," replied Bartlett. " Didn't she play the young sister in ' The Cad ' ? "

" Yes, with Harold Hodgson and Marie Blythe."

" I thought I'd seen her. I remember her as very pretty and vivacious."

" She certainly was! And she is yet! I mean she's even prettier, but of course she ain't a kid, though she looks it. I mean she was only seventeen in that picture and that was ten years ago. I mean she's twenty-seven years old now. But I never met a girl with as much zip as she had in those days. It's remarkable how marriage changes them. I mean nobody would ever thought Celia Sayles would turn out to be a sit-by-the-fire. I mean she still likes a good time, but her home and kiddies come first. I mean her home and kiddies come first."

" I see what you mean," said Bartlett.

An hour's drive brought them to Ardsley-on-Hudson and the great man's home.

" A wonderful place! " Bartlett exclaimed with a heroic semblance of enthusiasm as the car turned in at an *arc de triomphe* of a gateway and approached a white house that might have been mistaken for the Yale Bowl.

" It ought to be! " said Gregg. " I mean I've spent enough on it. I mean these things cost money."

He indicated with a gesture the huge house and Urbanesque landscaping.

" But no amount of money is too much to spend on home. I mean it's a good investment if it tends to make your family proud and satisfied with their home. I mean every nickel I've spent here is like so much insurance; it insures me of a happy wife and family. And what more can a man ask! "

Bartlett didn't know, but the topic was forgotten in the business of leaving the resplendent Rolls and entering the even more resplendent reception hall.

" Forbes will take your things," said Gregg. "And, Forbes, you may tell Dennis that Mr. Bartlett will spend the night." He faced the wide stairway and raised his voice. " Sweetheart ! " he called.

From above came the reply in contralto : " Hello, sweetheart ! "

" Come down, sweetheart. I've brought you a visitor."

" All right, sweetheart, in just a minute."

Gregg led Bartlett into a living-room that was five laps to the mile and suggestive of an Atlantic City auction sale.

" Sit there," said the host, pointing to a balloon-stuffed easy chair, " and I'll see if we can get a drink. I've got some real old Bourbon that I'd like you to try. You know I come from Chicago and I always liked Bourbon better than Scotch. I mean I always preferred it to Scotch. Forbes," he addressed the servant, " we want a drink. You'll find a full bottle of that Bourbon in the cupboard."

" It's only half full, sir," said Forbes.

" Half full! That's funny! I mean I opened it last night and just took one drink. I mean it ought to be full."

" It's only half full," repeated Forbes, and went to fetch it.

" I'll have to investigate," Gregg told his guest. " I mean this ain't the first time lately that some of my good stuff has disappeared. When you keep so many servants, it's hard to get all honest ones. But here's Celia ! "

Bartlett rose to greet the striking brunette who at this moment made an entrance so Delsarte as to be almost painful. With never a glance at him, she minced across the room to her husband and took a half interest in a convincing kiss.

" Well, sweetheart," she said when it was at last over.

" This is Mr. Bartlett, sweetheart," said her husband. " Mr. Bartlett, meet Mrs. Gregg."

Bartlett shook his hostess's proffered two fingers.

" I'm so pleased ! " said Celia in a voice reminiscent of Miss Claire's imitation of Miss Barrymore.

" Mr. Bartlett," Gregg went on, " is with Mankind, Ralph Doane's magazine. He is going to write me up; I mean us."

" No, you mean you," said Celia. " I'm sure the public is not interested in great men's wives."

" I am sure you are mistaken, Mrs. Gregg," said Bartlett politely. " In this case at least. You are worth writing up aside from being a great man's wife."

" I'm afraid you're a flatterer, Mr. Bartlett," she returned. " I have been out of the limelight so long that I doubt if anybody remembers me.   I'm no longer an artist; merely a happy wife and mother."

"And I claim, sweetheart," said Gregg, "that it takes an artist to be that."

"Oh, no, sweetheart!" said Celia. "Not when they have you for a husband!"

The exchange of hosannahs was interrupted by the arrival of Forbes with the tray.

"Will you take yours straight or in a high-ball?" Gregg inquired of his guest. "Personally I like good whisky straight. I mean mixing it with water spoils the flavor. I mean whisky like this, it seems like a crime to mix it with water."

"I'll have mine straight," said Bartlett, who would have preferred a high-ball.

While the drinks were being prepared, he observed his hostess more closely and thought how much more charming she would be if she had used finesse in improving on nature. Her cheeks, her mouth, her eyes, and lashes had been, he guessed, far above the average in beauty before she had begun experimenting with them. And her experiments had been clumsy. She was handsome in spite of her efforts to be handsomer.

"Listen, sweetheart," said her husband. "One of the servants has been helping himself to this Bourbon. I mean it was a full bottle last night and I only had one little drink out of it. And now it's less than half full. Who do you suppose has been at it?"

"How do I know, sweetheart? Maybe the groceryman or the iceman or somebody."

"But you and I and Forbes are the only ones that have a key. I mean it was locked up."

"Maybe you forgot to lock it."

"I never do. Well, anyway, Bartlett, here's a go!"

"Doesn't Mrs. Gregg indulge?" asked Bartlett.

"Only a cocktail before dinner," said Celia. "Lou objects to me drinking whisky, and I don't like it much anyway."

"I don't object to you drinking whisky, sweetheart. I just object to you drinking to excess. I mean I think it coarsens a woman to drink. I mean it makes them coarse."

"Well, there's no argument, sweetheart. As I say, I don't care whether I have it or not."

"It certainly is great Bourbon!" said Bartlett, smacking his lips and putting his glass back on the tray.

"You bet it is!" Gregg agreed. "I mean you can't buy that

kind of stuff any more. I mean it's real stuff. You help yourself
when you want another. Mr. Bartlett is going to stay all night,
sweetheart. I told him he could get a whole lot more of a line on
us that way than just interviewing me in the office. I mean I'm
tongue-tied when it comes to talking about my work and my success. I mean it's better to see me out here as I am, in my home,
with my family. I mean my home life speaks for itself without
me saying a word."

"But, sweetheart," said his wife, "what about Mr. Latham?"

"Gosh! I forgot all about him! I must phone and see if I can
call it off. That's terrible! You see," he explained to Bartlett, "I
made a date to go up to Tarrytown tonight, to K. L. Latham's, the
sugar people. We're going to talk over the new club. We're going
to have a golf club that will make the rest of them look like a toy.
I mean a real golf club! They want me to kind of run it. And I
was to go up there tonight and talk it over. I'll phone and see if I
can postpone it."

"Oh, don't postpone it on my account!" urged Bartlett. "I
can come out again some other time, or I can see you in town."

"I don't see how you *can* postpone it, sweetheart," said Celia.
"Didn't he say old Mr. King was coming over from White Plains?
They'll be mad at you if you don't go."

"I'm afraid they would resent it, sweetheart. Well, I'll tell you.
You can entertain Mr. Bartlett and I'll go up there right after
dinner and come back as soon as I can. And Bartlett and I can
talk when I get back. I mean we can talk when I get back. How
is that?"

"That suits me," said Bartlett.

"I'll be as entertaining as I can," said Celia, "but I'm afraid
that isn't very entertaining. However, if I'm too much of a bore,
there's plenty to read."

"No danger of my being bored," said Bartlett.

"Well, that's all fixed then," said the relieved host. "I hope
you'll excuse me running away. But I don't see how I can get out
of it. I mean with old King coming over from White Plains. I
mean he's an old man. But listen, sweetheart—where are the
kiddies? Mr. Bartlett wants to see them."

"Yes, indeed!" agreed the visitor.

"Of course you'd say so!" Celia said. "But we *are* proud of
them! I suppose all parents are the same. They all think their
own children are the only children in the world. Isn't that so, Mr.
Bartlett? Or haven't you any children?"

"I'm sorry to say I'm not married."

"Oh, you poor thing! We pity him, don't we, sweetheart? But why aren't you, Mr. Bartlett? Don't tell me you're a woman hater!"

"Not now, anyway," said the gallant Bartlett.

"Do you get that, sweetheart? He's paying you a pretty compliment."

"I heard it, sweetheart. And now I'm sure he's a flatterer. But I must hurry and get the children before Hortense puts them to bed."

"Well," said Gregg when his wife had left the room, "would you say she's changed?"

"A little, and for the better. She's more than fulfilled her early promise."

"I think so," said Gregg. "I mean I think she was a beautiful girl and now she's an even more beautiful woman. I mean wifehood and maternity have given her a kind of a—well, you know—I mean a kind of a pose. I mean a pose. How about another drink?"

They were emptying their glasses when Celia returned with two of her little girls.

"The baby's in bed and I was afraid to ask Hortense to get her up again. But you'll see her in the morning. This is Norma and this is Grace. Girls, this is Mr. Bartlett."

The girls received this news calmly.

"Well, girls," said Bartlett.

"What do you think of them, Bartlett?" demanded their father. "I mean what do you think of them?"

"They're great!" replied the guest with creditable warmth.

"I mean aren't they pretty?"

"I should say they are!"

"There, girls! Why don't you thank Mr. Bartlett?"

"Thanks," murmured Norma.

"How old are you, Norma?" asked Bartlett.

"Six," said Norma.

"Well," said Bartlett. "And how old is Grace?"

"Four," replied Norma.

"Well," said Bartlett. "And how old is baby sister?"

"One and a half," answered Norma.

"Well," said Bartlett.

As this seemed to be final, "Come, girls," said their mother. "Kiss daddy good night and I'll take you back to Hortense."

"I'll take them," said Gregg. "I'm going up-stairs anyway. And you can show Bartlett around. I mean before it gets any darker."

"Good night, girls," said Bartlett, and the children murmured a good night.

"I'll come and see you before you're asleep," Celia told them. And after Gregg had led them out, "Do you really think they're pretty?" she asked Bartlett.

"I certainly do. Especially Norma. She's the image of you," said Bartlett.

"She looks a little like I used to," Celia admitted. "But I hope she doesn't look like me now. I'm too old looking."

"You look remarkably young!" said Bartlett. "No one would believe you were the mother of three children."

"Oh, Mr. Bartlett! But I mustn't forget I'm to 'show you around.' Lou is so proud of our home!"

"And with reason," said Bartlett.

"It *is* wonderful! I call it our love nest. Quite a big nest, don't you think? Mother says it's too big to be cosy; she says she can't think of it as a home. But I always say a place is whatever one makes of it. A woman can be happy in a tent if they love each other. And miserable in a royal palace without love. Don't you think so, Mr. Bartlett?"

"Yes, indeed."

"Is this really such wonderful Bourbon? I think I'll just take a sip of it and see what it's like. It can't hurt me if it's so good. Do you think so, Mr. Bartlett?"

"I don't believe so."

"Well then, I'm going to taste it and if it hurts me it's your fault."

Celia poured a whisky glass two-thirds full and drained it at a gulp.

"It *is* good, isn't it?" she said. "Of course I'm not much of a judge as I don't care for whisky and Lou won't let me drink it. But he's raved so about this Bourbon that I did want to see what it was like. You won't tell on me, will you, Mr. Bartlett?"

"Not I!"

"I wonder how it would be in a high-ball. Let's you and I have just one. But I'm forgetting I'm supposed to show you the place. We won't have time to drink a high-ball and see the place too before Lou comes down. Are you so crazy to see the place?"

" Not very."

" Well, then, what do you say if we have a high-ball? And it'll
be a secret between you and I."

They drank in silence and Celia pressed a button by the door.

" You may take the bottle and tray," she told Forbes. "And
now," she said to Bartlett, " we'll go out on the porch and see as
much as we can see. You'll have to guess the rest."

Gregg, having changed his shirt and collar, joined them.

" Well," he said to Bartlett, " have you seen everything? "

" I guess I have, Mr. Gregg," lied the guest readily. " It's a
wonderful place! "

" We like it. I mean it suits us. I mean it's my idear of a real
home. And Celia calls it her love nest."

" So she told me," said Bartlett.

" She'll always be sentimental," said her husband.

He put his hand on her shoulder, but she drew away.

" I must run up and dress," she said.

" Dress! " exclaimed Bartlett, who had been dazzled by her
flowered green chiffon.

" Oh, I'm not going to really dress," she said. " But I couldn't
wear this thing for dinner! "

" Perhaps you'd like to clean up a little, Bartlett," said Gregg.
" I mean Forbes will show you your room if you want to go up."

" It might be best," said Bartlett.

Celia, in a black lace dinner gown, was rather quiet during the
elaborate meal. Three or four times when Gregg addressed her,
she seemed to be thinking of something else and had to ask, " What
did you say, sweetheart? " Her face was red and Bartlett imagined that she had " sneaked " a drink or two besides the two help-
ings of Bourbon and the cocktail that had preceded dinner.

" Well, I'll leave you," said Gregg when they were in the living-
room once more. " I mean the sooner I get started, the sooner I'll
be back. Sweetheart, try and keep your guest awake and don't let
him die of thirst. *Au revoir*, Bartlett. I'm sorry, but it can't be
helped. There's a fresh bottle of the Bourbon, so go to it. I mean
help yourself. It's too bad you have to drink alone."

" It *is* too bad, Mr. Bartlett," said Celia when Gregg had gone.

" What's too bad? " asked Bartlett.

" That you have to drink alone. I feel like I wasn't being a good
hostess to let you do it. In fact, I refuse to let you do it. I'll
join you in just a little wee sip."

" But it's so soon after dinner ! "

" It's never too soon ! I'm going to have a drink myself and if you don't join me, you're a quitter."

She mixed two life-sized high-balls and handed one to her guest.

" Now we'll turn on the radio and see if we can't stir things up. There ! No, no ! Who cares about the old baseball ! Now ! This is better ! Let's dance."

" I'm sorry, Mrs. Gregg, but I don't dance."

" Well, you're an old cheese ! To make me dance alone ! ' All alone, yes, I'm all alone.' "

There was no affectation in her voice now and Bartlett was amazed at her unlabored grace as she glided around the big room.

" But it's no fun alone," she complained. " Let's shut the damn thing off and talk."

" I love to watch you dance," said Bartlett.

" Yes, but I'm no Pavlowa," said Celia as she silenced the radio. "And besides, it's time for a drink."

" I've still got more than half of mine."

" Well, you had that wine at dinner, so I'll have to catch up with you."

She poured herself another high-ball and went at the task of " catching up."

" The trouble with you, Mr.—now isn't that a scream ! I can't think of your name."

" Bartlett."

" The trouble with you, Barker—do you know what's the trouble with you? You're too sober. See? You're too damn sober ! That's the whole trouble, see? If you weren't so sober, we'd be better off. See? What I can't understand is how you can be so sober and me so high."

" You're not used to it."

" Not used to it ! That's the cat's pajamas ! Say, I'm like this half the time, see? If I wasn't, I'd die ! "

" What does your husband say ? "

" He don't say because he don't know. See, Barker? There's nights when he's out and there's a few nights when I'm out my-self. And there's other nights when we're both in and I pretend I'm sleepy and I go up-stairs. See? But I don't go to bed. See? I have a little party all by myself. See? If I didn't, I'd die ! "

" What do you mean, you'd die ? "

" You're dumb, Barker ! You may be sober, but you're dumb !

Did you fall for all that apple sauce about the happy home and the contented wife? Listen, Barker—I'd give anything in the world to be out of this mess. I'd give anything to never see him again."

"Don't you love him any more? Doesn't he love you? Or what?"

"Love! I never did love him! I didn't know what love was! And all his love is for himself!"

"How did you happen to get married?"

"I was a kid; that's the answer. A kid and ambitious. See? He was a director then and he got stuck on me and I thought he'd make me a star. See, Barker? I married him to get myself a chance. And now look at me!"

"I'd say you were fairly well off."

"Well off, am I? I'd change places with the scum of the earth just to be free! See, Barker? And I could have been a star without any help if I'd only realized it. I had the looks and I had the talent. I've got it yet. I could be a Swanson and get myself a marquis; maybe a prince! And look what I did get! A self-satisfied, self-centered——! I thought he'd *make* me! See, Barker? Well, he's made me all right; he's made me a chronic mother and it's a wonder I've got any looks left.

"I fought at first. I told him marriage didn't mean giving up my art, my life work. But it was no use. He wanted a beautiful wife and beautiful children for his beautiful home. Just to show us off. See? I'm part of his chattels. See, Barker? I'm just like his big diamond or his cars or his horses. And he wouldn't stand for his wife 'lowering' herself to act in pictures. Just as if pictures hadn't made him!

"You go back to your magazine tomorrow and write about our love nest. See, Barker? And be sure and don't get mixed and call it a baby ranch. Babies! You thought little Norma was pretty. Well, she is. And what is it going to get her? A rich —— of a husband that treats her like a ——! That's what it'll get her if I don't interfere. I hope I don't last long enough to see her grow up, but if I do, I'm going to advise her to run away from home and live her own life. And *be* somebody! Not a *thing* like I am! See, Barker?"

"Did you ever think of a divorce?"

"Did I ever think of one! Listen—but there's no chance. I've got nothing on him, and no matter what he had on me, he'd never let the world know it. He'd keep me here and torture me like he does now, only worse. But I haven't done anything wrong, see? The men I might care for, they're all scared of him and his money and power. See, Barker? And the others are just as bad as him. Like fat old Morris, the hotel man, that everybody thinks he's a model husband. The reason he don't step out more is because he's too stingy. But I could have him if I wanted him. Every time he gets near enough to me, he squeezes my hand. I guess he thinks it's a nickel, the tight old ——! But come on, Barker. Let's have a drink. I'm running down."

" I think it's about time you were running up—up-stairs," said Bartlett. " If I were you, I'd try to be in bed and asleep when Gregg gets home."

" You're all right, Barker. And after this drink I'm going to do just as you say. Only I thought of it before you did, see? I think of it lots of nights. And tonight you can help me out by telling him I had a bad headache."

Left alone, Bartlett thought a while, then read, and finally dozed off. He was dozing when Gregg returned.

" Well, well, Bartlett," said the great man, " did Celia desert you? "

" It was perfectly all right, Mr. Gregg. She had a headache and I told her to go to bed."

" She's had a lot of headaches lately; reads too much, I guess. Well, I'm sorry I had this date. It was about a new golf club and I had to be there. I mean I'm going to be president of it. I see you consoled yourself with some of the Bourbon. I mean the bottle doesn't look as full as it did."

" I hope you'll forgive me for helping myself so generously," said Bartlett. " I don't get stuff like that every day! "

" Well, what do you say if we turn in? We can talk on the way to town tomorrow. Though I guess you won't have much to ask me. I guess you know all about us. I mean you know all about us now."

" Yes, indeed, Mr. Gregg. I've got plenty of material if I can just handle it."

Celia had not put in an appearance when Gregg and his guest were ready to leave the house next day.

" She always sleeps late," said Gregg. " I mean she never wakes up very early. But she's later than usual this morning. Sweetheart! " he called up the stairs.

" Yes, sweetheart," came the reply.

" Mr. Bartlett's leaving now. I mean he's going."

"Oh, good-by, Mr. Bartlett. Please forgive me for not being down to see you off."

"You're forgiven, Mrs. Gregg. And thanks for your hospitality."

"Good-by, sweetheart!"

"Good-by, sweetheart!"

XVII

EX PARTE

MOST always when a man leaves his wife, there's no excuse in the world for him. She may have made whoop-whoop-whoopee with the whole ten commandments, but if he shows his disapproval to the extent of walking out on her, he will thereafter be a total stranger to all his friends excepting the two or three bums who will tour the night clubs with him so long as he sticks to his habits of paying for everything.

When a woman leaves her husband, she must have good and sufficient reasons. He drinks all the time, or he runs around, or he doesn't give her any money, or he uses her as the heavy bag in his home gymnasium work. No more is he invited to his former playmates' houses for dinner and bridge. He is an outcast just the same as if he had done the deserting. Whichever way it happens, it's his fault. He can state his side of the case if he wants to, but there is nobody around listening.

Now I claim to have a little chivalry in me, as well as a little pride. So in spite of the fact that Florence has broadcast her grievances over the red and blue network both, I intend to keep mine to myself till death do me part.

But after I'm gone, I want some of my old pals to know that this thing wasn't as lopsided as she has made out, so I will write the true story, put it in an envelope with my will and appoint Ed Osborne executor. He used to be my best friend and would be yet if his wife would let him. He'll have to read all my papers, including this, and he'll tell everybody else about it and maybe they'll be a little sorry that they treated me like an open manhole.

(Ed, please don't consider this an attempt to be literary. You know I haven't written for publication since our days on "The Crimson and White," and I wasn't so hot then. Just look on it as a statement of facts. If I were still alive, I'd take a bible oath that nothing herein is exaggerated. And whatever else may have been my imperfections, I never lied save to shield a woman or myself.)

Well, a year ago last May I had to go to New York. I called up Joe Paxton and he asked me out to dinner. I went, and met Flor-

ence. She and Marjorie Paxton had been at school together and
she was there for a visit. We fell in love with each other and got
engaged. I stopped off in Chicago on the way home, to see her
people. They liked me all right, but they hated to have Florence
marry a man who lived so far away. They wanted to postpone her
leaving home as long as possible and they made us wait till April
this year.

I had a room at the Belden and Florence and I agreed that when
we were married, we would stay there awhile and take our time
about picking out a house. But the last day of March, two weeks
before the date of our wedding, I ran into Jeff Cooper and he told
me his news, that the Standard Oil was sending him to China in
some big job that looked permanent.

" I'm perfectly willing to go," he said. " So is Bess. It's a lot
more money and we think it will be an interesting experience.
But here I am with a brand-new place on my hands that cost me
$45,000, including the furniture, and no chance to sell it in a
hurry except at a loss. We were just beginning to feel settled.
Otherwise we would have no regrets about leaving this town. Bess
hasn't any real friends here and you're the only one I can claim."

" How much would you take for your house, furniture and all? "
I asked him.

" I'd take a loss of $5,000," he said. " I'd take $40,000 with
the buyer assuming my mortgage of $15,000, held by the Phillips
Trust and Mortgage Company in Seattle."

I asked him if he would show me the place. They had only been
living there a month and I hadn't had time to call. He said, what
did I want to look at it for and I told him I would buy it if it looked
o. k. Then I confessed that I was going to be married; you know
I had kept it a secret around here.

Well, he took me home with him and he and Bess showed me
everything, all new and shiny and a bargain if you ever saw one.
In the first place, there's the location, on the best residential street
in town, handy to my office and yet with a whole acre of ground,
and a bed of cannas coming up in the front yard that Bess had
planted when they bought the property last fall. As for the house,
I always liked stucco, and this one is *built!* You could depend
on old Jeff to see to that.

But the furniture was what decided me. Jeff had done the smart
thing and ordered the whole works from Wolfe Brothers, taking
their advice on most of the stuff, as neither he nor Bess knew much
about it. Their total bill, furnishing the entire place, rugs, beds,

tables, chairs, everything, was only $8,500, including a mahogany upright player-piano that they ordered from Seattle. I had my mother's old mahogany piano in storage and I kind of hoped Jeff wouldn't want me to buy this, but it was all or nothing, and with a bargain like that staring me in the face, I didn't stop to argue, not when I looked over the rest of the furniture and saw what I was getting.

The living-room had, and still has, three big easy chairs and a couch, all over-stuffed, as they call it, to say nothing of an Oriental rug that alone had cost $500. There was a long mahogany table behind the couch, with lamps at both ends in case you wanted to lie down and read. The dining-room set was solid mahogany—a table and eight chairs that had separated Jeff from $1,000.

The floors downstairs were all oak parquet. Also he had blown himself to an oak mantelpiece and oak woodwork that must have run into heavy dough. Jeff told me what it cost him extra, but I don't recall the amount.

The Coopers were strong for mahogany and wanted another set for their bedroom, but Jake Wolfe told them it would get monotonous if there was too much of it. So he sold them five pieces —a bed, two chairs, a chiffonier and a dresser—of some kind of wood tinted green, with flowers painted on it. This was $1,000 more, but it certainly was worth it. You never saw anything prettier than that bed when the lace spreads were on.

Well, we closed the deal and at first I thought I wouldn't tell Florence, but would let her believe we were going to live at the Belden and then give her a surprise by taking her right from the train to our own home. When I got to Chicago, though, I couldn't keep my mouth shut. I gave it away and it was I, not she, that had the surprise.

Instead of acting tickled to death, as I figured she would, she just looked kind of funny and said she hoped I had as good taste in houses as I had in clothes. She tried to make me describe the house and the furniture to her, but I wouldn't do it. To appreciate a layout like that, you have to see it for yourself.

We were married and stopped in Yellowstone for a week on our way here. That was the only really happy week we had together. From the minute we arrived home till she left for good, she was a different woman than the one I thought I knew. She never smiled and several times I caught her crying. She wouldn't tell me what ailed her and when I asked if she was just homesick, she said no and choked up and cried some more.

You can imagine that things were not as I expected they would be. In New York and in Chicago and Yellowstone, she had had more *life* than any girl I ever met. Now she acted all the while as if she were playing the title rôle at a funeral.

One night late in May the telephone rang. It was Mrs. Dwan and she wanted Florence. If I had known what this was going to mean, I would have slapped the receiver back on the hook and let her keep on wanting.

I had met Dwan a couple of times and had heard about their place out on the Turnpike. But I had never seen it or his wife either.

Well, it developed that Mildred Dwan had gone to school with Florence and Marjorie Paxton, and she had just learned from Marjorie that Florence was my wife and living here. She said she and her husband would be in town and call on us the next Sunday afternoon.

Florence didn't seem to like the idea and kind of discouraged it. She said we would drive out and call on them instead. Mrs. Dwan said no, that Florence was the newcomer and it was her (Mrs. Dwan's) first move. So Florence gave in.

They came and they hadn't been in the house more than a minute when Florence began to cry. Mrs. Dwan cried, too, and Dwan and I stood there first on one foot and then the other, trying to pretend we didn't know the girls were crying. Finally, to relieve the tension, I invited him to come and see the rest of the place. I showed him all over and he was quite enthusiastic. When we returned to the living-room, the girls had dried their eyes and were back in school together.

Florence accepted an invitation for one-o'clock dinner a week from that day. I told her, after they had left, that I would go along only on condition that she and our hostess would both control their tear-ducts. I was so accustomed to solo sobbing that I didn't mind it any more, but I couldn't stand a duet of it either in harmony or unison.

Well, when we got out there and had driven down their private lane through the trees and caught a glimpse of their house, which people around town had been talking about as something wonderful, I laughed harder than any time since I was single. It looked just like what it was, a reorganized barn. Florence asked me what was funny, and when I told her, she pulled even a longer face than usual.

" I think it's beautiful," she said.

Tie that!

I insisted on her going up the steps alone. I was afraid if the two of us stood on the porch at once, we'd fall through and maybe founder before help came. I warned her not to smack the knocker too hard or the door might crash in and frighten the horses.

" If you make jokes like that in front of the Dwans," she said, " I'll never speak to you again.

" I'd forgotten you ever did," said I.

I was expecting a hostler to let us in, but Mrs. Dwan came in person.

" Are we late? " said Florence.

" A little," said Mrs. Dwan, " but so is dinner. Helga didn't get home from church till half past twelve."

" I'm glad of it," said Florence. " I want you to take me all through this beautiful, beautiful house right this minute."

Mrs. Dwan called her husband and insisted that he stop in the middle of mixing a cocktail so he could join us in a tour of the beautiful, beautiful house.

" You wouldn't guess it," said Mrs. Dwan, " but it used to be a barn."

I was going to say I had guessed it. Florence gave me a look that changed my mind.

" When Jim and I first came here," said Mrs. Dwan, " we lived in an ugly little rented house on Oliver Street. It was only temporary, of course; we were just waiting till we found what we really wanted. We used to drive around the country Saturday afternoons and Sundays, hoping we would run across the right sort of thing. It was in the late fall when we first saw this place. The leaves were off the trees and it was visible from the Turnpike.

" ' Oh, Jim! ' I exclaimed. ' Look at that simply gorgeous old barn! With those wide shingles! And I'll bet you it's got hand-hewn beams in that middle, main section.' Jim bet me I was wrong, so we left the car, walked up the driveway, found the door open and came brazenly in. I won my bet as you can see."

She pointed to some dirty old rotten beams that ran across the living-room ceiling and looked as if five or six generations of rats had used them for gnawing practise.

" They're beautiful! " said Florence.

" The instant I saw them," said Mrs. Dwan, " I knew this was going to be our home! "

" I can imagine! " said Florence.

" We made inquiries and learned that the place belonged to a

family named Taylor," said Mrs. Dwan. "The house had burned
down and they had moved away. It was suspected that they had
started the fire themselves, as they were terribly hard up and it
was insured. Jim wrote to old Mr. Taylor in Seattle and asked
him to set a price on the barn and the land, which is about four
acres. They exchanged several letters and finally Mr. Taylor accepted Jim's offer. We got it for a song."

"Wonderful!" said Florence.

"And then, of course," Mrs. Dwan continued, "we engaged a
house-wrecking company to tear down the other four sections of
the barn—the stalls, the cow-shed, the tool-shed, and so forth—
and take them away, leaving us just this one room. We had a man
from Seattle come and put in these old pine walls and the floor-
ing, and plaster the ceiling. He was recommended by a friend
of Jim's and he certainly knew his business."

"I can see he did," said Florence.

"He made the hay-loft over for us, too, and we got the wings
built by day-labor, with Jim and me supervising. It was so much
fun that I was honestly sorry when it was finished."

"I can imagine!" said Florence.

Well, I am not very well up in Early American, which was the
name they had for pretty nearly everything in the place, but for
the benefit of those who are not on terms with the Dwans I will
try and describe from memory the *objets d'art* they bragged of
the most and which brought forth the loudest squeals from
Florence.

The living-room walls were brown bare boards without a picture or scrap of wall-paper. On the floor were two or three
"hooked rugs," whatever that means, but they needed five or six
more of them, or one big carpet, to cover up all the knots in the
wood. There was a maple "low-boy"; a "dough-trough" table
they didn't have space for in the kitchen; a pine "stretcher" table
with sticks connecting the four legs near the bottom so you
couldn't put your feet anywhere; a "Dutch" chest that looked as
if it had been ordered from the undertaker by one of Singer's
Midgets, but he got well; and some "Windsor" chairs in which
the only position you could get comfortable was to stand up behind them and lean your elbows on their back.

Not one piece that matched another, and not one piece of mahogany anywhere. And the ceiling, between the beams, had apparently been plastered by a workman who was that way, too.

"Some day soon I hope to have a piano," said Mrs. Dwan. "I

can't live much longer without one. But so far I haven't been able to find one that would fit in."

"Listen," I said. "I've got a piano in storage that belonged to my mother. It's a mahogany upright and not so big that it wouldn't fit in this room, especially when you get that 'trough' table out. It isn't doing me any good and I'll sell it to you for $250. Mother paid $1,250 for it new."

"Oh, I couldn't think of taking it!" said Mrs. Dwan.

"I'll make it $200 even just because you're a friend of Florence's," I said.

"Really, I couldn't!" said Mrs. Dwan.

"You wouldn't have to pay for it all at once," I said.

"Don't you see," said Florence, "that a mahogany upright piano would be a perfect horror in here? Mildred wouldn't have it as a gift, let alone buy it. It isn't in the period."

"She could get it tuned," I said.

The answer to this was, "I'll show you the up-stairs now and we can look at the dining-room later on."

We were led to the guest-chamber. The bed was a maple four-poster, with pineapple posts, and a "tester" running from pillar to post. You would think a "tester" might be a man that went around trying out beds, but it's really a kind of frame that holds a canopy over the bed in case it rains and the roof leaks. There was a quilt made by Mrs. Dwan's great-grandmother, Mrs. Anthony Adams, in 1859, at Lowell, Mass. How is that for a memory?

"This used to be the hay-loft," said Mrs. Dwan.

"You ought to have left some of the hay so the guests could hit it," I said.

The dressers, or chests of drawers, and the chairs were all made of maple. And the same in the Dwans' own room; everything maple.

"If you had maple in one room and mahogany in the other," I said, "people wouldn't get confused when you told them that so and so was up in Maple's room."

Dwan laughed, but the women didn't.

The maid hollered up that dinner was ready.

"The cocktails aren't ready," said Dwan.

"You will have to go without them," said Mrs. Dwan. "The soup will be cold."

This put me in a great mood to admire the "sawbuck" table

and the " slat back " chairs, which were evidently the *chef-d'œuvre* and the *pièce de résistance* of the *chez Dwan*.

" It came all the way from Pennsylvania," said Mildred, when Florence's outcries, brought on by her first look at the table, had died down. " Mother picked it up at a little place near Strouds-burg and sent it to me. It only cost $550, and the chairs were $45 apiece."

" How reasonable ! " exclaimed Florence.

That was before she had sat in one of them. Only one thing was more unreasonable than the chairs, and that was the table it-self, consisting of big planks nailed together and laid onto a rail-road tie, supported underneath by a whole forest of cross-pieces and beams. The surface was as smooth on top as the trip to Cata-lina Island and all around the edges, great big divots had been taken out with some blunt instrument, probably a bayonet. There were stains and scorch marks that Florence fairly crowed over, but when I tried to add to the general ensemble by laying a lighted cigaret right down beside my soup-plate, she and both the Dwans yelled murder and made me take it off.

They planted me in an end seat, a location just right for a man who had stretched himself across a railway track and had both legs cut off at the abdomen. Not being that kind of man, I had to sit so far back that very few of my comestibles carried more than half-way to their target.

After dinner I was all ready to go home and get something to eat, but it had been darkening up outdoors for half an hour and now such a storm broke that I knew it was useless trying to per-suade Florence to make a start.

" We'll play some bridge," said Dwan, and to my surprise he produced a card-table that was nowhere near " in the period."

At my house there was a big center chandelier that lighted up a bridge game no matter in what part of the room the table was put. But here we had to waste forty minutes moving lamps and wires and stands and when they were all fixed, you could tell a red suit from a black suit, but not a spade from a club. Aside from that and the granite-bottomed " Windsor " chairs and the fact that we played " families " for a cent a point and Florence and I won $12 and didn't get paid, it was one of the pleasantest afternoons I ever spent gambling.

The rain stopped at five o'clock and as we splashed through the puddles of Dwan's driveway, I remarked to Florence that I had never known she was such a kidder.

" What do you mean? " she asked me.

" Why, your pretending to admire all that junk," I said.

" Junk! " said Florence. " That is one of the most beautifully furnished homes I have ever seen! "

And so far as I can recall, that was her last utterance in my presence for six nights and five days.

At lunch on Saturday I said : " You know I like the silent drama one evening a week, but not twenty-four hours a day every day. What's the matter with you? If it's laryngitis, you might write me notes."

" I'll tell you what's the matter! " she burst out. " I hate this house and everything in it! It's too new! Everything shines! I loathe new things! I want a home like Mildred's, with things in it that I can look at without blushing for shame. I can't invite anyone here. It's too hideous. And I'll never be happy here a single minute as long as I live! "

Well, I don't mind telling that this kind of got under my skin. As if I hadn't intended to give her a pleasant surprise! As if Wolfe Brothers, in business thirty years, didn't know how to furnish a home complete! I was pretty badly hurt, but I choked it down and said, as calmly as I could :

" If you'll be a little patient, I'll try to sell this house and its contents for what I paid for it and them. It oughtn't to be much trouble; there are plenty of people around who know a bargain. But it's too bad you didn't confess your barn complex to me long ago. Only last February, old Ken Garrett had to sell his establishment and the men who bought it turned it into a garage. It was a livery-stable which I could have got for the introduction of a song, or maybe just the vamp. And we wouldn't have had to spend a nickel to make it as nice and comfortable and homey as your friend Mildred's dump."

Florence was on her way upstairs before I had finished my speech.

I went down to Earl Benham's to see if my new suit was ready. It was and I put it on and left the old one to be cleaned and pressed.

On the street I met Harry Cross.

" Come up to my office," he said. " There's something in my desk that may interest you."

I accepted his invitation and from three different drawers he pulled out three different quart bottles of Early American rye.

Just before six o'clock I dropped in Kane's store and bought myself a pair of shears, a blow torch and an ax. I started home, but stopped among the trees inside my front gate and cut big holes in my coat and trousers. Alongside the path to the house was a sizable mud puddle. I waded in it. And I bathed my gray felt hat.

Florence was sitting on the floor of the living-room, reading. She seemed a little upset by my appearance.

" Good heavens! What's happened? "

" Nothing much," said I. " I just didn't want to look too new."

" What are those things you're carrying? "

" Just a pair of shears, a blow torch and an ax. I'm going to try and antique this place and I think I'll begin on the dining-room table."

Florence went into her scream, dashed upstairs and locked herself in. I went about my work and had the dinner-table looking pretty Early when the maid smelled fire and rushed in. She rushed out again and came back with a pitcher of water. But using my vest as a snuffer, I had had the flames under control all the while and there was nothing for her to do.

" I'll just nick it up a little with this ax," I told her, " and by the time I'm through, dinner ought to be ready."

" It will never be ready as far as I'm concerned," she said. " I'm leaving just as soon as I can pack."

And Florence had the same idea—vindicating the old adage about great minds.

I heard the front door slam and the back door slam, and I felt kind of tired and sleepy, so I knocked off work and went up to bed.

That's my side of the story, Eddie, and it's true so help me my bootlegger. Which reminds me that the man who sold Harry the rye makes this town once a week, or did when this was written. He's at the Belden every Tuesday from nine to six and his name is Mike Farrell.

XVIII

THE GOLDEN HONEYMOON

MOTHER says that when I start talking I never know when to stop.
But I tell her the only time I get a chance is when she ain't around,
so I have to make the most of it. I guess the fact is neither one
of us would be welcome in a Quaker meeting, but as I tell Mother,
what did God give us tongues for if He didn't want we should use
them? Only she says He didn't give them to us to say the same
thing over and over again, like I do, and repeat myself. But I say:

" Well, Mother," I say, " when people is like you and I and been
married fifty years, do you expect everything I say will be something you ain't heard me say before? But it may be new to others,
as they ain't nobody else lived with me as long as you have."

So she says:

" You can bet they ain't, as they couldn't nobody else stand you
that long."

" Well," I tell her, " you look pretty healthy."

" Maybe I do," she will say, " but I looked even healthier before I married you."

You can't get ahead of Mother.

Yes, sir, we was married just fifty years ago the seventeenth day
of last December and my daughter and son-in-law was over from
Trenton to help us celebrate the Golden Wedding. My son-in-
law is John H. Kramer, the real estate man. He made $12,000
one year and is pretty well thought of around Trenton; a good,
steady, hard worker. The Rotarians was after him a long time to
join, but he kept telling them his home was his club. But Edie
finally made him join. That's my daughter.

Well, anyway, they come over to help us celebrate the Golden
Wedding and it was pretty crimpy weather and the furnace don't
seem to heat up no more like it used to and Mother made the remark that she hoped this winter wouldn't be as cold as the last,
referring to the winter previous. So Edie said if she was us, and
nothing to keep us home, she certainly wouldn't spend no more
winters up here and why didn't we just shut off the water and close
up the house and go down to Tampa, Florida? You know we
was there four winters ago and staid five weeks, but it cost us over

three hundred and fifty dollars for hotel bill alone. So Mother said we wasn't going no place to be robbed. So my son-in-law spoke up and said that Tampa wasn't the only place in the South, and besides we didn't have to stop at no high price hotel but could rent us a couple rooms and board out somewheres, and he had heard that St. Petersburg, Florida, was *the* spot and if we said the word he would write down there and make inquiries.

Well, to make a long story short, we decided to do it and Edie said it would be our Golden Honeymoon and for a present my son-in-law paid the difference between a section and a compartment so as we could have a compartment and have more privacy. In a compartment you have an upper and lower berth just like the regular sleeper, but it is a shut in room by itself and got a wash bowl. The car we went in was all compartments and no regular berths at all. It was all compartments.

We went to Trenton the night before and staid at my daughter and son-in-law and we left Trenton the next afternoon at 3.23 P. M.

This was the twelfth day of January. Mother set facing the front of the train, as it makes her giddy to ride backwards. I set facing her, which does not affect me. We reached North Philadelphia at 4.03 P. M. and we reached West Philadelphia at 4.14, but did not go into Broad Street. We reached Baltimore at 6.30 and Washington, D.C., at 7.25. Our train laid over in Washington two hours till another train come along to pick us up and I got out and strolled up the platform and into the Union Station. When I come back, our car had been switched on to another track, but I remembered the name of it, the La Belle, as I had once visited my aunt out in Oconomowoc, Wisconsin, where there was a lake of that name, so I had no difficulty in getting located. But Mother had nearly fretted herself sick for fear I would be left.

" Well," I said, " I would of followed you on the next train."

" You could of," said Mother, and she pointed out that she had the money.

" Well," I said, " we are in Washington and I could of borrowed from the United States Treasury. I would of pretended I was an Englishman."

Mother caught the point and laughed heartily.

Our train pulled out of Washington at 9.40 P. M. and Mother and I turned in early, I taking the upper. During the night we passed through the green fields of old Virginia, though it was too dark to tell if they was green or what color. When we got up in the morning, we was at Fayetteville, North Carolina. We had breakfast in the dining car and after breakfast I got in conversation with the man in the next compartment to ours. He was from Lebanon, New Hampshire, and a man about eighty years of age. His wife was with him, and two unmarried daughters and I made the remark that I should think the four of them would be crowded in one compartment, but he said they had made the trip every winter for fifteen years and knowed how to keep out of each other's way. He said they was bound for Tarpon Springs.

We reached Charleston, South Carolina, at 12.50 P. M. and arrived at Savannah, Georgia, at 4.20. We reached Jacksonville, Florida, at 8.45 P. M. and had an hour and a quarter to lay over there, but Mother made a fuss about me getting off the train, so we had the darky make up our berths and retired before we left Jacksonville. I didn't sleep good as the train done a lot of hemming and hawing, and Mother never sleeps good on a train as she says she is always worrying that I will fall out. She says she would rather have the upper herself, as then she would not have to worry about me, but I tell her I can't take the risk of having it get out that I allowed my wife to sleep in an upper berth. It would make talk.

We was up in the morning in time to see our friends from New Hampshire get off at Tarpon Springs, which we reached at 6.53 A. M.

Several of our fellow passengers got off at Clearwater and some at Belleair, where the train backs right up to the door of the mammoth hotel. Belleair is the winter headquarters for the golf dudes and everybody that got off there had their bag of sticks, as many as ten and twelve in a bag. Women and all. When I was a young man we called it shinny and only needed one club to play with and about one game of it would of been a-plenty for some of these dudes, the way we played it.

The train pulled into St. Petersburg at 8.20 and when we got off the train you would think they was a riot, what with all the darkies barking for the different hotels.

I said to Mother, I said:

" It is a good thing we have got a place picked out to go to and don't have to choose a hotel, as it would be hard to choose amongst them if every one of them is the best."

She laughed.

We found a jitney and I give him the address of the room my son-in-law had got for us and soon we was there and introduced ourselves to the lady that owns the house, a young widow about forty-eight years of age. She showed us our room, which was light and airy with a comfortable bed and bureau and washstand. It was twelve dollars a week, but the location was good, only three blocks from Williams Park.

St. Pete is what folks calls the town, though they also call it the Sunshine City, as they claim they's no other place in the country where they's fewer days when Old Sol don't smile down on Mother Earth, and one of the newspapers gives away all their copies free every day when the sun don't shine. They claim to of only give them away some sixty-odd times in the last eleven years. Another nickname they have got for the town is " the Poor Man's Palm Beach," but I guess they's men that comes there that could borrow as much from the bank as some of the Willie boys over to the other Palm Beach.

During our stay we paid a visit to the Lewis Tent City, which is the headquarters for the Tin Can Tourists. But maybe you ain't heard about them. Well, they are an organization that takes their vacation trips by auto and carries everything with them. That is, they bring along their tents to sleep in and cook in and they don't patronize no hotels or cafeterias, but they have got to be bona fide auto campers or they can't belong to the organization.

They tell me they's over 200,000 members to it and they call themselves the Tin Canners on account of most of their food being put up in tin cans. One couple we seen in the Tent City was a couple from Brady, Texas, named Mr. and Mrs. Pence, which the old man is over eighty years of age and they had come in their auto all the way from home, a distance of 1,641 miles. They took five weeks for the trip, Mr. Pence driving the entire distance.

The Tin Canners hails from every State in the Union and in the summer time they visit places like New England and the Great Lakes region, but in the winter the most of them comes to Florida and scatters all over the State. While we was down there, they was a national convention of them at Gainesville, Florida, and they elected a Fredonia, New York, man as their president. His title is Royal Tin Can Opener of the World. They have got a song wrote up which everybody has got to learn it before they are a member:

> "The tin can forever! Hurrah, boys! Hurrah!
> Up with the tin can! Down with the foe!
> We will rally round the campfire, we'll rally once again,
> Shouting, 'We auto camp forever!'"

That is something like it. And the members has also got to have a tin can fastened on to the front of their machine.

I asked Mother how she would like to travel around that way and she said:

"Fine, but not with an old rattle brain like you driving."

"Well," I said, "I am eight years younger than this Mr. Pence who drove here from Texas."

"Yes," she said, "but he is old enough to not be skittish."

You can't get ahead of Mother.

Well, one of the first things we done in St. Petersburg was to go to the Chamber of Commerce and register our names and where we was from as they's great rivalry amongst the different States in regards to the number of their citizens visiting in town and of course our little State don't stand much of a show, but still every little bit helps, as the fella says. All and all, the man told us, they was eleven thousand names registered, Ohio leading with some fifteen hundred-odd and New York State next with twelve hundred. Then come Michigan, Pennsylvania and so on down, with one man each from Cuba and Nevada.

The first night we was there, they was a meeting of the New York-New Jersey Society at the Congregational Church and a man from Ogdensburg, New York State, made the talk. His subject was Rainbow Chasing. He is a Rotarian and a very convicting speaker, though I forget his name.

Our first business, of course, was to find a place to eat and after trying several places we run on to a cafeteria on Central Avenue that suited us up and down. We eat pretty near all our meals there and it averaged about two dollars per day for the two of us, but the food was well cooked and everything nice and clean. A man don't mind paying the price if things is clean and well cooked.

On the third day of February, which is Mother's birthday, we spread ourselves and eat supper at the Poinsettia Hotel and they charged us seventy-five cents for a sirloin steak that wasn't hardly big enough for one.

I said to Mother: "Well," I said, "I guess it's a good thing every day ain't your birthday or we would be in the poorhouse."

"No," says Mother, "because if every day was my birthday, I would be old enough by this time to of been in my grave long ago."

You can't get ahead of Mother.

In the hotel they had a card-room where they was several men and ladies playing five hundred and this new fangled whist bridge. We also seen a place where they was dancing, so I asked Mother would she like to trip the light fantastic toe and she said no, she was too old to squirm like you have got to do now days. We watched some of the young folks at it awhile till Mother got disgusted and said we would have to see a good movie to take the taste out of our mouth. Mother is a great movie heroyne and we go twice a week here at home.

But I want to tell you about the Park. The second day we was there we visited the Park, which is a good deal like the one in Tampa, only bigger, and they's more fun goes on here every day than you could shake a stick at. In the middle they's a big bandstand and chairs for the folks to set and listen to the concerts, which they give you music for all tastes, from Dixie up to classical pieces like Hearts and Flowers.

Then all around they's places marked off for different sports and games—chess and checkers and dominoes for folks that enjoys those kind of games, and roque and horse-shoes for the nimbler ones. I used to pitch a pretty fair shoe myself, but ain't done much of it in the last twenty years.

Well, anyway, we bought a membership ticket in the club which costs one dollar for the season, and they tell me that up to a couple years ago it was fifty cents, but they had to raise it to keep out the riffraff.

Well, Mother and I put in a great day watching the pitchers and she wanted I should get in the game, but I told her I was all out of practice and would make a fool of myself, though I seen several men pitching who I guess I could take their measure without no practice. However, they was some good pitchers, too, and one boy from Akron, Ohio, who could certainly throw a pretty shoe. They told me it looked like he would win the championship of the United States in the February tournament. We come away a few days before they held that and I never did hear if he win. I forget his name, but he was a clean cut young fella and he has got a brother in Cleveland that's a Rotarian.

Well, we just stood around and watched the different games for two or three days and finally I set down in a checker game with a man named Weaver from Danville, Illinois. He was a pretty fair checker player, but he wasn't no match for me, and I hope that don't sound like bragging. But I always could hold my own on a checker-board and the folks around here will tell you the same thing. I played with this Weaver pretty near all morning for two or three mornings and he beat me one game and the only other time it looked like he had a chance, the noon whistle blowed and we had to quit and go to dinner.

While I was playing checkers, Mother would set and listen to the band, as she loves music, classical or no matter what kind, but anyway she was setting there one day and between selections the woman next to her opened up a conversation. She was a woman about Mother's own age, seventy or seventy-one, and finally she asked Mother's name and Mother told her her name and where she was from and Mother asked her the same question, and who do you think the woman was?

Well, sir, it was the wife of Frank M. Hartsell, the man who was engaged to Mother till I stepped in and cut him out, fifty-two years ago!

Yes, sir!

You can imagine Mother's surprise! And Mrs. Hartsell was surprised, too, when Mother told her she had once been friends with her husband, though Mother didn't say how close friends they had been, or that Mother and I was the cause of Hartsell going out West. But that's what we was. Hartsell left his town a month after the engagement was broke off and ain't never been back since. He had went out to Michigan and become a veterinary, and that is where he had settled down, in Hillsdale, Michigan, and finally married his wife.

Well, Mother screwed up her courage to ask if Frank was still living and Mrs. Hartsell took her over to where they was pitching horse-shoes and there was old Frank, waiting his turn. And he knowed Mother as soon as he seen her, though it was over fifty years. He said he knowed her by her eyes.

" Why, it's Lucy Frost! " he says, and he throwed down his shoes and quit the game.

Then they come over and hunted me up and I will confess I wouldn't of knowed him. Him and I is the same age to the month, but he seems to show it more, some way. He is balder for one thing. And his beard is all white, where mine has still got a streak of brown in it. The very first thing I said to him, I said:

" Well, Frank, that beard of yours makes me feel like I was back north. It looks like a regular blizzard."

" Well," he said, " I guess yourn would be just as white if you had it dry cleaned."

But Mother wouldn't stand that.

" Is that so! " she said to Frank. " Well, Charley ain't had no tobacco in his mouth for over ten years! "

And I ain't!

Well, I excused myself from the checker game and it was pretty

close to noon, so we decided to all have dinner together and they
was nothing for it only we must try their cafeteria on Third Avenue. It was a little more expensive than ours and not near as
good, I thought. I and Mother had about the same dinner we had
been having every day and our bill was $1.10. Frank's check was
$1.20 for he and his wife. The same meal wouldn't of cost them
more than a dollar at our place.

After dinner we made them come up to our house and we all set
in the parlor, which the young woman had give us the use of to entertain company. We begun talking over old times and Mother
said she was a-scared Mrs. Hartsell would find it tiresome listening to we three talk over old times, but as it turned out they wasn't
much chance for nobody else to talk with Mrs. Hartsell in the
company. I have heard lots of women that could go it, but Hartsell's wife takes the cake of all the women I ever seen. Sho told us
the family history of everybody in the State of Michigan and
bragged for a half hour about her son, who she said is in the drug
business in Grand Rapids, and a Rotarian.

When I and Hartsell could get a word in edgeways we joked one
another back and forth and I chafed him about being a horse
doctor.

"Well, Frank," I said, "you look pretty prosperous, so I suppose they's been plenty of glanders around Hillsdale."

"Well," he said, "I've managed to make more than a fair living. But I've worked pretty hard."

"Yes," I said, "and I suppose you get called out all hours of
the night to attend births and so on."

Mother made me shut up.

Well, I thought they wouldn't never go home and I and Mother
was in misery trying to keep awake, as the both of us generally always takes a nap after dinner. Finally they went, after we had
made an engagement to meet them in the Park the next morning,
and Mrs. Hartsell also invited us to come to their place the next
night and play five hundred. But she had forgot that they was a
meeting of the Michigan Society that evening, so it was not till
two evenings later that we had our first card game.

Hartsell and his wife lived in a house on Third Avenue North
and had a private setting room besides their bedroom. Mrs.
Hartsell couldn't quit talking about their private setting room
like it was something wonderful. We played cards with them, with
Mother and Hartsell partners against his wife and I. Mrs. Hartsell is a miserable card player and we certainly got the worst of it.

After the game she brought out a dish of oranges and we had to pretend it was just what we wanted, though oranges down there is like a young man's whiskers; you enjoy them at first, but they get to be a pesky nuisance.

We played cards again the next night at our place with the same partners and I and Mrs. Hartsell was beat again. Mother and Hartsell was full of compliments for each other on what a good team they made, but the both of them knowed well enough where the secret of their success laid. I guess all and all we must of played ten different evenings and they was only one night when Mrs. Hartsell and I come out ahead. And that one night wasn't no fault of hern.

When we had been down there about two weeks, we spent one evening as their guest in the Congregational Church, at a social give by the Michigan Society. A talk was made by a man named Bitting of Detroit, Michigan, on How I was Cured of Story Telling. He is a big man in the Rotarians and give a witty talk.

A woman named Mrs. Oxford rendered some selections which Mrs. Hartsell said was grand opera music, but whatever they was my daughter Edie could of give her cards and spades and not made such a hullaballoo about it neither.

Then they was a ventriloquist from Grand Rapids and a young woman about forty-five years of age that mimicked different kinds of birds. I whispered to Mother that they all sounded like a chicken, but she nudged me to shut up.

After the show we stopped in a drug store and I set up the refreshments and it was pretty close to ten o'clock before we finally turned in. Mother and I would of preferred tending the movies, but Mother said we mustn't offend Mrs. Hartsell, though I asked her had we came to Florida to enjoy ourselves or to just not offend an old chatter-box from Michigan.

I felt sorry for Hartsell one morning. The women folks both had an engagement down to the chiropodist's and I run across Hartsell in the Park and he foolishly offered to play me checkers.

It was him that suggested it, not me, and I guess he repented himself before we had played one game. But he was too stubborn to give up and set there while I beat him game after game and the worst part of it was that a crowd of folks had got in the habit of watching me play and there they all was, looking on, and finally they seen what a fool Frank was making of himself, and they began to chafe him and pass remarks. Like one of them said:

" Who ever told you you was a checker player ! "

And:

"You might maybe be good for tiddle-de-winks, but not checkers!"

I almost felt like letting him beat me a couple games. But the crowd would of knowed it was a put up job.

Well, the women folks joined us in the Park and I wasn't going to mention our little game, but Hartsell told about it himself and admitted he wasn't no match for me.

"Well," said Mrs. Hartsell, "checkers ain't much of a game anyway, is it?" She said: "It's more of a children's game, ain't it? At least, I know my boy's children used to play it a good deal."

"Yes, ma'am," I said. "It's a children's game the way your husband plays it, too."

Mother wanted to smooth things over, so she said:

"Maybe they's other games where Frank can beat you."

"Yes," said Mrs. Hartsell, "and I bet he could beat you pitching horse-shoes."

"Well," I said, "I would give him a chance to try, only I ain't pitched a shoe in over sixteen years."

"Well," said Hartsell, "I ain't played checkers in twenty years."

"You ain't never played it," I said.

"Anyway," says Frank, "Lucy and I is your master at five hundred."

Well, I could of told him why that was, but had decency enough to hold my tongue.

It had got so now that he wanted to play cards every night and when I or Mother wanted to go to a movie, any one of us would have to pretend we had a headache and then trust to goodness that they wouldn't see us sneak into the theater. I don't mind playing cards when my partner keeps their mind on the game, but you take a woman like Hartsell's wife and how can they play cards when they have got to stop every couple seconds and brag about their son in Grand Rapids?

Well, the New York-New Jersey Society announced that they was goin to give a social evening too and I said to Mother, I said:

"Well, that is one evening when we will have an excuse not to play five hundred."

"Yes," she said, "but we will have to ask Frank and his wife to go to the social with us as they asked us to go to the Michigan social."

"Well," I said, " I had rather stay home than drag that chatterbox everywheres we go."

So Mother said:

"You are getting too cranky. Maybe she does talk a little too much but she is good hearted. And Frank is always good company."

So I said:

"I suppose if he is such good company you wished you had of married him."

Mother laughed and said I sounded like I was jealous. Jealous of a cow doctor!

Anyway we had to drag them along to the social and I will say that we give them a much better entertainment than they had given us.

Judge Lane of Paterson made a fine talk on business conditions and a Mrs. Newell of Westfield imitated birds, only you could really tell what they was the way she done it. Two young women from Red Bank sung a choral selection and we clapped them back and they gave us Home to Our Mountains and Mother and Mrs. Hartsell both had tears in their eyes. And Hartsell, too.

Well, some way or another the chairman got wind that I was there and asked me to make a talk and I wasn't even going to get up, but Mother made me, so I got up and said:

"Ladies and gentlemen," I said. "I didn't expect to be called on for a speech on an occasion like this or no other occasion as I do not set myself up as a speech maker, so will have to do the best I can, which I often say is the best anybody can do."

Then I told them the story about Pat and the motorcycle, using the brogue, and it seemed to tickle them and I told them one or two other stories, but altogether I wasn't on my feet more than twenty or twenty-five minutes and you ought to of heard the clapping and hollering when I set down. Even Mrs. Hartsell admitted that I am quite a speechifier and said if I ever went to Grand Rapids, Michigan, her son would make me talk to the Rotarians.

When it was over, Hartsell wanted we should go to their house and play cards, but his wife reminded him that it was after 9.30 P. M., rather a late hour to start a card game, but he had went crazy on the subject of cards, probably because he didn't have to play partners with his wife. Anyway, we got rid of them and went home to bed.

It was the next morning, when we met over to the Park, that

Mrs. Hartsell made the remark that she wasn't getting no exercise so I suggested that why didn't she take part in the roque game.

She said she had not played a game of roque in twenty years, but if Mother would play she would play. Well, at first Mother wouldn't hear of it, but finally consented, more to please Mrs. Hartsell than anything else.

Well, they had a game with a Mrs. Ryan from Eagle, Nebraska, and a young Mrs. Morse from Rutland, Vermont, who Mother had met down to the chiropodist's. Well, Mother couldn't hit a flea and they all laughed at her and I couldn't help from laughing at her myself and finally she quit and said her back was too lame to stoop over. So they got another lady and kept on playing and soon Mrs. Hartsell was the one everybody was laughing at, as she had a long shot to hit the black ball, and as she made the effort her teeth fell out on to the court. I never seen a woman so flustered in my life. And I never heard so much laughing, only Mrs. Hartsell didn't join in and she was madder than a hornet and wouldn't play no more, so the game broke up.

Mrs. Hartsell went home without speaking to nobody, but Hartsell stayed around and finally he said to me, he said:

"Well, I played you checkers the other day and you beat me bad and now what do you say if you and me play a game of horseshoes?"

I told him I hadn't pitched a shoe in sixteen years, but Mother said:

"Go ahead and play. You used to be good at it and maybe it will come back to you."

Well, to make a long story short, I give in. I oughtn't to of never tried it, as I hadn't pitched a shoe in sixteen years, and I only done it to humor Hartsell.

Before we started, Mother patted me on the back and told me to do my best, so we started in and I seen right off that I was in for it, as I hadn't pitched a shoe in sixteen years and didn't have my distance. And besides, the plating had wore off the shoes so that they was points right where they stuck into my thumb and I hadn't throwed more than two or three times when my thumb was raw and it pretty near killed me to hang on to the shoe, let alone pitch it.

Well, Hartsell throws the awkwardest shoe I ever seen pitched and to see him pitch you wouldn't think he would ever come nowheres near, but he is also the luckiest pitcher I ever seen and he made some pitches where the shoe lit five and six feet short and then schoonered up and was a ringer. They's no use trying to beat that kind of luck.

They was a pretty fair size crowd watching us and four or five other ladies besides Mother, and it seems like, when Hartsell pitches, he has got to chew and it kept the ladies on the anxious seat as he don't seem to care which way he is facing when he leaves go.

You would think a man as old as him would of learnt more manners.

Well, to make a long story short, I was just beginning to get my distance when I had to give up on account of my thumb, which I showed it to Hartsell and he seen I couldn't go on, as it was raw and bleeding. Even if I could of stood it to go on myself, Mother wouldn't of allowed it after she seen my thumb. So anyway I quit and Hartsell said the score was nineteen to six, but I don't know what it was. Or don't care, neither.

Well, Mother and I went home and I said I hoped we was through with the Hartsells as I was sick and tired of them, but it seemed like she had promised we would go over to their house that evening for another game of their everlasting cards.

Well, my thumb was giving me considerable pain and I felt kind of out of sorts and I guess maybe I forgot myself, but anyway, when we was about through playing Hartsell made the remark that he wouldn't never lose a game of cards if he could always have Mother for a partner.

So I said:

" Well, you had a chance fifty years ago to always have her for a partner, but you wasn't man enough to keep her."

I was sorry the minute I had said it and Hartsell didn't know what to say and for once his wife couldn't say nothing. Mother tried to smooth things over by making the remark that I must of had something stronger than tea or I wouldn't talk so silly. But Mrs. Hartsell had froze up like an iceberg and hardly said good night to us and I bet her and Frank put in a pleasant hour after we was gone.

As we was leaving, Mother said to him: " Never mind Charley's nonsense, Frank. He is just mad because you beat him all hollow pitching horseshoes and playing cards."

She said that to make up for my slip, but at the same time she certainly riled me. I tried to keep ahold of myself, but as soon as we was out of the house she had to open up the subject and begun to scold me for the break I had made.

Well, I wasn't in no mood to be scolded. So I said:

" I guess he is such a wonderful pitcher and card player that you wished you had married him."

" Well," she said, " at least he ain't a baby to give up pitching because his thumb has got a few scratches."

" And how about you," I said, " making a fool of yourself on the roque court and then pretending your back is lame and you can't play no more ! "

" Yes," she said, " but when you hurt your thumb I didn't laugh at you, and why did you laugh at me when I sprained my back ? "

" Who could help from laughing ! " I said.

" Well," she said, " Frank Hartsell didn't laugh."

" Well," I said, " why didn't you marry him ? "

" Well," said Mother, " I almost wished I had ! "

" And I wished so, too ! " I said.

" I'll remember that ! " said Mother, and that's the last word she said to me for two days.

We seen the Hartsells the next day in the Park and I was willing to apologize, but they just nodded to us. And a couple days later we heard they had left for Orlando, where they have got relatives.

I wished they had went there in the first place.

Mother and I made it up setting on a bench.

" Listen, Charley," she said. " This is our Golden Honeymoon and we don't want the whole thing spoilt with a silly old quarrel."

" Well," I said, " did you mean that about wishing you had married Hartsell ? "

" Of course not," she said, " that is, if you didn't mean that you wished I had, too."

So I said:

" I was just tired and all wrought up. I thank God you chose me instead of him as they's no other woman in the world who I could of lived with all these years."

" How about Mrs. Hartsell ? " says Mother.

" Good gracious ! " I said. " Imagine being married to a woman that plays five hundred like she does and drops her teeth on the roque court ! "

" Well," said Mother, " it wouldn't be no worse than being married to a man that expectorates towards ladies and is such a fool in a checker game."

So I put my arm around her shoulder and she stroked my hand and I guess we got kind of spoony.

They was two days left of our stay in St. Petersburg and the next to the last day Mother introduced me to a Mrs. Kendall from Kingston, Rhode Island, who she had met at the chiropodist's.

Mrs. Kendall made us acquainted with her husband, who is in the grocery business. They have got two sons and five grandchildren and one great-grandchild. One of their sons lives in Providence and is way up in the Elks as well as a Rotarian.

We found them very congenial people and we played cards with them the last two nights we was there. They was both experts and I only wished we had met them sooner instead of running into the Hartsells. But the Kendalls will be there again next winter and we will see more of them, that is, if we decide to make the trip again.

We left the Sunshine City on the eleventh day of February, at 11 A. M. This give us a day trip through Florida and we seen all the country we had passed through at night on the way down.

We reached Jacksonville at 7 P. M. and pulled out of there at 8.10 P. M. We reached Fayetteville, North Carolina, at nine o'clock the following morning, and reached Washington, D. C., at 6.30 P. M., laying over there half an hour.

We reached Trenton at 11.01 P. M. and had wired ahead to my daughter and son-in-law and they met us at the train and we went to their house and they put us up for the night. John would of made us stay up all night, telling about our trip, but Edie said we must be tired and made us go to bed. That's my daughter.

The next day we took our train for home and arrived safe and sound, having been gone just one month and a day.

Here comes Mother, so I guess I better shut up.

XIX

NOW AND THEN

Nassau, Bahamas, Feb. 3.

DEAREST ESTHER:

Bob is asleep and I will snatch these few minutes to write you a letter, but it may not be very long because he is liable to wake up any moment and insist that I stop writing and " pay some attention " to him. He is honestly jealous of you and I being friends or of me caring for anybody besides him enough to write to them. Isn't that too silly for words and yet it thrills me to have him be that way and shows that I am really everything in his life. He is a regular child where I am concerned and can't bear to have me even mention my old friends or things that happened before I met him.

Esther, I am tickled to death now that we didn't go on our honeymoon right after we were married, but waited these seven months when Bob can have a real vacation and don't have to be worrying about business all of the time. Just think we might never have seen this place if we hadn't made up our minds to wait and Esther it is just heaven, so beautiful and quaint that it is like a place in some other world.

Well I will begin at the beginning and tell you everything about our trip like I promised though I am afraid it won't be very interesting as in the first place I was deathly seasick all the way down on the boat, but it may sound funny but I am honestly glad I was because Bob was so perfectly dear and would not leave me for a minute though he is a wonderful sailor himself and I being sick must have simply ruined the trip for him. Well I was just in misery for three nights and two days, but as soon as the boat stopped Monday morning I was all right again and able to take in all the sights.

The boat has to anchor out in the harbor on account of the water being too shallow near land so we were all loaded on to a tender and brought to the dock here and then we had to wait around while they inspected our baggage because this is a British port though they didn't open anything at all but just put chalk marks on it and Bob says about the only thing the customs inspectors look for these

237

days is liquor and they realize nobody would try and smuggle liquor to this place as it would be like bringing coal to New Castle, Pa.

Next we got into a two seated carriage and drove to the hotel and Bob talked to the Negro driver and of course all the drivers and people like that here are Negros but not like our Negros at home, they talk with a kind of English accent and you can't hardly understand them half the time. Our room is wonderful and faces on the water which is wonderful, all different shades of green and blue and purple, it makes a person wish they were a painter it is so wonderful in coloring.

At lunch time Bob told the head waiter to put us as far as he could from other people. Bob says he used to be one of the most sociable men in the world but since he married me he don't want anything to do with other people and the more we can keep to ourselves just we two the better he likes it. The head waiter gave us a table in a corner near a window and when another couple came in and sat at the next table Bob actually got mad at them like nobody had a right to be in the same dining room with us almost.

After lunch I unpacked or rather I directed the unpacking and Bob did the real work as he won't let me lift my hand to really do anything as he says he would never forgive himself if I overdid. At five o'clock the hotel orchestra began playing out on the lawn where they have a dance floor and serve tea and drinks and Bob and I had some tea and cakes and danced four dances.

Most of the other people around us were drinking highballs and things and Bob said he didn't blame them, if he had to dance with some of the women here he would want to drink enough first to blind him. But he said he wanted his eyes clear when he looked at me and as for drinking anything why just being with me and touching me made him intoxicated. He does say the nicest things and puts them so differently.

He is beginning to wake up so this will have to be " continued in our next."

With love,

Irma.

DEAREST ESTHER: *Nassau, Bahamas, Feb. 6.*

We are having such a heavenly time that it seems criminal to not share it with somebody but of course it is just us being here together alone that makes it so heavenly. It is simply heavenly here and I don't see why people go other places when they can come here and I guess maybe they don't know about this place or perhaps it seems more wonderful to me than it really is on account of being here with Bob and that is what makes it so wonderful. Anyway I was never so happy in my life and am already dreading the time when it will be time to start home.

The first day we got here there was a young couple introduced themselves to Bob after dinner that evening and wanted to know did we want to play bridge with them. As you know I don't play bridge and Bob says he can't take any interest in games unless I am in them so he told these people we were going out for a sail and after we were alone he said he hated to tell a lie so we would have to go out for a sail so he would not have told those people a lie, so he hired a sail boat and it was simply heavenly sailing in the moonlight just Bob and I and the man sailing the boat who never looked at us.

The moonlight here is heavenly and I don't believe there is any other place where it is so wonderful and it was so wonderful that Bob and I had to laugh at the idea of staying in a stuffy hotel and playing cards when you could be out sailing in the moonlight though I suppose it would bore some people.

The next morning we got on the hotel boat and went over to the bathing beach and went in swimming and the water was wonderful but Bob didn't like it at first as he said there was too many people around and he hated to have other men see me in my bathing suit so he and I walked away along the beach where there was nobody else and we went in the water there. It was kind of weedy and not as nice as the regular beach as there was also some rocks in the place we went in and I stubbed my toe on one of them, but Bob said he would rather I stubbed my toe than have a lot of men staring at me, but he was awfully nice about my toe and kept asking me how it felt.

Bob is a wonderful swimmer and I tried to make him go out and enjoy himself in the deep water, but he wouldn't leave me for a second and he said he would never forgive himself if he left me and something happened to me. I told him I would stay in shallow water and there would be no danger, but he said he had heard that sharks and baracudas sometimes came right up to the beach and bit women if they were alone.

We came back to the hotel for lunch and in the afternoon we took a ride on the glass bottom boat to the sea garden. It is a boat with a glass bottom and you can see right through it and they took us to a place where the bottom of the sea is just like a garden with things growing in it and fish. It was simply heavenly, but Bob got kind of mad because there was a man that spoke to me, the man didn't mean anything, but Bob gave him a terrible look and the incident kind of spoiled the trip.

We had dinner in our room as Bob said there was too many people in the dining room. We went to bed early and the orchestra was playing out on the lawn and it was heavenly just lying there listening and finally they sang some native Bahamian songs and Bob just loved them and is going to try and get them to take home with us.

He is through shaving and all dressed and this will have to be " continued in our next " as he gets impatient if I am not ready to do things with him when he is ready to do them.

Yours,
IRMA.

Nassau, Bahamas, Feb. 10.

DEAREST ESTHER:

What do you think I did today? Well you will never guess so I may as well tell you. I played golf. I suppose I ought not to say I really played it but I played at it though Bob said I had a beautiful swing and he was amazed at how quickly I picked it up.

Bob of course is a splendid golf player and brought his clubs along, but up to today I couldn't make him play as he said it was no fun for him to do anything if I was not doing it with him, but yesterday we took a carriage ride and went past the golf course and Bob said he would like to try it and I said why didn't he and then he said he would if I would go along and play with him. Well at first I thought he was joking, but he was in dead earnest and he said he did not see any reason why I did not learn the game and then in the summer time we could play together and he would not have to play around with a lot of stupid men who always wanted to bet and then get sore when he beats them.

Well I finally agreed to try it and he borrowed some clubs from Jock Hutchinson who is the teacher down here and we went out on the linx and the first time I swang at the ball I missed it entirely, but I hit it the next time and did better after that and we played nine holes and Bob said my score was 92 which was good for a beginner. We are going to play again tomorrow and every day we are down here. It is really wonderful exercise and as long as Bob won't play without me I feel like I really ought to play with him because he really enjoys the game so much.

It took us an hour to get out there and an hour to get back, but we could have made it in ten minutes each way if we had gone in an automobile, but Bob won't use the automobiles here as he says the carriages look more in keeping with the place they are so quaint and it would be sacrilegious to use the automobiles. Well Esther won't you be proud of me when I am a real golfer and maybe I will have a chance to teach you the game some time when Bob is away on business.

We had a narrow escape when we got back to the hotel. Just as we were coming in the door a man got out of a car right behind us that Bob knows and it was just luck that he didn't see Bob. He is from Chicago and Bob says he is an awfully nice man and he does business with him sometimes, but he says our whole trip would be ruined if we couldn't be alone just by ourselves all the time we are here and not see anybody else, that is to talk to them. So we are having dinner in our room again so as not to take any chance of seeing this man and maybe his wife is here with him and we would have to spend an evening with them or something. I hope they will go away soon and not bother us.

I had some pictures taken the second day we were here by a man who takes pictures of all the hotel guests and then if you like them you can buy some of them. They were finished today and the man showed them to us and I wanted to buy two or three of each as they were awfully good, but Bob said I could only buy one of each and that would be for him and he didn't want me sending my pictures around to other people, so I guess you will just have to remember what I look like and get along without my picture.

Last night the orchestra played out on the lawn and Bob and I danced a couple of dances and were sitting there watching the others and the assistant manager of the hotel was there and he came to our table and asked me to dance and I almost started to get up when Bob answered for me and said he was sorry but I had turned my ankle in swimming.

I know the man had seen me dancing just a few minutes before and I don't know what he thought, but he was awfully nice about it and said maybe we could have a dance some other time.

After he had gone away Bob said I wasn't to speak to him next time I saw him or he would take it as an encouragement and ask me to dance with him again.

Must close now as Bob has finished the letters he was writing and wants to be read aloud to. I don't read aloud very well, but he says he loves to have me as he can sit and look at me while I read and it don't make any difference if I read well or not because he is too busy looking at me to pay any attention to what I am reading.

Love,

IRMA

DEAREST ESTHER: *Nassau, Bahamas, Feb. 13.*

I know I promised to write you every other day while we were down here, but I am afraid I will have to ask you to release me from my promise. I suppose I could tell you a fib and say I don't have time to write, but that would be a fib and the real reason I can't write to you any more is because it makes Bob mad and I won't do anything behind his back so I know you will understand if you don't hear from me again and as soon as I get home and Bob's vacation is over, I will come and see you and tell you about the rest of our trip, that is anything that might be interesting.

Bob don't like to have me write for two reasons, in the first place he is jealous of all my old friends and he says I am his wife now and all my time belongs to him and he don't want me wasting it writing to other people even if they are old friends and secondly he don't like the idea of me telling anybody the things we do down here as he says this belated honeymoon as he calls it is sacred between him and me and it is nobody's else business what we do down here.

Please try and understand Esther and forgive me and you know I love you and wouldn't do anything in the world to hurt your feelings, but I am married to Bob now and his feelings are to be considered above everything else. We are having such a heavenly time that I simply can't do anything that would spoil it in any way.

Your friend,

IRMA

DEAREST ESTHER: *Nassau, Bahamas, Feb. 5.*

Well Esther here we are Bob and I " honeymooning " again and it hardly seems possible that three years have gone by since we were in Nassau before, but don't you think it was a wonderful idea coming back to the place where we had such a heavenly time the winter after we were married and this is the first time Bob has had a real vacation since then and he has certainly earned it and I know he will enjoy every minute down here even if we keep to ourselves and just rest and " loaf."

I am feeling all right again after being terribly seasick all the way down from New York. I thought it was quite rough, but Bob said it was just like a billiard table and he was quite provoked at me being sick and threatened to leave me home the next time he was going anywhere on a boat. He said he did not see how I ever sat through a dinner party as he would think the waves in the finger bowl would upset me. Bob just loves to tease me.

When we went in the dining room for lunch today the same head waiter was there as the last time and he remembered us after three years and gave us the same corner table we had the last time. Imagine him remembering us after three years, but after lunch Bob stopped and talked to him about giving us another table in the middle of the room and not so far off from everybody as he said it would not seem like we were in a big hotel way off from everybody like that. So tonight he is going to change us.

I have had quite a busy afternoon unpacking and getting settled. Bob went out with some men he met on the boat to play golf as he said he couldn't very well get out of it and he thought I would be too worn out to play with him after my seasickness. I am afraid he will be bothered to death by all the different people he met on the boat which he couldn't help because of course I was unable to leave my stateroom for meals and they put him at a big table with a lot of other people but he can always manage to discourage new acquaintances if they begin to make a nuisance of themselves.

Will have to close as Bob promised he would be back in time for a few dances before it is time to dress for dinner, but it is after six now and the orchestra will soon stop playing, but I suppose they were slow getting their golf game started the first day or maybe he has had trouble getting away from those other men.

With love,

IRMA

Nassau, Bahamas, Feb. 7.

DEAREST ESTHER:

Well it is nearly bed time but I don't feel like going to bed till Bob comes in and he is downstairs playing bridge with a woman and her husband and the woman's sister that he met on the boat. I have hardly seen him at all today as he was not feeling well this morning and would not go to the beach swimming as he said he thought it had upset his stomach swallowing the salt water, but he insisted on me going without him and he introduced me to a friend of his from Chicago a Mr. Granville who was here three years ago

with his wife but his wife has since died. Bob said Mr. Granville
was a great swimmer and would see that I did not drown and
would teach me to swim.

Well I wouldn't let him teach me to swim because I hate to have
a strange man come near me in swimming, but he was awfully nice
to me, but I didn't stay in long as I hate to enjoy myself when Bob
is not feeling well.

Bob and I had lunch together and he felt better and arranged
a golf game with some people he met on the boat. I asked him if
he was sure he ought to play when he didn't feel well, but he said
it was swimming that upset him and not golf. I asked him if he
wasn't ever going to play golf again with me and he said yes some
time, but he said it wasn't much fun playing with me as I am so
terrible that we can't play any kind of a match and he likes to play
with people he can bet with and he also said I look so awkward
when I try to play that he is afraid people will laugh at me.

Yesterday I asked him if he didn't want to go out in the glass
bottom boat and look at the sea garden as we did when we were
here before and he said yes we would go tomorrow, meaning today,
but when I reminded him of it he told me to go alone or find somebody else to go with as he couldn't get any thrill out of looking at a
bunch of dirty sea weed. He did keep his promise to take me to
tea out on the lawn where they dance.

The golf match had tired him out though and he wouldn't dance
but he would not admit he was tired but said he didn't like the
music and wished the orchestra would get up to date and play
something besides old native tunes that the Negros down here
made up. They really only played the native songs for one dance,
but Bob has no ear and don't know one tune from another. He insisted on me dancing with Mr. Granville whom he invited to our
table.

We had tea and Bob said he felt like he needed something
stronger than tea and he drank four highballs so I knew he wasn't
telling the truth when he said the golf hadn't made him tired.

I was really very tired myself and I suggested that it would be a
good thing for both of us if we had dinner in our room and we
would go to bed right after and I would read to him. He said he
wouldn't like anything better though he could hardly understand
me when I read because I mumble my words so, but he had asked
some people he met on the boat to have a cocktail with him and
they were people who might help him in a business way so he
couldn't get out of it, but if I met them too why it would mean we

would probably have them on our hands the rest of the time we are here so he thought it would be a good idea for me to have dinner by myself and go to bed when I felt like it.

After dinner he phoned up to say that he got tangled up in a bridge game with these people and I had better go to bed and not wait for him. But I know he will have some things to tell me about these people when he comes in and he tells things in such an amusing way that I hate to miss it and maybe by tomorrow morning he won't remember half the things that happened.

The weather has been heavenly and we are having a simply wonderful time and I wish some time you could come down here and spend a week or two as it is simply heavenly and I don't believe there is another place like it in the world.

Am out of stationery so this will have to be " continued in our next."

Love,

Irma

Nassau, Bahamas, Feb. 8.

Dearest Esther:

I have been having dinner in the room again as I did not feel like dressing up and going downstairs. Bob was tired out too and wanted to stay here with me, but those people he met on the boat insisted on him having a cocktail with them and as long as he had to get dressed for that he thought he might as well eat in the dining room and now he is playing bridge with them again as they couldn't find a fourth without him. They are a Mr. and Mrs. Griffin and Mrs. Griffin's sister, Miss Cutts, and he met them on the boat coming down. Mr. Griffin is in a position to do Bob some good in a business way and that is why Bob don't like to refuse their invitations.

This morning I went over to the beach with Mr. Granville and Bob played golf with some people he met on the boat. As we were coming back from the beach a man stopped us who takes pictures and he wanted to take a picture of Mr. Granville and me together but I thought that wouldn't look right so I let him take my picture alone and while he was taking it Bob came along and he had just come back from his golf game and when he saw me getting my picture taken he teased me about it and said I must think I was a movie star, or somebody, getting my picture taken all the time.

I said I was just having it taken for him and he said I needn't waste money on pictures of myself for him as he already had enough of them and I better send these to my friends who were always asking me for my picture. So if they are good I will send you one and send some to the other girls too.

This afternoon Bob went out to play golf and I was sitting on the porch reading and Mr. Granville came along and invited me to take a drive with him and I was tired reading so I accepted and we took a carriage though Bob says it is silly to ride in the old broken down carriages they have got here when you can get a car and get to places ten times as fast but we were in no hurry so we took a carriage and drove past the golf club and they have got a bathing beach out there too and we stopped for a minute to watch the people in swimming and there was Bob swimming with Miss Cutts whom he met on the boat coming down.

Well he didn't see us and I didn't say anything to him about it when he came home but he is just a child Esther and he knew I would think it was bad for him to go in swimming when the salt water affects him so and that is why he went in swimming where he thought I wouldn't see him and I only hope he don't get sick again.

He had promised to take me for a moonlight sail tonight, but I could see that his golf and his swim had worn him out and besides that the Griffins made him stay down on the lawn when they got back from the golf club and he didn't want to offend them but felt so tired that he had to take some highballs and then Miss Cutts practically made him dance with her twice and he was tired enough without that, but he never would have told me all the things he had had to do and probably would have gone sailing with me if I had reminded him of it, but I had watched him dancing from my window which fronts on the lawn and I knew how he must feel so I pretended I had forgotten all about our sail.

Poor Bob he wasn't a bit like his usual cheerful self when he got up in the room and he would have given anything to get out of his engagement tonight and he was so cross that when I tried to persuade him to stay here by hinting that I was getting lonesome staying all by myself with nothing to do, he said, " What would you do if I was here? All you ever do is read or write letters. Why don't you write to your friend Esther and tell her your troubles? "

So I just laughed it off but I do get a little lonesome sometimes and wish he could get rid of these people he met on the boat. It is so heavenly here and such a wonderful place and we could be having such a heavenly time if it wasn't for the Griffins. Isn't it a darn shame that a man can't get away from business even on his vacation when he hasn't had one in three years?

With love,

IRMA.

Miami, Fla., Feb. 11.

DEAREST ESTHER:

You will probably be surprised at me writing to you from this place. I arrived here by boat from Nassau this morning and was sick all the way and now I am waiting for train time. I leave here tonight for home and will arrive there Thursday forenoon. I am crazy to see you Esther and I am writing to know if you can't come and visit me for a few days next week. We will go to a show every night or do anything you want to do. I just want to see you and have a nice visit.

Bob is staying on at Nassau for two more weeks as he loves it there and it agrees with him so well. I love it too and think it is the most heavenly place I ever went to, but there is so much to do there that a person simply gets worn out and both Bob and I agreed that I wasn't strong enough to stand the pace and would be better off at home.

I will be expecting a wire from you as soon as you get this. Wire me at home and I will try and get tickets for things I know you will want to see. Please come Esther. Any day will do and the sooner the better, but don't disappoint me.

Your friend,

IRMA.

XX

HORSESHOES

THE series ended Tuesday, but I had stayed in Philadelphia an extra day on the chance of there being some follow-up stuff worth sending. Nothing had broken loose; so I filed some stuff about what the Athletics and Giants were going to do with their dough, and then caught the eight o'clock train for Chicago.

Having passed up supper in order to get my story away and grab the train, I went to the buffet car right after I'd planted my grips. I sat down at one of the tables and ordered a sandwich. Four salesmen were playing rum at the other table and all the chairs in the car were occupied; so it didn't surprise me when somebody flopped down in the seat opposite me.

I looked up from my paper and with a little thrill recognized my companion. Now I've been experting round the country with ball players so much that it doesn't usually excite me to meet one face to face, even if he's a star. I can talk with Tyrus without getting all fussed up. But this particular player had jumped from obscurity to fame so suddenly and had played such an important though brief part in the recent argument between the Macks and McGraws that I couldn't help being a little awed by his proximity.

It was none other than Grimes, the utility outfielder Connie had been forced to use in the last game because of the injury to Joyce— Grimes, whose miraculous catch in the eleventh inning had robbed Parker of a home run and the Giants of victory, and whose own homer—a fluky one—had given the Athletics another World's Championship.

I had met Grimes one day during the spring he was with the Cubs, but I knew he wouldn't remember me. A ball player never recalls a reporter's face on less than six introductions or his name on less than twenty. However, I resolved to speak to him, and had just mustered sufficient courage to open a conversation when he saved me the trouble.

" Whose picture have they got there? " he asked, pointing to my paper.

" Speed Parker's," I replied.

249

" What do they say about him? " asked Grimes.

" I'll read it to you," I said:

" ' Speed Parker, McGraw's great third baseman, is ill in a local hospital with nervous prostration, the result of the strain of the World's Series, in which he played such a stellar rôle. Parker is in such a dangerous condition that no one is allowed to see him. Members of the New York team and fans from Gotham called at the hospital to-day, but were unable to gain admittance to his ward. Philadelphians hope he will recover speedily and will suffer no permanent ill effects from his sickness, for he won their admiration by his work in the series, though he was on a rival team. A lucky catch by Grimes, the Athletics' substitute outfielder, was all that prevented Parker from winning the title for New York. According to Manager Mack, of the champions, the series would have been over in four games but for Parker's wonderful exhibition of nerve and——' "

" That'll be a plenty," Grimes interrupted. "And that's just what you might expect from one o' them doughheaded reporters. If all the baseball writers was where they belonged they'd have to build an annex to Matteawan."

I kept my temper with very little effort—it takes more than a peevish ball player's remarks to insult one of our fraternity; but I didn't exactly understand his peeve.

" Doesn't Parker deserve the bouquet? " I asked.

" Oh, they can boost him all they want to," said Grimes; " but when they call that catch lucky and don't mention the fact that Parker is the luckiest guy in the world, somethin' must be wrong with 'em. Did you see the serious? "

" No," I lied glibly, hoping to draw from him the cause of his grouch.

" Well," he said, " you sure missed somethin'. They never was a serious like it before and they won't never be one again. It went the full seven games and every game was a bear. They was one big innin' every day and Parker was the big cheese in it. Just as Connie says, the Ath-a-letics would of cleaned 'em in four games but for Parker; but it wasn't because he's a great ball player—it was because he was born with a knife, fork and spoon in his mouth, and a rabbit's foot hung round his neck.

" You may not know it, but I'm Grimes, the guy that made the lucky catch. I'm the guy that won the serious with a hit—a home-run hit; and I'm here to tell you that if I'd had one-tenth o' Parker's luck they'd of heard about me long before yesterday.

They say my homer was lucky. Maybe it was; but, believe me, it was time things broke for me. They been breakin' for him all his life."

"Well," I said, "his luck must have gone back on him if he's in a hospital with nervous prostration."

"Nervous prostration nothin'," said Grimes. "He's in a hospital because his face is all out o' shape and he's ashamed to appear on the street. I don't usually do so much talkin' and I'm ravin' a little to-night because I've had a couple o' drinks; but——"

"Have another," said I, ringing for the waiter, "and talk some more."

"I made two hits yesterday," Grimes went on, "but the crowd only seen one. I busted up the game and the serious with the one they seen. The one they didn't see was the one I busted up a guy's map with—and Speed Parker was the guy. That's why he's in a hospital. He may be able to play ball next year; but I'll bet my share o' the dough that McGraw won't reco'nize him when he shows up at Marlin in the spring."

"When did this come off?" I asked. "And why?"

"It come off outside the clubhouse after yesterday's battle," he said; "and I hit him because he called me a name—a name I won't stand for from him."

"What did he call you?" I queried, expecting to hear one of the delicate epithets usually applied by conquered to conqueror on the diamond.

"'Horseshoes!'" was Grimes' amazing reply.

"But, good Lord!" I remonstrated, "I've heard of ball players calling each other that, and Lucky Stiff, and Fourleaf Clover, ever since I was a foot high, and I never knew them to start fights about it."

"Well," said Grimes, "I might as well give you all the dope; and then if you don't think I was justified I'll pay your fare from here to wherever you're goin'. I don't want you to think I'm kickin' about trifles—or that I'm kickin' at all, for that matter. I just want to prove to you that he didn't have no license to pull that Horseshoes stuff on me and that I only give him what was comin' to him."

"Go ahead and shoot," said I.

"Give us some more o' the same," said Grimes to the passing waiter. And then he told me about it.

Maybe you've heard that me and Speed Parker was raised in the same town—Ishpeming, Michigan. We was kids together, and though he done all the devilment I got all the lickin's. When we was about twelve years old Speed throwed a rotten egg at the teacher and I got expelled. That made me sick o' schools and I wouldn't never go to one again, though my ol' man beat me up and the truant officers threatened to have me hung.

Well, while Speed was learnin' what was the principal products o' New Hampshire and Texas I was workin' round the freight-house and drivin' a dray.

We'd both been playin' ball all our lives; and when the town organized a semi-pro club we got jobs with it. We was to draw two bucks apiece for each game and they played every Sunday. We played four games before we got our first pay. They was a hole in my pants pocket as big as the home plate, but I forgot about it and put the dough in there. It wasn't there when I got home. Speed didn't have no hole in his pocket—you can bet on that! Afterward the club hired a good outfielder and I was canned. They was huntin' for another third baseman too; but, o' course, they didn't find none and Speed held his job.

The next year they started the Northern Peninsula League. We landed with the home team. The league opened in May and blowed up the third week in June. They paid off all the outsiders first and then had just money enough left to settle with one of us two Ishpeming guys. The night they done the payin' I was out to my uncle's farm, so they settled with Speed and told me I'd have to wait for mine. I'm still waitin'!

Gene Higgins, who was manager o' the Battle Creek Club, lived in Houghton, and that winter we goes over and strikes him for a job. He give it to us and we busted in together two years ago last spring.

I had a good year down there. I hit over .300 and stole all the bases in sight. Speed got along good too, and they was several big-league scouts lookin' us over. The Chicago Cubs bought Speed outright and four clubs put in a draft for me. Three of 'em—Cleveland and the New York Giants and the Boston Nationals—needed outfielders bad, and it would of been a pipe for me to of made good with any of 'em. But who do you think got me? The same Chicago Cubs; and the only outfielders they had at that time was Schulte and Leach and Good and Williams and Stewart, and one or two others.

Well, I didn't figure I was any worse off than Speed. The Cubs had Zimmerman at third base and it didn't look like they was any danger of a busher beatin' him out; but Zimmerman goes and breaks his leg the second day o' the season—that's a year ago last April—and Speed jumps right in as a regular. Do you think anything like that could happen to Schulte or Leach, or any o' them outfielders? No, sir! I wore out my uniform slidin' up and down the bench and wonderin' whether they'd ship me to Fort Worth or Siberia.

Now I want to tell you about the miserable luck Speed had right off the reel. We was playin' at St. Louis. They had a one-run lead in the eighth, when their pitcher walked Speed with one out. Saier hits a high fly to centre and Parker starts with the crack o' the bat. Both coachers was yellin' at him to go back, but he thought they was two out and he was clear round to third base when the ball come down. And Oakes muffs it! O' course he scored and the game was tied up.

Parker come in to the bench like he'd did something wonderful.

"Did you think they was two out?" ast Hank.

"No," says Speed, blushin'.

"Then what did you run for?" says Hank.

"I had a hunch he was goin' to drop the ball," says Speed; and Hank pretty near falls off the bench.

The next day he come up with one out and the sacks full, and the score tied in the sixth. He smashes one on the ground straight at Hauser and it looked like a cinch double play; but just as Hauser was goin' to grab it the ball hit a rough spot and hopped a mile over his head. It got between Oakes and Magee and went clear to the fence. Three guys scored and Speed pulled up at third. The papers come out and said the game was won by a three-bagger from the bat o' Parker, the Cubs' sensational kid third baseman. Gosh!

We go home to Chi and are havin' a hot battle with Pittsburgh. This time Speed's turn come when they was two on and two out, and Pittsburgh a run to the good—I think it was the eighth innin'. Cooper gives him a fast one and he hits it straight up in the air. O' course the runners started goin', but it looked hopeless because they wasn't no wind or high sky to bother anybody. Mowrey and Gibson both goes after the ball; and just as Mowrey was set for the catch Gibson bumps into him and they both fall down. Two runs scored and Speed got to second. Then what does he do but try to steal third—with two out too! And Gibson's peg pretty near hits the left field seats on the fly.

When Speed comes to the bench Hank says:

" If I was you I'd quit playin' ball and go to Monte Carlo."

" What for ? " says Speed.

" You're so dam' lucky ! " says Hank.

" So is Ty Cobb," says Speed. That's how he hated himself !

First trip to Cincy we run into a couple of old Ishpeming boys. They took us out one night, and about twelve o'clock I said we'd have to go back to the hotel or we'd get fined. Speed said I had cold feet and he stuck with the boys. I went back alone and Hank caught me comin' in and put a fifty-dollar plaster on me. Speed stayed out all night long and Hank never knowed it. I says to myself : " Wait till he gets out there and tries to play ball without no sleep ! " But the game that day was called off on account o' rain. Can you beat it ?

I remember what he got away with the next afternoon the same as though it happened yesterday. In the second innin' they walked him with nobody down, and he took a big lead off first base like he always does. Benton throwed over there three or four times to scare him back, and the last time he throwed, Hobby hid the ball. The coacher seen it and told Speed to hold the bag ; but he didn't pay no attention. He started leadin' right off again and Hobby tried to tag him, but the ball slipped out of his hand and rolled about a yard away. Parker had plenty o' time to get back ; but, instead o' that, he starts for second. Hobby picked up the ball and shot it down to Groh—and Groh made a square muff.

Parker slides into the bag safe and then gets up and throws out his chest like he'd made the greatest play ever. When the ball's throwed back to Benton, Speed leads off about thirty foot and stands there in a trance. Clarke signs for a pitch-out and pegs down to second to nip him. He was caught flatfooted—that is, he would of been with a decent throw ; but Clarke's peg went pretty near to Latonia. Speed scored and strutted over to receive our hearty congratulations. Some o' the boys was laughin' and he thought they was laughin' with him instead of at him.

It was in the ninth, though, that he got by with one o' the worst I ever seen. The Reds was a run behind and Marsans was on third base with two out. Hobby, I think it was, hit one on the ground right at Speed and he picked it up clean. The crowd all got up and started for the exits. Marsans run toward the plate in the faint hope that the peg to first would be wild. All of a sudden the boys on the Cincy bench begun yellin' at him to slide, and he done so. He was way past the plate when Speed's throw got to Archer. The bonehead had shot the ball home instead o' to first base, thinkin' they was only one down. We was all crazy, believin' his nut play had let 'em tie it up; but he comes tearin' in, tellin' Archer to tag Marsans. So Jim walks over and tags the Cuban, who was brushin' off his uniform.

" You're out! " says Klem. " You never touched the plate."

I guess Marsans knowed the umps was right because he didn't make much of a holler. But Speed sure got a pannin' in the club-house.

" I suppose you knowed he was goin' to miss the plate! " says Hank sarcastic as he could.

Everybody on the club roasted him, but it didn't do no good.

Well, you know what happened to me. I only got into one game with the Cubs—one afternoon when Leach was sick. We was play-in' the Boston bunch and Tyler was workin' against us. I always had trouble with lefthanders and this was one of his good days. I couldn't see what he throwed up there. I got one foul durin' the afternoon's entertainment; and the wind was blowin' a hun-dred-mile gale, so that the best outfielder in the world couldn't judge a fly ball. That Boston bunch must of hit fifty of 'em and they all come to my field.

If I caught any I've forgot about it. Couple o' days after that I got notice o' my release to Indianapolis.

Parker kept right on all season doin' the blamedest things you ever heard of and gettin' by with 'em. One o' the boys told me about it later. If they was playin' a double-header in St. Louis, with the thermometer at 130 degrees, he'd get put out by the umps in the first innin' o' the first game. If he started to steal the catcher'd drop the pitch or somebody'd muff the throw. If he hit a pop fly the sun'd get in somebody's eyes. If he took a swell third strike with the bases full the umps would call it a ball. If he cut first base by twenty feet the umps would be readin' the mornin' paper.

Zimmerman's leg mended, so that he was all right by June; and then Saier got sick and they tried Speed at first base. He'd never saw the bag before; but things kept on breakin' for him and he played it like a house afire. The Cubs copped the pennant and Speed got in on the big dough, besides playin' a whale of a game through the whole serious.

Speed and me both went back to Ishpeming to spend the winter —though the Lord knows it ain't no winter resort. Our homes was there; and besides, in my case, they was a certain girl livin' in the old burg.

Parker, o' course, was the hero and the swell guy when we got home. He'd been in the World's Serious and had plenty o' dough in his kick. I come home with nothin' but my suitcase and a hard-luck story, which I kept to myself. I hadn't even went good enough in Indianapolis to be sure of a job there again.

That fall—last fall—an uncle o' Speed's died over in the Soo and left him ten thousand bucks. I had an uncle down in the Lower Peninsula who was worth five times that much—but he had good health!

This girl I spoke about was the prettiest thing I ever see. I'd went with her in the old days, and when I blew back I found she was still strong for me. They wasn't a great deal o' variety in Ishpeming for a girl to pick from. Her and I went to the dance every Saturday night and to church Sunday nights. I called on her Wednesday evenin's, besides takin' her to all the shows that come along—rotten as the most o' them was.

I never knowed Speed was makin' a play for this doll till along last Feb'uary. The minute I seen what was up I got busy. I took her out sleigh-ridin' and kept her out in the cold till she'd promised to marry me. We set the date for this fall—I figured I'd know better where I was at by that time.

Well, we didn't make no secret o' bein' engaged; down in the poolroom one night Speed come up and congratulated me. He says:

" You got a swell girl, Dick! I wouldn't mind bein' in your place. You're mighty lucky to cop her out—you old Horseshoes, you! "

" Horseshoes! " I says. " You got a fine license to call anybody Horseshoes! I suppose you ain't never had no luck? "

" Not like you," he says.

I was feelin' too good about grabbin' the girl to get sore at the time; but when I got to thinkin' about it a few minutes after-ward it made me mad clear through. What right did that bird have to talk about me bein' lucky?

Speed was playin' freeze-out at a table near the door, and when I started home some o' the boys with him says:

" Good night, Dick."

I said good night and then Speed looked up.

" Good night, Horseshoes! " he says.

That got my nanny this time.

" Shut up, you lucky stiff! " I says. " If you wasn't so dam' lucky you'd be sweepin' the streets." Then I walks on out.

I was too busy with the girl to see much o' Speed after that. He left home about the middle o' the month to go to Tampa with the Cubs. I got notice from Indianapolis that I was sold to Baltimore. I didn't care much about goin' there and I wasn't anxious to leave home under the circumstances, so I didn't report till late.

When I read in the papers along in April that Speed had been traded to Boston for a couple o' pitchers I thought: " Gee! He must of lost his rabbit's foot!" Because, even if the Cubs didn't cop again, they'd have a city serious with the White Sox and get a bunch o' dough that way. And they wasn't no chance in the world for the Boston Club to get nothin' but their salaries.

It wasn't another month, though, till Shafer, o' the Giants, quit baseball and McGraw was up against it for a third baseman. Next thing I knowed Speed was traded to New York and was with another winner—for they never was out o' first place all season.

I was gettin' along all right at Baltimore and Dunnie liked me; so I felt like I had somethin' more than just a one-year job—somethin' I could get married on. It was all framed that the weddin' was comin' off as soon as this season was over; so you can believe I was pullin' for October to hurry up and come.

One day in August, two months ago, Dunnie come in the clubhouse and handed me the news.

" Rube Oldring's busted his leg," he says, " and he's out for the rest o' the season. Connie's got a youngster named Joyce that he can stick in there, but he's got to have an extra outfielder. He's made me a good proposition for you and I'm goin' to let you go. It'll be pretty soft for you, because they got the pennant cinched and they'll cut you in on the big money."

" Yes," I says; " and when they're through with me they'll ship me to Hellangone, and I'll be draggin' down about seventy-five bucks a month next year."

" Nothin' like that," says Dunnie. " If he don't want you next season he's got to ask for waivers; and if you get out o' the big league you come right back here. That's all framed."

So that's how I come to get with the Ath-a-letics. Connie give me a nice, comf'table seat in one corner o' the bench and I had the pleasure o' watchin' a real ball club perform once every afternoon and sometimes twice.

Connie told me that as soon as they had the flag cinched he was goin' to lay off some o' his regulars and I'd get a chance to play.

Well, they cinched it the fourth day o' September and our next engagement was with Washin'ton on Labor Day. We had two

games and I was in both of 'em. And I broke in with my usual
lovely luck, because the pitchers I was ast to face was Boehling, a
nasty lefthander, and this guy Johnson.

The mornin' game was Boehling's and he wasn't no worse than
some o' the rest of his kind. I only whiffed once and would of
had a triple if Milan hadn't run from here to New Orleans and
stole one off me.

I'm not boastin' about my first experience with Johnson though.
They can't never tell me he throws them balls with his arm. He's
got a gun concealed about his person and he shoots 'em up there.
I was leadin' off in Murphy's place and the game was a little delayed in startin', because I'd watched the big guy warm up and
wasn't in no hurry to get to that plate. Before I left the bench
Connie says:

" Don't try to take no healthy swing. Just meet 'em and you'll
get along better."

So I tried to just meet the first one he throwed; but when I
stuck out my bat Henry was throwin' the pill back to Johnson.
Then I thought: Maybe if I start swingin' now at the second one
I'll hit the third one. So I let the second one come over and the
umps guessed it was another strike, though I'll bet a thousand
bucks he couldn't see it no more'n I could.

While Johnson was still windin' up to pitch again I started to
swing—and the big cuss crosses me with a slow one. I lunged at
it twice and missed it both times, and the force o' my wallop
throwed me clean back to the bench. The Ath-a-letics was all
laughin' at me and I laughed too, because I was glad that much
of it was over.

McInnes gets a base hit off him in the second innin' and I ast
him how he done it.

" He's a friend o' mine," says Jack, " and he lets up when he
pitches to me."

I made up my mind right there that if I was goin' to be in the
league next year I'd go out and visit Johnson this winter and get
acquainted.

I wished before the day was over that I was hittin' in the catcher's place, because the fellers down near the tail-end of the battin'
order only had to face him three times. He fanned me on three
pitched balls again in the third, and when I come up in the sixth
he scared me to death by pretty near beanin' me with the first one.

" Be careful! " says Henry. " He's gettin' pretty wild and he's
liable to knock you away from your uniform."

"Don't he never curve one?" I ast.

"Sure!" says Henry. "Do you want to see his curve?"

"Yes," I says, knowin' the hook couldn't be no worse'n the fast one.

So he give me three hooks in succession and I missed 'em all; but I felt more comf'table than when I was duckin' his fast ball. In the ninth he hit my bat with a curve and the ball went on the ground to McBride. He booted it, but throwed me out easy—because I was so surprised at not havin' whiffed that I forgot to run!

Well, I went along like that for the rest o' the season, runnin' up against the best pitchers in the league and not exactly murderin' 'em. Everything I tried went wrong, and I was smart enough to know that if anything had depended on the games I wouldn't of been in there for two minutes. Joyce and Strunk and Murphy wasn't jealous o' me a bit; but they was glad to take turns restin', and I didn't care much how I went so long as I was sure of a job next year.

I'd wrote to the girl a couple o' times askin' her to set the exact date for our weddin'; but she hadn't paid no attention. She said she was glad I was with the Ath-a-letics, but she thought the Giants was goin' to beat us. I might of suspected from that that somethin' was wrong, because not even a girl would pick the Giants to trim that bunch of ourn. Finally, the day before the serious started, I sent her a kind o' sassy letter sayin' I guessed it was up to me to name the day, and askin' whether October twentieth was all right. I told her to wire me yes or no.

I'd been readin' the dope about Speed all season, and I knowed he'd had a whale of a year and that his luck was right with him; but I never dreamed a man could have the Lord on his side as strong as Speed did in that World's Serious! I might as well tell you all the dope, so long as you wasn't there.

The first game was on our grounds and Connie give us a talkin' to in the clubhouse beforehand.

"The shorter this serious is," he says, "the better for us. If it's a long serious we're goin' to have trouble, because McGraw's got five pitchers he can work and we've got about three; so I want you boys to go at 'em from the jump and play 'em off their feet. Don't take things easy, because it ain't goin' to be no snap. Just because we've licked 'em before ain't no sign we'll do it this time."

Then he calls me to one side and ast me what I knowed about Parker.

"You was with the Cubs when he was, wasn't you?" he says.

"Yes," I says; "and he's the luckiest stiff you ever seen! If he got stewed and fell in the gutter he'd catch a fish."

"I don't like to hear a good ball player called lucky," says Connie. "He must have a lot of ability or McGraw wouldn't use him regular. And he's been hittin' about .340 and played a bang-up game at third base. That can't be all luck."

"Wait till you see him," I says; "and if you don't say he's the luckiest guy in the world you can sell me to the Boston Bloomer Girls. He's so lucky," I says, "that if they traded him to the St. Louis Browns they'd have the pennant cinched by the Fourth o' July."

And I'll bet Connie was willin' to agree with me before it was over.

Well, the Chief worked against the Big Rube in that game. We beat 'em, but they give us a battle and it was Parker that made it close. We'd gone along nothin' and nothin' till the seventh, and then Rube walks Collins and Baker lifts one over that little old wall. You'd think by this time them New York pitchers would know better than to give that guy anything he can hit.

In their part o' the ninth the Chief still had 'em shut out and two down, and the crowd was goin' home; but Doyle gets hit in the sleeve with a pitched ball and it's Speed's turn. He hits a foul pretty near straight up, but Schang misjudges it. Then he lifts another one and this time McInnes drops it. He'd ought to of been out twice. The Chief tries to make him hit at a bad one then, because he'd got him two strikes and nothin'. He hit at it all right—kissed it for three bases between Strunk and Joyce! And it was a wild pitch that he hit. Doyle scores, o' course, and the bugs suddenly decide not to go home just yet. I fully expected to see him steal home and get away with it, but Murray cut into the first ball and lined out to Barry.

Plank beat Matty two to one the next day in New York, and again Speed and his rabbit's foot give us an awful argument. Matty wasn't so good as usual and we really ought to of beat him bad. Two different times Strunk was on second waitin' for any kind o' wallop, and both times Barry cracked 'em down the third-base line like a shot. Speed stopped the first one with his stomach and extricated the pill just in time to nail Barry at first base and retire the side. The next time he throwed his glove in front of his face in self-defense and the ball stuck in it.

In the sixth innin' Schang was on third base and Plank on first, and two down, and Murphy combed an awful one to Speed's left.

He didn't have time to stoop over and he just stuck out his foot. The ball hit it and caromed in two hops right into Doyle's hands on second base before Plank got there. Then in the seventh Speed bunts one and Baker trips and falls goin' after it or he'd of threw him out a mile. They was two gone; so Speed steals second, and, o' course, Schang has to make a bad peg right at that time and lets him go to third. Then Collins boots one on Murray and they've got a run. But it didn't do 'em no good, because Collins and Baker and McInnes come up in the ninth and walloped 'em where Parker couldn't reach 'em.

Comin' back to Philly on the train that night, I says to Connie: " What do you think o' that Parker bird now? "

" He's lucky, all right," says Connie smilin'; " but we won't hold it against him if he don't beat us with it."

" It ain't too late," I says. " He ain't pulled his real stuff yet."

The whole bunch was talkin' about him and his luck, and sayin' it was about time for things to break against him. I warned 'em that they wasn't no chance—that it was permanent with him.

Bush and Tesreau hooked up next day and neither o' them had much stuff. Everybody was hittin' and it looked like anybody's game right up to the ninth. Speed had got on every time he come up—the wind blowin' his fly balls away from the outfielders and the infielders bootin' when he hit 'em on the ground.

When the ninth started the score was seven apiece. Connie and McGraw both had their whole pitchin' staffs warmin' up. The crowd was wild, because they'd been all kinds of action. They wasn't no danger of anybody's leavin' their seats before this game was over.

Well, Bescher is walked to start with and Connie's about ready to give Bush the hook; but Doyle pops out tryin' to bunt. Then Speed gets two strikes and two balls, and it looked to me like the next one was right over the heart; but Connolly calls it a ball and gives him another chance. He whales the groove ball to the fence in left center and gets round to third on it, while Bescher scores. Right then Bush comes out and the Chief goes in. He whiffs Murray and has two strikes on Merkle when Speed makes a break for home—and, o' course, that was the one ball Schang dropped in the whole serious!

They had a two-run lead on us then and it looked like a cinch for them to hold it, because the minute Tesreau showed a sign o' weakenin' McGraw was sure to holler for Matty or the Rube. But you know how quick that bunch of ourn can make a two-run lead look sick. Before McGraw could get Jeff out o' there we had two on the bases.

Then Rube comes in and fills 'em up by walkin' Joyce. It was Eddie's turn to wallop and if he didn't do nothin' we had Baker comin' up next. This time Collins saved Baker the trouble and whanged one clear to the woods. Everybody scored but him—and he could of, too, if it'd been necessary.

In the clubhouse the boys naturally felt pretty good. We'd copped three in a row and it looked like we'd make it four straight, because we had the Chief to send back at 'em the followin' day.

"Your friend Parker is lucky," the boys says to me, "but it don't look like he could stop us now."

I felt the same way and was consultin' the time-tables to see whether I could get a train out o' New York for the West next evenin'. But do you think Speed's luck was ready to quit? Not yet! And it's a wonder we didn't all go nuts durin' the next few days. If words could kill, Speed would of died a thousand times. And I wish he had!

They wasn't no record-breakin' crowd out when we got to the Polo Grounds. I guess the New York bugs was pretty well discouraged and the bettin' was eight to five that we'd cop that battle and finish it. The Chief was the only guy that warmed up for us and McGraw didn't have no choice but to use Matty, with the whole thing dependin' on this game.

They went along like the two swell pitchers they was till Speed's innin', which in this battle was the eighth. Nobody scored, and it didn't look like they was ever goin' to till Murphy starts off that round with a perfect bunt and Joyce sacrifices him to second. All Matty had to do then was to get rid o' Collins and Baker—and that's about as easy as sellin' silk socks to an Eskimo.

He didn't give Eddie nothin' he wanted to hit, though; and finally he slaps one on the ground to Doyle. Larry made the play to first base and Murphy moved to third. We all figured Matty'd walk Baker then, and he done it. Connie sends Baker down to second on the first pitch to McInnes, but Meyers don't pay no attention to him—they was playin' for McInnes and wasn't takin' no chances o' throwin' the ball away.

Well, the count goes to three and two on McInnes and Matty comes with a curve—he's got some curve too; but Jack happened to meet it and—Blooie! Down the left foul line where he always hits! I never seen a ball hit so hard in my life. No infielder in the world could of stopped it. But I'll give you a thousand bucks if that ball didn't go kerplunk right into the third bag and stop as dead as George Washington! It was child's play for Speed to pick it up and heave it over to Merkle before Jack got there. If anybody else had been playin' third base the bag would of ducked out o' the way o' that wallop; but even the bases themselves was helpin' him out.

The two runs we ought to of had on Jack's smash would of been just enough to beat 'em, because they got the only run o' the game in their half—or, I should say, the Lord give it to 'em.

Doyle'd been throwed out and up come Parker, smilin'. The minute I seen him smile I felt like somethin' was comin' off and I made the remark on the bench.

Well, the Chief pitched one right at him and he tried to duck. The ball hit his bat and went on a line between Jack and Eddie. Speed didn't know he'd hit it till the guys on the bench wised him up. Then he just had time to get to first base. They tried the hit-and-run on the second ball and Murray lifts a high fly that Murphy didn't have to move for. Collins pulled the old bluff about the ball bein' on the ground and Barry yells, " Go on! Go on!" like he was the coacher. Speed fell for it and didn't know where the ball was no more'n a rabbit; he just run his fool head off and we was gettin' all ready to laugh when the ball come down and Murphy dropped it!

If Parker had stuck near first base, like he ought to of done, he couldn't of got no farther'n second; but with the start he got he was pretty near third when Murphy made the muff, and it was a cinch for him to score. The next two guys was easy outs; so they wouldn't of had a run except for Speed's boner. We couldn't do nothin' in the ninth and we was licked.

Well, that was a tough one to lose; but we figured that Matty was through and we'd wind it up the next day, as we had Plank ready to send back at 'em. We wasn't afraid o' the Rube, because he hadn't never bothered Collins and Baker much.

The two lefthanders come together just like everybody'd doped it and it was about even up to the eighth. Plank had been goin' great and, though the score was two and two, they'd got their two on boots and we'd hit ourn in. We went after Rube in our part o' the eighth and knocked him out. Demaree stopped us after we'd scored two more.

" It's all over but the shoutin'! " says Davis on the bench.

" Yes," I says, " unless that seventh son of a seventh son gets up there again."

He did, and he come up after they'd filled the bases with a boot, a base hit and a walk with two out. I says to Davis:

"If I was Plank I'd pass him and give 'em one run."

"That wouldn't be no baseball," says Davis—"not with Murray comin' up."

Well, it mayn't of been no baseball, but it couldn't of turned out worse if they'd did it that way. Speed took a healthy at the first ball; but it was a hook and he caught it on the handle, right up near his hands. It started outside the first-base line like a foul and then changed its mind and rolled in. Schang run away from the plate, because it looked like it was up to him to make the play. He picked the ball up and had to make the peg in a hurry.

His throw hit Speed right on top o' the head and bounded off like it had struck a cement sidewalk. It went clear over to the seats and before McInnes could got it three guys had scored and Speed was on third base. He was left there, but that didn't make no difference. We was licked again and for the first time the gang really begun to get scared.

We went over to New York Sunday afternoon and we didn't do no singin' on the way. Some o' the fellers tried to laugh, but it hurt 'em. Connie sent us to bed early, but I don't believe none o' the bunch got much sleep—I know I didn't; I was worryin' too much about the serious and also about the girl, who hadn't sent me no telegram like I'd ast her to. Monday mornin' I wired her askin' what was the matter and tellin' her I was gettin' tired of her foolishness. O' course I didn't make it so strong as that— but the telegram cost me a dollar and forty cents.

Connie had the choice o' two pitchers for the sixth game. He could use Bush, who'd been slammed round pretty hard last time out, or the Chief, who'd only had two days' rest. The rest of 'em —outside o' Plank—had a epidemic o' sore arms. Connie finally picked Bush, so's he could have the Chief in reserve in case we had to play a seventh game. McGraw started Big Jeff and we went at it.

It wasn't like the last time these two guys had hooked up. This time they both had somethin', and for eight innin's runs was as scarce as Chinese policemen. They'd been chances to score on both sides, but the big guy and Bush was both tight in the pinches. The crowd was plumb nuts and yelled like Indians every time a fly ball was caught or a strike called. They'd of got their money's worth if they hadn't been no ninth; but, believe me, that was some round!

They was one out when Barry hit one through the box for a base. Schang walked, and it was Bush's turn. Connie told him to bunt, but he whiffed in the attempt. Then Murphy comes up and walks—and the bases are choked. Young Joyce had been pie for Tesreau all day or else McGraw might of changed pitchers right there. Anyway he left Big Jeff in and he beaned Joyce with a fast one. It sounded like a tire blowin' out. Joyce falls over in a heap and we chase out there, thinkin' he's dead; but he ain't, and pretty soon he gets up and walks down to first base. Tesreau had forced in a run and again we begun to count the winner's end. Matty comes in to prevent further damage and Collins flies the side out.

"Hold 'em now! Work hard!" we says to young Bush, and he walks out there just as cool as though he was goin' to hit fungoes.

McGraw sends up a pinch hitter for Matty and Bush whiffed him. Then Bescher flied out. I was prayin' that Doyle would end it, because Speed's turn come after his'n; so I pretty near fell dead when Larry hit safe.

Speed had his old smile and even more chest than usual when he come up there, swingin' five or six bats. He didn't wait for Doyle to try and steal, or nothin'. He lit into the first ball, though Bush was tryin' to waste it. I seen the ball go high in the air toward left field, and then I picked up my glove and got ready to beat it for the gate. But when I looked out to see if Joyce was set, what do you think I seen? He was lyin' flat on the ground! That blow on the head had got him just as Bush was pitchin' to Speed. He'd flopped over and didn't no more know what was goin' on than if he'd croaked.

Well, everybody else seen it at the same time; but it was too late. Strunk made a run for the ball, but they wasn't no chance for him to get near it. It hit the ground about ten feet back o' where Joyce was lyin' and bounded way over to the end o' the foul line. You don't have to be told that Doyle and Parker both scored and the serious was tied up.

We carried Joyce to the clubhouse and after a while he come to. He cried when he found out what had happened. We cheered him up all we could, but he was a pretty sick guy. The trainer said he'd be all right, though, for the final game.

They tossed up a coin to see where they'd play the seventh battle and our club won the toss; so we went back to Philly that night and cussed Parker clear across New Jersey. I was so sore I kicked the stuffin' out o' my seat.

You probably heard about the excitement in the burg yesterday mornin'. The demand for tickets was somethin' fierce and some of 'em sold for as high as twenty-five bucks apiece. Our club hadn't been lookin' for no seventh game and they was some tall hustlin' done round that old ball park.

I started out to the grounds early and bought some New York papers to read on the car. They was a big story that Speed Parker, the Giants' hero, was goin' to be married a week after the end o' the serious. It didn't give the name o' the girl, sayin' Speed had refused to tell it. I figured she must be some dame he'd met round the circuit somewheres.

They was another story by one o' them smart baseball reporters sayin' that Parker, on his way up to the plate, had saw that Joyce was about ready to faint and had hit the fly ball to left field on purpose. Can you beat it?

I was goin' to show that to the boys in the clubhouse, but the minute I blowed in there I got some news that made me forget about everything else. Joyce was very sick and they'd took him to a hospital. It was up to me to play!

Connie come over and ast me whether I'd ever hit against Matty. I told him I hadn't, but I'd saw enough of him to know he wasn't no worse'n Johnson. He told me he was goin' to let me hit second—in Joyce's place—because he didn't want to bust up the rest of his combination. He also told me to take my orders from Strunk about where to play for the batters.

"Where shall I play for Parker?" I says, tryin' to joke and pretend I wasn't scared to death.

"I wisht I could tell you," says Connie. "I guess the only thing to do when he comes up is to get down on your knees and pray."

The rest o' the bunch slapped me on the back and give me all the encouragement they could. The place was jammed when we went out on the field. They may of been bigger crowds before, but they never was packed together so tight. I doubt whether they was even room enough left for Falkenberg to sit down.

The afternoon papers had printed the stuff about Joyce bein' out of it, so the bugs was wise that I was goin' to play. They watched me pretty close in battin' practice and give me a hand whenever I managed to hit one hard. When I was out catchin' fungoes the guys in the bleachers cheered me and told me they was with me; but I don't mind tellin' you that I was as nervous as a bride.

They wasn't no need for the announcers to tip the crowd off to the pitchers. Everybody in the United States and Cuba knowed that the Chief'd work for us and Matty for them. The Chief didn't have no trouble with 'em in the first innin'. Even from where I stood I could see that he had a lot o' stuff. Bescher and Doyle popped out and Speed whiffed.

Well, I started out makin' good, with reverse English, in our part. Fletcher booted Murphy's ground ball and I was sent up to sacrifice. I done a complete job of it—sacrificin' not only myself but Murphy with a pop fly that Matty didn't have to move for. That spoiled whatever chance we had o' gettin' the jump on 'em; but the boys didn't bawl me for it.

"That's all right, old boy. You're all right!" they said on the bench—if they'd had a gun they'd of shot me.

I didn't drop no fly balls in the first six innin's—because none was hit out my way. The Chief was so good that they wasn't hittin' nothin' out o' the infield. And we wasn't doin' nothin' with Matty, either. I led off in the fourth and fouled the first one. I didn't molest the other two. But if Connie and the gang talked about me they done it internally. I come up again—with Murphy on third base and two gone in the sixth, and done my little whiffin' specialty. And still the only people that panned me was the thirty thousand that had paid for the privilege!

My first fieldin' chance come in the seventh. You'd of thought that I'd of had my nerve back by that time; but I was just as scared as though I'd never saw a crowd before. It was just as well that they was two out when Merkle hit one to me. I staggered under it and finally it hit me on the shoulder. Merkle got to second, but the Chief whiffed the next guy. I was gave some cross looks on the bench and I shouldn't of blamed the fellers if they'd cut loose with some language; but they didn't.

They's no use in me tellin' you about none o' the rest of it— except what happened just before the start o' the eleventh and durin' that innin', which was sure the big one o' yesterday's pastime—both for Speed and yours sincerely.

The scoreboard was still a row o' ciphers and Speed'd had only a fair amount o' luck. He'd made a scratch base hit and robbed our bunch of a couple o' real ones with impossible stops.

When Schang flied out and wound up our tenth I was leanin' against the end of our bench. I heard my name spoke, and I turned round and seen a boy at the door.

"Right here!" I says; and he give me a telegram.

"Better not open it till after the game," says Connie.

"Oh, no; it ain't no bad news," I said, for I figured it was an answer from the girl. So I opened it up and read it on the way to my position. It said:

"Forgive me, Dick—and forgive Speed too. Letter follows."

Well, sir, I ain't no baby, but for a minute I just wanted to sit down and bawl. And then, all of a sudden, I got so mad I couldn't see. I run right into Baker as he was pickin' up his glove. Then I give him a shove and called him some name, and him and Barry both looked at me like I was crazy—and I was. When I got out in left field I stepped on my own foot and spiked it. I just had to hurt somebody.

As I remember it the Chief fanned the first two of 'em. Then Doyle catches one just right and lams it up against the fence back o' Murphy. The ball caromed round some and Doyle got all the way to third base. Next thing I seen was Speed struttin' up to the plate. I run clear in from my position.

"Kill him!" I says to the Chief. "Hit him in the head and kill him, and I'll go to jail for it!"

"Are you off your nut?" says the Chief. "Go out there and play ball—and quit ravin'."

Barry and Baker led me away and give me a shove out toward left. Then I heard the crack o' the bat and I seen the ball comin' a mile a minute. It was headed between Strunk and I and looked like it would go out o' the park. I don't remember runnin' or nothin' about it till I run into the concrete wall head first. They told me afterward and all the papers said that it was the greatest catch ever seen. And I never knowed I'd caught the ball!

Some o' the managers have said my head was pretty hard, but it wasn't as hard as that concrete. I was pretty near out, but they tell me I walked to the bench like I wasn't hurt at all. They also tell me that the crowd was a bunch o' ravin' maniacs and was throwin' money at me. I guess the ground-keeper'll get it.

The boys on the bench was all talkin' at once and slappin' me on the back, but I didn't know what it was about. Somebody told me pretty soon that it was my turn to hit and I picked up the first bat I come to and starts for the plate. McInnes come runnin' after me and ast me whether I didn't want my own bat. I cussed him and told him to mind his own business.

I didn't know it at the time, but I found out afterward that they was two out. The bases was empty. I'll tell you just what I had in my mind: I wasn't thinkin' about the ball game; I was determined that I was goin' to get to third base and give that guy my spikes. If I didn't hit one worth three bases, or if I didn't hit one at all, I was goin' to run till I got round to where Speed was, and then slide into him and cut him to pieces!

Right now I can't tell you whether I hit a fast ball, or a slow ball, or a hook, or a fader—but I hit somethin'. It went over Bescher's head like a shot and then took a crazy bound. It must of struck a rock or a pop bottle, because it hopped clear over the fence and landed in the bleachers.

Mind you, I learned this afterward. At the time I just knowed I'd hit one somewheres and I starts round the bases. I speeded up when I got near third and took a runnin' jump at a guy I thought was Parker. I missed him and sprawled all over the bag. Then, all of a sudden, I come to my senses. All the Ath-a-letics was out there to run home with me and it was one o' them I'd tried to cut. Speed had left the field. The boys picked me up and seen to it that I went on and touched the plate. Then I was carried into the clubhouse by the crazy bugs.

Well, they had a celebration in there and it was a long time before I got a chance to change my clothes. The boys made a big fuss over me. They told me they'd intended to give me five hundred bucks for my divvy, but now I was goin' to get a full share.

"Parker ain't the only lucky guy!" says one of 'em. "But even if that ball hadn't of took that crazy hop you'd of had a triple."

A triple! That's just what I'd wanted; and he called me lucky for not gettin' it!

The Giants was dressin' in the other part o' the clubhouse; and when I finally come out there was Speed, standin' waitin' for some o' the others. He seen me comin' and he smiled. "Hello, Horseshoes!" he says.

He won't smile no more for a while—it'll hurt too much. And if any girl wants him when she sees him now—with his nose over shakin' hands with his ear, and his jaw a couple o' feet foul— she's welcome to him. They won't be no contest!

Grimes leaned over to ring for the waiter.

"Well," he said, "what about it?"

"You won't have to pay my fare," I told him.

"I'll buy a drink anyway," said he. "You've been a good listener—and I had to get it off my chest."

"Maybe they'll have to postpone the wedding," I said.

" No," said Grimes. " The weddin' will take place the day after tomorrow—and I'll bat for Mr. Parker. Did you think I was goin' to let him get away with it ? "

" What about next year ? " I asked.

" I'm goin' back to the Ath-a-letics," he said. "And I'm goin' to hire somebody to call me ' Horseshoes ! ' before every game—because I can sure play that old baseball when I'm mad."

XXI

THERE ARE SMILES

AT the busy corner of Fifth Avenue and Forty-sixth Street there was, last summer, a traffic policeman who made you feel that he didn't have such a terrible job after all. Lots of traffic policemen seem to enjoy abusing you, sadistic complex induced by exposure to bad weather and worse drivers, and, possibly, brutal wives. But Ben Collins just naturally appeared to be having a good time whether he was scolding you or not; his large freckled face fairly beamed with joviality and refused to cloud up even under the most trying conditions.

It heartened you to look at him. It amused you to hear him talk. If what he said wasn't always so bright, the way he said it was.

Ben was around thirty years old. He was six feet four inches tall and weighed two hundred and eighteen pounds. This describes about eighty per cent of all the traffic officers between Thirty-second Street and the Park. But Ben was distinguished from the rest by his habitual good humor and—well, I guess you'd have to call it his subtlety.

For example, where Noonan or Wurtz or Carmody was content with the stock " Hey! Get over where you belong! " or " Where the hell do you think you're going? " Ben was wont to finesse.

" How are you, Barney? " he would say to a victim halted at the curb.

" My name isn't Barney."

" I beg your pardon. The way you was stepping along, I figured you must be Barney Oldfield."

Or, " I suppose you didn't see that red light."

" No."

" Well, what did you think the other cars was stopped for? Did you think they'd all ran out of gas at once? "

Or, " What business are you in? "

" I'm a contractor."

" Well, that's a good, honorable business and, if I was you, I wouldn't be ashamed of it. I'd quit trying to make people believe I was in the fire department."

Or, " How do you like London ? "

" Me ? I've never been there."

" I thought that's where you got the habit of driving on the wrong side of the street."

Transgressions at Ben's corner, unless they resulted seriously, were seldom punished beyond these sly rebukes, which were delivered in such a nice way that you were kind of glad you had done wrong.

Off duty he was " a big good-natured boy," willing to take Grace to a picture, or go over to the Arnolds' and play cards, or just stay at home and do nothing.

And then one morning in September, a dazzlingly new Cadillac roadster, blue with yellow trimmings, flashed down from the north, violating all the laws of common sense and of the State and City of New York. Shouts and whistles from Carmody and Noonan, at Forty-eighth and Forty-seventh, failed to check its crazy career, but Ben, first planting his huge bulk directly in its path, giving the driver the choice of slackening speed or running into him, and then, with an alertness surprising in one so massive, sidestepping and jumping onto the running-board, succeeded in forcing a surrender at the curb half-way between his post and Forty-fifth Street.

He was almost mad and about to speak his mind in words beginning with capitals when he got his first look at the miscreant's face. It was the prettiest face he had ever seen and it wore a most impudent, ill-timed, irresistible smile, a smile that spoiled other smiles for you once for all.

" Well—" Ben began falteringly ; then recovering something of his stage presence : " Where's your helmet ? "

She made no reply, but continued to smile.

" If you're in the fire department," said Ben, " you ought to wear a helmet and a badge. Or paint your car red and get a sireen."

Still no reply.

" Maybe I look like a bobby. Maybe you thought you was in London where they drive on the left side of the street."

" You're cute," she said, and her voice was as thrilling as her smile. " I could stay here all morning and listen to you. That is, I could, but I can't. I've got a date down on Eighth Street and I'm late for it now. And I know you're busy, too. So we mustn't keep each other any longer now. But I'd like to hear your whole line some day."

" Oh, you would ! "

" Where do you live? "

" At home."

" That isn't very polite, is it? I was thinking you might live in the Bronx——"

" I do."

"—and that's on the way to Rye, where I live, so I might drive you."

" Thanks. When I die, I want to die of old age."

" Oh, I'm not a bad driver, really. I do like to go fast, but I'm careful. In Buffalo, where we lived before, the policemen all knew I was careful and they generally let me go as fast as I wanted to."

" This ain't Buffalo. And this ain't no speedway. If you want to go fast, stay off Fifth Avenue."

The girl looked him right in the eye. " Would you like that? "

" No," said Ben.

She smiled at him again. " What time are you through? "

" Four o'clock," said Ben.

" Well," said the girl, " some afternoon I may be going home about then——"

" I told you I wasn't ready to die."

" I'd be extra careful."

Ben suddenly realized that they were playing to a large staring audience and that, for once, he was not the star.

" Drive on ! " he said in his gruffest tone. " I'm letting you go because you're a stranger, but you won't get off so easy next time."

" I'm very, very grateful," said the girl. " Just the same I don't like being a stranger and I hope you won't excuse me on that ground again."

Which remark, accompanied by her radiant smile, caused Mr. Collins, hitherto only a bathroom singer, to hum quite loudly all the rest of his working day snatches of a gay Ohman and Arden record that his wife had played over and over the night before.

His relief, Tim Martin, appeared promptly at four, but Ben seemed in no hurry to go home. He pretended to listen to two new ones Tim had heard on the way in from Flushing, one about a Scotchman and some hotel towels and one about two Heebs in a night club. He managed to laugh in the right place, but his attention was on the northbound traffic, which was now none of his business.

At twenty minutes past four he said good-by to Martin and

walked slowly south on the east side of the street. He walked as far as Thirty-sixth, in vain. Usually he caught a ride home with some Bronx or north suburban motorist, but now he was late and had to pay for his folly by hurrying to Grand Central and standing up in a subway express.

"I was a sucker!" he thought. "She probably drove up some other street on purpose to miss me. Or she might have came in on one of them cross streets after I'd walked past it. I ought to stuck at Forty-fourth a while longer. Or maybe some other fella done his duty and had her locked up. Not if she smiled at him, though."

But she wouldn't smile like that at everybody. She had smiled at him because she liked him, because she really thought he was cute. Yes, she did! That was her regular line. That was how she had worked on them Buffalo fellas. "Cute!" A fine word to use on a human Woolworth Building. She was kidding. No, she wasn't; not entirely. She'd liked his looks as plenty other gals had, and maybe that stuff about the fire department and London had tickled her.

Anyway, he had seen the most wonderful smile in the world and he still felt warm from it when he got home, so warm that he kissed his wife with a fervor that surprised her.

When Ben was on the day shift, he sometimes entertained Grace at supper with an amusing incident or two of his work. Sometimes his stories were pure fiction and she suspected as much, but what difference did it make? They were things that ought to have happened even if they hadn't.

On this occasion he was wild to talk about the girl from Rye, but he had learned that his wife did not care much for anecdotes concerning pretty women. So he recounted one-sided arguments with bungling drivers of his own sex which had very little foundation in fact.

"There was a fella coming south in a 1922 Buick and the light changed and when it was time to go again, he thought he was starting in second, and it was reverse instead, and he backed into a big Pierce from Greenwich. He didn't do no damage to the Pierce and only bent himself a little. But they'd have held up the parade ten minutes talking it over if I hadn't bore down.

"I got the Buick fella over to the curb and I said to him, 'What's the matter? Are you homesick?' So he said what did I mean, homesick, and I said, 'Well, you was so anxious to get back to wherever you come from that you couldn't even wait to turn around.'

" Then he tried to explain what was the matter, just like I didn't know. He said this was his first trip in a Buick and he was used to a regular gear shift.

" I said, ' That's fine, but this ain't no training-camp. The place to practice driving is four blocks farther down, at Forty-second. You'll find more automobiles there and twicet as many pedestrians and policemen, and besides, they've got street-cars and a tower to back into.'

" I said, ' You won't never learn nothing in a desert like this.' You ought to heard the people laugh."

" I can imagine ! " said Grace.

" Then there was a Jordan, an old guy with a gray beard. He was going to park right in front of Kaskel's. He said he wouldn't be more than half an hour. I said, ' Oh, that's too bad ! I wished you could spend the weekend.' I said, ' If you'd let us knew you was coming, we'd have arranged some parties for you.' So he said, ' I've got a notion to report you for being too fresh.'

" So I said, ' If you do that, I'll have you arrested for driving without your parents' consent.' You ought to have heard them laugh. I said, ' Roll, Jordan, roll ! ' You ought to have heard them."

" I'll bet ! " said Grace.

Ben fell into a long, unaccustomed silence.

" What are you thinking about ? "

It came out against his better judgment. " There was a gal in a blue Cadillac."

" Oh ! There was ! What about her ? "

" Nothing. Only she acted like it was her Avenue and I give her hell."

" What did you say to her ? "

" I forget."

" Was she pretty ? "

" I didn't notice. I was sore."

" You ! "

" She all but knocked me for a corpse."

" And you probably just smiled at her."

" No. She done the smiling. She smiled——" He broke off and rose from the table. " Come on, babe. Let's go to the Franklin. Joe Frisco's there. And a Chaplin picture."

Ben saw nothing of the blue Cadillac or its mistress the rest of that week, but in all his polemics he was rehearsing lines aimed to strengthen her belief in his "cuteness." When she suddenly appeared, however, late on the following Tuesday afternoon, he was too excited to do anything but stare, and he would have lost an opportunity of hearing her enchanting voice if she hadn't taken the initiative. Northbound, she stopped at the curb a few feet above his corner and beckoned to him.

"It's after four," she said. "Can't I drive you home?"

What a break! It was his week on the late shift.

"I just come to work. I won't be off till midnight."

"You're mean! You didn't tell me you were going to change."

"I change every week. Last week, eight to four; this week, four to twelve."

"And next week eight to four?"

"Yes'm."

"Well, I'll just have to wait."

He couldn't say a word.

"Next Monday?"

He made an effort. "If you live."

She smiled that smile. "I'll live," she said. "There's an incentive."

She was on her way and Ben returned to his station, dizzy.

"Incentive, incentive, incentive," he repeated to himself, memorizing it, but when he got home at half past one, he couldn't find it in Grace's abridged Webster; he thought it was spelled with an *s*.

The longest week in history ended. A little before noon on Monday the Cadillac whizzed past him going south and he caught the word "later." At quitting time, while Tim Martin was still in the midst of his first new one about two or more Heebs, Ben was all at once aware that she had stopped right beside him, was blocking the traffic, waiting for him.

Then he was in her car, constricting his huge bulk to fit it and laughing like a child at Tim's indelicate ejaculation of surprise.

"What are you laughing at?"

"Nothing. I just feel good."

"Are you glad to be through?"

"Yes. Today."

"Not always?"

"I don't generally care much."

"I don't believe you do. I believe you enjoy your job. And I don't see how you can because it seems to me such a hard job. I'm going to make you tell me all about it as soon as we get out of this jam."

A red light stopped them at Fifty-first Street and she turned and looked at him amusedly.

" It's a good thing the top is down," she said. " You'd have been hideously uncomfortable in one more fold."

" When I get a car of my own," said Ben, " it'll have to be a Mack, and even then I'll have to hire a man to drive it."

" Why a man? "

" Men ain't all crazy."

" Honestly, I'm not crazy. Have I come near hitting anything? "

" You've just missed everything. You drive too fast and you take too many chances. But I knew it before I got in, so I can't kick."

" There isn't room for you to, anyway. Do you want to get out? "

" No."

" I doubt if you could. Where do you live? "

" Hundred and sixty-fourth, near the Concourse," said Ben.

" How do you usually go home? "

" Like this."

" And I thought I was saving you from a tiresome subway ride or something. I ought to have known you'd never lack invitations. Do you? "

" Hardly ever."

" Do the people ask you all kinds of questions? "

" Yes."

" I'm sorry. Because I wanted to and now I can't."

" Why not? "

" You must be tired of answering."

" I don't always answer the same."

" Do you mean you lie to people, to amuse yourself? "

" Sometimes."

" Oh, that's grand! Come on, lie to me! I'll ask you questions, probably the same questions they all ask, and you answer them as if I were a fool. Will you? "

" I'll try."

" Well, let's see. What shall I ask first? Oh, yes. Don't you get terribly cold in winter? "

He repeated a reply he had first made to an elderly lady, obviously a visitor in the city, whose curiosity had prompted her to cross-examine him for over twenty minutes on one of the busiest days he had ever known.

" No. When I feel chilly, I stop a car and lean against the radiator."

His present interviewer rewarded him with more laughter than was deserved.

" That's wonderful ! " she said. "And I suppose when your ears are cold, you stop another car and borrow its hood."

" I'll remember that one."

" Now what next? Do you ever get hit? "

" Right along, but only glancing blows. I very seldom get knocked down and run over."

" Doesn't it almost kill you, standing on your feet all day ? "

" It ain't near as bad as if it was my hands. Seriously, Madam, I get so used to it that I sleep that way nights."

" Don't the gasoline fumes make you sick ? "

" They did at first, but now I can't live without them. I have an apartment near a public garage so I can run over there any time and re-fume myself."

" How tall are you ? "

" Six feet ten."

" Not really ! "

" You know better, don't you? I'm six feet four, but when women ask me, I tell them anything from six feet eight to seven feet two. And they always say, ' Heavens ! ' "

" Which do you have the most trouble with, men drivers or women drivers? "

" Men drivers."

" Honestly ? "

" Sure. There's fifty times as many of them."

" Do lots of people ask you questions? "

" No. You're the first one."

" Were you mad at me for calling you cute the other day ? "

" I couldn't be mad at you."

A silence of many blocks followed. The girl certainly did drive fast and Ben might have been more nervous if he had looked ahead, but mostly his eyes were on her profile which was only a little less alluring than her smile.

" Look where we are ! " she exclaimed as they approached Fordham Road. "And you live at a Hundred and sixty-fourth ! Why didn't you tell me ? "

" I didn't notice."

" Don't get out. I'll drive you back."

" No, you won't. I'll catch a ride. There's a fella up this way I want to see."

" You were nice to take a chance with me and not to act scared. Will you do it again? "

" Whenever you say."

" I drive in once a week. I go down to Greenwich Village to visit my sister. Generally on Mondays."

" Next Monday I'll be on the late shift."

" Let's make it the Monday after."

" That's a long ways off."

" The time will pass. It always does."

It did, but so haltingly! And the day arrived with such a threat of rain that Ben was afraid she wouldn't come in. Later on, when the threat was fulfilled and the perils of motoring trebled by a steady drizzle and slippery pavements, he was afraid she would. Prudence, he knew, was not in her make-up and if she had an engagement with her sister, nothing short of a flood would prevent her keeping it.

Just before his luncheon time, the Cadillac passed, going south. Its top was up and its squeegee flying back and forth across the front glass.

Through the rain he saw the girl smile and wave at him briefly. Traffic was thick and treacherous and both must keep their minds on it.

It was still drizzling when she reappeared and stopped for him at four.

" Isn't this a terrible day? " she said.

" Not now! "

She smiled, and in an instant he forgot all the annoyance and discomfort of the preceding hours.

" If we leave the top up, you'll get stoop-shouldered, and if we take it down, we'll be drowned."

" Leave it up. I'm all right."

" Do you mind if we don't talk much? I feel quiet."

He didn't answer and nothing more was said until they turned east at Mount Morris Park. Then:

" I could find out your name," she said, " by remembering your number and having somebody look it up. But you can save me the trouble by telling me."

" My name is Ben Collins. And I could learn yours by demanding to see your driver's license."

" Heavens! Don't do that! I haven't any. But my name is Edith Dole."

" Edith Dole. Edith Dole," said Ben.

" Do you like it? "

" It's pretty."

" It's a funny combination. Edith means happiness and Dole means grief."

" Well," said Ben, " you'll have plenty of grief if you drive without a license. You'll have it anyway if you drive fast on these kind of streets. There's nothing skiddier than car-tracks when it's raining."

They were on upper Madison and the going was dangerous. But that was not the only reason he wanted her to slow down.

Silence again until they were on the Concourse.

" Are you married? " she asked him suddenly.

" No," he lied. "Are you? "

" I will be soon."

" Who to? "

" A man in Buffalo."

" Are you stuck on him? "

" I don't know. But he wants me and my father wants him to have me."

" Will you live in Buffalo? "

" No. He's coming here to be my father's partner."

" And yours."

" Yes. Oh, dear! Here's a Hundred and sixty-fourth and I mustn't take you past it today, not in this weather. Do you think you can extricate yourself? "

He managed it with some difficulty.

" I don't suppose I'll see you again for two weeks."

" I'm afraid not," she said.

He choked down the words that wanted to come out. " Miss Dole," he said, " take my advice and don't try for no records getting home. Just loaf along and you'll be there an hour before your supper's ready. Will you? For that guy's sake in Buffalo? "

" Yes."

" And my sake, too."

Gosh! What a smile to remember!

He must walk slow and give himself a chance to calm down before he saw Grace. Why had he told the girl he wasn't married? What did she care?

Grace's greeting was a sharp command. " Take a hot bath right away! And wear your bath-robe afterwards. We won't be going anywhere tonight."

She and Mary Arnold had been in Mount Vernon at a card-party. They had got soaked coming home. She talked about it all through supper, thank the Lord!

After supper he tried to read, but couldn't. He listened awhile to the Ohman and Arden record which his wife couldn't get enough of. He went to bed, wishing he could sleep and dream, wishing he could sleep two weeks.

He was up early, early enough to look at the paper before breakfast. "Woman Motorist Killed By Street-Car in Bronx." His eyes felt funny as he read: "Miss Edith Dole, twenty-two, of Rye, was instantly killed when the automobile she was driving skidded and struck a street-car at the corner of Fordham Road and Webster Avenue, the Bronx, shortly after four-thirty yesterday afternoon.

"Grace," he said in a voice that was not his own, "I forgot. I'm supposed to be on the job at seven this morning. There's some kind of a parade."

Out of the house, alone, he talked aloud to himself for the first time since he was a kid.

"I can't feel as bad as I think I do. I only seen her four or five times. I can't really feel this bad."

Well, on an afternoon two or three weeks later, a man named Hughes from White Plains, driving a Studebaker, started across Forty-sixth Street out of turn and obeyed a stern order to pull over to the curb.

"What's your hurry?" demanded the grim-faced traffic policeman. "Where the hell do you think you're going? What's the matter with you, you so-and-so!"

"I forgot myself for a minute. I'm sorry," said Mr. Hughes. "If you'll overlook it, I'll pick you up on my way home and take you to the Bronx. Remember, I give you a ride home last month? Remember? That is, it was a fella that looked like you. That is, he looked something like you. I can see now it wasn't you. It was a different fella."

XXII

ANNIVERSARY

MRS. TAYLOR shuffled a worn pack of cards and began her evening session at solitaire. She would play probably forty games before she went to bed, and she would win thirty of them. What harm if she cheated a little? Russian Bank was more fun, but it cannot be played alone, and her husband was bored by it. He had been unable to learn bridge in spite of the patient and more or less expert teaching of the Hammonds, who lived three blocks away.

The thirty-four-dollar synthetic radio had done nothing but croak since the day following its installation. The cheap piano's D and G above middle C were mute. The town's Carnegie Library acquired very few " hot " books and the few were nearly always out. Picture plays hurt Louis' eyes and he would not let her go out nights by herself, though he had no scruples against leaving her at home from eight to eleven Wednesdays, when he attended lodge and bowled.

So Mrs. Taylor shuffled her cards and tried to listen when Louis read aloud from the Milton Daily Star or the Milton Weekly Democrat, or recounted stories she had heard six times before and would hear six times again.

She had awakened this morning to the realization that it was the twelfth day of November, the ninth anniversary of her marriage. Louis had remembered that date for the first six years of their life together; for the last three years it had been to him just November the twelfth.

Nine years ago the Star and the Democrat had called her one of Milton's most charming and beautiful young women, and they had been right. They had referred to Louis as a model young man, sober, industrious and " solid "; a young man whom any girl should be proud and glad to have as a husband. They were right again.

Now Mrs. Taylor, at thirty-three, was good-looking, but in a cold, indifferent sort of way. She no longer bothered to embellish her natural attractiveness and she lacked the warmth and vivacity which had won the adoration of most of Milton's male youth, notably Walter Frayne, Jim Satterly and Louis Taylor himself.

Louis was still a model young man, sober, industrious and "solid." When you thought of the precarious existence of the women who had married his chief rivals, you couldn't help feeling that wisdom and good luck had been on Mrs. Taylor's side when she made her choice.

Walter had attended college for one semester, at the end of which he came home with a perfect record of studies, 4; Flunks, 4. He had run amuck in Milton and ultimately, turned down by the girl he really cared for, had married an orphan whose parents had left her $150,000—but not for long. After this tidy sum had been poured away Walter was almost continuously unemployed and people wondered how he and his wife lived. And why.

There was nothing of the gay dog about Jim Satterly. He had graduated from high school and gone into the Milton Gas Company's office as bookkeeper at eight dollars per week. He was now thirty-five years old and still with the gas company, but his salary had been steadily increased until it was twenty-two dollars. His wife gave weekly piano lessons to a class of four pupils at fifty cents a half-hour each. She had borne Jim three children, or kiddies. The Satterlys seemed to enjoy their kiddies and an occasional picture show, but no magazine editor had ever sent a staff man to get a success story out of Jim.

Louis Taylor was secretary to the town's only wealthy man, old Thomas Parvis, who owned a controlling interest in the Interurban Railway. Louis worked long hours and was paid four thousand a year, big money in Milton. It was enough to keep the childless Taylors in comfort; in comparative luxury, even. Couples with smaller incomes owned cars, took trips to near-by lake resorts and to Harper City, where a stock company presented worth-while plays. But Louis was saving for a rainy day and his wife had long ago given up praying for rain.

Mrs. Taylor was winning her fourth successive victory over solitaire by the simple expedient of pretending that a black queen was red.

"It says here," stated her husband, "that there are 27,650,267 automobiles in the world, according to a census just completed."

It was Mrs. Taylor's own fault that Louis had contracted the habit of reciting interesting tidbits from the paper. Back in May, 1924, he had asked her whether she would like to hear the news of the Loeb-Leopold case. She had already read it, but she said yes, thinking it would be more thrilling, even in repetition, than one of Louis' own experiences, also in repetition. Since then, she had listened every evening—except Wednesday, when Louis went out, and Sundays, when there was no paper—to excerpts from the Star, consisting principally of what is known in newspaper offices as filler—incontrovertible statistics about men and things in all parts of the world, facts that seemed to smite her husband like a bolt from the blue.

"Think of it!" he said. "Nearly twenty-eight million automobiles!"

"Heavens!" said Mrs. Taylor.

"And speaking of automobiles: 'Storms have made roads so bad in parts of Chile that drivers have not dared to go into the rural districts.' That's the trouble with owning a car. If you don't stay right on the paved streets or paved roads, you're liable to get stuck and maybe walk home. Besides that, you've got to be a mechanic yourself or else, when there's something wrong, you have to take it to a garage and lay it up a week till they consent to look at it and find out what's the matter, and then they don't know themselves nine times out of ten. But they charge you just the same and they charge you plenty. Did I tell you about Walter Trumbull's trip to Harper City?"

"Yes," said Mrs. Taylor.

"I don't believe I did. It was only last Friday night; no, Thursday night, the night after the Spartans beat us by one pin, when I had a chance to get a 202 and hit the head pin just a little too full and they split on me. That was the night Berger showed up so drunk he couldn't bowl and we had to use Tommy and he shot 123.

"So it was the night after that when Walter and Marjorie started over to the City to see the 'Seventh Heaven,' and about five miles the other side of Two Oaks the engine died and Walter couldn't get it going again. His flash-light wouldn't work and Marjorie wouldn't let him strike matches with the hood up to see what the trouble was. As it turned out, it wouldn't have done him any good anyway.

"Finally he left poor Marjorie in the car and walked way back to Two Oaks, but the garage was closed up for the night and the whole town was asleep, so he went back to the car and by that time of course it was too late to see the show. He hailed three or four cars coming from the other way, trying to get a ride home, but it wasn't till after ten o'clock that he could get a car to stop and pick them up. The next morning he sent Charlie Thomas out to fix up the car so it would run or else tow it in, and Charlie found out there was nothing the matter with it except it was out of gas. When Walter told me about it, I said that was what he deserved for not patronizing the Interurban."

" We don't patronize it ourselves."

" I hear enough about it in the daytime without riding on it at night."

Mrs. Taylor shuffled the cards and Louis resumed perusal of the Star.

" The old U. S. is a pretty good country after all," he said presently. " Listen to this: ' The Netherlands' unemployed now include 26,000 skilled and 24,000 unskilled workers.' And listen: 'A large proportion of Belgium's population still wear wooden shoes.' You wouldn't think that was possible in this day and age ! "

" I imagine," said Mrs. Taylor, " that there are some places in the United States where people don't wear any shoes at all."

" Oh, sure, but not a large proportion; probably a few of those backwoods Tennessee mountaineers. And of course the colored people in the small towns in Georgia and South Carolina. You see lots of them, passing through on the train, that never had a shoe on in their life. I remember a place named Jesup, Georgia, a kind of junction. There was—— No, that wasn't Jesup; it was some other place, some place the boss and I went through on the way to Daytona that time. I guess I told you about it."

" Yes," said Mrs. Taylor.

" You wouldn't believe the way some of those people live. Not all colored people, either; white people, too. Poor white trash, they call them. Or rather, ' po' white trash.' Families of four and five in one room. Mr. Parvis said it was a crime and kept wishing he could do something for them."

" Why didn't he ? "

" Well, he's hardly got money enough to house and clothe the whole South and it wouldn't do any good to just pick out some one town and try and better conditions there."

" Why not ? "

" It would be a drop in the bucket, and besides, other towns would hear about it and pester the life out of him. I reminded him he was taking the trip to get away from care and worry for a while and he ought not to fret himself about other people's busi-

ness. Then, too, if he was going to practise some of his philan-
throphy down there, I'd probably be put in charge of it. We might
have even had to live there a year or two. I guess you wouldn't
like that, would you?"

" It wouldn't make any difference to me," said Mrs. Taylor.

" What! Live in one of those God-forsaken holes, without any
friends or anybody you'd want to make friends with! Nothing to
do all day and all night but eat and sleep and——"

" Play solitaire," suggested Mrs. Taylor.

" You may think you wouldn't mind it, but that's because you've
never seen it. Those Georgia villages are an interesting study, but
as for making your home in one of them, you'd die of loneliness.
Of course there's some spots in Florida that are pretty close to
heaven. Take Daytona, for instance. But I've told you what it's
like."

" Yes."

" They've got a beach that's so hard and smooth that they have
automobile races on it. It's beautiful. And it's right close to Ormond, where Rockefeller spends his winters. Mr. Parvis and I
saw him playing golf on the Ormond course. I can't see anything
in golf myself, but maybe I would if I had a chance to get interested in it. When I'm as old as he is, I'll try it out, providing I've
got as much time and one-millionth as much money."

" There's no reason why you shouldn't have fully as much
money."

" I know what you mean by that. You're digging at my thrifti-
ness, though I suppose you call it stinginess. You'll look at it differently when we're old."

" I hope I won't be here to look at it at all."

" No, you don't. But what was I saying? Oh, yes. Daytona is
where I'd like to live in winter, if I had the means. I must have
told you about running into Harry Riker down there."

" You did."

" It certainly was a funny thing, running into him! We hadn't
seen each other for twenty-two years and he recognized me the
minute he set eyes on me. I wouldn't have known him from
Adam's off ox.

" It sure did take me back, running into Harry. He recalled
one time, just before I left Shelbyville, when his father and mother
were away on a visit somewhere. Harry's aunt, Mr. Riker's sister,
was supposed to be taking care of Harry while his father and

mother was away, but she was kind of old and she used to go to sleep right after supper.

" Well, there were a couple of girls, sisters, named Lindsay. They lived out in the country, but came in town to school. Harry and I thought we were stuck on them, so one night after supper, when Harry's aunt had gone to sleep, we hitched up Mr. Riker's horse and buggy and drove seven miles out in the country to call on the Lindsay girls. When we got out there it was raining, so we unhitched the horse and put him in the barn and——"

" He got loose, didn't he? And ran all the way home? "

" Yes, but that comes later. We put him in Lindsay's barn and we thought we had him tied all right, and Harry and I went in the house and sat around with the girls. Mrs. Lindsay stayed right in the room with us and did most of the talking——"

" You're sure of that? "

" I certainly am! She was one of these women that talk all the time. She never stopped. So about half past nine she said the girls would have to go to bed, and that was telling us to get out. Well, to make a long story short, the horse wasn't in the barn and Harry and I walked home seven miles in the pouring rain. We found the horse in his own stall and Harry had to ride him out to Lindsay's next day and get the buggy. That was the last time we ever called on the Lindsay girls."

" Kind of hard on them," said Mrs. Taylor.

" Oh, we were all just kids and there wasn't anything serious between us. Harry's in the insurance business now in Indianapolis, doing fine, he told me."

Louis was almost, but not quite, through with his paper.

" Here's a funny thing," he said. "Although Edinburgh, Scotland, had only 237 ice-cream parlors last season, the number was fifty more than were in the city a year ago."

" I should think that was enough ice-cream parlors."

" Not for the size of the town. Let's see. How big is Edinburgh? I'll have to look it up."

He was on his way to the bookcase when the door-bell rang. He went to the door and admitted Florence Hammond.

" Hello, Louis. Hello, Bess. This isn't a social call. We're out here with a flat tire and Perce wants to borrow your flash."

" There's automobiles for you! " said Louis. " More trouble than they're worth."

" I tried to persuade Perce to take it to the garage and have them fix it, but he's afraid driving it even that far would ruin the rim or the shoe or whatever you call it."

"I'll get the flash and see if I can help him," said Louis.

"And you sit down, Florence, and keep me company," said Mrs. Taylor. "I haven't been out of the house for three days and I'm dying to hear what's going on in Milton."

"You take the Star, don't you?"

"I'm afraid we do, but it hasn't been very thrilling lately."

"You can't blame the paper for that," said Mrs. Hammond. "Nothing exciting has happened; that is, in Milton."

"Has anything happened anywhere?"

"Yes. In Clyde."

"Clyde. That's where your sister lives, isn't it?"

"If you call it living. I'd rather be dead! Honestly, Bess, you and I ought to thank the Lord that we married men who are at least sane and normal. Louis and Perce may not be as good-looking or 'brilliant' as Ed, but anyway we always know where they are and what to expect of them."

"That's true," said Mrs. Taylor.

"I wrote Grace a letter today and told her she was simply crazy not to leave him, especially after this last mess. But she won't give him up. I believe he's got her hypnotized. And she still loves him. She admits his faults and excuses him and expects everybody to do the same. If she didn't, she'd keep her troubles to herself and not write me all the details. I realize everybody has their weakness, but it seems to me there are some things I couldn't forgive. And one of them is a punch in the eye."

"You don't mean——"

"Yes, I do. And Grace took it and accepted his apology when he made one. When I think of it, I simply boil!"

"What was the occasion?"

"No special occasion. Just Saturday night. Everybody in Clyde goes to the Yacht Club Saturday nights. There's no river or lake and no yachts, but they have a sunset gun, so I suppose they're entitled to call it a yacht club. Grace hated it at first and let Ed go alone, but that only made him drink more and get home later Sunday mornings. Besides, she's always been a little jealous, and probably with reason. So she decided to go with him and try to enjoy herself. Grace loves to dance and there are some awfully good dancers in Clyde; that is, early in the evening, before they begin to flounder and reel.

"Of course nobody can say Ed married her under false pretenses. She went into it with her eyes wide open. She saw him for the first time at one of those parties and she fell in love with him when he got mad at a man and knocked him down for cutting in on a dance. The man was about half Ed's size and Ed hit him when he wasn't looking. That didn't make any difference to Grace. And it didn't seem to make any difference to the Yacht Club. Anybody else would have been expelled, but Ed begged everyone's pardon and wasn't even scolded.

"That first night he asked Grace to let him drive her home. She was visiting Helen Morse, and Helen advised her not to take the chance. Ed didn't seem to be in very good driving condition. But Grace was so crazy about him that she told him yes. And then he forgot all about it, went home with another girl and left Grace at the club with some people she hardly knew. She had to call up the Morses and get them to come back after her.

"Well, they met again the next week and Grace thought she would put him in his place by ignoring him entirely, but that didn't work because he didn't remember having seen her before. He was comparatively sober this time and awfully nice and attentive. I'll admit Ed can be nice when he wants to. After that they played tennis together two or three times and then Ed proposed and Grace accepted him and he said he couldn't wait for a big wedding and she agreed to marry him secretly at Colby, a town about thirty miles from Clyde. She was to be in front of the Clyde post-office at twelve o'clock on a certain day and he was to pick her up in his car and drive to Colby and be married.

"The day came and she waited for him an hour and then went back to the Morses'. That evening he telephoned that he had made a mistake in the day and had just discovered it, and would she please forgive him and meet him the next day at the same place. I blush to say she succumbed, though she suspected what she found out later to be true—Ed had been on a bat and was sleeping it off at the time he was supposed to do his eloping.

"They were married and Ed behaved beautifully on the honeymoon. They spent two weeks in New York and went to the theatre every night and sightseeing in the mornings and afternoons. He had men friends of his to dinner once or twice and gave them all they wanted to drink, but wouldn't touch anything himself.

"When they got back to Clyde, Ed bought a lovely house already furnished, and the furniture was just what Grace would have picked out. Grace was so happy it seemed as if it couldn't last, and it didn't.

"They had been in Clyde a week when Ed announced that he had to go away on a trip. He didn't trouble to say where or why or how long. He just went, stayed away five days and came home looking as if he had had five or six operations. Grace tried to get him to tell her where he had been, but he just laughed and said it was a secret.

"And that's the way things have gone on ever since. Ed's got plenty of money and he gives Grace all she can possibly spend, besides buying her presents that are always lovely and terribly expensive. He'll be as good as pie for weeks and weeks—except for the Saturday night carousal—and then he'll disappear for a few days and she won't know where he is or when to expect him home. Her life is one surprise after another. But when he suddenly hits her in the eye, it's more than a surprise. It's a kind of a shock. At least it would be to me."

"When did it happen?" asked Mrs. Taylor.

"A week ago Saturday," said Mrs. Hammond. "There was the usual party at the Yacht Club and Ed took more than his usual amount to drink. Along about midnight he disappeared, and so did a girl named Eva Grayson.

"Finally Grace went home, but she sat up and waited for Ed. He came in about four o'clock, pie-eyed. He walked right to where Grace was sitting and without saying anything at all, he hit her, not hard enough to knock her out of her chair but with enough force to really hurt. Then, still not saying anything, he went to bed without taking the time to undress.

"In the morning, or whenever he woke up, he noticed that Grace's eye was discolored and asked her what had happened. She told him and he made no attempt to deny it. All he said was, ' Dearest, I can't tell you how sorry I am. You must believe me when I say I had no idea it was you. I thought it was Eva Grayson. And she deserved to be hit.'

"Can you imagine forgiving a man for a thing like that? Can you imagine continuing to live with him and love him? I'd kill myself before I'd stand it! And Grace excuses him and writes me the full details, just as if it were something she was proud of. I tell you, Bess, you and I can consider ourselves lucky——"

The front door opened and Louis came in with his flash-light.

"You're all set, Florence," said he. "I asked Perce in, but he thinks it's time to drive on."

"I know it is," said Mrs. Hammond. "We're going to play bridge out at the Cobbs' and we're terribly late. I ought to have

phoned them, but I guess they'll sit up for us. Good night, Bess.
I hope I didn't bore you with my long monolog."

"You didn't," said Mrs. Taylor.

Louis sat down to finish the Star. Mrs. Taylor shuffled her
cards and started a new game, but in the middle of it she rose
from the table and went close to her husband's chair.

"Do you know what day this is?" she said.

"Why, yes," Louis replied. "It's Tuesday."

"It's Tuesday, November twelfth. Our anniversary."

"Gosh! That's right! I wish I'd remembered it. I'd have
bought you some flowers. Will it do tomorrow?"

"I don't want any flowers. But there is something I would like
you to give me. And you don't have to wait till tomorrow."

"What is it?"

"A punch in the eye," said Mrs. Taylor.

"You're feeling kind of funny, aren't you? Did Florence have
a shot of their home-made gin in her bag?"

"No. And I'm not feeling funny. I'm just sleepy. I think
I'll go to bed."

Louis was reading again.

"It says: 'Experiments in the raising of sisal are being made
in Haiti.' I don't suppose you happen to know what sisal is."

But Mrs. Taylor was on her way up-stairs.

XXIII

REUNION

THIS is one about a brother and sister and the sister's husband and the brother's wife. The sister's name was Rita Mason Johnston; she was married to Stuart Johnston, whose intimates called him Stu, which was appropriate only on special occasions. The brother was Bob Mason, originally and recently from Buchanan, Michigan, and in between whiles a respected resident of Los Angeles. His wife was a woman he had found in San Bernardino and married for some reason.

Rita had been named after a Philadelphia aunt with money. The flattered aunt had made Rita's mother bring Rita east for a visit when the child was three or four. After that, until she met Stu, she had spent two-thirds of her time with her aunt or at schools of her aunt's choosing. Her brother Bob, in bad health at fourteen, had gone to California to live with cousins or something. He had visited home only three times in nearly twenty years, and not once while Rita was there. So he and Rita hardly knew each other, you might say.

Johnston and Rita had become acquainted at a party following a Cornell-Pennsylvania football game. Johnston's people were decent and well-off, and Rita's aunt had encouraged the romance, which resulted in a wedding and a comfortable home at Sands Point, Long Island.

Bob Mason had first worked for a cousin in a Los Angeles real estate office, then had gone into business for himself, and finally saved enough to bring his wife to the old Michigan homestead, which had been left him by his father.

He and Jennie were perfectly satisfied with small-town life. Once in a while they visited Chicago, less than a hundred miles away, or drove up the lake shore or down into Indiana in Bob's two-thousand-dollar automobile. In the past year they had been to Chicago three times and had attended three performances of Abie's Irish Rose. It was the best play ever played; better, even, than Lightnin'.

"I honestly think we ought to do something about Rita," said

Jennie to Bob one June day. "Imagine a person not seeing their own sister in nearly twenty years!"

"I'd love to see her," replied Bob, "and I wish you'd write her a letter. She don't pay no attention to mine. I've asked her time and time again to come out here and stay as long as she likes, but she hasn't even answered."

"Well," said Jennie, "I'll write to her, although she still owes me a letter from last Christmas."

"Stu," said Rita to her husband, "we've simply got to do something about Bob and his wife. Heaven knows how many times he's asked us to go out there and visit and now here is a letter from Jennie, inviting us again."

"Well, why don't you go? You'd enjoy it, seeing the old home and the people you used to play around with. I'd go along, but I haven't the time."

"Time! You have time to go to the Water Gap or up to Manchester for golf every two or three weeks. As for me wanting to see the old home, you know that's silly!"

"Well, we won't argue about it, but I'm certainly not going to waste my vacation in any hick town where they've probably got a six-hole course that you have to putt on with a niblick! Why can't they come here?"

"I don't suppose they could, but if you want me to, I'll ask them."

"Suit yourself. It's your brother."

The Bob Masons boarded The Wolverine at the near-by metropolis of Niles and got off some twenty hours later in New York's Grand Central Station. Compared with the jump from California to Michigan, it seemed like once around on a roller coaster.

Rita met them and identified Bob by the initials on his suitcase. He wouldn't have known her. She was the same age as Jennie, thirty-five, and he had expected her to look it. Instead, she looked ten years younger and was prettier than a member of the Buchanan Mason family had any right to be. And what clothes! Like those of the movie gals who had infested his Los Angeles.

"Why, sis, are you sure it's you?"

"Am I changed?" she said, laughing.

"Not as much as you ought to be," replied Bob. "That's what makes it so hard to recognize you."

"Well, *you've* changed," said Rita. "Let's see—it's twenty years, isn't it? You were fourteen and naturally you didn't have that mustache. But even if you were clean shaven, you wouldn't be a bit like the Bob I remember. And this is Jennie," she added. " Well ! "

" Yes," admitted Bob's wife.

She smiled and Rita noticed her teeth for the first time. Most of the visible ones were of gold, and the work had evidently been done by a dentist for whom three members of a foursome were waiting. Rita, Bob, and Bob's wife, escorted by a red cap, walked through the Biltmore and across Forty-third Street to where Gates was parked with Rita's sedan. Gates observed the newcomers as he relieved the red cap of their meager baggage. " Sears, Roebuck," he said to himself, for he had lived in Janesville, Wisconsin.

" Oh, we forgot to see about your trunks ! " exclaimed Rita when the car had started.

" We didn't bring no trunks," said Bob.

" We can only stay two weeks," said his wife.

" That seems like an awfully short visit," Rita said.

" I know, but Bob don't feel like he can stay away from the garden this time of year. We left old Jimmy Preston to take care of it, but nobody can be trusted to tend to another person's garden like you would yourself."

" Does the place look just the same ? "

" I should say not ! It was in terrible condition when he first came East."

" Came East ? "

" I mean, to Michigan. But Bob spent—— How much did you spend fixing things up, Bob, about ? "

" Over two thousand dollars," said Bob.

" I thought it was nearer twenty-one or twenty-two hundred," said his wife.

" Well, somewhere over two thousand."

" It was more than two thousand," insisted his wife.

" Look out ! " yelled Bob, and the two women jumped.

They were on the Fifty-ninth Street bridge and Gates was worming his way through the myriad trucks and funerals that prevail on that structure at 11 A. M.

" What's the matter? You scared me to death ! " said Rita.

" I thought we was going to hit that Reo," Bob explained.

" Bob's a nervous wreck when anybody else is driving," apologized Jennie. " I often think a person who drives themselves is more liable to be nervous when somebody else is driving."

"I guess that's true," agreed Rita, and reflected that she had heard this theory expounded before.

"And I do believe," continued Jennie, "that Bob is just about the best driver in the world, and that's not because he's my husband, either."

This remark caused Gates to turn around suddenly and look the speaker in the eye, and the sedan missed another Reo by a flea's upper lip.

The road leading from New York to the towns on Long Island's north shore is, for the most part, as scenically attractive as an incinerating plant. Nevertheless, Jennie kept saying "How beautiful!" and asking Rita who were the owners of various places which looked as if they had been disowned these many years. Bob was too nervous to make any effort to talk and Rita sighed with relief when the drive was over.

"I'll show you your room," she said, "and then you can rest till lunch. Stu is in the city and won't be home till dinner. But he only goes in once or twice a week, and he said he would arrange not to go at all while you're here, so he'd have plenty of time to visit."

Jennie was impressed with the luxurious guest room and its outlook on the Sound, but Bob had slept badly on the train and dozed off while she was still marveling.

"I don't suppose you feel like doing much this afternoon," said Rita when lunch was over. "Maybe we'd better just loaf. I imagine that tomorrow and the rest of the week will be pretty strenuous. Stu has all kinds of plans."

So they loafed, and Jennie and Rita took naps, and Bob walked around the yard and plotted the changes he would make in it if it were his.

Seven o'clock brought Stu, who was introduced to the in-laws and then ordered to his room to make himself presentable for dinner. Rita followed him upstairs.

"Well?" he said.

"I'm not sure yet," said Rita, "but I'm kind of afraid—— Bob is awfully quiet and I guess she's embarrassed to death. I hope they've brought some other clothes, but then I don't know—— A change might be for the worse, though it doesn't seem possible."

"Does she think," asked Stu, "that just because she's from the Golden State she has to run around with a mouthful of nuggets?"

"She's all right when she doesn't smile. You mustn't say anything what will make her smile."

"That's going to be tough," said Stu. "You know what I am when I get started!"

"And another thing I just thought of," said Rita. "He didn't bring any golf clubs."

"Oh, that doesn't matter. I can fit him out."

The host and hostess joined their guests on the porch. A Swedish girl served cocktails.

"Are these—is it liquor?" asked Jennie.

"Just Bacardi, and they're awfully mild," said Rita.

"But Bob and I don't indulge at all," said Jennie.

"This wouldn't be indulging," urged Stu. "This is practically a soft drink."

"I know, but it would be violating the letter of the law," said Jennie.

So Rita and Stu drank alone and the four moved in to dinner.

"What time do you get up, Bob?" asked the host, at table.

"Six o'clock, in the summer," replied his brother-in-law.

"Oh, well, there's no need of that! But it would be nice if we could get through breakfast tomorrow at, say, nine o'clock. I'm going to take you to Piping Rock. We'll make a day of it."

"That'll be fine," said Bob.

"What do you go around in?" inquired his brother-in-law.

"I've got a 1924 Studebaker," said Bob.

"No, no," said Stu. "I mean your golf game."

"Me? I haven't any golf game. I never played golf in my life."

Stu's expression would have made Rita laugh if she hadn't felt so sorry for him.

"Bob can't see anything in golf," explained Jennie. "He says it's a sissy game. I tell him he ought to try it some time and he might change his mind. Why don't you try it while you're here, Bob? Maybe Stuart would show you the fine points."

The host seemed not to have heard this suggestion.

"They have got a links near Buchanan, between Buchanan and Niles," said Bob, "but they charge fifty dollars to join and thirty-five dollars annual dues. That seems exorbitant."

"It's an outrage!" is what Stu was going to say, but Rita shook her head at him. "I think you'd find it was worth the money," is what he said.

"Lots of our friends play," said Jennie. "Some of the nicest people in both Niles and Buchanan belong to the club, so it can't be as silly as Bob thinks. But he gets an idear in his head and you can't change him."

"What's on tonight?" asked Stu as the dessert was served.

"Well," said Rita, "I thought these people would want to get to bed early after their trip, so we won't go anywhere. We might have a little bridge. Do you feel like bridge, Jennie?"

"I'm awfully sorry, but neither Bob or I play. I know it must be a wonderful game and some of our best friends play it a great deal, but somehow or other, Bob and I just never took it up."

This was a terrific blow to Rita, who counted that day lost which was without its twenty or thirty rubbers.

"You miss something," she said with remarkable self-control. "Shall we have our coffee on the porch? I think it's pleasanter."

"What do you smoke, Bob? Cigars or cigarettes?" inquired the host.

"Neither, thanks," Bob replied. "I never cared for tobacco."

"You're lucky," said Stu. "A cigarette, Jennie?"

"Mercy! It would kill me! Even the smell of smoke makes me dizzy."

Stu and Rita evidently missed this statement for they proceeded to light their cigarettes.

"Is bridge hard to learn?" asked Jennie presently.

"Not very," said Rita.

"I was wondering if maybe you and Stuart couldn't teach it to Bob and I. Then we could have some games while we're here."

"Well," said Rita, "it's—it's a terribly hard game to learn, that is, to play it right."

"You said it wasn't," put in Bob.

"Well, it isn't, if you don't care—if you just—— But to learn to play it right, it's impossible!"

"Have you got a radio?" asked Bob. He pronounced the "a" short, as in Buchanan.

"I'm sorry to say we haven't," said Stu, who wasn't sorry at all.

"I don't know how you get along without one," said Bob.

"We just live for ours!" said Jennie.

"What is it, an Atwater-Kent?" asked Rita.

She had seen that name in some paper yesterday.

"No," replied Bob. "It's a Ware Neutrodyne, with a Type X receiver."

"And an Ethovox horn," added Jennie. "We had Omaha one night."

"You did!" said Rita.

There was a silence, which was broken by Bob's asking his sister how often she went to New York.

"Only when I can't help myself, when I simply have to get something."

"Don't you never go to the theater?"

"Oh, yes, if it's something especially good."

"Of course," said Jennie, "you've seen Abie's Irish Rose?"

"Heavens, no!" said Rita. "Everybody says it's terrible!"

"Well, it's not terrible!" said Bob indignantly. "That is, if you've got anywheres near as good a company here as they have in Chicago."

"I'd like to see the New York company," said Jennie, "and see how they do compare."

This met with no encouragement and another silence followed.

"Well, Bob," said Stu at length, "you must do *something* for exercise. How about a little tennis in the morning?"

"That's another game I don't play," Bob replied. "As for exercise, I get plenty of it fooling around the garden and monkeying with the car."

"Then all I can suggest is that we put in the day fishing or swimming or just riding around in the launch."

Bob was silent, but his wife spoke up.

"You know, Stuart, Bob's ashamed to admit it, but being on the water makes him deathly sick, even if it's as smooth as glass. And he can't swim."

Bob didn't seem to relish this topic and turned to his sister.

"Do you remember the Allens in Buchanan, old Tom Allen and his family?"

"Kind of."

"Did you hear about Louise Allen running away and getting married?"

"No."

"Well, she ran away with Doc Marshall and got married. And at first old Tom was pretty near wild, but when Doc and Louise came back, why one day Doc was walking along the street and old Tom came along from the opposite direction and Doc spoke to him and called him by name and old Tom looked at him and asked him what he wanted, and Doc said he wanted to know if he'd forgave him. So old Tom said, 'Forgiven you! Have *you* forgiven *me*, is the question.' So Doc said, forgiven him for what, and old Tom said, for not killing her when she was a baby. This put the laugh on Doc and the boys have all been kidding him about it. I guess you didn't know Doc."

" No, I didn't," admitted Rita.

" Quite a card," said Bob.

Jennie had picked up a book. " May Fair," she read. " Is it good? "

" Yes," said Rita. " It's short stories by Michael Arlen; you know, the man who wrote The Green Hat."

" A detective story? " asked Bob.

" No, Michael Arlen. He was here last spring and we met him. He's awfully nice. He's really an Armenian."

" There's an Armenian comes to Buchanan two or three times a year," said Jennie. " But he sells linen."

Upstairs, two or three hours later, Stu made a brief speech:

" My God! He doesn't play golf, he doesn't play tennis, he doesn't play bridge, he doesn't swim, fish, drink, or smoke. And I'd arranged these two weeks for a kind of a vacation! Hell's bells! "

In the guest room Bob said:

" I certainly miss the old radio."

" Yes," said Jennie. " We'd be getting the Drake Hotel now."

" I'd like to see the New York company in Abie's Irish Rose," said Jennie at breakfast next morning. " I'd like to compare them with the companies that's in Chicago."

" Did you see it in Chicago? " asked Stu.

" Three times," said Jennie.

" You must be sick of it," said Stu.

" I couldn't get sick of it," replied Jennie, " not if I saw it every night in the year."

After breakfast Bob tried to read the *Herald-Tribune,* the *World,* and the *Times,* but couldn't make head or tail of them. He wished he had a copy of the Chi *Trib,* even if it was two or three days old.

" Do you go to pictures much? " inquired Jennie of her hostess.

" Hardly ever," said Rita.

" We're very fond of them," said Jennie. " You know, we lived in Los Angeles for a long time, and that's right near Hollywood. So we often saw different stars in person. And some friends of ours knew Harold Lloyd and introduced us to him. You'd never know him without those glasses. He's really handsome! And democratic! "

" What is he running for? " asked Stu.

"Nothing that I know of," said Jennie. "Is he running for anything, Bob?"

"I don't think so," said Bob.

The morning dragged along and finally it was time for lunch and Stu broke a precedent by having seven highballs with his meal.

"They'll make you sleepy," warned Rita.

"What of it?" he said, and there seemed to be no answer.

Sure enough, Stu slept on the porch swing all afternoon while Jennie struggled with the first volume of The Peasants and Rita took Bob for a walk.

"Do you remember Tom Allen?" Bob asked her.

"I don't believe so," she answered.

"Oh, you must remember the Allens! They lived next door to the Deans. Well, anyway, Tom had a daughter, Louise, about our age, and she ran away with Doc Marshall and got married. Everybody thought old Tom would shoot Doc on sight, but when they met and Doc asked Tom to forgive him, old Tom said he was the one that ought to be asking forgiveness. So Doc said forgiveness for what, and old Tom said, for not killing Louise when she was a baby."

Near the end of their walk, Bob asked:

"Don't you never go to New York?"

"Hardly ever, and especially at this time of year. It's so hot! But I suppose you and Jennie would like to see something of it. We'll arrange to drive in before you go home."

Stu woke up a little after five and took on a fresh cargo of Scotch before dinner.

"You certainly ought to get a radio!" said Bob as the clock struck nine.

At half past, everybody went to bed.

"This will be our third day here," said Bob, dressing. "We don't start home till a week from next Thursday."

"Yes," said Jennie absently.

"I'd wear my other suit today, but it's all wrinkled up," said Bob.

"I'll ask Rita for an iron and press it out for you. Or maybe we could send it to a tailor."

"Tailor! There's no tailor within miles of here, or anything else as far as I can see!"

Stu wasn't up for breakfast, but joined the party on the porch a little before lunch time. He had started in on a new bottle.

"Bob," he said, "you ought to fall off the wagon. I've got some of the most able-bodied Scotch on Long Island."

"Thanks," said his brother-in-law. "I may be tempted before long."

It was late in the afternoon when Bob said to Rita:

"Do you remember old Tom Allen?"

"I think so," his sister replied. "Didn't his daughter run away with some doctor?"

"Yes," said Bob, "and——"

He was interrupted by Stu's voice, calling Rita from upstairs.

"Listen," said Stu when she had answered his summons, "A telegram is coming for me tonight, saying that my grandfather is sick up in Bennington, Vermont, or some place, and for me to come at once. And he's going to stay sick for at least ten days, so sick that I can't leave him."

"No, sir!" said Rita firmly. "You don't do that to me!"

"Well, then, how about this? Suppose it's one of our dearest friends that's sick and we've both got to go. Do you think they'd go home? You see, we could pack up some baggage and run in to New York and stay over night if necessary, and come back here after they're gone."

"If they ever found out, I couldn't forgive myself."

"They won't. You let me plan it and we'll spring it after dinner. I wouldn't be so desperate if I hadn't just got so I could break an eighty-five and if I don't keep after it I'll be back in the nineties."

But after dinner, while Rita and Stu were sparring for an opening, Jennie said:

"Folks, I hope you won't think we are crazy, but Bob is, almost. He's worried to death about his garden. He read in the paper this morning that there's a regular drought threatened all through southern Michigan. We were afraid of it, because it hadn't rained for a long time before we left. And now it looks like everything would be ruined unless he gets back there and tends to things himself. We left old Jimmy Preston to look out for things, but you can't trust things to an outsider. Bob feels like if he was there, he could see that things were taken care of. The garden will get plenty of water if Bob is there to see to it, but if he isn't, there's no telling what will happen. So if you'll forgive us, we're thinking about starting home on The Wolverine tomorrow afternoon."

"Well!" said Rita.

"Well!" said Stu.

" Of course," said Rita, " you know best, and it would be a shame to have your whole garden spoiled. But it does seem—— But of course we wouldn't dream of urging——"

" We've simply got to go, sis," said Bob. "And another thing: Don't bother about coming in to New York with us. Just send us in your car tomorrow forenoon, say, and we'll have time to look around a little before we catch the train."

．　．　．　．　．　．　．　．　．　．　．　．

The Masons were in their room at the Biltmore.

" It's eight dollars a day without meals," said Bob, " but we can eat out, some place where it's not expensive, and besides, it's only for a week. Tonight," he went on, "Abie's Irish Rose. Tomorrow morning the top of the Woolworth Building. Tomorrow afternoon, Coney. Thursday night, Abie again. After that, we'll see."

Jennie laughed nervously.

" I'll be petrified every time we leave the hotel," she said. " Suppose we should meet them on the street ! "

" There's no danger of that," said Bob. " Sis never comes to town in summer and Stuart is taking a vacation. What I'm afraid of is that they'll run acrost some article on the weather conditions in the Middle West and see where we've had the rainiest summer since 1902."

XXIV

TRAVELOGUE

They met for the first time at luncheon in the diner of the west-bound limited that had left Chicago the night before. The girls, it turned out, were Hazel Dignan and her friend Mildred Orr. The man was Dan Chapman.

He it was who broke the ice by asking if they minded riding backwards. It was Hazel who answered. She was a seasoned traveler and knew how to talk to strangers. Mildred had been hardly anywhere and had little to say, even when she knew people.

"Not at all," was Hazel's reply to his polite query. "I'm so used to trains that I believe I could ride on top of them and not be uncomfortable."

"Imagine," put in Mildred, "riding on top of a train!"

"Many's the time I've done it!" said their new acquaintance. "Freight-trains, though; not passenger-trains. And it was when I was a kid."

"I don't see how you dared," said Mildred.

"I guess I was a kind of a reckless, wild kid," he said. "It's a wonder I didn't get killed, the chances I took. Some kids takes lots of chances; that is, boys."

"Girls do, too," said Hazel quickly. "Girls take just as many chances as boys."

"Oh, no, Hazel!" remonstrated her friend, and received an approving look from the male.

"Where are you headed for?" he asked.

"Frisco first and then Los Angeles," Hazel replied.

"Listen—let me give you a tip. Don't say 'Frisco' in front of them native sons. They don't like that nickname."

"I should worry what they like and don't like!" said Hazel, rather snootily, Mildred thought.

"This your first trip out there?" Chapman inquired.

"No," Hazel answered to Mildred's surprise, for the purpose of the journey, she had been led to believe, was to give Hazel a glimpse of one of the few parts of America that she had never visited.

"How long since you was out there last?" asked Chapman.

"Let's see," said Hazel. "It's been——" She was embarrassed by Mildred's wondering look. "I don't know exactly. I've forgotten."

"This is about my fiftieth trip," said Chapman. "If you haven't been——"

"I like Florida better," interrupted Hazel. "I generally go there in the winter."

"'Generally!'" thought Mildred, who had reliable information that the previous winter had been her friend's first in the South.

"I used to go to Palm Beach every year," said Chapman, "but that was before it got common. It seems to be that the people that goes to Florida now, well, they're just riffraff."

"The people that go to Tampa aren't riffraff," said Hazel. "I met some lovely people there last winter, especially one couple, the Babcocks. From Racine. They were perfectly lovely to me. We played Mah Jongg nearly every evening. They wanted me to come up and visit them in Racine this last summer, but something happened. Oh, yes; Sis's nurse got married. She was a Swedish girl. Just perfect! And Sis had absolute confidence in her.

"I always say that when a Swede is good, they're *good!* Now she's got a young girl about nineteen that's wild about movie actors and so absent-minded that Sis is scared to death she'll give Junior coffee and drink his milk herself. Just crazy! Jennie, her name is. So I didn't get up to Racine."

"Ever been out to Yellowstone?"

"Oh, isn't it wonderful!" responded Hazel. "Isn't 'Old Faithful' just fascinating! You see," she explained to Mildred, "It's one of the geysers and they call it 'Old Faithful' because it spouts every hour and ten minutes or something, just as regular as clockwork. Wonderful! And the different falls and canyons! Wonderful! And what a wonderful view from Inspiration Point!"

"Ever been to the Thousand Islands?" asked Chapman.

"Wonderful! And I was going up there again last summer with a girl friend of mine, Bess Eldridge. She was engaged to a man named Harley Bateman. A wonderful fellow when he wasn't drinking, but when he'd had a few drinks, he was just terrible. So Bess and I were in Chicago and we went to a show; Eddie Cantor. It was the first time I ever saw him when he wasn't blacked up. Well, we were walking out of the theater that night and who should we run into but Harley Bateman, terribly boiled, and a girl from Elkhart, Joan Killian. So Bess broke off her engagement and last fall she married a man named Wannop who's interested in flour-mills or something up in Minneapolis. So I didn't get to the Thousand Islands after all. That is, a second time.

" But I always think that if a person hasn't taken that trip, they haven't seen anything. And Bess would have certainly enjoyed it. She used to bite her finger-nails till she didn't have any left. But she married this man from Minneapolis."

After luncheon the three moved to the observation-car and made a brave effort to be interested in what passes for scenery in Nebraska.

For no possible reason, it reminded Chapman of Northern Michigan.

" Have you ever been up in Northern Michigan? "

" Yes, indeed," said Hazel. " I visited a week once in Petoskey. Some friends of mine named Gilbert. They had their own launch. Ina Gilbert—that's Mrs. Gilbert—her hair used to be the loveliest thing in the world and she had typhoid or something and lost nearly all of it. So we played Mah Jongg every afternoon and evening."

" I mean 'way up," said Chapman. " Mackinac Island and the Upper Peninsula, the Copper Country."

" Oh, wonderful! " said Hazel. " Calumet and Houghton and Hancock! Wonderful! And the boat trip is wonderful! Though I guess I was about the only one that thought so. Everybody else was sick. The captain said it was the roughest trip he'd ever been on, and he had lived on the Great Lakes for forty years. And another time I went across from Chicago to St. Joseph. But that wasn't so rough. We visited the House of David in Benton Harbor. They wear long beards. We were almost in hysterics, Marjorie Trumbull and I. But the time I went to Petoskey, I went alone."

" You see a lot of Finns up in that Northern Peninsula," remarked Chapman.

" Yes, and Sis had a Finnish maid once. She couldn't hardly understand a word of English. She was a Finn. Sis finally had to let her go. Now she has an Irish girl for a maid and Jennie takes care of the kiddies. Poor little Dickie, my nephew, he's nearly seven and of course he's lost all his front teeth. He looks terrible! Teeth do make such a difference! My friends always say they envy me my teeth."

"Talking about teeth," said Chapman, "you see this?" He opened his mouth and pointed to a large, dark vacancy where once had dwelt a molar. "I had that one pulled in Milwaukee the day before yesterday. The fella said I better take gas, but I said no. So he said, 'Well, you must be pretty game.' I said I faced German shell-fire for sixteen months and I guess I ain't going to be a-scared of a little forceps. Well, he said afterwards that it was one of the toughest teeth he ever pulled. The roots were the size of your little finger. And the tooth itself was full of——"

"I only had one tooth pulled in my life," said Hazel. "I'd been suffering from rheumatism and somebody suggested that it might be from a tooth, but I couldn't believe it at first because my teeth are so perfect. But I hadn't slept in months on account of these pains in my arms and limbs. So finally, just to make sure, I went to a dentist, old Doctor Platt, and he pulled this tooth"— she showed him where it had been—"and my rheumatism disappeared just like that. It was terrible not to be able to sleep because I generally sleep like a log. And I do now, since I got my tooth pulled."

"I don't sleep very good on trains," said Chapman.

"Oh, I do. Probably on account of being so used to it. I slept just beautifully last night. Mildred here insisted on taking the upper. She said if she was where she could look out the window, she never would go to sleep. Personally, I'd just as lief have the upper. I don't mind it a bit. I like it really better. But this is Mildred's first long trip and I thought she ought to have her choice. We tried to get a compartment or drawing-room, but they were all gone. Sis and I had a compartment the time we went to New Orleans. I slept in the upper."

Mildred wished she had gone places so she could take part in the conversation. Mr. Chapman must think she was terribly dumb.

She had nothing to talk about that people would care to hear, and it was kind of hard to keep awake when you weren't talking yourself, even with such interesting, traveled people to listen to as Mr. Chapman and Hazel. Mr. Chapman was a dandy-looking man and it was terrible to have to appear dumb in front of him.

But after all, she *was* dumb and Hazel's erudition made her

seem all the dumber. No wonder their new acquaintance had
scarcely looked at her since luncheon.

"Have you ever been to San Antone?" Chapman asked his
companions.

"Isn't it wonderful!" Hazel exclaimed. "The Alamo! Wonderful! And those dirty Mexicans! And Salt Lake City is wonderful, too! That temple! And swimming in the lake itself is one
of the most fascinating experiences! You know, Mildred, the water is so salt that you can't sink in it. You just lie right on top of
it like it was a floor. You can't sink. And another wonderful
place is Lake Placid. I was going back there last summer with
Bess Eldridge, but she was engaged at the time to Harley Bateman, an awfully nice boy when he wasn't drinking, but perfectly
terrible when he'd had a few drinks. He went to college with my
brother, to Michigan. Harley tried for the football nine, but the
coach hated him. His father was a druggist and owned the first
automobile in Berrien County. So we didn't go to Placid last
summer, but I'm going next summer sure. And it's wonderful in
winter, too!"

"It feels funny, where that tooth was," said Chapman.

"Outside of one experience," said Hazel, "I've never had any
trouble with my teeth. I'd been suffering from rheumatism and
somebody suggested it might be a bad tooth, but I couldn't believe
it because my teeth are perfect——"

"This was all shot to pieces," said Chapman.

"But my friends always say they envy me my teeth; my teeth
and my complexion. I try to keep my mouth clean and my face
clean, and I guess that's the answer. But it's hard to keep clean
on a train."

"Where are you going? Out to the coast?"

"Yes. Frisco and then Los Angeles."

"Don't call it Frisco in front of them Californians. They don't
like their city to be called Frisco. Is this your first trip out
there?"

"No. I was there a good many years ago."

She turned to Mildred.

"You didn't know that, did you?" she said. But Mildred was
asleep. "Poor Mildred! She's worn out. She isn't used to traveling. She's quite a pretty girl, don't you think so?"

"Very pretty!"

" Maybe not exactly pretty," said her friend, " but kind of sweet-looking, like a baby. You'd think all the men would be crazy about her, but they aren't. Lots of people don't even think she's pretty and I suppose you can't be really pretty unless you have more expression in your face than she's got. Poor Mildred hasn't had many advantages."

" At this time of year, I'd rather be in Atlantic City than San Francisco."

" Oh, isn't Atlantic City wonderful! There's only one Atlantic City! And I really like it better in the winter. Nobody but nice people go there in the winter. In the summer-time it's different. I'm no snob, but I don't mind saying that I hate to mix up with some people a person has to meet at these resort places. Terrible! Two years ago I went to Atlantic City with Bess Eldridge. Like a fool I left it to her to make the reservations and she wired tho Traymore, she says, but they didn't have anything for us. We tried the Ritz and the Ambassador and everywhere else, but we couldn't get in anywhere, that is, anywhere a person would want to stay. Bess was engaged to Harley Bateman at the time. Now she's married a man named Wannop from Minneapolis. But this time I speak of, we went to Philadelphia and stayed all night with my aunt and we had scrapple and liver and bacon for breakfast. Harley was a dandy boy when he wasn't drinking. But give me Atlantic City any time of the year! "

" I've got to send a telegram at Grand Island."

" Oh, if I sent one from there, when would it get to Elkhart? "

" Tonight or tomorrow morning."

" I want to wire my sister."

" Well, wire her from Grand Island."

" I think I'll wait and wire her from Frisco."

" But we won't be in San Francisco for over two days yet."

" But we change time before then, don't we? "

" Yes, we change at North Platte."

" Then I think I'll wire her from Grand Island."

" Your sister, you say? "

" Yes. My sister Lucy. She married Jack Kingston, the Kingston tire people."

" It certainly feels empty, where that tooth was," said Chapman.

As the train pulled out of North Platte, later in the afternoon, Chapman rejoined the two girls in the observation-car.

" Now, girls," he said, " you can set your watches back an hour. We change time here. We were Central time and now we're Mountain time."

" Mountain time," repeated Mildred. " I suppose that's where the expression started, ' it's high time.' "

Hazel and Chapman looked blank and Mildred blushed. She felt she had made a mistake saying anything at all. She opened her book, " Carlyle on Cromwell and Others," which Rev. N. L. Veach had given her for Christmas.

" Have you ever been to Washington? " Chapman asked Hazel.

" Oh, isn't it beautiful! ' The City of Magnificent Distances.' Wonderful! I was there two years ago with Bess Eldridge. We were going to meet the President, but something happened. Oh, yes; Bess got a wire from Harley Bateman that he was going to get in that afternoon. And he never came at all. He was awfully nice when he wasn't drinking, and just terrible when he drank. Bess broke off her engagement to him and married a man named Wannop, who owned some flour-mills in Minneapolis. She was a dandy girl, but bit her finger-nails just terribly. So we didn't get to see the President, but we sat through two or three sessions of the Senate and House. Do you see how they ever get anything done? And we went to Rock Creek Park and Mount Vernon and Arlington Cemetery and Keith's.

" Moran and Mack were there; you know, the black-face comedians. Moran, or maybe it's Mack, whichever is the little one, he says to the other—I've forgotten just how it went, but they were simply screaming and I thought Bess and I would be put out. We just howled. And the last night we were there we saw Thomas Meighan in ' Old Home Week.' Wonderful! Harley Bateman knows Thomas Meighan personally. He's got a beautiful home out on Long Island. He invited Harley out there to dinner one night, but something happened. Oh, yes; Harley lost a front tooth once and he had a false one put in and this day he ate some caramels and the tooth came out——"

" Look here," said Chapman, opening his mouth and pointing in it. " I got that one pulled in Milwaukee——"

" Harley was a perfect peach when he was sober, but terrible when——"

It occurred to Mildred that her presence might be embarrassing. Here were evidently kindred spirits, two people who had been everywhere and seen everything. But of course they couldn't talk anything but geography and dentistry before her.

"I think I'll go to our car and take a little nap," she said.

"Oh, don't——" began Chapman surprisingly, but stopped there.

She was gone and the kindred spirits were alone.

"I suppose," said Chapman, "you've been to Lake Louise."

"Wonderful!" Hazel responded. "Did you ever see anything as pretty in your life? They talk about the lakes of Ireland and Scotland and Switzerland, but I don't believe they can compare with Lake Louise. I was there with Bess Eldridge just before she got engaged to Harley Bateman. He was——"

"Your friend's a mighty pretty girl."

"I suppose some people would think her pretty. It's a matter of individual taste."

"Very quiet, isn't she?"

"Poor Mildred hasn't much to say. You see, she's never had any advantages and there's really nothing she can talk about. But what was I saying? Oh, yes; about Harley Bateman——"

"I think that's a good idea, taking a little nap. I believe I'll try it, too."

Hazel and Chapman lunched alone next day.

"I'm afraid Mildred is a little train sick," said Hazel. "She says she is all right but just isn't hungry. I guess the trip has been a little too much for her. You see, this is the first time she's ever been anywhere at all."

The fact was that Mildred did not like to be stared at and Chapman had stared at her all through dinner the night before, stared at her, she thought, as if she were a curiosity, as if he doubted that one so dumb could be real. She liked him, too, and it would have been so nice if she had been more like Hazel, never at a loss for something to say and able to interest him in her conversation.

"We'll be in Ogden in half an hour," said Chapman. "We stay there twenty-five minutes. That ought to give your friend a chance to get over whatever ails her. She should get out and walk around and get some air."

"You seem quite interested in Mildred," Hazel said.

"She's a mighty attractive girl," he replied. "And besides, I feel sorry for anybody that——"

"Men don't usually find her attractive. She's pretty in a way, but it's a kind of a babyish face."

" I don't think so at all——"

" We change time here again, don't we? "

" Yes. Another hour back. We've been on Mountain time and now we go to Pacific time. Some people say it's bad for a watch to turn it backwards, but it never seemed to hurt mine any. This watch——"

" I bought this watch of mine in New York," said Hazel. " It was about two years ago, the last time Bess Eldridge and I went East. Let's see; was that before or after she broke her engagement to Harley Bateman? It was before. But Harley said he knew the manager of the Belmont and he would wire him and get us a good room. Well, of course, he forgot to wire, so we finally got into the Pennsylvania, Room 1012. No, Room 1014. It was some people from Pittsburgh, a Mr. and Mrs. Bradbury, in 1012. He was lame. Bess wanted to see Jeanne Eagels in ' Rain ' and we tried to get tickets at the newsstand, but they said fifteenth row. We finally went to the Palace that night. Ina Claire was on the bill. So the next morning we came down to breakfast and who should we run into but Dave Homan! We'd met him at French Lick in the spring. Isn't French Lick wonderful !

" Well, Dave insisted on ' showing ' us New York, like we didn't know it backwards. But we did have a dandy time. Dave kept us in hysterics. I remember he took us to the Aquarium and of course a lot of other people were in there and Dave gave one of the attendants a quarter to page Mr. Fish. I thought they'd put us out, we screamed so ! Dave asked me to marry him once, just jokingly, and I told him I wouldn't think of it because I had heard it made people fat to laugh and if I lived with him I would soon have to buy my clothes from a tent-maker. Dave said we would make a great pair as we both have such a keen sense of humor. Honestly, I wouldn't give up my sense of humor for all the money in the world. I don't see how people can live without a sense of humor. Mildred, for instance; she never sees the funny side of things unless you make her a diagram and even then she looks at you like she thought you were deranged.

" But I was telling you about Dave Homan. We were talking along about one thing and another and I happened to mention Harley Bateman and Dave said, ' Harley Bateman! Do you know Harley Bateman? ' and Bess and I smiled at each other and I said I guessed we did. Well, it seems that Dave and Harley had been at Atlantic City together at a Lions' convention or something and they had some drinks and Dave had a terrible time keeping a policeman from locking Harley up. He's just as different when he's drinking as day and night. Dave got him out of it all right and they met again later on, in Chicago. Or was it Duluth? So the next day was Wednesday and Dave asked Bess and I to go to the matinée of 'Rain,' but Bess had an engagement with a dentist——"

"Do you see this?" interrupted Chapman, opening his mouth wide.

"So Dave took me alone and he said he had been hoping for that chance right along. He said three was a crowd. I believe if I had given him any encouragement—— But the man I marry must be something more than clever and witty. I like men that have been around and seen things and studied human nature and have a background. Of course they must see the funny side, too. That's the trouble with Dave Homan—he can't be serious. Harley Bateman is twice as much of a man if he wouldn't drink. It's like two different people when he drinks. He's terrible! Bess Eldridge was engaged to him, but she broke it off after we happened to see him in Chicago one time with Joan Killian, from Elkhart. Bess is married now, to a man named Wannop, a flour man from Minneapolis. So after the matinée we met Bess. She'd been to the dentist——"

"Three days ago, in Milwaukee——" began Chapman.

"So the next afternoon we were taking the boat for Boston. I'd been to Boston before, of course, but never by boat. Harley Bateman told us it was a dandy trip, so we decided to try it. Well, we left New York at five o'clock and Bess and I were up on deck when somebody came up behind us and put their hands over my eyes and said, 'Guess who it is?' Well, I couldn't have guessed in a hundred years. It was Clint Poole from South Bend. Imagine Harley Bateman's brother-in-law!"

"Here's Ogden," said Chapman as the train slowed down.

"Oh, and I've got to send Sis a telegram! My sister Lucy Kingston."

"I think I'll get out and get some air," said Chapman, but he went first to the car where Mildred sat reading.

"Miss Mildred," he said, "suppose you have breakfast with me early tomorrow morning. I'd like to show you the snow-sheds."

"That would be wonderful!" said Mildred. "I'll tell Hazel.

"No," said Chapman. "Please don't tell Hazel. I'd like to show them to you alone."

Well, even if Mildred had been used to trains, that remark would have interfered seriously with her night's sleep.

Mildred found Chapman awaiting her in the diner next morning, an hour west of Truckee.

" Are those the snow-sheds you spoke of ? "

" Yes," he replied, " but we'll talk about them later. First I want to ask you a few questions."

" Ask *me* questions ! " said Mildred. " Well, they'll have to be simple ones or I won't be able to answer them."

" They're simple enough," said Chapman. " The first one is, do you know Harley Bateman ? "

" I know *of* him, but I don't know him."

" Do you know Bess Eldridge ? "

" Just to speak to; that's all."

" What other trips have you taken besides this ? "

" None at all. This is really the first time I've ever been anywhere."

" Has your friend ever been engaged ? "

" Yes; twice. It was broken off both times."

" I bet I know why. There was no place to take her on a honeymoon."

" What do you mean ? "

" Oh, nothing. Say, did I tell you about getting my tooth pulled in Milwaukee ? "

" I don't believe so," said Mildred.

" Well, I had a terrible toothache. It was four days ago. And I thought there was no use fooling with it, so I went to a dentist and told him to pull it. He said I'd better take gas, but I wouldn't. So he pulled it and it pretty near killed me, but I never batted an eye. He said it was one of the toughest teeth he'd ever seen ; roots as big as your little finger. And the tooth itself full of poison."

" How terrible ! You must be awfully brave ! "

" Look here, at the hole," said Chapman, opening his mouth.

" Why, Mr. Chapman, it must have hurt horribly ! "

" Call me Dan."

" Oh, I couldn't."

" Well, listen—are you going to be with Miss Hazel all the time you're in San Francisco ? "

" Why, no," said Mildred. " Hazel is going to visit her aunt in Berkeley part of the time. And I'm going to stop at the Fairmont."

" When is she going to Berkeley? "

" Next Tuesday, I think."

" Can I phone you next Wednesday? "

" But Hazel will be gone then."

" Yes, I know," said Chapman, " but if you don't mind, I'll phone you just the same. Now about these snow-sheds——"

XXV

WHO DEALT?

You know, this is the first time Tom and I have been with real friends since we were married. I suppose you'll think it's funny for me to call you *my* friends when we've never met before, but Tom has talked about you so much and how much he thought of you and how crazy he was to see you and everything—well, it's just as if I'd known you all my life, like he has.

We've got our little crowd out there, play bridge and dance with them; but of course we've only been there three months, at least I have, and people you've known that length of time, well, it isn't like knowing people all your life, like you and Tom. How often I've heard Tom say he'd give any amount of money to be with Arthur and Helen, and how bored he was out there with just poor little me and his new friends!

Arthur and Helen, Arthur and Helen—he talks about you so much that it's a wonder I'm not jealous; especially of you, Helen. You must have been his real pal when you were kids.

Nearly all of his kid books, they have your name in front—to Thomas Cannon from Helen Bird Strong. This is a wonderful treat for him to see you! And a treat for me, too. Just think, I've at last met the wonderful Helen and Arthur! You must forgive me calling you by your first names; that's how I always think of you and I simply can't say Mr. and Mrs. Gratz.

No, thank you, Arthur; no more. Two is my limit and I've already exceeded it, with two cocktails before dinner and now this. But it's a special occasion, meeting Tom's best friends. I bet Tom wishes he could celebrate too, don't you, dear? Of course he could if he wanted to, but when he once makes up his mind to a thing, there's nothing in the world can shake him. He's got the strongest will power of any person I ever saw.

I do think it's wonderful, him staying on the wagon this long, a man that used to—well, you know as well as I do; probably a whole lot better, because you were with him so much in the old days, and all I know is just what he's told me. He told me about once in

Pittsburgh—— All right, Tommie; I won't say another word.
But it's all over now, thank heavens! Not a drop since we've been
married; three whole months! And he says it's forever, don't you,
dear? Though I don't mind a person drinking if they do it in
moderation. But you know Tom! He goes the limit in everything he does. Like he used to in athletics——

All right, dear; I won't make you blush. I know how you hate
the limelight. It's terrible, though, not to be able to boast about
your own husband; everything he does or ever has done seems so
wonderful. But is that only because we've been married such a
short time? Do you feel the same way about Arthur, Helen?
You do? And you married him four years ago, isn't that right?
And you eloped, didn't you? You see I know all about you.

Oh, are you waiting for me? Do we cut for partners? Why
can't we play families? I don't feel so bad if I do something
dumb when it's Tom I'm playing with. He never scolds, though
he does give me some terrible looks. But not very often lately; I
don't make the silly mistakes I used to. I'm pretty good now,
aren't I, Tom? You better say so, because if I'm not, it's your
fault. You know Tom had to teach me the game. I never played
at all till we were engaged. Imagine! And I guess I was pretty
awful at first, but Tom was a dear, so patient! I know he thought
I never would learn, but I fooled you, didn't I, Tommie?

No, indeed, I'd rather play than do almost anything. But
you'll sing for us, won't you, Helen? I mean after a while. Tom
has raved to me about your voice and I'm dying to hear it.

What are we playing for? Yes, a penny's perfectly all right.
Out there we generally play for half a cent a piece, a penny a family. But a penny apiece is all right. I guess we can afford it now,
can't we, dear? Tom hasn't told you about his raise. He was——
All right, Tommie; I'll shut up. I know you hate to be talked
about, but your wife can't help being just a teeny bit proud of you.
And I think your best friends are interested in your affairs, aren't
you, folks?

But Tom is the most secretive person I ever knew. I believe he
even keeps things from me! Not very many, though. I can usually tell when he's hiding something and I keep after him till he
confesses. He often says I should have been a lawyer or a detective, the way I can worm things out of people. Don't you, Tom?

For instance, I never would have known about his experience
with those horrid football people at Yale if I hadn't just made him
tell me. Didn't you know about that? No, Tom, I'm going to tell

Arthur even if you hate me for it. I know you'd be interested, Arthur, not only because you're Tom's friend, but on account of you being such a famous athlete yourself. Let me see, how was it, Tom? You must help me out. Well, if I don't get it right, you correct me.

Well, Tom's friends at Yale had heard what a wonderful football player he was in high school so they made him try for a place on the Yale nine. Tom had always played half-back. You have to be a fast runner to be a half-back and Tom could run awfully fast. He can yet. When we were engaged we used to run races and the prize was—— All right, Tommie, I won't give away our secrets. Anyway, he can beat me to pieces.

Well, he wanted to play half-back at Yale and he was getting along fine and the other men on the team said he would be a wonder and then one day they were having their practice and Tex Jones, no, Ted Jones—he's the main coach—he scolded Tom for having the signal wrong and Tom proved that Jones was wrong and he was right and Jones never forgave him. He made Tom quit playing half-back and put him tackle or end or some place like that where you can't do anything and being a fast runner doesn't count. So Tom saw that Jones had it in for him and he quit. Wasn't that it, Tom? Well, anyway, it was something.

Oh, are you waiting for me? I'm sorry. What did you bid, Helen? And you, Tom? You doubled her? And Arthur passed? Well, let's see. I wish I could remember what that means. I know that sometimes when he doubles he means one thing and sometimes another. But I always forget which is which. Let me see; it was two spades that he doubled, wasn't it? That means I'm to leave him in, I'm pretty sure. Well, I'll pass. Oh, I'm sorry, Tommie! I knew I'd get it wrong. Please forgive me. But maybe we'll set them anyway. Whose lead?

I'll stop talking now and try and keep my mind on the game. You needn't look that way, Tommie. I *can* stop talking if I try. It's kind of hard to concentrate though, when you're, well, excited. It's not only meeting you people, but I always get excited traveling. I was just terrible on our honeymoon, but then I guess a honeymoon's enough to make anybody nervous. I'll never forget when we went into the hotel in Chicago—— All right, Tommie, I won't. But I can tell about meeting the Bakers.

They're a couple about our age that I've known all my life. They were the last people in the world I wanted to see, but we ran into them on State Street and they insisted on us coming to their hotel for dinner and before dinner they took us up to their room and Ken—that's Mr. Baker—Ken made some cocktails, though I didn't want any and Tom was on the wagon. He said a honeymoon was a fine time to be on the wagon! Ken said.

"Don't tempt him, Ken," I said. "Tom isn't a drinker like you and Gertie and the rest of us. When he starts, he can't stop." Gertie is Mrs. Baker.

So Ken said why should he stop and I said there was good reason why he should because he had promised me he would and he told me the day we were married that if I ever saw him take another drink I would know that——

What did you make? Two odd? Well, thank heavens that isn't a game! Oh, that does make a game, doesn't it? Because Tom doubled and I left him in. Isn't that wicked! Oh, dearie, please forgive me and I'll promise to pay attention from now on! What do I do with these? Oh, yes, I make them for Arthur.

I was telling you about the Bakers. Finally Ken saw he couldn't make Tom take a drink, so he gave up in disgust. But imagine meeting them on our honeymoon, when we didn't want to see anybody! I don't suppose anybody does unless they're already tired of each other, and we certainly weren't, were we, Tommie? And aren't yet, are we, dear? And never will be. But I guess I better speak for myself.

There! I'm talking again! But you see it's the first time we've been with anybody we really cared about; I mean, you're Tom's best friends and it's so nice to get a chance to talk to somebody who's known him a long time. Out there the people we run around with are almost strangers and they don't talk about anything but themselves and how much money their husbands make. You never can talk to them about things that are worth while, like books. I'm wild about books, but I honestly don't believe half the women we know out there can read. Or at least they don't. If you mention some really worth while novel like, say, "Black Oxen," they think you're trying to put on the Ritz.

You said a no-trump, didn't you, Tom? And Arthur passed. Let me see; I wish I knew what to do. I haven't any five-card—it's terrible! Just a minute. I wish somebody could—I know I ought to take—but—well, I'll pass. Oh, Tom, this is the worst you ever saw, but I don't know what I could have done.

I do hold the most terrible cards! I certainly believe in the saying, "Unlucky at cards, lucky in love." Whoever made it up must have been thinking of me. I hate to lay them down, dear.

I know you'll say I ought to have done something. Well, there they are! Let's see your hand, Helen. Oh, Tom, she's—but I mustn't tell, must I? Anyway, I'm dummy. That's one comfort. I can't make a mistake when I'm dummy. I believe Tom overbids lots of times so I'll be dummy and can't do anything ridiculous. But at that I'm much better than I used to be, aren't I, dear?

Helen, do you mind telling me where you got that gown? Crandall and Nelsons's? I've heard of them, but I heard they were terribly expensive. Of course a person can't expect to get a gown like that without paying for it. I've got to get some things while I'm here and I suppose that's where I better go, if their things aren't too horribly dear. I haven't had a thing new since I was married and I've worn this so much I'm sick of it.

Tom's always after me to buy clothes, but I can't seem to get used to spending somebody else's money, though it was dad's money I spent before I did Tom's, but that's different, don't you think so? And of course at first we didn't have very much to spend, did we, dear? But now that we've had our raise—— All right, Tommie, I won't say another word.

Oh, did you know they tried to get Tom to run for mayor? Tom is making faces at me to shut up, but I don't see any harm in telling it to his best friends. They know we're not the kind that brag, Tommie. I do think it was quite a tribute; he'd only lived there a little over a year. It came up one night when the Guthries were at our house, playing bridge. Mr. Guthrie—that's A. L. Guthrie —he's one of the big lumbermen out there. He owns—just what does he own, Tom? Oh, I'm sorry. Anyway, he's got millions. Well, at least thousands.

He and his wife were at our house playing bridge. She's the queerest woman! If you just saw her, you'd think she was a janitor or something; she wears the most hideous clothes. Why, that night she had on a—honestly you'd have sworn it was a maternity gown, and for no reason. And the first time I met her—well, I just can't describe it. And she's a graduate of Bryn Mawr and one of the oldest families in Philadelphia. You'd never believe it!

She and her husband are terribly funny in a bridge game. He doesn't think there ought to be any conventions; he says a person might just as well tell each other what they've got. So he won't pay any attention to what-do-you-call-'em, informatory, doubles and so forth. And she plays all the conventions, so you can imagine how they get along. Fight! Not really fight, you know, but argue. That is, he does. It's horribly embarrassing to whoever is playing with them. Honestly, if Tom ever spoke to me like Mr. Guthrie does to his wife, well—aren't they terrible, Tom? Oh, I'm sorry!

She was the first woman in Portland that called on me and I thought it was awfully nice of her, though when I saw her at the door I would have sworn she was a book agent or maybe a cook looking for work. She had on a—well, I can't describe it. But it was sweet of her to call, she being one of the real people there and me—well, that was before Tom was made a vice-president. What? Oh, I never dreamed he hadn't written you about that!

But Mrs. Guthrie acted just like it was a great honor for her to meet me, and I like people to act that way even when I know it's all apple sauce. Isn't that a funny expression, "apple sauce"? Some man said it in a vaudeville show in Portland the Monday night before we left. He was a comedian—Jack Brooks or Ned Frawley or something. It means—well, I don't know how to describe it. But we had a terrible time after the first few minutes. She is the silentest person I ever knew and I'm kind of bashful myself with strangers. What are you grinning about, Tommie? I am, too, bashful when I don't know people. Not exactly bashful, maybe, but, well, bashful.

It was one of the most embarrassing things I ever went through. Neither of us could say a word and I could hardly help from laughing at what she had on. But after you get to know her you don't mind her clothes, though it's a terrible temptation all the time not to tell her how much nicer—— And her hair! But she plays a dandy game of bridge, lots better than her husband. You know he won't play conventions. He says it's just like telling you what's in each other's hand. And they have awful arguments in a game. That is, he does. She's nice and quiet and it's a kind of mystery how they ever fell in love. Though there's a saying or a proverb or something, isn't there, about like not liking like? Or is it just the other way?

But I was going to tell you about them wanting Tom to be mayor. Oh, Tom, only two down? Why, I think you did splendidly! I gave you a miserable hand and Helen had—what didn't you have, Helen? You had the ace, king of clubs. No, Tom had the king. No, Tom had the queen. Or was it spades? And you had the ace of hearts. No, Tom had that. No, he didn't. What did you have, Tom? I don't exactly see what you bid on. Of course I was terrible, but—what's the difference anyway?

What was I saying? Oh, yes, about Mr. and Mrs. Guthrie. It's funny for a couple like that to get married when they are so different in every way. I never saw two people with such different tastes. For instance, Mr. Guthrie is keen about motoring and Mrs. Guthrie just hates it. She simply suffers all the time she's in a car. He likes a good time, dancing, golfing, fishing, shows, things like that. She isn't interested in anything but church work and bridge work.

"Bridge work." I meant bridge, not bridge work. That's funny, isn't it? And yet they get along awfully well; that is when they're not playing cards or doing something else together. But it does seem queer that they picked each other out. Still, I guess hardly any husband and wife agree on anything.

You take Tom and me, though, and you'd think we were made for each other. It seems like we feel just the same about everything. That is, almost everything. The things we don't agree on are little things that don't matter. Like music. Tom is wild about jazz and blues and dance music. He adores Irving Berlin and Gershwin and Jack Kearns. He's always after those kind of things on the radio and I just want serious, classical things like "Humoresque" and "Indian Love Lyrics." And then there's shows. Tom is crazy over Ed Wynn and I can't see anything in him. Just the way he laughs at his own jokes is enough to spoil him for me. If I'm going to spend time and money on a theater I want to see something worth while—"The Fool" or "Lightnin'."

And things to eat. Tom insists, or that is he did insist, on a great big breakfast—fruit, cereal, eggs, toast, and coffee. All I want is a little fruit and dry toast and coffee. I think it's a great deal better for a person. So that's one habit I broke Tom of, was big breakfasts. And another thing he did when we were first married was to take off his shoes as soon as he got home from the office and put on bedroom slippers. I believe a person ought not to get sloppy just because they're married.

But the worst of all was pajamas! What's the difference, Tommie? Helen and Arthur don't mind. And I think it's kind of funny, you being so old-fashioned. I mean Tom had always worn a nightgown till I made him give it up. And it was a struggle, believe me! I had to threaten to leave him if he didn't buy pajamas. He certainly hated it. And now he's mad at me for telling, aren't you, Tommie? I just couldn't help it. I think it's so funny in this day and age. I hope Arthur doesn't wear them; nightgowns, I mean. You don't, do you, Arthur? I knew you didn't.

Oh, are you waiting for me? What did you say, Arthur? Two diamonds? Let's see what that means. When Tom makes an original bid of two it means he hasn't got the tops. I wonder—but of course you couldn't have the—heavens! What am I saying! I guess I better just keep still and pass.

But what was I going to tell you? Something about—oh, did I tell you about Tom being an author? I had no idea he was talented that way till after we were married and I was unpacking his old papers and things and came across a poem he'd written, the saddest, mushiest poem! Of course it was a long time ago he wrote it; it was dated four years ago, long before he met me, so it didn't make me very jealous, though it was about some other girl. You didn't know I found it, did you, Tommie?

But that wasn't what I refer to. He's written a story, too, and he's sent it to four different magazines and they all sent it back. I tell him though, that that doesn't mean anything. When you see some of the things the magazines do print, why, it's an honor to have them *not* like yours. The only thing is that Tom worked so hard over it and sat up nights writing and rewriting, it's a kind of a disappointment to have them turn it down.

It's a story about two men and a girl and they were all brought up together and one of the men was awfully popular and well off and good-looking and a great athlete—a man like Arthur. There, Arthur! How is that for a T. L.? The other man was just an ordinary man with not much money, but the girl seemed to like him better and she promised to wait for him. Then this man worked hard and got money enough to see him through Yale.

The other man, the well-off one, went to Princeton and made a big hit as an athlete and everything and he was through college long before his friend because his friend had to earn the money first. And the well-off man kept after the girl to marry him. He didn't know she had promised the other one. Anyway she got tired waiting for the man she was engaged to and eloped with the other one. And the story ends up by the man she threw down welcoming the couple when they came home and pretending everything was all right, though his heart was broken.

What are you blushing about, Tommie? It's nothing to be ashamed of. I thought it was very well written and if the editors had any sense they'd have taken it.

Still, I don't believe the real editors see half the stories that are sent to them. In fact I know they don't. You've either got to have a name or a pull to get your things published. Or else pay

the magazines to publish them. Of course if you are Robert
Chambers or Irving R. Cobb, they will print whatever you write
whether it's good or bad. But you haven't got a chance if you are
an unknown like Tom. They just keep your story long enough so
you will think they are considering it and then they send it back
with a form letter saying it's not available for their magazine and
they don't even tell why.

You remember, Tom, that Mr. Hastings we met at the Hammonds'. He's a writer and knows all about it. He was telling me
of an experience he had with one of the magazines; I forget which
one, but it was one of the big ones. He wrote a story and sent it
to them and they sent it back and said they couldn't use it.

Well, some time after that Mr. Hastings was in a hotel in Chicago and a bell-boy went around the lobby paging Mr.—— I forget the name, but it was the name of the editor of this magazine
that had sent back the story, Runkle, or Byers, or some such name.
So the man, whatever his name was, he was really there and answered the page and afterwards Mr. Hastings went up to him and
introduced himself and told the man about sending a story to his
magazine and the man said he didn't remember anything about it.
And he was the editor! Of course he'd never seen it. No wonder
Tom's story keeps coming back!

He says he is through sending it and just the other day he was
going to tear it up, but I made him keep it because we may meet
somebody some time who knows the inside ropes and can get a
hearing with some big editor. I'm sure it's just a question of pull.
Some of the things that get into the magazines sound like they had
been written by the editor's friends or relatives or somebody whom
they didn't want to hurt their feelings. And Tom really can
write!

I wish I could remember that poem of his I found. I memorized it once, but—wait! I believe I can still say it! Hush, Tommie! What hurt will it do anybody? Let me see; it goes:

> "I thought the sweetness of her song
> Would ever, ever more belong
> To me; I thought (O thought divine!)
> My bird was really mine!

> "But promises are made, it seems,
> Just to be broken. All my dreams
> Fade out and leave me crushed, alone.
> My bird, alas, has flown!"

Isn't that pretty. He wrote it four years ago. Why, Helen, you revoked! And, Tom, do you know that's Scotch you're drinking? You said—— *Why, Tom!*

XXVI

MY ROOMY

I

No—I ain't signed for next year; but there won't be no trouble about that. The dough part of it is all fixed up. John and me talked it over and I'll sign as soon as they send me a contract. All I told him was that he'd have to let me pick my own roommate after this and not sic no wild man on to me.

You know I didn't hit much the last two months o' the season. Some o' the boys, I notice, wrote some stuff about me gettin' old and losin' my battin' eye. That's all bunk! The reason I didn't hit was because I wasn't gettin' enough sleep. And the reason for that was Mr. Elliott.

He wasn't with us after the last part o' May, but I roomed with him long enough to get the insomny. I was the only guy in the club game enough to stand for him; but I was sorry afterward that I done it, because it sure did put a crimp in my little old average.

And do you know where he is now? I got a letter today and I'll read it to you. No—I guess I better tell you somethin' about him first. You fellers never got acquainted with him and you ought to hear the dope to understand the letter. I'll make it as short as I can.

He didn't play in no league last year. He was with some semi-pros over in Michigan and somebody writes John about him. So John sends Needham over to look at him. Tom stayed there Saturday and Sunday, and seen him work twice. He was playin' the outfield, but as luck would have it they wasn't a fly ball hit in his direction in both games. A base hit was made out his way and he booted it, and that's the only report Tom could get on his fieldin'. But he wallops two over the wall in one day and they catch two line drives off him. The next day he gets four blows and two o' them is triples.

So Tom comes back and tells John the guy is a whale of a hitter and fast as Cobb, but he don't know nothin' about his fieldin'. Then John signs him to a contract—twelve hundred or somethin'

327

like that. We'd been in Tampa a week before he showed up. Then he comes to the hotel and just sits round all day, without tellin' nobody who he was. Finally the bellhops was going to chase him out and he says he's one o' the ballplayers. Then the clerk gets John to go over and talk to him. He tells John his name and says he hasn't had nothin' to eat for three days, because he was broke. John told me afterward that he'd drew about three hundred in advance—last winter sometime. Well, they took him in the dinin' room and they tell me he inhaled about four meals at once. That night they roomed him with Heine.

Next mornin' Heine and me walks out to the grounds together and Heine tells me about him. He says:

"Don't never call me a bug again. They got me roomin' with the champion o' the world."

"Who is he?" I says.

"I don't know and I don't want to know," says Heine; "but if they stick him in there with me again I'll jump to the Federals. To start with, he ain't got no baggage. I ast him where his trunk was and he says he didn't have none. Then I ast him if he didn't have no suitcase, and he says: 'No. What do you care?' I was goin' to lend him some pajamas, but he put on the shirt o' the uniform John give him last night and slept in that. He was asleep when I got up this mornin'. I seen his collar layin' on the dresser and it looked like he had wore it in Pittsburgh every day for a year. So I throwed it out the window and he comes down to breakfast with no collar. I ast him what size collar he wore and he says he didn't want none, because he wasn't goin' out nowheres. After breakfast he beat it up to the room again and put on his uniform. When I got up there he was lookin' in the glass at himself, and he done it all the time I was dressin'."

When we got out to the park I got my first look at him. Pretty good-lookin' guy, too, in his unie—big shoulders and well put together; built somethin' like Heine himself. He was talkin' to John when I come up.

"What position do you play?" John was askin' him.

"I play anywheres," says Elliott.

"You're the kind I'm lookin' for," says John. Then he says: "You was an outfielder up there in Michigan, wasn't you?"

"I don't care where I play," says Elliott.

John sends him to the outfield and forgets all about him for a while. Pretty soon Miller comes in and says:

"I ain't goin' to shag for no bush outfielder!"

John ast him what was the matter, and Miller tells him that Elliott ain't doin' nothin' but just standin' out there; that he ain't makin' no attemp' to catch the fungoes, and that he won't even chase 'em. Then John starts watchin' him, and it was just like Miller said. Larry hit one pretty near in his lap and he stepped out o' the way. John calls him in and ast him:

"Why don't you go after them fly balls?"

"Because I don't want 'em," says Elliott.

John gets sarcastic and says:

"What do you want? Of course we'll see that you get anythin' you want!"

"Give me a ticket back home," says Elliott.

"Don't you want to stick with the club?" says John, and the busher tells him, no, he certainly did not. Then John tells him he'll have to pay his own fare home and Elliott don't get sore at all. He just says:

"Well, I'll have to stick, then—because I'm broke."

We was havin' battin' practice and John tells him to go up and hit a few. And you ought to of seen him bust 'em!

Lavender was in there workin' and he'd been pitchin' a little all winter, so he was in pretty good shape. He lobbed one up to Elliott, and he hit it 'way up in some trees outside the fence—about a mile, I guess. Then John tells Jimmy to put somethin' on the ball. Jim comes through with one of his fast ones and the kid slams it agin the right-field wall on a line.

"Give him your spitter!" yells John, and Jim handed him one. He pulled it over first base so fast that Bert, who was standin' down there, couldn't hardly duck in time. If it'd hit him it'd killed him.

Well, he kep' on hittin' everythin' Jim give him—and Jim had somethin' too. Finally John gets Pierce warmed up and sends him out to pitch, tellin' him to hand Elliott a flock o' curve balls. He wanted to see if lefthanders was goin' to bother him. But he slammed 'em right along, and I don't b'lieve he hit more'n two the whole mornin' that wouldn't of been base hits in a game.

They sent him out to the outfield again in the afternoon, and after a lot o' coaxin' Leach got him to go after fly balls; but that's all he did do—just go after 'em. One hit him on the bean and another on the shoulder. He run back after the short ones and 'way in after the ones that went over his head. He catched just one—a line drive that he couldn't get out o' the way of; and then he acted like it hurt his hands.

I come back to the hotel with John. He ast me what I thought of Elliott.

" Well," I says, " he'd be the greatest ballplayer in the world if he could just play ball. He sure can bust 'em."

John says he was afraid he couldn't never make an outfielder out o' him. He says:

" I'll try him on the infield to-morrow. They must be some place he can play. I never seen a lefthand hitter that looked so good agin lefthand pitchin'—and he's got a great arm; but he acts like he'd never saw a fly ball."

Well, he was just as bad on the infield. They put him at short and he was like a sieve. You could of drove a hearse between him and second base without him gettin' near it. He'd stoop over for a ground ball about the time it was bouncin' up agin the fence; and when he'd try to cover the bag on a peg he'd trip over it.

They tried him at first base and sometimes he'd run 'way over in the coachers' box and sometimes out in right field lookin' for the bag. Once Heine shot one acrost at him on a line and he never touched it with his hands. It went bam! right in the pit of his stomach—and the lunch he'd ate didn't do him no good.

Finally John just give up and says he'd have to keep him on the bench and let him earn his pay by bustin' 'em a couple o' times a week or so. We all agreed with John that this bird would be a whale of a pinch hitter—and we was right too. He was hittin' 'way over five hundred when the blowoff come, along about the last o' May.

II

Before the trainin' trip was over, Elliott had roomed with pretty near everybody in the club. Heine raised an awful holler after the second night down there and John put the bug in with Needham. Tom stood him for three nights. Then he doubled up with Archer, and Schulte, and Miller, and Leach, and Saier—and the whole bunch in turn, averagin' about two nights with each one before they put up a kick. Then John tried him with some o' the youngsters, but they wouldn't stand for him no more'n the others. They all said he was crazy and they was afraid he'd get violent some night and stick a knife in 'em.

He always insisted on havin' the water run in the bathtub all night, because he said it reminded him of the sound of the dam near his home. The fellers might get up four or five times a night and shut off the faucet, but he'd get right up after 'em and turn it on again. Carter, a big bush pitcher from Georgia, started a fight with him about it one night, and Elliott pretty near killed him. So the rest o' the bunch, when they'd saw Carter's map next mornin', didn't have the nerve to do nothin' when it come their turn.

Another o' his habits was the thing that scared 'em, though. He'd brought a razor with him—in his pocket, I guess—and he used to do his shavin' in the middle o' the night. Instead o' doin' it in the bathroom he'd lather his face and then come out and stand in front o' the lookin'-glass on the dresser. Of course he'd have all the lights turned on, and that was bad enough when a feller wanted to sleep; but the worst of it was that he'd stop shavin' every little while and turn round and stare at the guy who was makin' a failure o' tryin' to sleep. Then he'd wave his razor round in the air and laugh, and begin shavin' agin. You can imagine how comf'table his roomies felt!

John had bought him a suitcase and some clothes and things, and charged 'em up to him. He'd drew so much dough in advance that he didn't have nothin' comin' till about June. He never thanked John and he'd wear one shirt and one collar till some one throwed 'em away.

Well, we finally gets to Indianapolis, and we was goin' from there to Cincy to open. The last day in Indianapolis John come and ast me how I'd like to change roomies. I says I was perfectly satisfied with Larry. Then John says:

" I wisht you'd try Elliott. The other boys all kicks on him, but he seems to hang round you a lot and I b'lieve you could get along all right."

" Why don't you room him alone? " I ast.

" The boss or the hotels won't stand for us roomin' alone," says John. " You go ahead and try it, and see how you make out. If he's too much for you let me know; but he likes you and I think he'll be diff'rent with a guy who can talk to him like you can."

So I says I'd tackle it, because I didn't want to throw John down. When we got to Cincy they stuck Elliott and me in one room, and we was together till he quit us.

III

I went to the room early that night, because we was goin' to open next day and I wanted to feel like somethin'. First thing I done when I got undressed was turn on both faucets in the bathtub.

They was makin' an awful racket when Elliott finally come in about midnight. I was layin' awake and I opened right up on him. I says:

" Don't shut off that water, because I like to hear it run."

Then I turned over and pretended to be asleep. The bug got his clothes off, and then what did he do but go in the bathroom and shut off the water! Then he come back in the room and says:

" I guess no one's goin' to tell me what to do in here."

But I kep' right on pretendin' to sleep and didn't pay no attention. When he'd got into his bed I jumped out o' mine and turned on all the lights and begun stroppin' my razor. He says:

" What's comin' off? "

" Some o' my whiskers," I says. " I always shave along about this time."

" No, you don't! " he says. " I was in your room one mornin' down in Louisville and I seen you shavin' then."

" Well," I says, " the boys tell me you shave in the middle o' the night; and I thought if I done all the things you do mebbe I'd get so's I could hit like you."

" You must be superstitious! " he says. And I told him I was. " I'm a good hitter," he says, " and I'd be a good hitter if I never shaved at all. That don't make no diff'rence."

" Yes, it does," I says. " You prob'ly hit good because you shave at night; but you'd be a better fielder if you shaved in the mornin'."

You see, I was tryin' to be just as crazy as him—though that wasn't hardly possible.

" If that's right," says he, " I'll do my shavin' in the mornin'— because I seen in the papers where the boys says that if I could play the outfield like I can hit I'd be as good as Cobb. They tell me Cobb gets twenty thousand a year."

" No," I says; " he don't get that much—but he gets about ten times as much as you do."

" Well," he says, " I'm goin' to be as good as him, because I need the money."

" What do you want with money? " I says.

He just laughed and didn't say nothin'; but from that time on the water didn't run in the bathtub nights and he done his shavin' after breakfast. I didn't notice, though, that he looked any better in fieldin' practice.

IV

It rained one day in Cincy and they trimmed us two out o' the other three; but it wasn't Elliott's fault.

They had Larry beat four to one in the ninth innin' o' the first game. Archer gets on with two out, and John sends my roomy up to hit—though Benton, a lefthander, is workin' for them. The first thing Benton serves up there Elliott cracks it a mile over Hobby's head. It would of been good for three easy—only Archer—playin' safe, o' course—pulls up at third base. Tommy couldn't do nothin' and we was licked.

The next day he hits one out o' the park off the Indian; but we was 'way behind and they was nobody on at the time. We copped the last one without usin' no pinch hitters.

I didn't have no trouble with him nights durin' the whole series. He come to bed pretty late while we was there and I told him he'd better not let John catch him at it.

" What would he do ? " he says.

" Fine you fifty," I says.

" He can't fine me a dime," he says, " because I ain't got it."

Then I told him he'd be fined all he had comin' if he didn't get in the hotel before midnight; but he just laughed and says he didn't think John had a kick comin' so long as he kep' bustin' the ball.

" Some day you'll go up there and you won't bust it," I says.

" That'll be an accident," he says.

That stopped me and I didn't say nothin'. What could you say to a guy who hated himself like that?

The " accident " happened in St. Louis the first day. We needed two runs in the eighth and Saier and Brid was on, with two out. John tells Elliott to go up in Pierce's place. The bug goes up and Griner gives him two bad balls—'way outside. I thought they was goin' to walk him—and it looked like good judgment, because they'd heard what he done in Cincy. But no! Griner comes back with a fast one right over and Elliott pulls it down the right foul line, about two foot foul. He hit it so hard you'd of thought they'd sure walk him then; but Griner gives him another fast one. He slammed it again just as hard, but foul. Then Griner gives him one 'way outside and it's two and three. John says, on the bench:

" If they don't walk him now he'll bust that fence down."

I thought the same and I was sure Griner wouldn't give him nothin' to hit; but he come with a curve and Rigler calls Elliott out. From where we sat the last one looked low, and I thought Elliott'd make a kick. He come back to the bench smilin'.

John starts for his position, but stopped and ast the bug what was the matter with that one. Any busher I ever knowed would of said, " It was too low," or " It was outside," or " It was inside." Elliott says:

" Nothin' at all. It was right over the middle."

" Why didn't you bust it, then ? " says John.

" I was afraid I'd kill somebody," says Elliott, and laughed like a big boob.

John was pretty near chokin'.

" What are you laughin' at ? " he says.

" I was thinkin' of a nickel show I seen in Cincinnati," says the bug.

" Well," says John, so mad he couldn't hardly see, " that show and that laugh'll cost you fifty."

We got beat, and I wouldn't of blamed John if he'd fined him his whole season's pay.

Up 'n the room that night I told him he'd better cut out that laughin' stuff when we was gettin' trimmed or he never would have no pay day. Then he got confidential.

" Pay day wouldn't do me no good," he says. " When I'm all squared up with the club and begin to have a pay day I'll only get a hundred bucks at a time, and I'll owe that to some o' you fellers. I wisht we could win the pennant and get in on that World's Series dough. Then I'd get a bunch at once."

" What would you do with a bunch o' dough ? " I ast him.

" Don't tell nobody, sport," he says; " but if I ever get five hundred at once I'm goin' to get married."

" Oh ! " I says. " And who's the lucky girl ? "

" She's a girl up in Muskegon," says Elliott; " and you're right when you call her lucky."

" You don't like yourself much, do you ? " I says.

" I got reason to like myself," says he. " You'd like yourself, too, if you could hit 'em like me."

" Well," I says, " you didn't show me no hittin' to-day."

" I couldn't hit because I was laughin' too hard," says Elliott.

" What was it you was laughin' at ? " I says.

" I was laughin' at that pitcher," he says. " He thought he had somethin' and he didn't have nothin'."

" He had enough to whiff you with," I says.

" He didn't have nothin' ! " says he again. " I was afraid if I busted one off him they'd can him, and then I couldn't never hit agin him no more."

Naturally I didn't have no comeback to that. I just sort o' gasped and got ready to go to sleep; but he wasn't through.

" I wisht you could see this bird ! " he says.

" What bird ? " I says.

" This dame that's nuts about me," he says.

" Good-looker ? " I ast.

" No," he says; " she ain't no bear for looks. They ain't nothin' about her for a guy to rave over till you hear her sing. She sure can holler some."

" What kind o' voice has she got ? " I ast.

" A bear," says he.

" No," I says; " I mean is she a barytone or an air ? "

" I don't know," he says; " but she's got the loudest voice I ever hear on a woman. She's pretty near got me beat."

" Can you sing ? " I says; and I was sorry right afterward that I ast him that question.

I guess it must of been bad enough to have the water runnin' night after night and to have him wavin' that razor round; but that couldn't of been nothin' to his singin'. Just as soon as I'd pulled that boner he says, " Listen to me ! " and starts in on ' Silver Threads Among the Gold.' Mind you, it was after midnight and they was guests all round us tryin' to sleep !

They used to be noise enough in our club when we had Hofman and Sheckard and Richie harmonizin'; but this bug's voice was louder'n all o' theirn combined. We once had a pitcher named Martin Walsh—brother o' Big Ed's—and I thought he could drownd out the Subway; but this guy made a boiler factory sound like Dummy Taylor. If the whole hotel wasn't awake when he'd howled the first line it's a pipe they was when he cut loose, which he done when he come to " Always young and fair to me." Them words could of been heard easy in East St. Louis.

He didn't get no encore from me, but he goes right through it again—or starts to. I knowed somethin' was goin' to happen before he finished—and somethin' did. The night clerk and the house detective come bangin' at the door. I let 'em in and they had plenty to say. If we made another sound the whole club'd be canned out o' the hotel. I tried to salve 'em, and I says:

" He won't sing no more."

But Elliott swelled up like a poisoned pup.

" Won't I ? " he says. " I'll sing all I want to."

"You won't sing in here," says the clerk.

"They ain't room for my voice in here anyways," he says. "I'll go outdoors and sing."

And he puts his clothes on and ducks out. I didn't make no attemp' to stop him. I heard him bellowin' 'Silver Threads' down the corridor and down the stairs, with the clerk and the dick chasin' him all the way and tellin' him to shut up.

Well, the guests make a holler the next mornin'; and the hotel people tells Charlie Williams that he'll either have to let Elliott stay somewheres else or the whole club'll have to move. Charlie tells John, and John was thinkin' o' settlin' the question by releasin' Elliott.

I guess he'd about made up his mind to do it; but that afternoon they had us three to one in the ninth, and we got the bases full, with two down and Larry's turn to hit   Elliott had been sittin' on the bench sayin' nothin'.

"Do you think you can hit one today?" says John.

"I can hit one any day," says Elliott.

"Go up and hit that lefthander, then," says John, "and remember there's nothin' to laugh at."

Sallee was workin'—and workin' good; but that didn't bother the bug. He cut into one, and it went between Oakes and Whitted like a shot. He come into third standin' up and we was a run to the good. Sallee was so sore he kind o' forgot himself and took pretty near his full wind-up pitchin' to Tommy. And what did Elliott do but steal home and get away with it clean!

Well, you couldn't can him after that, could you? Charlie gets him a room somewheres and I was relieved of his company that night. The next evenin' we beat it for Chi to play about two weeks at home. He didn't tell nobody where he roomed there and I didn't see nothin' of him, 'cep' out to the park. I ast him what he did with himself nights and he says:

"Same as I do on the road—borrow some dough some place and go to the nickel shows."

"You must be stuck on 'em," I says.

"Yes," he says; "I like the ones where they kill people—because I want to learn how to do it. I may have that job some day."

"Don't pick on me," I says.

"Oh," says the bug, "you never can tell who I'll pick on."

It seemed as if he just couldn't learn nothin' about fieldin', and finally John told him to keep out o' the practice.

" A ball might hit him in the temple and croak him," says John. But he busted up a couple o' games for us at home, beatin' Pittsburgh once and Cincy once.

V

They give me a great big room at the hotel in Pittsburgh; so the fellers picked it out for the poker game. We was playin' along about ten o'clock one night when in come Elliott—the earliest he'd showed up since we'd been roomin' together. They was only five of us playin' and Tom ast him to sit in.

" I'm busted," he says.

" Can you play poker? " I ast him.

" They's nothin' I can't do! " he says. " Slip me a couple o' bucks and I'll show you."

So I slipped him a couple o' bucks and honestly hoped he'd win, because I knowed he never had no dough. Well, Tom dealt him a hand and he picks it up and says:

" I only got five cards."

" How many do you want? " I says.

" Oh," he says, " if that's all I get I'll try to make 'em do."

The pot was cracked and raised, and he stood the raise. I says to myself: " There goes my two bucks! " But no—he comes out with three queens and won the dough. It was only about seven bucks; but you'd of thought it was a million to see him grab it. He laughed like a kid.

" Guess I can't play this game! " he says; and he had me fooled for a minute—I thought he must of been kiddin' when he complained of only havin' five cards.

He copped another pot right afterward and was sittin' there with about eleven bucks in front of him when Jim opens a roodle pot for a buck. I stays and so does Elliott. Him and Jim both drawed one card and I took three. I had kings or queens—I forget which. I didn't help 'em none; so when Jim bets a buck I throws my hand away.

" How much can I bet? " says the bug.

" You can raise Jim a buck if you want to," I says.

So he bets two dollars. Jim comes back at him. He comes right back at Jim. Jim raises him again and he tilts Jim right back. Well, when he'd boosted Jim with the last buck he had, Jim says:

" I'm ready to call. I guess you got me beat. What have you got? "

" I know what I've got, all right," says Elliott. " I've got a straight." And he throws his hand down. Sure enough, it was a straight, eight high. Jim pretty near fainted and so did I.

The bug had started pullin' in the dough when Jim stops him.

"Here! Wait a minute!" says Jim. "I thought you had somethin'. I filled up." Then Jim lays down his nine full.

"You beat me, I guess," says Elliott, and he looked like he'd lost his last friend.

"Beat you?" says Jim. "Of course I beat you! What did you think I had?"

"Well," says the bug, "I thought you might have a small flush or somethin'."

When I regained consciousness he was beggin' for two more bucks.

"What for?" I says. "To play poker with? You're barred from the game for life!"

"Well," he says, "if I can't play no more I want to go to sleep, and you fellers will have to get out o' this room."

Did you ever hear o' nerve like that? This was the first night he'd came in before twelve and he orders the bunch out so's he can sleep! We politely suggested to him to go to Brooklyn.

Without sayin' a word he starts in on his 'Silver Threads'; and it wasn't two minutes till the game was busted up and the bunch—all but me—was out o' there. I'd of beat it too, only he stopped yellin' as soon as they'd went.

"You're some buster!" I says. "You bust up ball games in the afternoon and poker games at night."

"Yes," he says; "that's my business—bustin' things."

And before I knowed what he was about he picked up the pitcher of ice-water that was on the floor and throwed it out the window— through the glass and all.

Right then I give him a plain talkin' to. I tells him how near he come to gettin' canned down in St. Louis because he raised so much Cain singin' in the hotel.

"But I had to keep my voice in shape," he says. "If I ever get dough enough to get married the girl and me'll go out singin' together."

"Out where?" I ast.

"Out on the vaudeville circuit," says Elliott.

"Well," I says, "if her voice is like yours you'll be wastin' money if you travel round. Just stay up in Muskegon and we'll hear you, all right!"

I told him he wouldn't never get no dough if he didn't behave himself. That, even if we got in the World's Series, he wouldn't be with us—unless he cut out the foolishness.

"We ain't goin' to get in no World's Series," he says, "and I won't never get a bunch o' money at once; so it looks like I couldn't get married this fall."

Then I told him we played a city series every fall. He'd never thought o' that and it tickled him to death. I told him the losers always got about five hundred apiece and that we were about due to win it and get about eight hundred. "But," I says, "we still got a good chance for the old pennant; and if I was you I wouldn't give up hope o' that yet—not where John can hear you, anyway."

"No," he says, "we won't win no pennant, because he won't let me play reg'lar; but I don't care so long as we're sure o' that city-series dough."

"You ain't sure of it if you don't behave," I says.

"Well," says he, very serious, "I guess I'll behave." And he did—till we made our first Eastern trip.

VI

We went to Boston first, and that crazy bunch goes out and piles up a three-run lead on us in seven innin's the first day. It was the pitcher's turn to lead off in the eighth, so up goes Elliott to bat for him. He kisses the first thing they hands him for three bases; and we says, on the bench: "Now we'll get 'em!"—because, you know, a three-run lead wasn't nothin' in Boston.

"Stay right on that bag!" John hollers to Elliott.

Mebbe if John hadn't said nothin' to him everythin' would of been all right; but when Perdue starts to pitch the first ball to Tommy, Elliott starts to steal home. He's out as far as from here to Seattle.

If I'd been carryin' a gun I'd of shot him right through the heart. As it was, I thought John'd kill him with a bat, because he was standin' there with a couple of 'em, waitin' for his turn; but I guess John was too stunned to move. He didn't even seem to see Elliott when he went to the bench. After I'd cooled off a little I says:

"Beat it and get into your clothes before John comes in. Then go to the hotel and keep out o' sight."

When I got up in the room afterward, there was Elliott, lookin' as innocent and happy as though he'd won fifty bucks with a pair o' treys.

" I thought you might of killed yourself," I says.

" What for? " he says.

" For that swell play you made," says I.

" What was the matter with the play? " ast Elliott, surprised.
" It was all right when I done it in St. Louis."

" Yes," I says; " but they was two out in St. Louis and we
wasn't no three runs behind."

" Well," he says, " if it was all right in St. Louis I don't see why
it was wrong here."

" It's a diff'rent climate here," I says, too disgusted to argue
with him.

" I wonder if they'd let me sing in this climate? " says Elliott.

" No," I says. " Don't sing in this hotel, because we don't want
to get fired out o' here—the eats is too good."

" All right," he says. " I won't sing." But when I starts down
to supper he says: " I'm li'ble to do somethin' worse'n sing."

He didn't show up in the dinin' room and John went to the
boxin' show after supper; so it looked like him and Elliott wouldn't
run into each other till the murder had left John's heart. I was
glad o' that—because a Mass'chusetts jury might not consider it
justifiable hommercide if one guy croaked another for givin' the
Boston club a game.

I went down to the corner and had a couple o' beers; and then I
come straight back, intendin' to hit the hay. The elevator boy had
went for a drink or somethin', and they was two old ladies already
waitin' in the car when I stepped in. Right along after me comes
Elliott.

" Where's the boy that's supposed to run this car? " he says. I
told him the boy'd be right back; but he says: " I can't wait. I'm
much too sleepy."

And before I could stop him he'd slammed the door and him
and I and the poor old ladies was shootin' up.

" Let us off at the third floor, please! " says one o' the ladies, her
voice kind o' shakin'.

" Sorry, madam," says the bug; " but this is a express and we
don't stop at no third floor."

I grabbed his arm and tried to get him away from the machin-
ery; but he was as strong as a ox and he throwed me agin the side
o' the car like I was a baby. We went to the top faster'n I ever
rode in an elevator before. And then we shot down to the bottom,
hittin' the bumper down there so hard I thought we'd be smashed
to splinters.

The ladies was too scared to make a sound durin' the first trip; but while we was goin' up and down the second time—even faster'n the first—they begun to scream. I was hollerin' my head off at him to quit and he was makin' more noise than the three of us— pretendin' he was the locomotive and the whole crew o' the train.

Don't never ask me how many times we went up and down! The women fainted on the third trip and I guess I was about as near it as I'll ever get. The elevator boy and the bellhops and the waiters and the night clerk and everybody was jumpin' round the lobby screamin'; but no one seemed to know how to stop us.

Finally—on about the tenth trip, I guess—he slowed down and stopped at the fifth floor, where we was roomin'. He opened the door and beat it for the room, while I, though I was tremblin' like a leaf, run the car down to the bottom.

The night clerk knowed me pretty well and knowed I wouldn't do nothin' like that; so him and I didn't argue, but just got to work together to bring the old women to. While we was doin' that Elliott must of run down the stairs and slipped out o' the hotel, because when they sent the officers up to the room after him he'd blowed.

They was goin' to fire the club out; but Charlie had a good stand-in with Amos, the proprietor, and he fixed it up to let us stay—providin' Elliott kep' away. The bug didn't show up at the ball park next day and we didn't see no more of him till we got on the rattler for New York. Charlie and John both bawled him, but they give him a berth—an upper—and we pulled into the Grand Central Station without him havin' made no effort to wreck the train.

VII

I'd studied the thing pretty careful, but hadn't come to no conclusion. I was sure he wasn't no stew, because none o' the boys had ever saw him even take a glass o' beer, and I couldn't never detect the odor o' booze on him. And if he'd been a dope I'd of knew about it—roomin' with him.

There wouldn't of been no mystery about it if he'd been a left-hand pitcher—but he wasn't. He wasn't nothin' but a whale of a hitter and he throwed with his right arm. He hit lefthanded, o' course; but so did Saier and Brid and Schulte and me, and John himself; and none of us was violent. I guessed he must of been just a plain nut and li'ble to break out any time.

They was a letter waitin' for him at New York, and I took it, intendin' to give it to him at the park, because I didn't think they'd let him room at the hotel; but after breakfast he come up to the room, with his suitcase. It seems he'd promised John and Charlie to be good, and made it so strong they b'lieved him.

I give him his letter, which was addressed in a girl's writin' and come from Muskegon.

" From the girl? " I says.

" Yes," he says; and, without openin' it, he tore it up and throwed it out the window.

" Had a quarrel? " I ast.

" No, no," he says; " but she can't tell me nothin' I don't know already. Girls always writes the same junk. I got one from her in Pittsburgh, but I didn't read it."

" I guess you ain't so stuck on her," I says.

He swells up and says:

" Of course I'm stuck on her! If I wasn't, do you think I'd be goin' round with this bunch and gettin' insulted all the time? I'm stickin' here because o' that series dough, so's I can get hooked."

" Do you think you'd settle down if you was married? " I ast him.

" Settle down? " he says. " Sure, I'd settle down. I'd be so happy that I wouldn't have to look for no excitement."

Nothin' special happened that night 'cep' that he come in the room about one o'clock and woke me up by pickin' up the foot o' the bed and droppin' it on the floor, sudden-like.

" Give me a key to the room," he says.

" You must of had a key," I says, " or you couldn't of got in."

" That's right! " he says, and beat it to bed.

One o' the reporters must of told Elliott that John had ast for waivers on him and New York had refused to waive, because next mornin' he come to me with that dope.

" New York's goin' to win this pennant! " he says.

" Well," I says, " they will if some one else don't. But what of it? "

" I'm goin' to play with New York," he says, " so's I can get the World's Series dough."

" How you goin' to get away from this club? " I ast.

" Just watch me! " he says. " I'll be with New York before this series is over."

Well, the way he goes after the job was original, anyway. Rube'd had one of his good days the day before and we'd got a trimmin'; but this second day the score was tied up at two runs apiece in the tenth, and Big Jeff'd been wabblin' for two or three innin's.

Well, he walks Saier and me, with one out, and Mac sends for Matty, who was warmed up and ready. John sticks Elliott in in Brid's place and the bug pulls one into the right-field stand.

It's a cinch McGraw thinks well of him then, and might of went after him if he hadn't went crazy the next afternoon. We're tied up in the ninth and Matty's workin'. John sends Elliott up with the bases choked; but he doesn't go right up to the plate. He walks over to their bench and calls McGraw out. Mac tells us about it afterward.

"I can bust up this game right here!" says Elliott.

"Go ahead," says Mac; "but be careful he don't whiff you."

Then the bug pulls it.

"If I whiff," he says, "will you get me on your club?"

"Sure!" says Mac, just as anybody would.

By this time Bill Koem was hollerin' about the delay; so up goes Elliott and gives the worst burlesque on tryin' to hit that you ever see. Matty throws one a mile outside and high, and the bug swings like it was right over the heart. Then Matty throws one at him and he ducks out o' the way—but swings just the same. Matty must of been wise by this time, for he pitches one so far outside that the Chief almost has to go to the coachers' box after it. Elliott takes his third healthy and runs through the field down to the clubhouse.

We got beat in the eleventh; and when we went in to dress he has his street clothes on. Soon as he seen John comin' he says: "I got to see McGraw!" And he beat it.

John was goin' to the fights that night; but before he leaves the hotel he had waivers on Elliott from everybody and had sold him to Atlanta.

"And," says John, "I don't care if they pay for him or not."

My roomy blows in about nine and got the letter from John out of his box. He was goin' to tear it up, but I told him they was news in it. He opens it and reads where he's sold. I was still sore at him; so I says:

"Thought you was goin' to get on the New York club?"

"No," he says. "I got turned down cold. McGraw says he wouldn't have me in his club. He says he'd had Charlie Faust—and that was enough for him."

He had a kind o' crazy look in his eyes; so when he starts up to the room I follows him.

"What are you goin' to do now?" I says.

"I'm goin' to sell this ticket to Atlanta," he says, "and go back to Muskegon, where I belong."

"I'll help you pack," I says.

"No," says the bug. "I come into this league with this suit o' clothes and a collar. They can have the rest of it." Then he sits down on the bed and begins to cry like a baby. "No series dough for me," he blubbers, "and no weddin' bells! My girl'll die when she hears about it!"

Of course that made me feel kind o' rotten, and I says:

"Brace up, boy! The best thing you can do is go to Atlanta and try hard. You'll be up here again next year."

"You can't tell me where to go!" he says, and he wasn't cryin' no more. "I'll go where I please—and I'm li'ble to take you with me."

I didn't want no argument, so I kep' still. Pretty soon he goes up to the lookin'-glass and stares at himself for five minutes. Then, all of a sudden, he hauls off and takes a wallop at his reflection in the glass. Naturally he smashed the glass all to pieces and he cut his hand somethin' awful.

Without lookin' at it he come over to me and says: "Well, good-by, sport!"—and holds out his other hand to shake. When I starts to shake with him he smears his bloody hand all over my map. Then he laughed like a wild man and run out o' the room and out o' the hotel.

VIII

Well, boys, my sleep was broke up for the rest o' the season. It might of been because I was used to sleepin' in all kinds o' racket and excitement, and couldn't stand for the quiet after he'd went— or it might of been because I kep' thinkin' about him and feelin' sorry for him.

I of'en wondered if he'd settle down and be somethin' if he could get married; and finally I got to b'lievin' he would. So when we was dividin' the city series dough I was thinkin' of him and the girl. Our share o' the money—the losers', as usual—was twelve thousand seven hundred sixty bucks or somethin' like that. They was twenty-one of us and that meant six hundred seven

bucks apiece. We was just goin' to cut it up that way when I says:
"Why not give a divvy to poor old Elliott?"

About fifteen of 'em at once told me that I was crazy. You see, when he got canned he owed everybody in the club. I guess he'd stuck me for the most—about seventy bucks—but I didn't care nothin' about that. I knowed he hadn't never reported to Atlanta, and I thought he was prob'ly busted and a bunch o' money might make things all right for him and the other songbird.

I made quite a speech to the fellers, tellin' 'em how he'd cried when he left us and how his heart'd been set on gettin' married on the series dough. I made it so strong that they finally fell for it. Our shares was cut to five hundred eighty apiece, and John sent him a check for a full share.

For a while I was kind o' worried about what I'd did. I didn't know if I was doin' right by the girl to give him the chance to marry her.

He'd told me she was stuck on him, and that's the only excuse I had for tryin' to fix it up between 'em; but, b'lieve me, if she was my sister or a friend o' mine I'd just as soon of had her manage the Cincinnati Club as marry that bird. I thought to myself:

"If she's all right she'll take acid in a month—and it'll be my fault; but if she's really stuck on him they must be somethin' wrong with her too, so what's the diff'rence?"

Then along comes this letter that I told you about. It's from some friend of hisn up there—and they's a note from him. I'll read 'em to you and then I got to beat it for the station:

Dear Sir: They have got poor Elliott locked up and they are goin' to take him to the asylum at Kalamazoo. He thanks you for the check, and we will use the money to see that he is made comf'table.

When the poor boy come back here he found that his girl was married to Joe Bishop, who runs a soda fountain. She had wrote to him about it, but he did not read her letters. The news drove him crazy—poor boy—and he went to the place where they was livin' with a baseball bat and very near killed 'em both. Then he marched down the street singin' 'Silver Threads Among the Gold' at the top of his voice. They was goin' to send him to prison for assault with intent to kill, but the jury decided he was crazy.

He wants to thank you again for the money.

Yours truly,
Jim——

I can't make out his last name—but it don't make no diff'rence. Now I'll read you his note:

Old Roomy: I was at bat twice and made two hits; but I guess I did not meet 'em square. They tell me they are both alive yet, which I did not mean 'em to be. I hope they got good curve-ball pitchers where I am goin'. I sure can bust them curves—can't I, sport?

Yours,
B. Elliott.

P. S.—The B stands for Buster.

That's all of it, fellers; and you can see I had some excuse for not hittin'. You can also see why I ain't never goin' to room with no bug again—not for John or nobody else!

XXVII

RHYTHM

THIS story is slightly immoral, but so, I guess, are all stories based on truth. It concerns, principally, Harry Hart, whose frankness and naturalness were the traits that endeared him to fellow members of the Friars' Club and all red-blooded she-girls who met him in and out of show business. Music writers have never been noted for self-loathing and Harry was a refreshing exception to the general run. That was before " Upsy Daisy " began its year's tenancy of the Casino.

You can judge what sort of person he was by listening in on a talk he had at the club one night with Sam Rose, lyricist of "Nora's Nightie," " Sheila's Shirt " and a hundred popular songs. They were sitting alone at the table nearest the senile piano.

" Sam," said Harry, " I was wondering if they's a chance of you and I getting together."

" What's happened to Kane? " asked Sam.

" It's off between he and I," Harry replied. " That dame ruined him. I guess she married him to make an honest man of him. Anyways, he got so honest that I couldn't stand it no more. You know how I am, Sam—live and let live. I don't question nobody's ethics or whatever you call them, as long as they don't question mine. We're all trying to get along; that's the way I look at it. At that, I've heard better lyrics than he wrote for those two rhythm numbers of mine in ' Lottie ' ; in fact, between you and I, I thought he made a bum out of those two numbers. They sold like hymns, so I was really able to bear up when we reached the parting of the ways.

" But I'll tell you the climax just to show you how silly a guy can get. You remember our ' Yes, Yes, Eulalie.' Well, they was a spot for a swell love duet near the end of the first act and I had a tune for it that was a smash. You know I'm not bragging when I say that; I don't claim it as my tune, but it was and is a smash. I mean the ' Catch Me ' number."

" I'll say it's a smash ! " agreed Sam.

" But a smash in spite of the words," said Harry.

" You're right," said Sam.

" Well, the first time I played this tune for him, he went nuts over it and I gave him a lead sheet and he showed it to his wife. It seems she plays piano a little and she played this melody and she told him I had stole it from some opera; she thought it was ' Gioconda,' but she wasn't sure. So the next day Kane spoke to me about it and I told him it wasn't ' Gioconda ' ; it was Donizetti's ' Linda di Chamounix.' Well, he said he didn't feel like it was right to work on a melody that had been swiped from somewhere. So I said, ' Ain't it kind of late for you to be having all those scruples? ' So he said, ' Maybe it is, but better late than never.' So I said, ' Listen, Benny—this is your wife talking, not you.' And he said, ' Let's leave her out of this,' and I said, ' I wished to heaven we could.'

" I said, ' Benny, you'll admit that's a pretty melody,' and he said yes, he admitted it. So I said: ' Well, how many of the dumb-bells that goes to our shows has ever heard ' Linda di Chamounix " or ever will hear it? When I put this melody in our troupe I'm doing a million people a favor; I'm giving them a chance to hear a beautiful piece of music that they wouldn't never hear otherwise. Not only that, but they'll hear it at its best because I've improved it.' So Benny said, ' The first four bars is exactly the same and that's where people will notice.'

" So then I said : ' Now listen here, Benny—up to the present you haven't never criticized my music and I haven't criticized your lyrics. But now you say I'm a tune thief. I don't deny it, but if I wasn't, you'd of had a sweet time making a living for yourself, let alone get married. However, laying that to one side, I was over to my sister's house the other night and she had a soprano singer there and she sung a song something about " I love you, I love you; 'tis all my heart can say." It was a mighty pretty song and it come out about twenty or thirty years ago.'

" So then Benny said, ' What of it? ' So I said, ' Just this: I can recall four or five lyrics of yours where " I love you " comes in and I bet you've used the words " heart " and " say " and " all " at least twice apiece during your remarkable career as a song writer. Well, did you make those words up or did you hear them somewhere? ' That's what I said to him and of course he was stopped. But his ethics was ravaged just the same and it was understood we'd split up right after ' Eulalie.' And as I say, his words wasn't no help to my Donizetti number; they'd of slayed it if it could of been slayed."

" Well ? " said Sam.

" Well," said Harry, " Conrad Green wired me yesterday to come and see him, so I was up there today. He's so dumb that he thinks I'm better than Friml. And he's got a book by Jack Prendergast that he wanted Kane and I to work on. So I told him I wouldn't work with Kane and he said to get who I wanted. So that's why I gave you a ring."

" It sounds good to me," said Sam. " How is the book? "

" I only skimmed it through, but I guess it's all right. It's based on ' Cinderella,' so what with that idear combined with your lyrics and my tunes, it looks like we ought to give the public a novelty at least."

" Have you got any new tunes? "

" New? " Hart laughed. " I'm dirty with them." He sat down at the piano. " Get this rhythm number. If it ain't a smash, I'm Gatti-Casazza ! "

He played it, beautifully, first in F sharp—a catchy refrain that seemed to be waltz time in the right hand and two-four in the left.

" It's pretty down here, too," he said, and played it again, just as surely, in B natural, a key whose mere mention is henbane to the average pianist.

" A wow ! " enthused Sam Rose. " What is it? "

" Don't you know? "

" The Volga boat song."

" No," said Hart. " It's part of Aïda's number when she finds out the fella is going to war. And nobody that comes to our shows will spot it except maybe Deems Taylor and Alma Gluck."

" It's so pretty," said Sam, " that it's a wonder it never goes popular."

" The answer is that Verdi didn't know rhythm ! " said Hart.

Or go back and observe our hero at the Bucks' house on Long Island. Several of the boys and girls were there and thrilled to hear that Harry Hart was coming. He hardly had time to taste his first cocktail before they were after him to play something.

" Something of your own ! " pleaded the enraptured Helen Morse.

" If you mean something I made up," he replied with engaging frankness, " why, that's impossible; not exactly impossible, but it would be the homeliest tune you ever listened to. However, my name is signed to some mighty pretty things and I'll play you one or two of those."

Thus, without the conventional show of reluctance, Harry

played the two "rhythm numbers" and the love-song that were making Conrad Green's "Upsy Daisy" the hit of the season. And he was starting in on another, a thing his informal audience did not recognize, when he overheard his hostess introducing somebody to Mr. Rudolph Friml.

"Good night!" exclaimed Hart. "Let somebody play that can play!" And he resigned his seat at the piano to the newcomer and moved to a far corner of the room.

"I hope Friml didn't hear me," he confided to a Miss Silloh. "I was playing a thing he wrote himself and letting you people believe it was mine."

Or catch him in the old days at a football game with Rita Marlowe of Goldwyn. One of the college bands was playing "Yes, Sir! That's My Baby!"

"Walter Donaldson. There's the boy that can write the hits!" said Hart.

"Just as if you couldn't!" said his companion.

"I don't class with him," replied her modest escort.

Later on, Rita remarked that he must have been recognized by people in the crowd. Many had stared.

"Let's not kid ourselves, girlie," he said. "They're staring at you, not me."

Still later, on the way home from the game, he told her he had saved over $25,000 and expected to average at least $40,000 a year income while his vogue lasted.

"I'm good as long as I don't run out of pretty tunes," he said, "and they's no reason why I should with all those old masters to draw from. I'm telling you my financial status because—well, I guess you know why."

Rita did know, and it was the general opinion, shared by the two principals, that she and Harry were engaged.

When "Upsy Daisy" had been running two months and its hit numbers were being sung, played, and whistled almost to cloyment, Hart was discovered by Spencer Deal. That he was the pioneer in a new American jazz, that his rhythms would revolutionize our music—these things and many more were set forth by Deal in a four-thousand-word article called "Harry Hart, Harbinger," printed by the erudite Webster's Weekly. And Harry ate it up, though some of the words nearly choked him.

Interesting people were wont to grace Peggy Leech's drawing-room on Sunday afternoons. Max Reinhardt had been there. Reinald Werrenrath had been there. So had Heifetz and Jeritza and Michael Arlen, and Noel Coward and Dudley Malone. And

Charlie Chaplin, and Gene Tunney. In fact, Peggy's Sunday afternoons could be spoken of as salons and her apartment as a hotbed of culture.

It was to Peggy's that Spencer Deal escorted Hart a few weeks after the appearance of the article in Webster's. Deal, in presenting him, announced that he was at work on a "blue" symphony that would make George Gershwin's ultra rhythms and near dissonants sound like the doxology. "Oh!" exclaimed pretty Myra Hampton. "Will he play some of it for us?"

"Play, play, play!" said Hart querulously. "Don't you think I ever want a rest! Last night it was a party at Broun's and they kept after me and wouldn't take 'No' and finally I played just as rotten as I could, to learn them a lesson. But they didn't even know it was rotten. What do you do for a living?"

"I'm an actress," confessed the embarrassed young lady.

"Well, would you like it if, every time you went anywhere socially, people asked you to act?"

"Yes," she answered, but he had moved away.

He seemed to be seeking seclusion; sat down as far as possible from the crowd and looked hurt. He accepted a highball proffered by his hostess, but neglected to thank her. Not a bit discouraged, she brought him Signor Parelli of the Metropolitan.

"Mr. Hart," she said, "this is Mr. Parelli, one of the Metropolitan's conductors."

"Yay?" said Hart.

"Perhaps some day Mr. Parelli will conduct one of your operas."

"I hope so," said the polite Parelli.

"Do you?" said Hart. "Well, if I ever write an opera, I'll conduct it myself, or at least I won't take no chance of having it ruined by a foreigner."

The late war increased people's capacity for punishment and in about twenty minutes Peggy's guests began to act as if they would live in spite of Harry's refusal to perform. In fact, one of them, Roy Lattimer, full of Scotch courage and not so full of musical ability, went to the piano himself and began to play.

"Began" is all, for he had not completed four bars before Hart plunged across the room and jostled him off the bench.

"I hope you don't call yourself a pianist!" he said, pronouncing it as if it meant a cultivator of, or dealer in, peonies. And for two hours, during which everybody but Spencer Deal and the unfortunate hostess walked out on him, Harry played and played and played. Nor in all that time did he play anything by Kern, Gershwin, Stephen Jones, or Isham Jones, Samuels, Youmans, Friml, Stamper, Tours, Berlin, Tierney, Hubbell, Hein, or Gitz-Rice.

It was during this epoch that Harry had occasion one day to walk up Fifth Avenue from Forty-fifth Street to the Plaza. He noticed that almost everyone he passed on the line of march gazed at him intently. He recalled that his picture had been in two rotogravure sections the previous Sunday. It must have been a better likeness than he had thought.

New York was burning soft coal that winter and when Hart arrived in the Plaza wash-room he discovered a smudge on the left side of his upper lip. It made him look as if he had had a mustache, had decided to get it removed and then had changed his mind when the barber was half through.

Harry's date at the Plaza was with Rita Marlowe. He had put it off as long as he could. If the girl had any pride or sense, she'd have taken a hint. Why should he waste his time on a second-rate picture actress when he was hobnobbing with women like Elinor Deal and Thelma Warren and was promised an introduction to Mrs. Wallace Gerard? Girls ought to know that when a fella who has been taking them out three and four times a week and giving them a ring every morning, night and noon between whiles—they ought to know that when a fella stops calling them up and taking them out and won't even talk to them when they call up, there is only one possible answer. Yet this dame insists on you meeting her and probably having a scene. Well, she'll get a scene. No, she won't. No use being brutal. Just make it apparent in a nice way that things ain't like they used to be and get it over as quick as possible.

"Where can we go?" asked Rita. "I mean, to talk."

"Nowheres that'll take much time," said Harry. "I've got a date with Paul Whiteman to look over part of my symphony.'

"I don't want to interrupt your work," said Rita. "Maybe it would be better if you came up to the house tonight."

"I can't tonight," he told her.

"When can you?"

"I'll give you a ring. It's hard to get away. You see——"

"I think I do," said Rita, and left him.

"About time," said Harry to himself.

His symphony went over fairly "big." The critics seemed less impressed than with the modern compositions of Gershwin and

Deems Taylor. " But then," Harry reflected, " Gershwin was ahead of me and of course Taylor has friends on the paper."

A party instigated by Spencer Deal followed the concert and Harry met Mrs. Wallace Gerard, who took a great interest in young composers and had been known to give them substantial aid. Hart accepted an invitation to play to her at her Park Avenue apartment. He made the mistake of thinking she wanted to be petted, not played to, and his first visit was his last.

He had been engaged by Conrad Green to do the music for a new show, with a book by Guy Bolton. He balked at working again with Sam Rose, whose lyrics were hopelessly proletarian. Green told him to pick his own lyricist and Harry chose Spencer Deal. The result of the collaboration was a score that required a new signature at the beginning of each bar, and a collection of six-syllable rhymes that has as much chance of being unriddled, let alone sung, by chorus girls as a pandect on biotaxy by Ernest Boyd.

" Terrible ! " was Green's comment on advice of his musical adviser, Frank Tours.

" You're a fine judge ! " said Hart. " But it don't make no difference what you think. Our contract with you is to write music and lyrics for this show and that's what we've done. If you don't like it, you can talk to my lawyer."

" Your lawyer is probably one of mine, too," replied Green. " He must be if he practises in New York. But that is neither here or there. If you think you can compel me to accept a score which Tours tells me that if it was orchestrated, Stokowski himself couldn't even read the triangle part, to say nothing of lyrics which you would have to ring up every night at seven o'clock to get the words in the opening chorus all pronounced in time for Bayside people to catch the one-twenty train—well, Hart, go along home now, because you and I are going to see each other in court every day for the next forty years."

A year or so later, Harry's total cash on hand and in bank amounted to $214.60, including the $56 he had cleaned up on the sale of sheet music and mechanical records of his symphony. He read in the Sunday papers that Otto Harbach had undertaken a book for Willis Merwin and the latter was looking around for a composer. Merwin was one of the younger producers and had been a pal of Harry's at the Friars'. Hart sought him there. He found Merwin and came to the point at once.

" It's too late," said the young entrepreneur. " I did consider you at first, but—well, I didn't think you were interested now in anything short of oratorio. The stuff you used to write would have been great, but this piece couldn't stand the ponderous junk you've been turning out lately. It needs light treatment and I've signed Donaldson and Gus Kahn."

"Maybe I could interpolate——" Harry began.

"I don't believe so," Merwin interrupted. "I don't recall a spot where we could use either a fugue or a dirge."

On his way out, Hart saw Benny Kane, his collaborator of other years. Benny made as if to get up and greet him, but changed his mind and sank back in his sequestered chair.

"He don't look as cocky as he used to," thought Harry, and wished that Kane had been more cordial. "What I'll have to do is turn out a hit song, just to tide me over. Of course I can write the words myself, but Benny had good idears once in a while."

Hart stopped in at his old publishers' where, in the halcyon days, he had been as welcome as more beer at the Pastry Cooks' Ball. He had left them for a more esthetic firm at the suggestion of Spencer Deal.

"Well, Harry," said Max Wise, one of the partners, "you're quite a stranger. We don't hear much of you lately."

"Maybe you will again," said Hart. "What would you say if I was to write another smash?"

"I'd say," replied Wise, "that it wasn't any too soon."

"How would you like to have me back here?"

"With a smash, yes. Go get one and you'll find the door wide open. Who are you working with?"

"I haven't nobody."

"You could do a lot worse," said Wise, "than team up again with Benny Kane. You and him parting company was like separating Baltimore and Ohio or pork and beans."

"He hasn't done nothing since he left me," said Hart.

"No," replied Wise, "but you can't hardly claim to have been glutting the country with sensations yourself!"

Hart went back to his hotel and wished there was no such thing as pride. He'd like to give Benny a ring.

He answered the telephone and recognized Benny's voice.

"I seen you at the Friars' today," said Benny, "and it reminded me of an idear. Where could we get together?"

"At the club," Harry replied. "I'll be there in a half-hour."

"I was thinking," said Benny, when they were seated at the table near the piano, "that nobody has wrote a rhythm song lately about ' I love you'; that is, not in the last two or three months. And one time you was telling me about being over to your sister's and they was a soprano there that sung a song that went ' I love you, I love you; 'tis all my heart can say.' "

" What of it ? "

" Well," said Benny, " let's take that song and I'll just fix up the words a little and you can take the tune and put it into your rhythm and we're all set. That is, if the tune's o. k. What is it like ? "

" Oh, 'Arcady' and 'Marcheta' and maybe that 'Buzz Around' song of Dave Stamper's. But then, what ain't ? "

" Well, let's go to it."

" Where is your ethics ? "

" Listen," said Benny Kane—" I and Rae was talking this afternoon, and we didn't disgust ethics. She was just saying she thought that all God's children had shoes except her."

" All right," said Hart. " I can remember enough of the tune. But I'll look the song up tomorrow and give it to you and you can rewrite the words."

" Fine! And now how about putting on the feed bag ? "

" No," said Harry. " I promised to call up a dame."

Whereupon he kept his ancient promise.

" You've got a lot of nerve," said Rita at the other end of the wire, " imagining a girl would wait for you this long. And I'd say ' No ' and say it good and loud, except that my piano has just been tuned and you've never played me your symphony."

" I ain't going to, neither," said Harry. " But I want to try out a new rhythm number that ought to be a smash. It starts off ' I love you, I love you.' "

" It sounds wonderful! " said Rita.

XXVIII

SOME LIKE THEM COLD

N. Y., Aug. 3.

Dear Miss Gillespie: How about our bet now as you bet me I would forget all about you the minute I hit the big town and would never write you a letter. Well girlie it looks like you lose so pay me. Seriously we will call all bets off as I am not the kind that bet on a sure thing and it sure was a sure thing that I would not forget a girlie like you and all that is worrying me is whether it may not be the other way round and you are wondering who this fresh guy is that is writeing you this letter. I bet you are so will try and refreshen your memory.

Well girlie I am the handsome young man that was wondering round the Lasalle st. station Monday and " happened " to sit down beside of a mighty pretty girlie who was waiting to meet her sister from Toledo and the train was late and I am glad of it because if it had not of been that little girlie and I would never of met. So for once I was a lucky guy but still I guess it was time I had some luck as it was certainly tough luck for you and I to both be liveing in Chi all that time and never get together till a half hour before I was leaveing town for good.

Still " better late than never " you know and maybe we can make up for lost time though it looks like we would have to do our makeing up at long distants unless you make good on your threat and come to N. Y. I wish you would do that little thing girlie as it looks like that was the only way we would get a chance to play round together as it looks like they was little or no chance of me comeing back to Chi as my whole future is in the big town. N. Y. is the only spot and specially for a man that expects to make my liveing in the song writeing game as here is the Mecca for that line of work and no matter how good a man may be they don't get no recognition unless they live in N. Y.

Well girlie you asked me to tell you all about my trip. Well I remember you saying that you would give anything to be makeing it yourself but as far as the trip itself was conserned you ought to be thankfull you did not have to make it as you would of sweat your head off. I know I did specially wile going through Ind.

Monday P. M. but Monday night was the worst of all trying to sleep and finely I give it up and just layed there with the presspiration rolling off of me though I was laying on top of the covers and nothing on but my underwear.

Yesterday was not so bad as it rained most of the A. M. comeing through N. Y. state and in the P. M. we road along side of the Hudson all P. M. Some river girlie and just looking at it makes a man forget all about the heat and everything else except a certain girlie who I seen for the first time Monday and then only for a half hour but she is the kind of a girlie that a man don't need to see her only once and they would be no danger of forgetting her. There I guess I better lay off that subject or you will think I am a " fresh guy."

Well that is about all to tell you about the trip only they was one amuseing incidence that come off yesterday which I will tell you. Well they was a dame got on the train at Toledo Monday and had the birth opp. mine but I did not see nothing of her that night as I was out smoking till late and she hit the hay early but yesterday A. M. she come in the dinner and sit at the same table with me and tried to make me and it was so raw that the dinge waiter seen it and give me the wink and of course I paid no tension and I waited till she got through so as they would be no danger of her folling me out but she stopped on the way out to get a tooth pick and when I come out she was out on the platform with it so I tried to brush right by but she spoke up and asked me what time it was and I told her and she said she geussed her watch was slow so I said maybe it just seemed slow on acct. of the company it was in.

I don't know if she got what I was driveing at or not but any way she give up trying to make me and got off at Albany. She was a good looker but I have no time for gals that tries to make strangers on a train.

Well if I don't quit you will think I am writeing a book but will expect a long letter in answer to this letter and we will see if you can keep your promise like I have kept mine. Don't dissapoint me girlie as I am all alone in a large city and hearing from you will keep me from getting home sick for old Chi though I never thought so much of the old town till I found out you lived there. Don't think that is kidding girlie as I mean it.

You can address me at this hotel as it looks like I will be here right along as it is on 47th st. right off of old Broadway and handy to everything and am only paying $21 per wk. for my rm. and could of got one for $16 but without bath but am glad to pay the differents as am lost without my bath in the A. M. and sometimes at night too.

Tomorrow I expect to commence fighting the "battle of Broadway" and will let you know how I come out that is if you answer this letter. In the mean wile girlie au reservoir and don't do nothing I would not do.

Your new friend (?)

Chas. F. Lewis.

Chicago, Ill., Aug. 6.

My Dear Mr. Lewis: Well, that certainly was a "surprise party" getting your letter and you are certainly a "wonder man" to keep your word as I am afraid most men of your sex are gay deceivers but maybe you are "different." Any way it sure was a surprise and will gladly pay the bet if you will just tell me what it was we bet. Hope it was not money as I am a "working girl" but if it was not more than a dollar or two will try to dig it up even if I have to "beg, borrow or steal."

Suppose you will think me a "case" to make a bet and then forget what it was, but you must remember, Mr. Man, that I had just met you and was "dazzled." Joking aside I was rather "fussed" and will tell you why. Well, Mr. Lewis, I suppose you see lots of girls like the one you told me about that you saw on the train who tried to "get acquainted" but I want to assure you that I am not one of those kind and sincerely hope you will believe me when I tell you that you was the first man I ever spoke to meeting them like that and my friends and the people who know me would simply faint if they knew I ever spoke to a man without a "proper introduction."

Believe me, Mr. Lewis, I am not that kind and I don't know now why I did it only that you was so "different" looking if you know what I mean and not at all like the kind of men that usually try to force their attentions on every pretty girl they see. Lots of times I act on impulse and let my feelings run away from me and sometimes I do things on the impulse of the moment which I regret them later on, and that is what I did this time, but hope you won't give me cause to regret it and I know you won't as I know you are not that kind of a man a specially after what you told me about the girl on the train. But any way as I say, I was in a "daze" so can't remember what it was we bet, but will try and pay it if it does not "break" me.

Sis's train got in about ten minutes after yours had gone and when she saw me what do you think was the first thing she said? Well, Mr. Lewis, she said: " Why Mibs (That is a pet name some of my friends have given me) what has happened to you? I never seen you have as much color." So I passed it off with some remark about the heat and changed the subject as I certainly was not going to tell her that I had just been talking to a man who I had never met or she would of dropped dead from the shock. Either that or she would not of believed me as it would be hard for a person who knows me well to imagine me doing a thing like that as I have quite a reputation for " squelching " men who try to act fresh. I don't mean anything personal by that, Mr. Lewis, as am a good judge of character and could tell without you telling me that you are not that kind.

Well, Sis and I have been on the " go " ever since she arrived as I took yesterday and today off so I could show her the " sights " though she says she would be perfectly satisfied to just sit in the apartment and listen to me " rattle on." Am afraid I am a great talker, Mr. Lewis, but Sis says it is as good as a show to hear me talk as I tell things in such a different way as I cannot help from seeing the humorous side of everything and she says she never gets tired of listening to me, but of course she is my sister and thinks the world of me, but she really does laugh like she enjoyed my craziness.

Maybe I told you that I have a tiny little apartment which a girl friend of mine and I have together and it is hardly big enough to turn round in, but still it is " home " and I am a great home girl and hardly ever care to go out evenings except occasionally to the theatre or dance. But even if our " nest " is small we are proud of it and Sis complimented us on how cozy it is and how " homey " it looks and she said she did not see how we could afford to have everything so nice and Edith (my girl friend) said: " Mibs deserves all the credit for that. I never knew a girl who could make a little money go a long ways like she can." Well, of course she is my best friend and always saying nice things about me, but I do try and I hope I get results. Have always said that good taste and being careful is a whole lot more important than lots of money though it is nice to have it.

You must write and tell me how you are getting along in the " battle of Broadway " (I laughed when I read that) and whether the publishers like your songs though I know they will. Am crazy to hear them and hear you play the piano as I love good jazz music even better than classical, though I suppose it is terrible to say such a thing. But I usually say just what I think though sometimes I wish afterwards I had not of. But still I believe it is better for a girl to be her own self and natural instead of always acting. But am afraid I will never have a chance to hear you play unless you come back to Chi and pay us a visit as my "threat" to come to New York was just a "threat" and I don't see any hope of ever getting there unless some rich New Yorker should fall in love with me and take me there to live. Fine chance for poor little me, eh Mr. Lewis?

Well, I guess I have "rattled on" long enough and you will think I am writing a book unless I quit and besides, Sis has asked me as a special favor to make her a pie for dinner. Maybe you don't know it, Mr. Man, but I am quite famous for my pie and pastry, but I don't suppose a "genius" is interested in common things like that.

Well, be sure and write soon and tell me what N.Y. is like and all about it and don't forget the little girlie who was "bad" and spoke to a strange man in the station and have been blushing over it ever since.

Your friend (?)
Mabelle Gillespie.

N. Y., Aug. 10.

Dear Girlie: I bet you will think I am a fresh guy commencing that way but Miss Gillespie is too cold and a man can not do nothing cold in this kind of weather specially in this man's town which is the hottest place I ever been in and I guess maybe the reason why New Yorkers is so bad is because they think they are all ready in H—— and can not go no worse place no matter how they behave themselves. Honest girlie I certainly envy you being where there is a breeze off the old Lake and Chi may be dirty but I never heard of nobody dying because they was dirty but four people died here yesterday on acct. of the heat and I seen two different women flop right on Broadway and had to be taken away in the ambulance and it could not of been because they was dressed too warm because it would be impossible for the women here to leave off any more cloths.

Well have not had much luck yet in the battle of Broadway as all the heads of the big music publishers is out of town on their vacation and the big boys is the only ones I will do business with as it would be silly for a man with the stuff I have got to waste my time on somebody that is just on the staff and have not got the final say. But I did play a couple of my numbers for the people up to Levy's and Goebel's and they went crazy over them in both places. So it looks like all I have to do is wait for the big boys to get back and then play my numbers for them and I will be all set. What I want is to get taken on the staff of one of the big firms as that gives a man the inside and they will plug your numbers more if you are on the staff. In the mean wile have not got nothing to worry me but am just seeing the sights of the big town as have saved up enough money to play round for a wile and any way a man that can play piano like I can don't never have to worry about starveing. Can certainly make the old music box talk girlie and am always good for a $75 or $100 job.

Well have been here a week now and on the go every minute and I thought I would be lonesome down here but no chance of that as I have been treated fine by the people I have met and have sure met a bunch of them. One of the boys liveing in the hotel is a vaudeville actor and he is a member of the Friars club and took me over there to dinner the other night and some way another the bunch got wise that I could play piano so of course I had to sit down and give them some of my numbers and everybody went crazy over them. One of the boys I met there was Paul Sears the song writer but he just writes the lyrics and has wrote a bunch of hits and when he heard some of my melodies he called me over to one side and said he would like to work with me on some numbers. How is that girlie as he is one of the biggest hit writers in N. Y.

N. Y. has got some mighty pretty girlies and I guess it would not be hard to get acquainted with them and in fact several of them has tried to make me since I been here but I always figure that a girl must be something wrong with her if she tries to make a man that she don't know nothing about so I pass them all up. But I did meet a couple of pips that a man here in the hotel went up on Riverside Drive to see them and insisted on me going along and they got on some way that I could make a piano talk so they was nothing but I must play for them so I sit down and played some of my own stuff and they went crazy over it.

One of the girls wanted I should come up and see her again, and I said I might but I think I better keep away as she acted like she wanted to vamp me and I am not the kind that likes to play round with a gal just for their company and dance with them etc. but when I see the right gal that will be a different thing and she won't have to beg me to come and see her as I will camp right on her trail till she says yes. And it won't be none of these N. Y. fly by nights neither. They are all right to look at but a man would be a sucker to get serious with them as they might take you up and next thing you know you would have a wife on your hands that don't know a dish rag from a waffle iron.

Well girlie will quit and call it a day as it is too hot to write any more and I guess I will turn on the cold water and lay in the tub a wile and then turn in. Don't forget to write to

Your friend,
Chas. F. Lewis.

Chicago, Ill., Aug. 13.

Dear Mr. Man: Hope you won't think me a " silly Billy " for starting my letter that way but " Mr. Lewis " is so formal and " Charles " is too much the other way and any way I would not dare call a man by their first name after only knowing them only two weeks. Though I may as well confess that Charles is my favorite name for a man and have always been crazy about it as it was my father's name. Poor old dad, he died of cancer three years ago, but left enough insurance so that mother and we girls were well provided for and do not have to do anything to support ourselves though I have been earning my own living for two years to make things easier for mother and also because I simply can't bear to be doing nothing as I feel like a " drone." So I flew away from the " home nest " though mother felt bad about it as I was her favorite and she always said I was such a comfort to her as when I was in the house she never had to worry about how things would go.

But there I go gossiping about my domestic affairs just like you would be interested in them though I don't see how you could be though personly I always like to know all about my friends, but I know men are different so will try and not bore you any longer. Poor Man, I certainly feel sorry for you if New York is as hot as all that. I guess it has been very hot in Chi, too, at least everybody has been complaining about how terrible it is. Suppose you will wonder why I say " I guess " and you will think I ought to know if it is hot. Well, sir, the reason I say " I guess " is because I don't feel the heat like others do or at least I don't let myself feel it. That sounds crazy I know, but don't you think there is a good deal in mental suggestion and not letting yourself feel things? I believe that if a person simply won't allow themselves to be affected by disagreeable things, why such things won't bother them near as much. I know it works with me and that is the reason why I am never cross when things go wrong and "keep smiling" no matter what happens and as far as the heat is concerned, why I just don't let myself feel it and my friends say I don't even look hot no matter if the weather is boiling and Edith, my girl friend, often says that I am like a breeze and it cools her off just to have me come in the room. Poor Edie suffers terribly during the hot weather and says it almost makes her mad at me to see how cool and unruffled I look when everybody else is perspiring and have red faces etc.

I laughed when I read what you said about New York being so hot that people thought it was the "other place." I can appreciate a joke, Mr. Man, and that one did not go "over my head." Am still laughing at some of the things you said in the station though they probably struck me funnier than they would most girls as I always see the funny side and sometimes something is said and I laugh and the others wonder what I am laughing at as they cannot see anything in it themselves, but it is just the way I look at things so of course I cannot explain to them why I laughed and they think I am crazy. But I had rather part with almost anything rather than my sense of humour as it helps me over a great many rough spots.

Sis has gone back home though I would of liked to of kept her here much longer, but she had to go though she said she would of liked nothing better than to stay with me and just listen to me "rattle on." She always says it is just like a show to hear me talk as I always put things in such a funny way and for weeks after she has been visiting me she thinks of some of the things I said and laughs over them. Since she left Edith and I have been pretty quiet though poor Edie wants to be on the "go" all the time and tries to make me go out with her every evening to the pictures and scolds me when I say I had rather stay home and read and calls me a "book worm." Well, it is true that I had rather stay home with a good book than go to some crazy old picture and the last two nights I have been reading myself to sleep with Robert W. Service's poems. Don't you love Service or don't you care for "highbrow" writings?

Personly there is nothing I love more than to just sit and read a good book or sit and listen to somebody play the piano, I mean if they can really play and I really believe I like popular music better than the classical though I suppose that is a terrible thing to confess, but I love all kinds of music but a specially the piano when it is played by somebody who can really play.

Am glad you have not " fallen " for the " ladies " who have tried to make your acquaintance in New York. You are right in thinking there must be something wrong with girls who try to " pick up " strange men as no girl with self respect would do such a thing and when I say that, Mr. Man, I know you will think it is a funny thing for me to say on account of the way our friendship started, but I mean it and I assure you that was the first time I ever done such a thing in my life and would never of thought of doing it had I not known you were the right kind of a man as I flatter myself that I am a good judge of character and can tell pretty well what a person is like by just looking at them and I assure you I had made up my mind what kind of a man you were before I allowed myself to answer your opening remark. Otherwise I am the last girl in the world that would allow myself to speak to a person without being introduced to them.

When you write again you must tell me all about the girl on Riverside Drive and what she looks like and if you went to see her again and all about her. Suppose you will think I am a little old " curiosity shop " for asking all those questions and will wonder why I want to know. Well, sir, I won't tell you why, so there, but I insist on you answering all questions and will scold you if you don't. Maybe you will think that the reason why I am so curious is because I am " jealous " of the lady in question. Well, sir, I won't tell you whether I am or not, but will keep you " guessing." Now, don't you wish you knew?

Must close or you will think I am going to " rattle on " forever or maybe you have all ready become disgusted and torn my letter up. If so all I can say is poor little me—she was a nice little girl and meant well, but the man did not appreciate her.

There! Will stop or you will think I am crazy if you do not all ready.

Yours (?)
Mabelle.

N. Y., Aug. 20.

Dear Girlie : Well girlie I suppose you thought I was never going to answer your letter but have been busier than a one armed paper hanger the last week as have been working on a number with Paul Sears who is one of the best lyric writers in N. Y. and has turned out as many hits as Berlin or Davis or any of them. And believe me girlie he has turned out another hit this time that is he and I have done it together. It is all done now and we are just waiting for the best chance to place it but will not place it nowheres unless we get the right kind of a deal but maybe will publish it ourselves.

The song is bound to go over big as Sears has wrote a great lyric and I have give it a great tune or at least every body that has heard it goes crazy over it and it looks like it would go over bigger than any song since Mammy and would not be surprised to see it come out the hit of the year. If it is handled right we will make a bbl. of money and Sears says it is a cinch we will clean up as much as $25000 apiece which is pretty fair for one song but this one is not like the most of them but has got a great lyric and I have wrote a melody that will knock them out of their seats. I only wish you could hear it girlie and hear it the way I play it. I had to play it over and over about 50 times at the Friars last night.

I will copy down the lyric of the chorus so you can see what it is like and get the idea of the song though of course you can't tell much about it unless you hear it played and sang. The title of the song is When They're Like You and here is the chorus:

> "Some like them hot, some like them cold.
> Some like them when they're not too darn old.
> Some like them fat, some like them lean.
> Some like them only at sweet sixteen.
> Some like them dark, some like them light.
> Some like them in the park, late at night.
> Some like them fickle, some like them true,
> But the time I like them is when they're like you."

How is that for a lyric and I only wish I could play my melody for you as you would go nuts over it but will send you a copy as soon as the song is published and you can get some of your friends to play it over for you and I know you will like it though it is a different melody when I play it or when somebody else plays it.

Well girlie you will see how busy I have been and am libel to keep right on being busy as we are not going to let the grass grow under our feet but as soon as we have got this number placed we will get busy on another one as a couple like that will put me on Easy st. even if they don't go as big as we expect but even 25 grand is a big bunch of money and if a man could only turn out one hit a year and make that much out of it I would be on Easy st. and no more hammering on the old music box in some cabaret.

Who ever we take the song to we will make them come across with one grand for advance royaltys and that will keep me going till I can turn out another one. So the future looks bright and rosey to yours truly and I am certainly glad I come to the big town though sorry I did not do it a whole lot quicker.

This is a great old town girlie and when you have lived here a wile you wonder how you ever stood for a burg like Chi which is just a hick town along side of this besides being dirty etc. and a man is a sucker to stay there all their life specially a man in my line of work as N. Y. is the Mecca for a man that has got the musical gift. I figure that all the time I spent in Chi I was just wasteing my time and never really started to live till I come down here and I have to laugh when I think of the boys out there that is trying to make a liveing in the song writeing game and most of them starve to death all their life and the first week I am down here I meet a man like Sears and the next thing you know we have turned out a song that will make us a fortune.

Well girlie you asked me to tell you about the girlie up on the Drive that tried to make me and asked me to come and see her again. Well I can assure you you have no reasons to be jealous in that quarter as I have not been back to see her as I figure it is wasteing my time to play round with a dame like she that wants to go out somewheres every night and if you married her she would want a house on 5th ave. with a dozen servants so I have passed her up as that is not my idea of home.

What I want when I get married is a real home where a man can stay home and work and maybe have a few of his friends in once in a wile and entertain them or go to a good musical show once in a wile and have a wife that is in sympathy with you and not nag at you all the wile but be a real help mate. The girlie up on the Drive would run me ragged and have me in the poor house inside of a year even if I was makeing 25 grand out of one song. Besides she wears a make up that you would have to blast to find out what her face looks like. So I have not been back there and don't intend to see her again so what is the use of me telling you about her. And the only other girlie I have met is a sister of Paul Sears who I met up to his house wile we was working on the song but she don't hardly count as she has not got no use for the boys but treats them like dirt and Paul says she is the coldest proposition he ever seen.

Well I don't know no more to write and besides have got a date to go out to Paul's place for dinner and play some of my stuff for him so as he can see if he wants to set words to some more of my melodies. Well don't do nothing I would not do and have as good

a time as you can in old Chi and will let you know how we come
along with the song.

                                                        Chas. F. Lewis.

                                        Chicago, Ill., Aug. 23.

Dear Mr. Man: I am thrilled to death over the song and think
the words awfully pretty and am crazy to hear the music which I
know must be great. It must be wonderful to have the gift of writing songs and then hear people play and sing them and just think
of making $25,000 in such a short time. My, how rich you will be
and I certainly congratulate you though am afraid when you are
rich and famous you will have no time for insignificant little me
or will you be an exception and remember your " old " friends
even when you are up in the world? I sincerely hope so.

Will look forward to receiving a copy of the song and will you
be sure and put your name on it? I am all ready very conceited
just to think that I know a man that writes songs and makes all
that money.

Seriously I wish you success with your next song and I laughed
when I read your remark about being busier than a one armed
paper hanger. I don't see how you think up all those compari-
sons and crazy things to say. The next time one of the girls asks
me to go out with them I am going to tell them I can't go because
I am busier than a one armed paper hanger and then they will
think I made it up and say: " The girl is clever."

Seriously I am glad you did not go back to see the girl on the
Drive and am also glad you don't like girls who makes themselves
up so much as I think it is disgusting and would rather go round
looking like a ghost than put artificial color on my face. Fortunately I have a complexion that does not need " fixing " but even
if my coloring was not what it is I would never think of lowering
myself to " fix " it. But I must tell you a joke that happened just
the other day when Edith and I were out at lunch and there was
another girl in the restaurant whom Edie knew and she introduced
her to me and I noticed how this girl kept staring at me and finally
she begged my pardon and asked if she could ask me a personal
question and I said yes and she asked me if my complexion was
really " mine." I assured her it was and she said: " Well, I thought
so because I did not think anybody could put it on so artistically.
I certainly envy you." Edie and I both laughed.

Well, if that girl envies me my complexion, why I envy you living in New York. Chicago is rather dirty though I don't let that

part of it bother me as I bathe and change my clothing so often that the dirt does not have time to " settle." Edie often says she cannot see how I always keep so clean looking and says I always look like I had just stepped out of a band box. She also calls me a fish (jokingly) because I spend so much time in the water. But seriously I do love to bathe and never feel so happy as when I have just " cleaned up " and put on fresh clothing.

Edie has just gone out to see a picture and was cross at me because I would not go with her. I told her I was going to write a letter and she wanted to know to whom and I told her and she said : " You write to him so often that a person would almost think you was in love with him." I just laughed and turned it off, but she does say the most embarrassing things and I would be angry if it was anybody but she that said them.

Seriously I had much rather sit here and write letters or read or just sit and dream than go out to some crazy old picture show except once in awhile I do like to go to the theater and see a good play and a specially a musical play if the music is catchy. But as a rule I am contented to just stay home and feel cozy and lots of evenings Edie and I sit here without saying hardly a word to each other though she would love to talk but she knows I had rather be quiet and she often says it is just like living with a deaf and dumb mute to live with me because I make so little noise round the apartment. I guess I was born to be a home body as I so seldom care to go " gadding."

Though I do love to have company once in awhile, just a few congenial friends whom I can talk to and feel at home with and play cards or have some music. My friends love to drop in here, too, as they say Edie and I always give them such nice things to eat. Though poor Edie has not much to do with it, I am afraid, as she hates anything connected with cooking which is one of the things I love best of anything and I often say that when I begin keeping house in my own home I will insist on doing most of my own work as I would take so much more interest in it than a servant, though I would want somebody to help me a little if I could afford it as I often think a woman that does all her own work is liable to get so tired that she loses interest in the bigger things of life like books and music. Though after all what bigger thing is there than home making a specially for a woman?

I am sitting in the dearest old chair that I bought yesterday at a little store on the North Side. That is my one extravagance, buying furniture and things for the house, but I always say it is economy in the long run as I will always have them and have use **for** them and when I can pick them up at a bargain I would be sil**ly** not to. Though heaven knows I will never be "poor" in regards to furniture and rugs and things like that as mother's house in Toledo is full of lovely things which she says she is going to give to Sis and myself as soon as we have real homes of our own. She is going to give me the first choice as I am her favorite. She has the loveliest old things that you could not buy now for love or money including lovely old rugs and a piano which Sis wanted to have a player attachment put on it but I said it would be an insult to the piano so we did not get one. I am funny about things like that, a specially old furniture and feel towards them like people whom I love.

Poor mother, I am afraid she won't live much longer to enjoy her lovely old things as she has been suffering for years from stomach trouble and the doctor says it has been worse lately instead of better and her heart is weak besides. I am going home to see her a few days this fall as it may be the last time. She is very cheerful and always says she is ready to go now as she has had enough joy out of life and all she would like would be to see her girls settled down in their own homes before she goes.

There I go, talking about my domestic affairs again and I will bet you are bored to death though personly I am never bored when my friends tell me about themselves. But I won't "rattle on" any longer, but will say good night and don't forget to write and tell me how you come out with the song and thanks for sending me the words to it. Will you write a song about me some time? I would be thrilled to death! But I am afraid I am not the kind of girl that inspires men to write songs about them, but am just a quiet "mouse" that loves home and am not giddy enough to be the heroine of a song.

Well, Mr. Man, good night and don't wait so long before writing again to

Yours (?)
Mabelle.

N. Y., Sept. 8.

Dear Girlie: Well girlie have not got your last letter with me so cannot answer what was in it as I have forgotten if there was anything I was supposed to answer and besides have only a little time to write as I have a date to go out on a party with the Sears. We are going to the Georgie White show and afterwards somewheres for supper. Sears is the boy who wrote the lyric to my song and it is him and his sister I am going on the party with. The sister is a cold fish that has no use for men but she is show crazy and insists on Paul takeing her to 3 or 4 of them a week.

Paul wants me to give up my room here and come and live with them as they have plenty of room and I am running a little low on money but don't know if I will do it or not as am afraid I would freeze to death in the same house with a girl like the sister as she is ice cold but she don't hang round the house much as she is always takeing trips or going to shows or somewheres.

So far we have not had no luck with the song. All the publishers we have showed it to has went crazy over it but they won't make the right kind of a deal with us and if they don't loosen up and give us a decent royalty rate we are libel to put the song out ourselves and show them up. The man up to Goebel's told us the song was O. K. and he liked it but it was more of a production number than anything else and ought to go in a show like the Follies but they won't be in N. Y. much longer and what we ought to do is hold it till next spring.

Mean wile I am working on some new numbers and also have taken a position with the orchestra at the Wilton and am going to work there starting next week. They pay good money $60 and it will keep me going.

Well girlie that is about all the news. I believe you said your father was sick and hope he is better and also hope you are getting along O. K. and take care of yourself. When you have nothing else to do write to your friend,

Chas. F. Lewis.

Chicago, Ill., Sept. 11.

Dear Mr. Lewis: Your short note reached me yesterday and must say I was puzzled when I read it. It sounded like you was mad at me though I cannot think of any reason why you should be. If there was something I said in my last letter that offended you I wish you would tell me what it was and I will ask your pardon though I cannot remember anything I could of said that you could take offense at. But if there was something, why I assure you, Mr. Lewis, that I did not mean anything by it. I certainly did not intend to offend you in any way.

Perhaps it is nothing I wrote you, but you are worried on account of the publishers not treating you fair in regards to your song and that is why your letter sounded so distant. If that is the case I hope that by this time matters have rectified themselves and the future looks brighter. But any way, Mr. Lewis, don't allow yourself to worry over business cares as they will all come right in the end and I always think it is silly for people to worry themselves sick over temporary troubles, but the best way is to " keep smiling " and look for the " silver lining " in the cloud. That is the way I always do and no matter what happens, I manage to smile and my girl friend, Edie, calls me Sunny because I always look on the bright side.

Remember also, Mr. Lewis, that $60 is a salary that a great many men would like to be getting and are living on less than that and supporting a wife and family on it. I always say that a person can get along on whatever amount they make if they manage things in the right way.

So if it is business troubles, Mr. Lewis, I say don't worry, but look on the bright side. But if it is something I wrote in my last letter that offended you I wish you would tell me what it was so I can apologize as I assure you I meant nothing and would not say anything to hurt you for the world.

Please let me hear from you soon as I will not feel comfortable until I know I am not to blame for the sudden change.

Sincerely,
Mabelle Gillespie.

N. Y. Sept. 24.

Dear Miss Gillespie: Just a few lines to tell you the big news or at least it is big news to me. I am engaged to be married to Paul Sears' sister and we are going to be married early next month and live in Atlantic City where the orchestra I have been playing with has got an engagement in one of the big cabarets.

I know this will be a surprise to you as it was even a surprise to me as I did not think I would ever have the nerve to ask the girlie the big question as she was always so cold and acted like I was just in the way. But she said she supposed she would have to marry somebody some time and she did not dislike me as much as most of the other men her brother brought round and she would marry me with the understanding that she would not have to be a slave and work round the house and also I would have to take her to a show or somewheres every night and if I could not take her myself she would " run wild " alone. Atlantic City will be O. K. for that as a lot of new shows opens down there and she will be able to see them before they get to the big town. As for her being a slave, I would hate to think of marrying a girl and then have them spend their lives in druggery round the house. We are going to live in a hotel till we find something better but will be in no hurry to start house keeping as we will have to buy all new furniture.

Betsy is some doll when she is all fixed up and believe me she knows how to fix herself up. I don't know what she uses but it is weather proof and I have been out in a rain storm with her and we both got drowned but her face stayed on. I would almost think it was real only she tells me different.

Well girlie I may write to you again once in a wile as Betsy says she don't give a damn if I write to all the girls in the world just so I don't make her read the answers but that is all I can think of to say now except good bye and good luck and may the right man come along soon and he will be a lucky man getting a girl that is such a good cook and got all that furniture etc.

But just let me give you a word of advice before I close and that is don't never speak to strange men who you don't know nothing about as they may get you wrong and think you are trying to make them. It just happened that I knew better so you was lucky in my case but the luck might not last.

Your friend,
Chas. F. Lewis.

Chicago, Ill., Sept. 27.

My Dear Mr. Lewis: Thanks for your advice and also thank your fiance for her generosity in allowing you to continue your correspondence with her " rivals," but personly I have no desire to take advantage of that generosity as I have something better to do than read letters from a man like you, a specially as I have a man friend who is not so generous as Miss Sears and would strongly object to my continuing a correspondence with another man. It is at his request that I am writing this note to tell you not to expect to hear from me again.

Allow me to congratulate you on your engagement to Miss Sears and I am sure she is to be congratulated too, though if I met the lady I would be tempted to ask her to tell me her secret, namely how she is going to " run wild " on $60.

Sincerely,
Mabelle Gillespie.

XXIX

NORA

"MR. HAZLETT, shake hands with Jerry Morris and Frank Moon. I guess you've heard of the both of them."

The speaker was Louie Brock, producer of musical shows, who had cleared over half a million dollars in two years through the popularity of " Jersey Jane," tunes by Morris and lyrics by Moon.

They were in Brock's inner office, the walls of which were adorned with autographed pictures of six or seven of the more celebrated musical comedy stars and a too-perfect likeness of Brock's wife, whom he had evidently married in a dense fog.

" Mr. Hazlett," continued Brock, " has got a book which he wrote as a straight play, but it struck me right off that it was great material for a musical, especially with you two fellas to do the numbers. It's a brand-new idear, entirely opposite from most of these here musical comedy books that's all the same thing and the public must be getting sick of them by this time. Don't you think so, Jerry ? "

" I certainly do," the tunesmith replied. " Give us a good novelty story, and with what I and Frank can throw in there to jazz it up, we'll run till the theatre falls down."

" Well, Mr. Hazlett," said Brock, " suppose you read us the book and we'll see what the boys thinks of it."

Hazlett was quite nervous in spite of Brock's approval of his work and the fact that friends to whom he had shown it had given it high praise and congratulated him on his good fortune in getting a chance to collaborate with Morris and Moon—Morris, who had set a new style in melodies and rhythms and whose tunes made up sixty percent of all dance programs, and Moon, the ideal lyricist who could fit Jerry's fast triplets with such cute-sounding three-syllable rhymes that no one ever went to the considerable trouble of trying to find out what they meant.

" I've tried to stay away from the stereotyped Cinderella theme," said Hazlett. " In my story, the girl starts out just moderately well off and winds up poor. She sacrifices everything for love and the end finds her alone with her lover, impoverished but happy. She——"

" Let's hear the book," said the producer.

Hazlett, with trembling fingers, opened to the first page of his script.

"Well," he began, "the title is 'Nora' and the first scene——"

"Excuse me a minute," Morris interrupted. "I promised a fella that I'd come over and look at a big second-hand Trinidad Twelve. Only eight grand and a bargain if there ever was one, hey, Frank?"

"I'll say it's a bargain," Moon agreed.

"The fella is going to hold it for me till half-past three and its nearly three o'clock now. So if you don't mind, Mr. Hazlett, I wish that instead of reading the book clear through, you'd kind of give us a kind of a synopsis and it will save time and we can tell just as good, hey, Frank?"

"Just as good," said Moon.

"All right, Mr. Hazlett," Brock put in. "Suppose you tell the story in your own way, with just the main idear and the situations."

"Well," said Hazlett, "of course, as a straight play, I wrote it in three acts, but when Mr. Brock suggested that I make a musical show out of it, I cut it to two. To start with, the old man, the girl's uncle, is an Irishman who came to this country when he was about twenty years old. He worked hard and he was thrifty and finally he got into the building business for himself. He's pretty well-to-do, but he's avaricious and not satisfied with the three or four hundred thousand he's saved up. He meets another Irish immigrant about his own age, a politician who has a lot to say about the letting of big city building contracts. This man, Collins, had a handsome young son, John, twenty-three or twenty-four.

"The old man, the girl's uncle—their name is Crowley—he tries his hardest to get in strong with old Collins so Collins will land him some of the city contracts, but Collins, though he's very friendly all the while, he doesn't do Crowley a bit of good in a business way.

"Well, Crowley gives a party at his house for a crowd of his Irish friends in New York, young people and people his own age, and during the party young John Collins sees a picture of Crowley's beautiful niece, Nora. She's still in Ireland and has never been to this country. Young Collins asks Crowley who it is and he tells him and young Collins says she is the only girl he will ever marry.

"Crowley then figures to himself that if he can connect up with the Collinses by having his niece marry young John, he can land

just about all the good contracts there are. So he cables for Nora
to come over and pay him a visit. She comes and things happen
just as Crowley planned—John and Nora fall in love.

"Now there's a big dinner and dance in honor of the Mayor
and one of the guests is Dick Percival, a transplanted Englishman
who has made fifty million dollars in the sugar business. He also
falls in love with Nora and confesses it to her uncle. Old Crowley
has always hated Englishmen, but his avarice is so strong that he
decides Nora must get rid of John and marry Dick. Nora refuses
to do this, saying John is ' her man ' and that she will marry him
or nobody.

"Crowley forbids her to see John, but she meets him whenever
she can get out. The uncle and niece had a long, stubborn battle
of wills, neither yielding an inch. Finally John's father, old Collins, is caught red-handed in a big bribery scandal and sent to the
penitentiary. It is also found out that he has gambled away all
his money and John is left without a dime.

"Crowley, of course, thinks this settles the argument, that Nora
won't have anything more to do with a man whose father is a crook
and broke besides, and he gets up a party to announce the engagement between her and Dick. Nora doesn't interfere at all, but insists that young John Collins be invited. When the announcement
is made, Nora says her uncle has got the name of her fiancé wrong;
she has been engaged to John Collins since the first day she came
to the United States, and if he will still have her, she is his. Then
she and John walk out alone into the world, leaving Dick disappointed and Crowley in a good old-fashioned Irish rage."

"Well, boys," said Brock, after a pause, "what do you think
of it?"

The "boys" were silent.

"You see," said Brock, "for natural ensembles, you got the
first party at What's-his-name's, the scene on the pier when the
gal lands from Ireland, the Mayor's party at some hotel maybe,
and another party at What's-his-name's, only this time it's out-
doors at his country place. You can have the boy sing a love-song
to the picture before he ever sees the gal; you can make that the
melody you want to carry clear through. You can have love duets
between she and the boy and she and the Englishman. You can
write a song like ' East Side, West Side ' for the Mayor's party.

"You can write a corking good number for the pier scene, where
the people of all nationalities are meeting their relatives and

friends. And you can run wild with all the good Irish tunes in the world."

"Where's your comic?" inquired Morris.

"Mr. Hazlett forgot to mention the comic," Brock said. "He's an old Irishman, a pal of What's-his-name's, a kind of a Jiggs."

"People don't want an Irish comic these days," said Morris. "Can't you make him a Wop or a Heeb?"

"I'd have to rewrite the part," said Hazlett.

"No you wouldn't," said Morris. "Give him the same lines with a different twist to them."

"It really would be better," Brock put in, "if you could change him to a Heeb or even a Dutchman. I've got to have a spot for Joe Stein and he'd be a terrible flop as a Turkey."

"And listen," said Morris. "What are you going to do with Enriqueta?"

"Gosh! I'd forgot her entirely!" said Brock. "Of course we'll have to make room for her."

"Who is she?" Hazlett inquired.

"The best gal in Spain," said Brock. "I brought her over here and I'm paying her two thousand dollars every week, with nothing for her to do. You'll have to write in a part for her."

"Write in a part!" exclaimed Morris. "She'll play the lead or she won't play."

"But how is a Spanish girl going to play Nora Crowley?" asked Hazlett.

"Why does your dame have to be Nora Crowley?" Morris retorted. "Why does she have to be Irish at all?"

"Because her uncle is Irish."

"Make him a Spaniard, too."

"Yes, and listen," said Moon. "While you're making the gal and her uncle Spaniards, make your boy a wop. If you do that, I and Jerry have got a number that'll put your troupe over with a bang! Play it for them, Jerry."

Morris went to the piano and played some introductory chords.

"This is a great break of luck," said Moon, "to have a number already written that fits right into the picture. Of course, I'll polish the lyric up a little more and I want to explain that the boy sings part of the lines, the gal the rest. But here's about how it is. Let's go, Jerry!"

Morris repeated his introduction and Moon began to sing:

"Somewhere in the old world
You and I belong.

It will be a gold world,
Full of light and song.
Why not let's divide our time
Between your native land and mine?
Move from Italy to Spain,
Then back to Italy again?

"In sunny Italy,
My Spanish queen,
You'll fit so prettily
In that glorious scene.
You will sing me 'La Paloma';
I will sing you 'Cara Roma';
We will build a little home, a
Bungalow serene.
Then in the Pyrenees,
Somewhere in Spain,
We'll rest our weary knees
Down in Lovers' Lane,
And when the breakers roll a-
Cross the azure sea,
Espanola, Gorgonzola;
Spain and Italy."

" A wow! " cried Brock. " Congratulations, Jerry! You, too, Frank! What do you think of that one, Mr. Hazlett? "

" Very nice," said Hazlett. " The tune sounds like ' Sole Mio ' and ' La Paloma.' "

" It sounds like them both and it's better than either," said the composer.

" That one number makes our troupe, Jerry," said Brock. " You don't need anything else."

" But we've got something else, hey, Frank? "

" You mean ' Montgomery ' ? " said Moon.

" Yeh."

" Let's hear it," requested Brock.

" It'll take a dinge comic to sing it."

" Well, Joe Stein can do a dinge."

" I'll say he can! I like him best in blackface. And he's just the boy to put over a number like this."

Morris played another introduction, strains that Hazlett was sure he had heard a hundred times before, and Moon was off again:

"I want to go to Alabam'.
That's where my lovin' sweetheart am,
And won't she shout and dance for joy
To see once more her lovin' boy!
I've got enough saved up, I guess,

To buy her shoes and a bran'-new dress.
She's black as coal, and yet I think
When I walk in, she'll be tickled pink.

"Take me to Montgomery
Where it's always summery.
New York's just a mummery.
Give me life that's real.
New York fields are rotten fields.
Give me those forgotten fields;
I mean those there cotton fields,
Selma and Mobile.
I done been away so long;
Never thought I'd stay so long.
Train, you'd better race along
To my honey lamb.
Train, you make it snappy till
('Cause I won't be happy till)
I am in the capital,
Montgomery, Alabam'."

"Another knock-out!" said Brock enthusiastically. "Boys, either one of those numbers are better than anything in 'Jersey Jane.' Either one of them will put our troupe over. And the two of them together in one show! Well, it's in!"

Hazlett mustered all his courage.

"They're a couple of mighty good songs," he said. "But I don't exactly see how they'll fit."

"Mr. Hazlett," said Jerry Morris. "I understand this is your first experience with a musical comedy. I've had five successes in four years and could have had five more if I wanted to work that hard. I know the game backwards and I hope you won't take offense if I tell you a little something about it."

"I'm always glad to learn," said Hazlett.

"Well, then," said Morris, "you've got a great book there, with a good novelty idear, but it won't go without a few changes, changes that you can make in a half-hour and not detract anything from the novelty. In fact, they will add to it. While you were telling your story, I was thinking of it from the practical angle, the angle of show business, and I believe I can put my finger right on the spots that have got to be fixed.

"In the first place, as Louie has told you, he's got a contract with Enriqueta and she won't play any secondary parts. That means your heroine must be Spanish. Well, why not make her uncle her father and have him a Spaniard, running a Spanish restaurant somewhere down-town? It's a small restaurant and he just gets by. He has to use her as cashier and she sits in the window where the people going past can see her.

"One day the boy, who is really an Italian count—we'll call him Count Pizzola—he is riding alone in a taxi and he happens to look in the window and see the gal. He falls in love with her at first sight, orders the driver to stop and gets out and goes in the restaurant. He sits down and has his lunch, and while he is eating we can put in a novelty dance number with the boys and gals from the offices that are also lunching in this place.

"When the number is over, I'd have a comedy scene between Stein, who plays a dinge waiter, and, say, a German customer who isn't satisfied with the food or the check or something. Louie, who would you suggest for that part?"

"How about Charlie Williams?" said Brock.

"Great!" said Morris. "Well, they have this argument and the dinge throws the waiter out. The scrap amuses Pizzola and the gal, too, and they both laugh and that brings them together. He doesn't tell her he is a count, but she likes him pretty near as well as he likes her. They gab a while and then go into the Spanish number I just played for you.

"Now, in your story, you've got a boat scene where the gal is landing from Ireland. You'd better forget that scene. There was a boat scene in 'Sunny' and a boat scene in 'Hit the Deck,' and a lot of other troupes. We don't wan't anything that isn't our own. But Pizzola is anxious to take the gal out somewhere and let's see —Frank, where can he take her?"

"Why not a yacht?" suggested Moon.

"Great! He invites her out on a yacht, but he's got to pretend it isn't his own yacht. He borrowed it from a friend. She refuses at first, saying she hasn't anything to wear. She's poor, see? So he tells her his sister has got some sport clothes that will fit her. He gets the clothes for her and then we have a scene in her room where she is putting them on with a bunch of girl friends helping her. We'll write a number for that.

"Now the clothes he gave her are really his sister's clothes and the sister has carelessly left a beautiful brooch pinned in them. We go to the yacht and the Spanish dame knocks everybody dead. They put on an amateur show. That will give Enriqueta a chance for a couple more numbers. She and Pizzola are getting more and more stuck on each other and they repeat the Spanish song on the yacht, in the moonlight.

"There's a Frenchman along on the party who is greatly attracted by Enriqueta's looks. The Frenchman hates Pizzola. He has found out in some way that Enriqueta is wearing Pizzola's sister's clothes and he notices the diamond brooch. He figures that if he can steal it off of her, why, suspicion will be cast on the gal herself on account of her being poor, and Pizzola, thinking her a thief, won't have anything more to do with her and he, the Frenchman, can have her. So, during a dance, he manages to steal the brooch and he puts it in his pocket.

"Of course Pizzola's sister is also on the yachting party. All of a sudden she misses her brooch. She recalls having left it in the clothes she lent to Enriqueta. She goes to Enriqueta and asks her for it and the poor Spanish dame can't find it. Then Pizzola's sister calls her a thief and Pizzola himself can't help thinking she is one.

"They demand that she be searched, but rather than submit to that indignity, she bribes a sailor to take her off the yacht in a small launch and the last we see of her she's climbing overboard to get into the launch while the rest of the party are all abusing her. That's your first act curtain.

"I'd open the second act with a paddock scene at the Saratoga race-track. We'll write a jockey number and have about eight boys and maybe twenty-four gals in jockey suits. Enriqueta's father has gone broke in the restaurant business and he's up here looking for a job as assistant trainer or something. He used to train horses for the bull-fights in Spain.

"The gal is along with him and they run into the Frenchman that stole the brooch. The Frenchman tries to make love to the gal, but she won't have anything to do with him. While they are talking, who should come up but Pizzola! He is willing to make up with Enriqueta even though he still thinks her a thief. She won't meet his advances.

"He asks the Frenchman for a light. The Frenchman has a patent lighter and in pulling it out of his pocket, he pulls the brooch out, too. Then Pizzola realizes what an injustice he has done the gal and he pretty near goes down on his knees to her, but she has been badly hurt and won't forgive him yet.

"Now we have a scene in the café in the club-house and Stein is one of the waiters there. He sings the Montgomery number with a chorus of waiters and lunchers and at the end of the number he and the Spanish gal are alone on the stage.

"She asks him if he is really going to Montgomery and he says yes, and she says she and her father will go with him. She is anxious to go some place where there is no danger of running into the Frenchman or Pizzola.

"The third scene in the second act ought to be a plantation in Alabama. Stein is working there and the negroes are having a celebration or revival of some kind. Louie, you can get a male quartet to sing us some spirituals.

"Enriqueta's father has landed a job as cook at the plantation and she is helping with the housework. Pizzola and his sister follow her to Montgomery and come out to see her at the plantation.

"They are about to go up on the porch and inquire for her when they hear her singing the Spanish number. This proves to Pizzola that she still loves him and he finally gets his sister to plead with her for forgiveness. She forgives him. He tells her who he really is and how much dough he's got. And that pretty near washes us up."

"But how about our Japanese number?" said Moon.

"That's right," Morris said. "We'll have to send them to Japan before we end it. I've got a cherry-blossom number that must have the right setting. But that's easy to fix. You make these few changes I've suggested, Mr. Hazlett, and I feel that we've got a hit.

"And I want to say that your book is a whole lot better than most of the books they hand us. About the fella falling in love with the gal's picture—that's a novelty idear."

Hazlett said good-by to his producer and collaborators, went home by taxi and called up his bootlegger.

"Harry," he said, "what kind of whiskey have you got?"

"Well, Mr. Hazlett, I can sell you some good Scotch, but I ain't so sure of the rye. In fact, I'm kind of scared of it."

"How soon can you bring me a case?"

"Right off quick. It's the Scotch you want, ain't it?"

"No," said Hazlett. "I want the rye."

XXX

MAN NOT OVERBOARD

BEN BRAINARD posed for the newspaper photographers on the deck of the Gargantua, saying to himself: "There's a picture for page one—'Young Novelist Kills Himself at Sea.'"

He went into his cabin and opened his two bags. In one were a couple of clean handkerchiefs. The other was empty. He would tell the steward he had come in a terrible hurry, had not had time to pack. The truth was that after eleven o'clock that night he would need nothing in the world, not even the clothes he was wearing. He wondered vacantly how long a man's clothes outlasted his body in salt water.

He sat down on the bed and felt pressing against him the little gun he had bought on Third Avenue a week ago, the day when he had planned this thing he was going to do. He would have been a week dead now but for his not exceptional aversion to funerals and his preference to die at sea, and the added fact that it was not quite a year since he had taken out insurance for $10,000 in in favor of his mother and sister and the suicide clause would still, five days ago, have been in force. The mother and sister had very little and he realized that he was hurting them enough by just killing himself without, in addition, leaving them penniless.

His plan had been carefully made. The Gargantua, on which his friend Phil Runyon was purser, would dock on the eighth and sail again on the tenth, just a week after his Third Avenue shopping tour. He would be on board and would have Phil for a witness of his death to avoid any balking on the part of the insurance company. And he would spend the intervening days and nights in boundless drinking, such as would cause him to be remembered around New York as something more than the writer of two popular books and one which no publisher would accept. (Perhaps they would accept it when he had made his name better known by doing what he was about to do; if so, the royalties would help his poor mother and sister.)

Well, he had had his orgy, opening and closing day clubs and night clubs till early yesterday morning, when he had been taken home and put to bed by his friend the purser after a party of whose details he remembered nothing at all.

The Gargantua was gliding smoothly out of New York Harbor. Ben Brainard went into the lounge and ordered three quick drinks to steady his hand so that he might write farewell letters to the members of his family and to the Girl whose heartless treatment of him had made life intolerable. His last act would be to entrust these letters to good old Phil Runyon, just previous to his embarkation to another World.

To his mother and sister he explained the reasons for his deed —the failure of his latest and greatest work to win appreciation, and the loss of the most wonderful and lovable of all girls. He asked their forgiveness. He knew they would understand.

To the Girl he wrote over two thousand words that would make her at least a little bit sorry even if she were really as hard-hearted as she had appeared at their last meeting. (The Girl was Pauline Lannin of the chorus of " Hit the Deck " and he might have known that a chorus girl, what with making quick changes and one thing and another, would never have time to digest two thousand words, especially as the ordinary daily extent of her reading was the captions in an evening tabloid.)

The bugle blew for dinner, but of what use was dinner to a man who had only four hours more to live? What Brainard needed was enough Scotch to sustain his resolution, for it really is tough to pass out at the age of thirty, when you are a genius and there is so much good writing God wants you to do. It was this fear of weakening at the last moment that had influenced him to buy a gun. He was an excellent swimmer and if he toppled overboard without shooting himself first, a natural instinct of self-preservation might keep him afloat until the Gargantua's sailors had rescued him.

He had had one drink and was about to order another when a stranger stopped at his table, a man of robust health, apparently about fifty-five years old.

" Do you mind if I join you? " he asked. " I am all alone and I like company when I have a drink."

Brainard was going to lie and say he expected a friend, but it occurred to him that the time would pass more quickly if he had someone to talk to; listen to, rather, for he was not in a mood to do much talking himself.

" Sit down," he invited. " I am ordering a Scotch high-ball. Perhaps you'd rather have a cocktail."

" No, make it two high-balls," said the stranger, and added to the waiter, " Bring me the check."

"You can buy the next one," Brainard said. "I suppose we ought to introduce ourselves. I am Benjamin Brainard, of New York."

"Not Benjamin Brainard the author!" the other exclaimed. "Why, I read two of your books and enjoyed them immensely. But I certainly never would have guessed you were such a young man; your novels show such a wide knowledge of life."

"I guess I've lived!" said Brainard with a bitter smile.

"My name," said his new companion, "is Fred Lemp. I'm just a plain business man, with very little business," he added good-naturedly.

"Where are you bound for?" Brainard inquired.

"Paris," said Lemp. "Paris and Château-Thierry. And you?"

Brainard's face wore a queer expression. "I don't know," he said.

"You don't know!"

"I only know that it's a long way off," said Brainard.

"Oh, I suppose you are just wandering around, in search of material for a new book."

"I have written my last book."

"You mustn't say that! A man your age and with your talent! You owe it to the world to keep on writing."

"Thank you, but I am sure I don't owe the world anything."

They had had four drinks and Brainard was now ordering another.

"I don't know whether I'd better or not," said Lemp hesitantly. "I hardly ever drink more than three, because after three I get talky and bore everybody to death."

"It doesn't matter to me if you get talky," said Brainard, and added to himself: "I don't have to listen to you."

"Well, it's on your own head," said Lemp, and ordered his fifth high-ball.

"Mr. Lemp," Brainard said, "what would you do—— Never mind. I guess I'm getting too talky myself."

"Not at all," said Lemp. "I'd like to hear what you were going to ask me."

"Well, I was going to ask what you would do if you were an artist in a certain line and nobody appreciated your work——"

"I'd keep at it anyway if I knew it was good work."

"I wasn't through. What would you do if you suddenly realized you were an unappreciated artist, and then, on top of that, a Girl broke your heart?"

"Is this autobiographical?"

"Perhaps."

"Well, I'd try my best to forget her and I'd go ahead and do such masterful work that she would be very sorry for what she had done to me."

"Forget her!" Brainard's tone was bitter in the extreme.

They were awaiting a sixth drink.

"You said you were going to Château-Thierry. I was in the fight there. I wish I'd been killed!"

"My boy was," said Lemp.

"Are you going to visit the grave?"

"Yes, and also to visit a little Frenchwoman who ought to have been his wife. Every year I pay her a call, to see if there is anything I can do for her and her child. Every year I try to coax her back to America with me, but she won't leave France. I wish she would. I'm all alone now and the youngster—he's nine years old —he's a mighty cute kid and would be company for me. A man gets lonesome sometimes. And my wife is worse than dead. She has lost her mind and has to be kept in a private sanitarium."

"Are you allowed to see her?"

"I do see her twice a year, on her birthday and on our anniversary. But I might as well stay away. She has no idea who I am. Poor Margaret! She is almost as beautiful as the day I met her."

"What type?"

"I suppose you would call her an Irish type—black hair and blue eyes. Just the type my first wife was; in fact, I believe it was her resemblance to Edith that made me fall in love with her."

"How old was your first wife when she died?"

"She didn't die. Poor Edith! I guess it was mostly my fault. She was too young to marry, too young to know her own mind. When we had lived together a little over a year, she fell desperately in love with a man I used to invite frequently to the house, a business acquaintance."

"Did she run away with him?"

"Yes. He had more money than I. I don't mean to say that Edith was money-mad, but she did like good times and our marriage came just at a period when I was in desperate financial straits; rather, just before that period, for naturally, if I had known what was going to happen, I wouldn't have married her."

" What did happen? " asked Brainard, sipping his eighth drink.

" You are an inquisitive young man."

" Oh, if you'd rather not tell me——"

" I might as well. I warned you I'd get talky. Well, my youngest brother went wrong. He was cashier in a small bank, out on Long Island, and he embezzled to the extent of twenty thousand dollars. He had gambled it all away at the race-tracks and in order to keep him out of jail, I liquidated all my assets and borrowed three thousand from a friend to make up the amount. I did it more for my mother's sake than for his; I knew that if she heard that he had stolen, it would kill her." Lemp brushed a hand across his eyes. " She found out about it anyway, and it did kill her."

" Horrible! "

" I worked like the devil to get back on my feet, and I did it. But it was too late. Edith had gone."

" What do you say if we have a drink? "

" I say yes."

" And how long after that did you get married the second time? "

" Four years, and the same thing nearly happened again. My other brother, older than I, fell in love with a woman in Garden City, another man's wife. The husband found it out and there was a fight in which my brother shot the husband dead. There was no chance in the world of my brother's getting off, but I felt it my duty to give him the best counsel obtainable. He had no money himself. I paid two lawyers forty thousand and my brother went to the chair. Well, I learned afterwards that on the very same day my brother committed murder, Margaret, my second wife, became friendly with a piano tuner. Of course he had nothing except his wages and she was not fool enough to give me up for him. But when those lawyers had taken all my capital she would have left me if Providence had not intervened. The piano tuner was hit by a truck on the Fifty-ninth Street bridge and lost his hearing."

" Did you have any other children besides the boy killed in the war? "

" Yes, a girl. But I'd rather not talk about her. Oh, well, what does it matter? Miriam was our first-born, a year and a half older than my son. One day she was driving a car up in Westchester County, going forty or fifty miles an hour, when she was stopped by a handsome young motorcycle policeman, and the rascal told her he would let her off if she would be his girl.

" She said to him, ' I don't know what you mean by being your girl, but I think you're awfully nice-looking and I'd just as soon be your wife.' They were married and had three children. Then it was discovered that he had another wife and family in Ardsley. He was sent to jail, she is a stenographer in an insurance office down-town and I am supporting the kiddies."

Brainard consumed his twelfth drink, then fumbled awkwardly in his pocket and drew out his gun.

" Mr. Lumps," he said, " I'm going to ask you to do me a favor. Put this right in your mouth, aim it upwards and shoot."

" What are you talking about, boy? Do you want me to commit suicide? Why, I'm only sixty-one years old and having a damn good time! "

" You do as I say and do it right in here so we won't lose the gun. I'm going to need it myself at eleven o'clock."

" What for? "

" To do the same thing you're going to do."

" But I'm not going to do anything except go to bed. What you intend to do is none of my business, though I would suggest that as you still have over two hours and a half to wait, you go to your cabin and take a nap and leave a call for eleven. I've always heard that the time to kill yourself with the best results is right after a nice nap."

Brainard had already started on one, but Lemp and a steward managed to get his room key out of his pocket and arouse him sufficiently to be conducted to the cabin, partly undressed and laid on his bed. Lemp then returned to the lounge and was soon joined by Phil Runyon.

" He's safe for the night anyway," said Lemp.

" You've done a good job, Fred, and I'm grateful to you," said the purser.

" I made him cry twice, and there were three or four times when I nearly broke down myself. Here's his gun."

" All right; I'll take charge of it if you're sure you don't want it. Though I don't know what good it would do you, as I emptied it yesterday morning after I'd got him to sleep, and I don't think we're selling any ammunition on the Gargantua, except what comes in bottles. That was a great party he took me on night before last. He insisted on dragging me to some night club and who should be there but this dame that's turned him down. She was with a man who could have been her father, but wouldn't want to if he was sober. I swear, Fred, she must be the manager's wife's sister ever to land a job in what they tell me is a pretty chorus.

" He was going to their table and make a scene, but I told him it would be cowardly to pick on a man as old as that. I finally got her eye and gave her the office to duck, and when she saw who was with me, she didn't hesitate a minute.

" Pretty soon Ben was worse than I ever saw him. He had his suicide plan all worked out and he gave me the details, thinking I was somebody else. He talked like this:

" ' I haven't much longer to live,' he said. ' In fact, this is the last time you'll see me. I've got it all fixed up to kill myself and a good old pal of mine is going to help me. I've bought a gun; it's over in my room now, all loaded and waiting for me. Well, this pal of mine is Phil Runyon, purser on the Gargantua, and she sails day after tomorrow. I'm going to be aboard and I'll make a date to meet Phil when we're out at sea and I'll coax him to one of the decks, telling him I want to discuss something with him where we can't be overheard. Then I'll sit up on the rail and I'll sit so that when I shoot myself, I'll be bound to fall overboard. You see, I've got to have him there, or somebody else that knows me, so there won't be any trouble about my insurance. How is that for an idea? '

" Imagine him asking *me* what kind of an idea I thought it was!

" And the funny part, along about five o'clock, when I finally succeeded in getting him out of the place, he knew me and was calling me Phil and talking about other times we'd been out together.

" Yesterday afternoon I called up his hotel and made sure he was out; then I went there and fixed it with a bell-hop and porter to go up in his room after he left this morning and pack up enough stuff for him to make the trip with and have it sent down to the ship in my name. He thinks he hasn't any baggage, but he's got enough to go over and back with, and I really think the crossing will do him a lot of good. Though writers are mostly all nutty and you never know what to expect of them."

" I haven't told you," said Lemp, " that when I was through with my story, he gave me the gun and ordered me to use it on myself."

" Oh, Ben was always a generous boy," said Runyon. " It surprises me that he didn't offer to take you out on deck, shoot you and throw you off the ship."

"Listen," said Lemp: "I need one more drink for courage and then I've got to find my wife and take my scolding. I explained to her that I'd met a man I thought I could do some business with and I might not be in for dinner. But what good is that explanation going to be when she sees me?"

"Probably none," Runyon said cheerfully. "But the drink is on me."

About noon next day Brainard woke up, summoned his steward and ordered him to send the purser to his cabin.

"Phil," he said when Runyon arrived, "didn't we have an engagement last night?"

"Yes, but you went to bed long before your bedtime."

"Phil, where did that steamer trunk come from?"

"I suppose it came from your hotel."

"I didn't bring any baggage except those two empty bags."

"Did you plan crossing the ocean without baggage?"

"I didn't plan crossing the ocean. And another thing, who was the fella I was with all evening, a fella about sixty years old, named Limp or Lemp or something?"

"Oh," said Runyon, "that's Fred Lemp, a big hosiery manufacturer from up-state."

"Say, he's had a tough life. He told me all about it. He told me stuff enough for a whale of a novel."

"Why don't you write it?"

"Because I can't remember a word he said."

"Well," said Runyon, "we'll get you together again some time."

"Do that, Phil," said Brainard. "But make it out on deck where he can't order so many drinks. A man as old as he ought not to drink so much. It's liable to get him."

XXXI

A CADDY'S DIARY

Wed. Apr. 12.

I AM 16 of age and am a caddy at the Pleasant View Golf Club but only temporary as I expect to soon land a job some wheres as asst pro as my game is good enough now to be a pro but to young looking. My pal Joe Bean also says I have not got enough swell head to make a good pro but suppose that will come in time, Joe is a wise cracker.

But first will put down how I come to be writeing this diary, we have got a member name Mr Colby who writes articles in the newspapers and I hope for his sakes that he is a better writer then he plays golf but any way I cadded for him a good many times last yr and today he was out for the first time this yr and I cadded for him and we got talking about this in that and something was mentioned in regards to the golf articles by Alex Laird that comes out every Sun in the paper Mr Colby writes his articles for so I asked Mr Colby did he know how much Laird got paid for the articles and he said he did not know but supposed that Laird had to split 50-50 with who ever wrote the articles for him. So I said don't he write the articles himself and Mr Colby said why no he guessed not. Laird may be a master mind in regards to golf he said, but that is no sign he can write about it as very few men can write decent let alone a pro. Writeing is a nag.

How do you learn it I asked him.

Well he said read what other people writes and study them and write things yourself, and maybe you will get on to the nag and maybe you wont.

Well Mr Colby I said do you think I could get on to it?

Why he said smileing I did not know that was your ambition to be a writer.

Not exactly was my reply, but I am going to be a golf pro myself and maybe some day I will get good enough so as the papers will want I should write them articles and if I can learn to write them myself why I will not have to hire another writer and split with them.

Well said Mr Colby smileing you have certainly got the right
temperament for a pro, they are all big hearted fellows.

But listen Mr Colby I said if I want to learn it would not do me
no good to copy down what other writers have wrote, what I would
have to do would be write things out of my own head.

That is true said Mr. Colby.

Well I said what could I write about?

Well said Mr Colby why don't you keep a diary and every night
after your supper set down and write what happened that day and
write who you cadded for and what they done only leave me out
of it. And you can write down what people say and what you think
and etc., it will be the best kind of practice for you, and once in a
wile you can bring me your writeings and I will tell you the truth
if they are good or rotten.

So that is how I come to be writeing this diary is so as I can get
some practice writeing and maybe if I keep at it long enough I can
get on to the nag.

Friday, Apr. 14.

We been haveing Apr. showers for a couple days and nobody out
on the course so they has been nothing happen that I could write
down in my diary but dont want to leave it go to long or will never
learn the trick so will try and write a few lines about a caddys life
and some of our members and etc.

Well I and Joe Bean is the 2 oldest caddys in the club and I been
cadding now for 5 yrs and quit school 3 yrs ago tho my mother did
not like it for me to quit but my father said he can read and write
and figure so what is the use in keeping him there any longer as
greek and latin dont get you no credit at the grocer, so they lied
about my age to the trunce officer and I been cadding every yr from
March till Nov and the rest of the winter I work around Heismans
store in the village.

Dureing the time I am cadding I genally always manage to play
at lease 9 holes a day myself on wk days and some times 18 and am
never more then 2 or 3 over par figures on our course but it is a cinch.

I played the engineers course 1 day last summer in 75 which is
some golf and some of our members who has been playing 20 yrs
would give their right eye to play as good as myself.

I use to play around with our pro Jack Andrews till I got so as I
could beat him pretty near every time we played and now he wont
play with me no more, he is not a very good player for a pro but
they claim he is a good teacher. Personly I think golf teachers is
a joke tho I am glad people is suckers enough to fall for it as I ex-

pect to make my liveing that way. We have got a member Mr
Dunham who must of took 500 lessons in the past 3 yrs and when
he starts to shoot he trys to remember all the junk Andrews has
learned him and he gets dizzy and they is no telling where the ball
will go and about the safest place to stand when he is shooting is
between he and the hole.

I dont beleive the club pays Andrews much salery but of course
he makes pretty fair money giveing lessons but his best graft is a
3 some which he plays 2 and 3 times a wk with Mr Perdue and Mr
Lewis and he gives Mr Lewis a stroke a hole and they genally break
some wheres near even but Mr Perdue made a 83 one time so he
thinks that is his game so he insists on playing Jack even, well they
always play for $5.00 a hole and Andrews makes $20.00 to $30.00
per round and if he wanted to cut loose and play his best he could
make $50.00 to $60.00 per round but a couple of wallops like that
and Mr Perdue might get cured so Jack figures a small stedy income is safer.

I have got a pal name Joe Bean and we pal around together as
he is about my age and he says some comical things and some times
will wisper some thing comical to me wile we are cadding and it is
all I can do to help from laughing out loud, that is one of the first
things a caddy has got to learn is never laugh out loud only when
a member makes a joke. How ever on the days when theys ladies
on the course I dont get a chance to caddy with Joe because for some
reason another the woman folks dont like Joe to caddy for them
wile on the other hand they are always after me tho I am no Othello
for looks or do I seek their flavors, in fact it is just the opp and I try
to keep in the back ground when the fair sex appears on the seen as
cadding for ladies means you will get just so much money and no
more as theys no chance of them loosning up. As Joe says the rule
against tipping is the only rule the woman folks keeps.

Theys one lady how ever who I like to caddy for as she looks like
Lillian Gish and it is a pleasure to just look at her and I would caddy
for her for nothing tho it is hard to keep your eye on the ball when
you are cadding for this lady, her name is Mrs Doane.

Sat. Apr. 15.

This was a long day and am pretty well wore out but must not
get behind in my writeing practice. I and Joe carried all day for
Mr Thomas and Mr Blake. Mr Thomas is the vice president of one
of the big banks down town and he always slips you a $1.00 extra
per round but beleive me you earn it cadding for Mr Thomas, there
is just 16 clubs in his bag includeing 5 wood clubs tho he has not

used the wood in 3 yrs but says he has got to have them along in case his irons goes wrong on him. I dont know how bad his irons will have to get before he will think they have went wrong on him but personly if I made some of the tee shots he made today I would certainly considder some kind of a change of weppons.

Mr Thomas is one of the kind of players that when it has took him more than 6 shots to get on the green he will turn to you and say how many have I had caddy and then you are suppose to pretend like you was thinking a minute and then say 4, then he will say to the man he is playing with well I did not know if I had shot 4 or 5 but the caddy says it is 4. You see in this way it is not him that is cheating but the caddy but he makes it up to the caddy afterwards with a $1.00 tip.

Mr Blake gives Mr Thomas a stroke a hole and they play a $10.00 nassua and niether one of them wins much money from the other one but even if they did why $10.00 is chickens food to men like they. But the way they crab and squak about different things you would think their last $1.00 was at stake. Mr Thomas started out this A. M. with a 8 and a 7 and of course that spoilt the day for him and me to. Theys lots of men that if they dont make a good score on the first 2 holes they will founder all the rest of the way around and raze H with their caddy and if I was laying out a golf course I would make the first 2 holes so darn easy that you could not help from getting a 4 or better on them and in that way everybody would start off good natured and it would be a few holes at lease before they begun to turn sour.

Mr Thomas was beat both in the A. M. and P. M. in spite of my help as Mr Blake is a pretty fair counter himself and I heard him say he got a 88 in the P. M. which is about a 94 but any way it was good enough to win. Mr Blakes regular game is about a 90 takeing his own figures and he is one of these cocky guys that takes his own game serious and snears at men that cant break 100 and if you was to ask him if he had ever been over 100 himself he would say not since the first yr he begun to play. Well I have watched a lot of those guys like he and I will tell you how they keep from going over 100 namely by doing just what he done this A. M. when he come to the 13th hole. Well he missed his tee shot and dubbed along and finely he got in a trap on his 4th shot and I seen him take 6 wallops in the trap and when he had took the 6th one his ball was worse off then when he started so he picked it up and marked a X down on his score card. Well if he had of played out the hole why the best he could of got was a 11 by holeing his next niblick shot but he would of probly got about a 20 which would of made him around

108 as he admitted takeing a 88 for the other 17 holes. But I bet
if you was to ask him what score he had made he would say O I was
terrible and I picked up on one hole but if I had of played them all
out I guess I would of had about a 92.

These is the kind of men that laughs themselfs horse when they
hear of some dub takeing 10 strokes for a hole but if they was made
to play out every hole and mark down their real score their card
would be decorated with many a big casino.

Well as I say I had a hard day and was pretty sore along towards
the finish but still I had to laugh at Joe Bean on the 15th hole which
is a par 3 and you can get there with a fair drive and personly I am
genally hole high with a midiron, but Mr Thomas topped his tee
shot and dubbed a couple with his mashie and was still quiet a ways
off the green and he stood studing the situation a minute and said
to Mr Blake well I wonder what I better take here. So Joe Bean
was standing by me and he said under his breath take my advice
and quit you old rascal.

Mon. Apr. 17.

Yesterday was Sun and I was to wore out last night to write as
I cadded 45 holes. I cadded for Mr Colby in the A. M. and Mr
Langley in the P. M. Mr Thomas thinks golf is wrong on the sabath
tho as Joe Bean says it is wrong any day the way he plays it.

This A. M. they was nobody on the course and I played 18 holes
by myself and had a 5 for a 76 on the 18th hole but the wind got a
hold of my drive and it went out of bounds. This P. M. they was
3 of us had a game of rummy started but Miss Rennie and Mrs
Thomas come out to play and asked for me to caddy for them, they
are both terrible.

Mrs Thomas is Mr Thomas wife and she is big and fat and shakes
like jell and she always says she plays golf just to make her skinny
and she dont care how rotten she plays as long as she is getting the
exercise, well maybe so but when we find her ball in a bad lie she
aint never sure it is hers till she picks it up and smells it and when
she puts it back beleive me she don't cram it down no gopher hole.

Miss Rennie is a good looker and young and they say she is engaged to Chas Crane, he is one of our members and is the best
player in the club and dont cheat hardly at all and he has got a
job in the bank where Mr Thomas is the vice president. Well I
have cadded for Miss Rennie when she was playing with Mr Crane
and I have cadded for her when she was playing alone or with another lady and I often think if Mr Crane could hear her talk when
he was not around he would not be so stuck on her. You would be
surprised at some of the words that falls from those fare lips.

Well the 2 ladies played for 2 bits a hole and Miss Rennie was haveing a terrible time wile Mrs Thomas was shot with luck on the greens and sunk 3 or 4 putts that was murder. Well Miss Rennie used some expressions which was best not repeated but towards the last the luck changed around and it was Miss Rennie that was sinking the long ones and when they got to the 18th tee Mrs Thomas was only 1 up.

Well we had started pretty late and when we left the 17th green Miss Rennie made the remark that we would have to hurry to get the last hole played, well it was her honor and she got the best drive she made all day about 120 yds down the fair way. Well Mrs Thomas got nervous and looked up and missed her ball a ft and then done the same thing right over and when she finely hit it she only knocked it about 20 yds and this made her lay 3. Well her 4th went wild and lit over in the rough in the apple trees. It was a cinch Miss Rennie would win the hole unless she dropped dead.

Well we all went over to hunt for Mrs Thomas ball but we would of been lucky to find it even in day light but now you could not hardly see under the trees, so Miss Rennie said drop another ball and we will not count no penalty. Well it is some job any time to make a woman give up hunting for a lost ball and all the more so when it is going to cost her 2 bits to play the hole out so there we stayed for at lease 10 minutes till it was so dark we could not see each other let alone a lost ball and finely Mrs Thomas said well it looks like we could not finish, how do we stand? Just like she did not know how they stood.

You had me one down up to this hole said Miss Rennie.

Well that is finishing pretty close said Mrs Thomas.

I will have to give Miss Rennie credit that what ever word she thought of for this occasion she did not say it out loud but when she was paying me she said I might of give you a quarter tip only I have to give Mrs Thomas a quarter she dont deserve so you dont get it.

Fat chance I would of had any way.

Thurs. Apr. 20.

Well we been haveing some more bad weather but today the weather was all right but that was the only thing that was all right. This P. M. I cadded double for Mr Thomas and Chas Crane the club champion who is stuck on Miss Rennie. It was a 4 some with he and Mr Thomas against Mr Blake and Jack Andrews the pro, they was only playing best ball so it was really just a match between Mr Crane and Jack Andrews and Mr Crane win by 1 up.

Joe Bean cadded for Jack and Mr Blake. Mr Thomas was terrible and I put in a swell P. M. lugging that heavy bag of his besides Mr Cranes bag.

Mr Thomas did not go off of the course as much as usual but he kept hitting behind the ball and he run me ragged replaceing his divots but still I had to laugh when we was playing the 4th hole which you have to drive over a ravine and every time Mr Thomas misses his tee shot on this hole why he makes a squak about the ravine and says it ought not to be there and etc.

Today he had a terrible time getting over it and afterwards he said to Jack Andrews this is a joke hole and ought to be changed. So Joe Bean wispered to me that if Mr Thomas kept on playing like he was the whole course would be changed.

Then a little wile later when we come to the long 9th hole Mr Thomas got a fair tee shot but then he whiffed twice missing the ball by a ft and the 3d time he hit it but it only went a little ways and Joe Bean said that is 3 trys and no gain, he will have to punt.

But I must write down about my tough luck, well we finely got through the 18 holes and Mr Thomas reached down in his pocket for the money to pay me and he genally pays for Mr Crane to when they play together as Mr Crane is just a employ in the bank and dont have much money but this time all Mr Thomas had was a $20.00 bill so he said to Mr Crane I guess you will have to pay the boy Charley so Charley dug down and got the money to pay me and he paid just what it was and not a dime over, where if Mr Thomas had of had the change I would of got a $1.00 extra at lease and maybe I was not sore and Joe Bean to because of course Andrews never gives you nothing and Mr Blake dont tip his caddy unless he wins.

They are a fine bunch of tight wads said Joe and I said well Crane is all right only he just has not got no money.

He aint all right no more than the rest of them said Joe.

Well at lease he dont cheat on his score I said.

And you know why that is said Joe, neither does Jack Andrews cheat on his score but that is because they play to good. Players like Crane and Andrews that goes around in 80 or better cant cheat on their score because they make the most of the holes in around 4 strokes and the 4 strokes includes their tee shot and a couple of putts which everybody is right there to watch them when they make them and count them right along with them. So if they make a 4 and claim a 3 why people would just laugh in their face and say how did the ball get from the fair way on to the green, did it fly? But the boys that takes 7 and 8 strokes to a hole can shave their score and you know they are shaveing it but you have to let them get away with it because you cant prove nothing. But that is one of the penaltys for being a good player, you cant cheat.

To hear Joe tell it pretty near everybody are born crooks, well maybe he is right.

Wed. Apr. 26.

Today Mrs Doane was out for the first time this yr and asked for me to caddy for her and you bet I was on the job. Well how are you Dick she said, she always calls me by name. She asked me what had I been doing all winter and was I glad to see her and etc.

She said she had been down south all winter and played golf pretty near every day and would I watch her and notice how much she had improved.

Well to tell the truth she was no better then last yr and wont never be no better and I guess she is just to pretty to be a golf player but of course when she asked me did I think her game was improved I had to reply yes indeed as I would not hurt her feelings and she laughed like my reply pleased her. She played with Mr and Mrs Carter and I carried the 2 ladies bags wile Joe Bean cadded for Mr Carter. Mrs Carter is a ugly dame with things on her face and it must make Mr Carter feel sore when he looks at Mrs Doane to think he married Mrs Carter but I suppose they could not all marry the same one and besides Mrs Doane would not be a sucker enough to marry a man like he who drinks all the time and is pretty near always stood, tho Mr Doane who she did marry aint such a H of a man himself tho dirty with money.

They all gave me the laugh on the 3d hole when Mrs Doane was makeing her 2d shot and the ball was in the fair way but laid kind of bad and she just ticked it and then she asked me if winter rules was in force and I said yes so we teed her ball up so as she could get a good shot at it and they gave me the laugh for saying winter rules was in force.

You have got the caddys bribed Mr Carter said to her.

But she just smiled and put her hand on my sholder and said Dick is my pal. That is enough of a bribe to just have her touch you and I would caddy all day for her and never ask for a cent only to have her smile at me and call me her pal.

Sat. Apr. 29.

Today they had the first club tournament of the yr and they have a monthly tournament every month and today was the first one, it is a handicap tournament and everybody plays in it and they have prizes for low net score and low gross score and etc. I cadded for Mr Thomas today and will tell what happened.

They played a 4 some and besides Mr Thomas we had Mr Blake and Mr Carter and Mr Dunham. Mr Dunham is the worst man player in the club and the other men would not play with him a specialy on a Saturday only him and Mr Blake is partners together in business. Mr Dunham has got the highest handicap in the club which is 50 but it would have to be 150 for him to win a prize. Mr Blake and Mr Carter has got a handicap of about 15 a piece I think and Mr Thomas is 30, the first prize for the low net score for the day was a dozen golf balls and the second low score a ½ dozen golf balls and etc.

Well we had a great battle and Mr Colby ought to been along to write it up or some good writer. Mr Carter and Mr Dunham played partners against Mr Thomas and Mr Blake which ment that Mr Carter was playing Thomas and Blakes best ball, well Mr Dunham took the honor and the first ball he hit went strate off to the right and over the fence outside of the grounds, well he done the same thing 3 times. Well when he finely did hit one in the course why Mr Carter said why not let us not count them 3 first shots of Mr Dunham as they was just practice. Like H we wont count them said Mr Thomas we must count every shot and keep our scores correct for the tournament.

All right said Mr. Carter.

Well we got down to the green and Mr Dunham had about 11 and Mr Carter sunk a long putt for a par 5, Mr Blake all ready had 5 strokes and so did Mr Thomas and when Mr Carter sunk his putt why Mr Thomas picked his ball up and said Carter wins the hole and I and Blake will take 6s. Like H you will said Mr Carter, this is a tournament and we must play every hole out and keep our scores correct. So Mr Dunham putted and went down in 13 and Mr Blake got a 6 and Mr Thomas missed 2 easy putts and took a 8 and maybe he was not boiling.

Well it was still their honor and Mr Dunham had one of his dizzy spells on the 2d tee and he missed the ball twice before he hit it and then Mr Carter drove the green which is only a midiron shot and then Mr Thomas stepped up and missed the ball just like Mr Dunham. He was wild and yelled at Mr Dunham no man could play golf playing with a man like you, you would spoil anybodys game.

Your game was all ready spoiled said Mr Dunham, it turned sour on the 1st green.

You would turn anybody sour said Mr Thomas.

Well Mr Thomas finely took a 8 for the hole which is a par 3 and

it certainly looked bad for him winning a prize when he started out
with 2 8s, and he and Mr Dunham had another terrible time on
No 3 and wile they was messing things up a 2 some come up behind
us and hollered fore and we left them go through tho it was Mr
Clayton and Mr Joyce and as Joe Bean said they was probly dissa-
pointed when we left them go through as they are the kind that
feels like the day is lost if they cant write to some committee and
preffer charges.

Well Mr Thomas got a 7 on the 3d and he said well it is no wonder I am off of my game today as I was up ½ the night with my
teeth.

Well said Mr Carter **if** I had your money why on the night before
a big tournament like this I would hire somebody else to set up
with my teeth.

Well I wished I could remember all that was said and done but
any way Mr Thomas kept getting sore and sore and we got to the
7th tee and he had not made a decent tee shot all day so Mr Blake
said to him why dont you try the wood as you cant do no worse?

By Geo I beleive I will said Mr Thomas and took his driver out
of the bag which he had not used it for 3 yrs.

Well he swang and zowie away went the ball pretty near 8 inchs
distants wile the head of the club broke off clean and saled 50 yds
down the course. Well I have got a hold on myself so as I dont
never laugh out loud and I beleive the other men was scarred to
laugh or he would of killed them so we all stood there in silents
waiting for what would happen.

Well without saying a word he come to where I was standing and
took his other 4 wood clubs out of the bag and took them to a tree
which stands a little ways from the tee box and one by one he swang
them with all his strength against the trunk of the tree and smashed
them to H and gone, all right gentlemen that is over he said.

Well to cut it short Mr Thomas score for the first 9 was a even 60
and then we started out on the 2d 9 and you would not think it was
the same man playing, on the first 3 holes he made 2 4s and a 5 and
beat Mr Carter even and followed up with a 6 and a 5 and that is
how he kept going up to the 17th hole.

What has got in to you Thomas said Mr Carter.

Nothing said Mr Thomas only I broke my hoodoo when I broke
them 5 wood clubs.

Yes I said to myself and if you had broke them 5 wood clubs 3 yrs
ago I would not of broke my back lugging them around.

Well we come to the 18th tee and Mr Thomas had a 39 which
give him a 99 for 17 holes, well everybody drove off and as we was

following along why Mr Klabor come walking down the course from the club house on his way to the 17th green to join some friends and Mr Thomas asked him what had he made and he said he had turned in a 93 but his handicap is only 12 so that give him a 81.

That wont get me no wheres he said as Charley Crane made a 75.

Well said Mr Thomas I can tie Crane for low net if I get a 6 on this hole.

Well it come his turn to make his 2d and zowie he hit the ball pretty good but they was a hook on it and away she went in to the woods on the left, the ball laid in behind a tree so as they was only one thing to do and that was waste a shot getting it back on the fair so that is what Mr Thomas done and it took him 2 more to reach the green.

How many have you had Thomas said Mr Carter when we was all on the green.

Let me see said Mr Thomas and then turned to me, how many have I had caddy?

I dont know I said.

Well it is either 4 or 5 said Mr Thomas.

I think it is 5 said Mr Carter.

I think it is 4 said Mr Thomas and turned to me again and said how many have I had caddy?

So I said 4.

Well said Mr Thomas personly I was not sure myself but my caddy says 4 and I guess he is right.

Well the other men looked at each other and I and Joe Bean looked at each other but Mr Thomas went ahead and putted and was down in 2 putts.

Well he said I certainly come to life on them last 9 holes.

So he turned in his score as 105 and with his handicap of 30 why that give him a net of 75 which was the same as Mr Crane so instead of Mr Crane getting 1 dozen golf balls and Mr Thomas getting ½ a dozen golf balls why they will split the 1st and 2d prize makeing 9 golf balls a piece.

Tues. May 2.

This was the first ladies day of the season and even Joe Bean had to carry for the fair sex. We cadded for a 4 some which was Miss Rennie and Mrs Thomas against Mrs Doane and Mrs Carter. I guess if they had of kept their score right the total for the 4 of them would of ran well over a 1000.

Our course has a great many trees and they seemed to have a traction for our 4 ladies today and we was in amongst the trees more then we was on the fair way.

Well said Joe Bean theys one thing about cadding for these dames, it keeps you out of the hot sun.

And another time he said he felt like a boy scout studing wood craft.

These dames is always up against a stump he said.

And another time he said that it was not fair to charge these dames regular ladies dues in the club as they hardly ever used the course.

Well it seems like they was a party in the village last night and of course the ladies was talking about it and Mrs Doane said what a lovely dress Miss Rennie wore to the party and Miss Rennie said she did not care for the dress herself.

Well said Mrs Doane if you want to get rid of it just hand it over to me.

I wont give it to you said Miss Rennie but I will sell it to you at ½ what it cost me and it was a bargain at that as it only cost me a $100.00 and I will sell it to you for $50.00.

I have not got $50.00 just now to spend said Mrs Doane and besides I dont know would it fit me.

Sure it would fit you said Miss Rennie, you and I are exactly the same size and figure, I tell you what I will do with you I will play you golf for it and if you beat me you can have the gown for nothing and if I beat you why you will give me $50.00 for it.

All right but if I loose you may have to wait for your money said Mrs Doane.

So this was on the 4th hole and they started from there to play for the dress and they was both terrible and worse then usual on acct of being nervous as this was the biggest stakes they had either of them ever played for tho the Doanes has got a bbl of money and $50.00 is chickens food.

Well we was on the 16th hole and Mrs Doane was 1 up and Miss Rennie sliced her tee shot off in the rough and Mrs Doane landed in some rough over on the left so they was clear across the course from each other. Well I and Mrs Doane went over to her ball and as luck would have it it had come to rest in a kind of a groove where a good player could not hardly make a good shot of it let alone Mrs Doane. Well Mrs Thomas was out in the middle of the course for once in her life and the other 2 ladies was over on the right side and Joe Bean with them so they was nobody near Mrs Doane and I.

Do I have to play it from there she said. I guess you do was my reply.

Why Dick have you went back on me she said and give me one of her looks.

Well I looked to see if the others was looking and then I kind of give the ball a shove with my toe and it come out of the groove and laid where she could get a swipe at it.

This was the 16th hole and Mrs Doane win it by 11 strokes to 10 and that made her 2 up and 2 to go. Miss Rennie win the 17th but they both took a 10 for the 18th and that give Mrs Doane the match.

Well I wont never have a chance to see her in Miss Rennies dress but if I did I aint sure that I would like it on her.

Fri. May 5.

Well I never thought we would have so much excitement in the club and so much to write down in my diary but I guess I better get busy writeing it down as here it is Friday and it was Wed. A. M. when the excitement broke loose and I was getting ready to play around when Harry Lear the caddy master come running out with the paper in his hand and showed it to me on the first page.

It told how Chas Crane our club champion had went south with $8000 which he had stole out of Mr Thomas bank and a swell looking dame that was a stenographer in the bank had elloped with him and they had her picture in the paper and I will say she is a pip but who would of thought a nice quiet young man like Mr Crane was going to prove himself a gay Romeo and a specialy as he was engaged to Miss Rennie tho she now says she broke their engagement a month ago but any way the whole affair has certainly give everybody something to talk about and one of the caddys Lou Crowell busted Fat Brunner in the nose because Fat claimed to of been the last one that cadded for Crane. Lou was really the last one and cadded for him last Sunday which was the last time Crane was at the club.

Well everybody was thinking how sore Mr Thomas would be and they would better not mention the affair around him and etc. but who should show up to play yesterday but Mr Thomas himself and he played with Mr Blake and all they talked about the whole P. M. was Crane and what he had pulled.

Well Thomas said Mr Blake I am curious to know if the thing come as a suprise to you or if you ever had a hunch that he was libel to do a thing like this.

Well Blake said Mr Thomas I will admit that the whole thing come as a complete suprise to me as Crane was all most like my son you might say and I was going to see that he got along all right and that is what makes me sore is not only that he has proved himself dishonest but that he could be such a sucker as to give up a bright future for a sum of money like $8000 and a doll face girl that cant be no good or she would not of let him do it. When you think how young he was and the carreer he might of had why it certainly seems like he sold his soul pretty cheap.

That is what Mr Thomas had to say or at lease part of it as I cant remember a ½ of all he said but any way this P. M. I cadded for Mrs Thomas and Mrs Doane and that is all they talked about to, and Mrs Thomas talked along the same lines like her husband and said she had always thought Crane was to smart a young man to pull a thing like that and ruin his whole future.

He was geting $4000 a yr said Mrs Thomas and everybody liked him and said he was bound to get ahead so that is what makes it such a silly thing for him to of done, sell his soul for $8000 and a pretty face.

Yes indeed said Mrs Doane.

Well all the time I was listening to Mr Thomas and Mr Blake and Mrs Thomas and Mrs Doane why I was thinking about something which I wanted to say to them but it would of ment me looseing my job so I kept it to myself but I sprung it on my pal Joe Bean on the way home tonight.

Joe I said what do these people mean when they talk about Crane selling his soul?

Why you know what they mean said Joe, they mean that a person that does something dishonest for a bunch of money or a gal or any kind of a reward why the person that does it is selling his soul.

All right I said and it dont make no differents does it if the reward is big or little?

Why no said Joe only the bigger it is the less of a sucker the person is that goes after it.

Well I said here is Mr Thomas who is vice president of a big bank and worth a bbl of money and it is just a few days ago when he lied about his golf score in order so as he would win 9 golf balls instead of a ½ a dozen.

Sure said Joe.

And how about his wife Mrs Thomas I said, who plays for 2 bits a hole and when her ball dont lie good why she picks it up and pretends to look at it to see if it is hers and then puts it back in a good lie where she can sock it.

And how about my friend Mrs Doane that made me move her ball out of a rut to help her beat Miss Rennie out of a party dress.

Well said Joe what of it?

Well I said it seems to me like these people have got a lot of nerve to pan Mr Crane and call him a sucker for doing what he done, it seems to me like $8000 and a swell dame is a pretty fair reward compared with what some of these other people sells their soul for, and I would like to tell them about it.

Well said Joe go ahead and tell them but maybe they will tell you something right back.

What will they tell me?

Well said Joe they might tell you this, that when Mr Thomas asks you how many shots he has had and you say 4 when you know he has had 5, why you are selling your soul for a $1.00 tip. And when you move Mrs Doanes ball out of a rut and give it a good lie, what are you selling your soul for? Just a smile.

O keep your mouth shut I said to him.

I am going to said Joe and would advice you to do the same.

XXXII

MR. AND MRS. FIX-IT

THEY'RE certainly a live bunch in this town. We ain't only been here three days and had calls already from people representin' four different organizations—the Chamber of Commerce, Kiwanis, and I forget who else. They wanted to know if we was comfortable and did we like the town and is they anything they can do for us and what to be sure and see.

And they all asked how we happened to come here instead of goin' somewheres else. I guess they keep a record of everybody's reasons for comin' so as they can get a line on what features tourists is most attracted by. Then they play up them features in next year's booster advertisin'.

Well, I told them we was perfectly comfortable and we like the town fine and they's nothin' nobody can do for us right now and we'll be sure and see all the things we ought to see. But when they asked me how did we happen to come here, I said it was just a kind of a accident, because the real reason makes too long a story.

My wife has been kiddin' me about my friends ever since we was married. She says that judgin' by the ones I've introduced her to, they ain't nobody in the world got a rummier bunch of friends than me. I'll admit that the most of them ain't, well, what you might call hot; they're different somehow than when I first hung around with them. They seem to be lost without a brass rail to rest their logs on. But of course they're old friends and I can't give 'em the air.

We have 'em to the house for dinner every little w'ile, they and their wives, and what my missus objects to is because they don't none of them play bridge or mah jong or do cross-word puzzles or sing or dance or even talk, but just set there and wait for somebody to pour 'em a fresh drink.

As I say, my wife kids me about 'em and they ain't really nothin' can offer in their defense. That don't mean, though, that the shoe is all on one foot. Because w'ile the majority of her friends may not be quite as dumb as mine, just the same they's a few she's picked out who I'd of had to be under the ether to allow anybody to introduce 'em to me in the first place.

Like the Crandalls, for instance. Mrs. Crandall come from my wife's home town and they didn't hardly know each other there, but they met again in a store in Chi and it went from bad to worse till finally Ada asked the dame and her husband to the house.

Well, the husband turns out to be the fella that win the war, w'ile it seems that Mrs. Crandall was in Atlantic City once and some movin' picture company was makin' a picture there and they took a scene of what was supposed to be society people walkin' up and down the Boardwalk and Mrs. Crandall was in the picture and people that seen it when it come out, they all said that from the way she screened, why if she wanted to go into the business, she could make Gloria Swanson look like Mrs. Gump.

Now it ain't only took me a few words to tell you these things, but when the Crandalls tells their story themselves, they don't hardly get started by midnight and no chance of them goin' home till they're through even when you drop 'em a hint that they're springin' it on you for the hundred and twelfth time.

That's the Crandalls, and another of the wife's friends is the Thayers. Thayer is what you might call a all-around handy man. He can mimic pretty near all the birds and beasts and fishes, he can yodel, he can play a ocarena, or he can recite Kipling or Robert H. Service, or he can do card tricks, and strike a light without no matches, and tie all the different knots.

And besides that, he can make a complete radio outfit and set it up, and take pictures as good as the best professional photographers and a whole lot better. He collects autographs. And he never had a sick day in his life.

Mrs. Thayer gets a headache playin' bridge, so it's mah jong or rhum when she's around. She used to be a teacher of elocution and she still gives readin's if you coax her, or if you don't, and her hair is such a awful nuisance that she would get it cut in a minute only all her friends tells her it would be criminal to spoil that head of hair. And when she talks to her husband, she always talks baby talk, maybe because somebody has told her that she'd be single if he wasn't childish.

And then Ada has got still another pal, a dame named Peggy Flood who is hospital mad and ain't happy unless she is just goin' under the knife or just been there. She's had everything removed that the doctors knew the name of and now they're probin' her for new giblets.

Well, I wouldn't mind if they cut her up into alphabet soup if they'd only do such a good job of it that they couldn't put her together again, but she always comes through O. K. and she spends the intermissions at our place, describin' what all they done or what they're plannin' to do next.

But the cat's nightgown is Tom Stevens and his wife. There's the team that wins the Olympics! And they're Ada's team, not mine.

Ada met Belle Stevens on the elevated. Ada was invited to a party out on the North Side and didn't know exactly where to get off and Mrs. Stevens seen her talkin' to the guard and horned in and asked her what was it she wanted to know and Ada told her, and Mrs. Stevens said she was goin' to get off the same station Ada wanted to get off, so they got off together.

Mrs. Stevens insisted on goin' right along to the address where Ada was goin' because she said Ada was bound to get lost if she wasn't familiar with the neighborhood.

Well, Ada thought it was mighty nice of her to do so much for a stranger. Mrs. Stevens said she was glad to because she didn't know what would of happened to her lots of times if strangers hadn't been nice and helped her out.

She asked Ada where she lived and Ada told her on the South Side and Mrs. Stevens said she was sure we'd like it better on the North Side if we'd leave her pick out a place for us, so Ada told her we had a year's lease that we had just signed and couldn't break it, so then Mrs. Stevens said her husband had studied law and he claimed they wasn't no lease that you couldn't break and some evening she would bring him out to call on us and he'd tell us how to break our lease.

Well, Ada had to say sure, come on out, though we was perfectly satisfied with our apartment and didn't no more want to break the lease than each other's jaw. Maybe not as much. Anyway, the very next night, they showed up, Belle and Tom, and when they'd gone, I give 'em the nickname—Mr. and Mrs. Fix-It.

After the introductions, Stevens made some remark about what a cozy little place we had and then he asked if I would mind tellin' what rent we paid. So I told him a hundred and a quarter a month. So he said, of course, that was too much and no wonder we wanted to break the lease. Then I said we was satisfied and didn't want to break it and he said I must be kiddin' and if I would show him the lease he would see what loopholes they was in it.

Well, the lease was right there in a drawer in the table, but I told him it was in my safety deposit box at the bank. I ain't got no safety deposit box and no more use for one than Judge Landis has for the deef and dumb alphabet.

Stevens said the lease was probably just a regular lease and if it was, they wouldn't be no trouble gettin' out of it, and meanw'ile him and his wife would see if they couldn't find us a place in the same buildin' with them.

And he was pretty sure they could even if the owner had to give some other tenant the air, because he, the owner, would do anything in the world for Stevens.

So I said yes, but suppose we want to stay where we are. So he said I looked like a man with better judgment than that and if I would just leave everything to him he would fix it so's we could move within a month. I kind of laughed and thought that would be the end of it.

He wanted to see the whole apartment so I showed him around and when we come to the bathroom he noticed my safety razor on the shelf. He said, "So you use one of them things," and I said, "Yes," and he asked me how I liked it, and I said I liked it fine and he said that must be because I hadn't never used a regular razor.

He said a regular razor was the only thing to use if a man wanted to look good. So I asked him if he used a regular razor and he said he did, so I said, "Well, if you look good, I don't want to."

But that didn't stop him and he said if I would meet him downtown the next day he would take me to the place where he bought all his razors and help me pick some out for myself. I told him I was goin' to be tied up, so just to give me the name and address of the place and I would drop in there when I had time.

But, no, that wouldn't do; he'd have to go along with me and introduce me to the proprietor because the proprietor was a great pal of his and would do anything in the world for him, and if the proprietor vouched for the razors, I could be sure I was gettin' the best razors money could buy. I told him again that I was goin' to be tied up and I managed to get him on some other subject.

Meanw'ile, Mrs. Stevens wanted to know where Ada had bought the dress she was wearin' and how much had it cost and Ada told her and Mrs. Stevens said it was a crime. She would meet Ada downtown tomorrow morning and take her to the shop where she bought her clothes and help her choose some dresses that really was dresses.

So Ada told her she didn't have no money to spend on dresses right then, and besides, the shop Mrs. Stevens mentioned was too high priced. But it seems the dame that run the shop was just like a sister to Mrs. Stevens and give her and her friends a big reduction and not only that, but they wasn't no hurry about payin'.

Well, Ada thanked her just the same, but didn't need nothin' new just at present; maybe later on she would take advantage of Mrs. Stevens's kind offer. Yes, but right now they was some models in stock that would be just beautiful on Ada and they might be gone later on. They was nothin' for it but Ada had to make a date with her; she wasn't obliged to buy nothin', but it would be silly not to go and look at the stuff that was in the joint and get acquainted with the dame that run it.

Well, Ada kept the date and bought three dresses she didn't want and they's only one of them she's had the nerve to wear. They cost her a hundred dollars a smash and I'd hate to think what the price would of been if Mrs. Stevens and the owner of the shop wasn't so much like sisters.

I was sure I hadn't made no date with Stevens, but just the same he called me up the next night to ask why I hadn't met him. And a couple of days later I got three new razors in the mail along with a bill and a note from the store sayin' that these was three specially fine razors that had been picked out for me by Thomas J. Stevens.

I don't know yet why I paid for the razors and kept 'em. I ain't used 'em and never intended to. Though I've been tempted a few times to test their edge on Stevens's neck.

That same week, Mrs. Stevens called up and asked us to spend Sunday with them and when we got out there, the owner of the buildin' is there, too. And Stevens has told him that I was goin' to give up my apartment on the South Side and wanted him to show me what he had.

I thought this was a little too strong and I said Stevens must of misunderstood me, that I hadn't no fault to find with the place I was in and wasn't plannin' to move, not for a year anyway. You can bet this didn't make no hit with the guy, who was just there on Stevens's say-so that I was a prospective tenant.

Well, it was only about two months ago that this cute little couple come into our life, but I'll bet we seen 'em twenty times at least. They was always invitin' us to their place or invitin' themselves to our place and Ada is one of these here kind of people that just can't say no. Which may be why I and her is married.

Anyway, it begin to seem like us and the Stevenses was livin' together and all one family, with them at the head of it. I never in my life seen anybody as crazy to run other people's business. Honest to heavens, it's a wonder they let us brush our own teeth!

Ada made the remark one night that she wished the ski jumper who was doin' our cookin' would get married and quit so's she wouldn't have to can her. Mrs. Stevens was there and asked Ada if she should try and get her a new cook, but Ada says no, the poor

gal might have trouble findin' another job and she felt sorry for
her.

Just the same, the next afternoon a Jap come to the apartment
and said he was ready to go to work and Mrs. Stevens had sent
him. Ada had to tell him the place was already filled.

Another night, Ada complained that her feet was tired. Belle
said her feet used to get tired, too, till a friend of hers recommended
a chiropodist and she went to him and he done her so much good
that she made a regular appointment with him for once every
month and paid him a flat sum and no matter how much runnin'
around she done, her dogs hadn't fretted her once since this corn-
husker started tendin' to 'em.

She wanted to call up the guy at his home right then and there
and make a date for Ada and the only way Ada could stop her
was by promisin' to go and see him the next time her feet hurt.
After that, whenever the two gals met, Belle's first question was
"How is your feet?" and the answer was always "Fine, thanks."

Well, I'm quite a football fan and Ada likes to go, too, when
it's a big game and lots of excitement. So we decided we'd see the
Illinois-Chicago game and have a look at this "Red" Grange. I
warned Ada to not say nothin' about it to Tom and Belle as I felt
like we was entitled to a day off.

But it happened that they was goin' to be a game up at Evanston that day and the Stevenses invited us to see that one with
them. So we used the other game as a alibi. And when Tom asked
me later on if I'd boughten my tickets yet, instead of sayin' yes, I
told him the truth and said no.

So then he said:

"I'm glad you ain't, because I and Belle has made up our mind
that the Chicago game is the one we ought to see. And we'll all
go together. And don't you bother about tickets because I can
get better ones than you can as Stagg and I is just like that."

So I left it to him to get the tickets and we might as well of set
on the Adams Street bridge. I said to Stevens, I said:

"If these is the seats Mr. Stagg digs up for his old pals, I suppose he leads strangers twenty or thirty miles out in the country
and blindfolds 'em and ties 'em to a tree."

Now of course it was the bunk about he and Stagg bein' so
close. He may of been introduced to him once, but he ain't the
kind of a guy that Stagg would go around holdin' hands with.
Just the same, most of the people he bragged about knowin', why
it turned out that he really did know 'em; yes, and stood ace high
with 'em, too.

Like, for instance, I got pinched for speedin' one night and they give me a ticket to show up in the Speeders' court and I told Stevens about it and he says, "Just forget it! I'll call up the judge and have it wiped off the book. He's a mighty good fella and a personal friend of mine."

Well, I didn't want to take no chances so I phoned Stevens the day before I was supposed to appear in court, and I asked him if he'd talked to the judge. He said he had and I asked him if he was sure. So he said, "If you don't believe me, call up the judge yourself." And he give me the judge's number. Sure enough, Stevens had fixed it and when I thanked the judge for his trouble, he said it was a pleasure to do somethin' for a friend of Tom Stevens's.

Now, I know it's silly to not appreciate favors like that and not warm up to people that's always tryin' to help you along, but still a person don't relish bein' treated like they was half-witted and couldn't button their shirt alone. Tom and Belle meant all right, but I and Ada got kind of tired of havin' fault found with everything that belonged to us and everything we done or tried to do.

Besides our apartment bein' no good and our clothes terrible, we learned that my dentist didn't know a bridge from a mustache cup, and the cigarettes I smoked didn't have no taste to them, and the man that bobbed Ada's hair must of been mad at her, and neither of us would ever know what it was to live till we owned a wire-haired fox terrier.

And we found out that the liquor I'd been drinkin' and enjoyin' was a mixture of bath salts and assorted paints, and the car we'd paid seventeen hundred smackers for wasn't nowheres near as much of a car as one that Tom could of got for us for eight hundred on account of knowin' a brother-in-law of a fella that used to go to school with the president of the company's nephew, and that if Ada would take up aesthetic dancin' under a dame Belle knew about, why she'd never have no more trouble with her tonsils.

Nothin' we had or nothin' we talked about gettin' or doin' was worth a damn unless it was recommended or suggested by the Stevenses.

Well, I done a pretty good business this fall and I and Ada had always planned to spend a winter in the South, so one night we figured it out that this was the year we could spare the money and the time and if we didn't go this year we never would. So the next thing was where should we go, and we finally decided on Miami. And we said we wouldn't mention nothin' about it to

Tom and Belle till the day we was goin'. We'd pretend we was doin' it out of a clear sky.

But a secret is just as safe with Ada as a police dog tethered with dental floss. It wasn't more than a day or two after we'd had our talk when Tom and Belle sprang the news that they was leavin' for California right after New Year's. And why didn't we go with them.

Well, I didn't say nothin' and Ada said it sounded grand, but it was impossible. Then Stevens said if it was a question of money, to not let that bother us as he would loan it to me and I could pay it back whenever I felt like it. That was more than Ada could stand, so she says we wasn't as poor as people seemed to think and the reason we couldn't go to California was because we was goin' to Miami.

This was such a surprise that it almost struck 'em dumb at first and all Tom could think of to say was that he'd been to Miami himself and it was too crowded and he'd lay off of it if he was us. But the next time we seen 'em they had our trip all arranged.

First, Tom asked me what road we was goin' on and I told him the Big Four. So he asked if we had our reservations and I told him yes.

"Well," he said, "we'll get rid of 'em and I'll fix you up on the C. & E. I. The general passenger agent is a friend of mine and they ain't nothin' he won't do for my friends. He'll see that you're treated right and that you get there in good shape."

So I said:

"I don't want to put you to all that trouble, and besides I don't know nobody connected with the Big Four well enough for them to resent me travelin' on their lines, and as for gettin' there in good shape, even if I have a secret enemy or two on the Big Four, I don't believe they'd endanger the lives of the other passengers just to see that I didn't get there in good shape."

But Stevens insisted on takin' my tickets and sellin' 'em back to the Big Four and gettin' me fixed on the C. & E. I. The berths we'd had on the Big Four was Lower 9 and Lower 10. The berths Tom got us on the C. & E. I. was Lower 7 and Lower 8, which he said was better. I suppose he figured that the nearer you are to the middle of the car, the less chance there is of bein' woke up if your car gets in another train's way.

He wanted to know, too, if I'd made any reservations at a hotel. I showed him a wire I had from the Royal Palm in reply to a wire I'd sent 'em.

"Yes," he says, "but you don't want to stop at the Royal Palm.

You wire and tell 'em to cancel that and I'll make arrangements for you at the Flamingo, over at the Beach. Charley Krom, the manager there, was born and raised in the same town I was. He'll take great care of you if he knows you're a friend of mine."

So I asked him if all the guests at the Flamingo was friends of his, and he said of course not; what did I mean?

"Well," I said, "I was just thinkin' that if they ain't, Mr. Krom probably makes life pretty miserable for 'em. What does he do, have the phone girl ring 'em up at all hours of the night, and hide their mail, and shut off their hot water, and put cracker crumbs in their beds?"

That didn't mean nothin' to Stevens and he went right ahead and switched me from one hotel to the other.

While Tom was reorganizin' my program and tellin' me what to eat in Florida, and what bait to use for barracuda and carp, and what time to go bathin' and which foot to stick in the water first, why Belle was makin' Ada return all the stuff she had boughten to wear down there and buy other stuff that Belle picked out for her at joints where Belle was so well known that they only soaked her twice as much as a stranger. She had Ada almost crazy, but I told her to never mind; in just a few more days we'd be where they couldn't get at us.

I suppose you're wonderin' why didn't we quarrel with 'em and break loose from 'em and tell 'em to leave us alone. You'd know why if you knew them. Nothin' we could do would convince 'em that we didn't want their advice and help. And nothin' we could say was a insult.

Well, the night before we was due to leave Chi, the phone rung and I answered it. It was Tom.

"I've got a surprise for you," he says. "I and Belle has give up the California idear. We're goin' to Miami instead, and on account of me knowin' the boys down at the C. & E. I., I've landed a drawin' room on the same train you're takin'. How is that for news?"

"Great!" I said, and I went back and broke it to Ada. For a minute I thought she was goin' to faint. And all night long she moaned and groaned and had hysterics.

So that's how we happened to come to Biloxi.

XXXIII

A FRAME–UP

I

I suppose you could call it a frame. But it wasn't like no frame that was ever pulled before. They's been plenty where one guy was paid to lay down. This is the first I heard of where a guy had to be bribed to win. And it's the first where a bird was bribed and didn't know it.

You know they've postponed the match with Britton. Nate said at first that his boy wasn't ready yet, but the papers all kidded him. Because anybody that seen Burke in the Kemp fight knows he's ready. So Nate had to change his story and say Burke had hurt one of his hands on Kemp's egg, and he wasn't going to take no chance boxing again till he was O. K., which mightn't be for a couple of months. Say, Kemp's head may be hard, but it ain't hard enough to hurt one of them hands of Burkey's. He could play catch with Big Bertha.

No, they's another reason why Nate ast for a postponement of the Britton date. It's got to be another frame-up that may take a long w'ile to fix, and he ain't got no plans made yet. And till he's all set, he'd be a dumbbell to send Burke against a man as good as Jack Britton.

The papers has printed a lot of stuff about Burke—how he ain't only been boxing a little over a year, and won't be twenty-one till next July, and five or six bouts is all he's been in, and now look at him, offered a match for the welterweight championship and $10,000 win, lose or draw! But if they knew Burke like some of us knows him, they could write a book. Because he certainly is Duke of the Cuckoos and the world's greatest sap. How they got him ready for the Kemp bout is a story in itself, but it won't come out till he's through with the game. So what I tell you is between you and I.

It was one afternoon about a year ago. Bill Brennan was in Kid Howard's gymnasium in Chi, working out, and they was a gang looking on. Howard seen one boy in the crowd that you couldn't help from noticing. He was made up for one of the hicks in "'Way Down East." He'd bought his collar in Akron and his coat sleeves died just south of his elbow. From his pants to his vest was a toll call. He hadn't never shaved and his w'iskers was just the right number and len'th to string a violin. Thinks Howard to himself: "If you seen a stage rube dressed like that, you'd say it was overdone."

Well, it got late and the gang thinned out till finally they wasn't nobody left but Howard and this sap. So Howard ast him if he wanted to see somebody.

"Yes," said the kid. "I want to see a man that can learn me to fight."

So Howard ast him if he meant box.

"Box or fight, I don't care which, just so's I can learn the rules," said the hick.

"Did you ever box?" says Howard.

"No," says the kid, "but I can learn quick and I'm willing to pay for it. I got plenty of money. I got pretty close to $700."

Howard ast him what was his name and where he come from and his business.

"My name's Burke and I work on my old man's farm," he says. "It's acrost the Lake, outside of Benton Harbor. We raise peaches."

"Has your old man got money?" ast Howard.

"Plenty," says the kid.

"Well," said Howard, "if you work on a farm, you're getting plenty of exercise. And if your old man's rich, you ain't after the sugar. So what's the idear of going into this game?"

"I don't want to go in no game," he says. "I just want to learn good enough so's I can win this one match and then I'm through."

"What one match?" says Howard.

"With Charley Porter," says Burke.

Well, of course you've heard of Charley Porter. He's a Benton Harbor boy too. He'd fought Lewis twice and Britton once and he'd give them both a sweet battle. He was considered about fourth or fifth best amongst the welters. So it struck Howard funny that this green rube, that hadn't never boxed, should think he could take a few lessons and then be good enough to beat a boy like Porter.

"You're an ambitious kid," he says to him, "but if I was you I'd take my seven hundred men and invest it some other way. Porter's had forty fights, and that's what counts. You could take all the lessons in the world, and he'd make a monkey out of you. Unless you're a boy wonder or something. But even if you are, you couldn't get no match with Porter till you'd proved it. And that means you'd have to beat some other good boys first."

So Burke said: "All I come to Chicago for is to take some boxing lessons. They told me you was the man to come and see. If

I'm willing to pay the money, it shouldn't ought to make no difference to you if I get a match with Porter or not. Or if I lick him or not."

"That's right," said Howard. "Only I ain't no burglar or no con man. I'm in this business for money, but I don't want to take nobody's money without they get what they think they're paying for. And if you had seven million smackers I couldn't guarantee to make you a good boxer, not good enough to land you a match with Porter."

"I ain't asking you to land no match," says Burke. "I'll tend to that part. He'll fight me as soon as I think I'm ready. If he don't, I'll run him out of Michigan. He wouldn't dast stay round there if everybody was saying I had him scared. And that's what they'd say if he wouldn't fight me."

"Why would they?" says Howard. "He's in the game for money, too, and he couldn't get no money for a bout with a guy like you that nobody ever heard of. They wouldn't no club match you up."

"I won't have no trouble getting matched up," says Burke. "Fitzsimmons will put us on right there in Benton Harbor. The town's nuts over Porter and they'll pay to see him any time. And whatever purse they offer is all his. I'll fight him for nothing."

"Oh!" says Howard. "That makes it different! You're sore at him!"

"No," says the hick, "I'm not sore at him."

"You just don't like him," says Howard.

"I don't know if I like him or not," said Burke. "I don't even know him."

"But for some reason you want to give him a trimming," says Howard. "Well, listen, boy: I understand they's no capital punishment in your State, so it looks to me like you'd run less risk of getting killed if you'd sneak in Porter's house some night w'ile he's asleep and kiss him on the brow with a meat ax."

Burke didn't crack a smile.

"That wouldn't get me nowheres," he said. "They's a reason I got to box him. If you can learn me, all right. If not, I'll go somewheres else."

So Howard made a date for him to come back the next day.

II

Well, when the kid stripped for action, Howard's eyes popped out. With them comic clothes on, he'd looked awkward; he was a picture with them off. Howard says he felt like inviting the best sculptures in Chi to come and take a look.

"I was going to box with him myself," says Howard, "but not after I seen them shoulder muscles. I figured I didn't have enough insurance to justify me putting on the gloves with this bird. So I made Joe Rivers take him."

Well, they could see in a minute that the rube was a born boxer. He was fast as a streak and in one lesson he learnt more than most boys picks up in a month. They just showed him how to stand and the rest seemed to come natural. In a little w'ile Joe, with all his experience, was having trouble to land, whereas Burkey was hitting Joe as often as he felt like. Only he didn't put no zip in his punches. He pulled them all.

"Cut loose once!" says Howard. "Let's see if you can knock him down!"

"Oh, no," said Burkey. "This ain't in earnest."

Rivers looked just as well satisfied, but Howard says:

"You got to be in earnest, even when you're just working out. They's lots of boys as strong as you that don't know how to get their stren'th into their punch. That's a thing that's got to be learnt, and I can't learn you if I can't see you wallop."

"No," says Burke. "I ain't going to hurt nobody for nothing."

And all Howard's coaxing done no good. He wouldn't cut loose.

But at the end of the six weeks he stuck round Howard's he was one of the sweetest boxers you ever seen and Howard thought so well of him that he tried to sign him up.

"Let me handle you, Burkey," he says. "I'll get you on in Milwaukee and I'll take you down east and make you some money. If you're handled right, they's no reason why you shouldn't be welterweight champion some day."

"I don't want to be welterweight champion," said Burke. "I just want to be champion of Charley Porter. And when I've beat him, I'm through."

"All right," says Howard. "You know what you want. But let me tell you one thing—you won't beat Porter or no one else if you just pet them. You've got to hit!"

The kid smiled.

"I'll hit when it's time," he says.

So that was the last Howard heard of him till pretty near a month later, when he picked up a paper and read where Young Burke, a farmer boy living outside of Benton Harbor, had stopped Charley Porter, an aspirant for the welterweight title, in one round.

III

About a month more went by before Burke showed up in Chi again and called on Nate. As soon as he mentioned his name and where he was from, Nate was interested. Because Howard had told him about his experience with the kid. But Burkey wasn't made up no more like Howard had described him. He was wearing the best suit of clothes twenty dollars could buy.

"I went to see Howard," he says, "but he's out of town. So I come to you. I want to go in the fight game."

"I understood from Howard," says Nate, "that you was going to quit after that one bout."

"I thought I was," says Burkey. "But it's different now. You see, I and my old man has busted up. So I got to make a living."

"What was the bust-up over?" ast Nate. "Didn't he like you boxing?"

"He didn't care nothing about that," says the kid. "But they was a gal he wanted I should marry. And I give her the air. So he done the same to me."

"Why did you quit the gal?" ast Nate.

"I figured I could do better," he says. "She's just a gal round home there, and why should I marry her? I can pretty near pick who I want to marry."

"Everybody can pick who they want to marry," said Nate.

"Yes, but who I pick, I can pretty near have," says the kid. "I thought I was stuck on this gal, but I found I wasn't. I hadn't seen hardly any other gals, and she was always round. So I thought she was about the only gal in the world. I know better now. But I did like her and my old man liked her and kept after me to ask her. So I ast her and she told me she was stuck on somebody else. So I ast her who was it and she said Charley Porter. She didn't know him, but she'd seen him on the street a lot of times, and he'd smiled at her. She thought he was handsome and made a hero out of him. He was the best fighter in the world, to her mind. So I said I could beat him and she laughed at me. She says, 'You might beat him plowing.' So I said, 'I can beat him boxing.' So she says, 'All right. You do it and I'll like you better than him.' So I come up here and took a few lessons and knocked him cock-eyed.

"When she seen me afterwards, she throwed her arms round my neck and said I was the best man in the world, and we got engaged. But during the time I was up here in Chi learning to box, I learnt to dance too. And I bought me these good clothes. So after I trimmed Porter I got to going over to St. Joe, to the pavilion, nights, and I seen all the gals was nuts over me. So I said to myself, 'What's the idear of tying up to this rube gal when you can marry somebody that is somebody—maybe one of these rich Chicago society dames.' So I give this hick the air and my old man throwed me out of the house."

Well, Nate's handled a lot of boxers and never seen one yet that despised himself, but after he'd listened to this bird a w'ile, he begin to think that all the rest of them was lilies of the valley.

"Which Chicago society gal have you picked out?" he says, to lead him on.

"I don't know yet," says Burkey. "Some of them at the dances in St. Joe looked good, but I want to see them all before I tie myself up."

If you ever been to St. Joe, you know the Chicago society gals that attends them dances. If you want to see one of them in the middle of the week, go up to the Draperies and ask for Min.

"You got the right dope," Nate says. "You'd be a sucker to make a choice till you'd looked over the whole field. And in the meanw'ile, I'll try and get you fixed up with a couple of matches so as you can grab some spending money."

But Burke was still thinking of the dames.

"I read a great story the other day," he says. "It was a young fella that was a boxer and one night he was walking along the street and he heard a gal scream. She was up on the porch of a big house and they was a dude there, trying to make love to her. So she didn't like him and that's why she screamed. So this young fella went in and grabbed the dude and knocked him for a long trip. So the gal got stuck on this young fella, the boxer, and married him and she turned out to be a millionaire."

"A great story!" said Nate. "I certainly wished I could of read it. But suppose he'd married her and then found out that her old man made automobiles and owed everybody. A young fella can't be too careful who he lets marry him. And if I was you I'd go slow. In the first place, most of the gals with the real class and the big money lives in New York. So why not wait till you've win a couple of bouts in Milwaukee or somewheres so's I can get you dated up in the Big Town? Then you can walk up and down Eighth Avenue and help yourself to the cream."

This was to stall him along so's he'd forget the skirts for a w'ile and tend to business.

Nate made him work out every day and box with some of the boys. But he was just as shy of a punch as when Howard had him.

"Cut loose and slug!" Nate told him.

"What for?" he says.

"To show me if you've got a haymaker," says Nate.

"Ask Porter if I have," said the kid.

Finally Nate got him matched with Red Harris in a semi-wind-up at Milwaukee. Harris can wallop, but he's slow. Well, Burkey made him look like he was handcuffed. Red never laid a glove on him the whole bout, w'ile Nate's boy played him like a piano. But it was soft music and when it was over neither of them had a mark. The crowd liked Burke at first on account of his speed. But they razzed him the last few rounds because it looked like he wasn't trying. The papers couldn't do nothing but give him the best of it, but said he wouldn't never get nowheres till he learned to punch. Nate had begged him all through to tear in and end it, but he might as well of tried to argue with Central.

Well, Fitzsimmons was putting on a show over to Benton Harbor and he wired Nate and ast him if he'd bring Burke there for a wind-up with a Grand Rapids boy named Hap Stein. This kid had met some of the best boys round Michigan and beat them all, and, of course, Burke'd draw good in his home town, especially after what he done to Porter.

So Nate took Burkey over there and Fitz ast Nate how the kid was coming and Nate told him:

"One of the sweetest boxers I ever seen, but he ain't showed enough of a wallop to annoy a soap bubble."

"It's a funny thing," said Fitz, "because he hit Porter just once and broke his jaw. And Charley's jaw ain't glass, neither. I know a punch when I see one and I doubt if Dempsey could hit harder than this bird plugged this baby."

"Well," says Nate, "I wished we had the prescription. He made a monkey out of Harris at Milwaukee, but he wouldn't even slap him hard. And the boys he works out with, I've had them rough him so's he'd get mad, but it didn't do no good."

"I don't suppose so," says Fitz, "because he wasn't sore at Porter. Charley didn't even know him."

"But he had a reason to show Porter up," said Nate, and he told Fitz about the rube gal.

"That's news to me," said Fitz. "Maybe he'll only fight when they's a dame for a prize. Why don't you hire some chorus doll to vamp him and have her tell him she's his as soon as he's knocked all the other welters for a corpse?"

"You don't know this bird!" said Nate. "Chorus gals would be beneath his notice. He wants a millionaire society belle and I'd have a fat chance of getting one of them to play the part."

Well, the bout with Stein was a farce. Burkey was so fast that Hap thought they'd ganged on him, but nothing Nate could say or do had any effect. He couldn't make the kid cut loose and punch.

IV

When they'd been back in Chi a couple of months and Burke had had one more fight in Milwaukee—he made a monkey out of Jimmy Mason—well, he begin fretting and wanted to know how soon Nate was going to take him east.

"As soon as I can get you matched," said Nate. "But if I do date you up down there, you'll have to cut out the cuddling and really fight or they won't want you a second time."

"Maybe I'll be different down there," said Burkey.

So along late in the fall Nate got him matched with Battling Igoe, in Boston.

"Now here's your chance," Nate told him. "I got Rickard's promise that if you trim Igoe he'll put you on in New York with Willie Kemp. And the man that beats Willie Kemp will get a whack at Britton and the big money."

All Burke said was:

"How's Boston for gals? Any class to them?"

"Not enough for you," says Nate. "You'd be throwing yourself away! They's no doubt but that you could go down to Scollay Square or Revere Beach and take your pick, but you'd be a sucker to do it. New York's the place. And suppose you get tied up to some Boston countess and then went to New York and win a couple of big bouts and got invited round to some of them big mansions on Mott Street or the Tenderloin, and next thing you know, you'd probably meet a dozen gals that never even heard of Boston. Then you'd wished you'd of been more careful and not financed yourself to no bean shooter."

You read about the Igoe bout? I seen it. When they was all in the ring beforehand, Nate said to Igoe, he says: "Well, Bat, we've decided to let you stay three rounds. That'll be enough to give you a boxing lesson. But in the fourth round, you're going to hear music that'll rock you to sleep." Nate had heard that the Battler wasn't no lion heart and this kind of gab fretted him.

"I'll rock him to sleep himself," he said, but his teeth was shimmying.

Burke was just the same like in his other bouts. He wrote his name and address all over Igoe's pan, and convinced the Battler that any time he wanted to he could knock him for a row of stumps. That went on for three rounds, with Nate, as usual, begging the kid to put over a haymaker, and Burke paying no attention. So when the bell rung for the fourth, Nate hollered, "Good night, Bat!" and Igoe thought sure he meant business. And he wasn't named after Nelson. So the first time Burke hit him in this round he folded up like a bass singer's chin and flopped on the floor, yelling foul. Well, we all seen the blow; it landed just under the green spot where he parks his collar button. And besides that, they wasn't no force to it. But Igoe was through for the evening, and the kid had win another soft one. Personally I'd of rather took fifty socks on the jaw than the razzing the crowd give Bat.

Well, Nate was going to New York and stay a w'ile and he wanted to send Burke back to Chi to wait till they'd chose a date for the fight with Kemp. But Burkey said no; he could lay round New York as easy as Chicago and if Nate wouldn't take him there he was through. He says:

"Here I am a coming champion, and what does it get me? I ain't having no fun. I want to meet some gals and dance with them and kid them."

"All right, come along," says Nate. "But I wished you'd remember one thing: When you do meet them swell East Side janes, don't treat them like toys. They've got feelings as well as riches and wealth, and I would rather see Kemp or Britton knock you lopsided than see you win fame and leave a trail of broken hearts."

"I'm no flirt!" says Burkey. "I can't help what they feel towards me, but I won't lead them on, not unlest I'm serious myself."

"Now you're talking like a man!" says Nate.

So they come to New York and stopped at the Spencer. Nate had a lot of business to tend to, and guys to see, and he didn't want this rube chasing round with him all the w'ile, so he turned him over to Jack Grace, the old lightweight. You know Jack, or at least you've heard of him. He'd kid Thomas A. Edison.

Nate had tipped off Jack about Burkey, and the second day they was in the Big Town, Jack took the boy for a walk. Every time they passed a car with a good-looking gal in it, Burke would ask, "Who's that?" And Jack pretended like he knew them all.

"That's Gwendolyn Weasel," he'd say. "Her old man owns part of the Grand Central Station—the Lower Level. And that one's Mildred Whiffletree, a niece of Bud Fisher, the ukulele king. And there's Honey Hives; she's a granddaughter of Old Man Bumble, the bee man. They got a big country place on Ellis Island."

"Where could a man meet these gals?" ast Burkey.

"Nowheres only at their home," said Jack. "And they's no chance of you getting invited round yet a w'ile. Nobody knows who you are. But wait till you've hung one on this Kemp guy's chin and I bet you'll have more invitations than a roach catcher."

Well, Nate landed the Kemp match sooner than he expected. Rickard said he'd put Burke on with Willie for the wind-up, three weeks from then. And he'd guarantee the winner a match with Britton.

Nate had got what he was after, but he was worried sick.

"I know he can beat Kemp if he fights," he says, "but I never yet been able to make him fight. And if he just babies along like he done in these other bouts, one of these New York referees is liable to say he ain't trying, and stop the bout. Or if it does go the limit, Kemp'll get the decision because he'll punch harder. And Kemp'll hit Burke too. He's far and away the best boy my kid's ever been against, too good to get showed up even by as fast and clever a boxer as Burkey. Our only chance is to make this little farmer slug—tear in there and sock him like he did Porter. But how we're going to do it is more than I know."

V

Jack Grace is the one that deserves the credit. He went to work the night of Miss Morgan's big show, when the receipts was turned over to devastated France. Nate had to buy four tickets and I and Jack and Burkey went with him.

Well, as you know, our best people was there that night.

The old Garden was full of the folks that generally goes there to the horse show, not to boxing bouts. The soup and fish was everywheres, and gals that would knock your eye out, dressed pretty near as warm as the fighters themselfs.

We couldn't keep Burke in his seat. He was scared that he wouldn't see all the janes, and just as scared that they wouldn't all see him. The guys behind him was yelling murder and the ushers bawled him out a dozen times.

Then all of a sudden, his eyes jumped right out of his head and he gave a gasp and flopped down in his chair. The three of us looked where he was looking. And no wonder he'd wilted! What a gal!

She was with a middle-aged man, probably her dad, and she set in the row just ahead of us and acrost the aisle. I guess it was the first time she'd ever been to this kind of a party and she was all flushed up with excitement. But she'd of been pretty enough without that.

"There she is!" says Burke. "There's the gal I want!"

"Who don't!" says Nate.

"Who is she?" Burke ast, and Nate was going to tell him he didn't know. But Jack Grace cut in.

"It's Esther Fester," he said. "That's her father with her, Lester Fester. He's the second richest man in New York. They claim he made three or four billion during the war, selling waffle irons to Belgium. And she's his only kid. Every young millionaire in town has proposed to her, but she won't have nothing to do with them, calls them all loafers.

"She says the man she marries will have to be a champion of something, whether it's football or boxing or halma. She don't care what, just so's he's better in one line than anybody else."

"She's quite a boxing fan," says Nate. "I seen her here several times before. She maybe wants to look all the boys over and see which one she likes the best."

"I understand she's a great admirer of Willie Kemp," says Jack. "She's always here when he boxes and she probably come to-night expecting to see him in the audience. Maybe he'll be introduced before the main bout, and if he is, we'll watch her close and see if she's interested."

"Why can't I get introduced?" ast Burke.

"You can," said Nate. "Wait till they're getting ready for the wind-up and then climb in the ring and tell Joe Humphreys who you are."

Well, he couldn't hardly wait till the preliminaries was over so's he could get up there and have her see him. And when he bowed, it was right at her.

"Young Burke, the Michigan Flash!" says Humphreys. "He is matched to box Willie Kemp in this ring two weeks from Friday night. The winner will meet Jack Britton for the welterweight title."

Coming back to his seat, Burkey had to pass the gal. He smiled right in her face and she smiled back. I guess it was all she could do to keep from laughing.

I don't suppose they's been more than three or four fights better than that Leonard-Mitchell scrap. It was certainly the best I ever seen. But I don't believe Burke knew they was fighting.

When it was over and the gang started out he would of overtook the gal and spoke to her only for Nate holding him.

"It'd make her sore and spoil everything," said Nate.

"How could it make her sore?" said Burke. "Didn't she smile at me?"

"Well, it'd make her old man sore," says Nate.

"What could he do?" says Burkey. "If he looked cross-eyed at me, I'd bust him."

"That'd be a sweet way to start a courtship!" said Jack. "Even New York gals ain't so far ahead of the times that they fall in love with every handsome young bud that introduces himself to their father with a smash in the jaw."

"But I just want her phone number," says the kid.

"You can get it at the hotel," says Jack. "The phone company got out a book three or four years ago that gives the names of a few of their rich subscribers, and what their number used to be, and if you call it up, they'll tell you what it's been changed to."

So as soon as we was back at the Spencer, Burkey run for the book. And he couldn't find no Lester Fester.

"I didn't think it'd be in there," says Jack. "They's very few New York millionaires has their number in the phone book. If they did, their wifes would bother them to death, calling up."

"But they must be some way to locate them," said the kid. "Somebody must know where they stay. A man as rich as him must have a big mansion somewheres. And you got to find out where it's at. If you don't find out for me to-morrow, why I'm through! I won't box Kemp or no one else."

And they knew he was cuckoo enough to mean it. But Jack Grace had his plans made already.

"I'll locate them to-morrow," he said, "that is, unless you hear from the gal herself."

"But she don't know where I'm staying," says Burke.

"She might maybe call up Rickard and find out," says Jack.

So the kid went to bed and Nate and Jack set up and talked it over.

"It looks like we got him," said Jack. "If we can make him think him and Kemp is rivals, he'll fight."

"But that gal can't be framed," says Nate. "I don't know who she is, but she ain't the kind we could get any help from."

"We don't need her help," says Jack. "He'll get a special delivery to-morrow afternoon, with her name signed to it; that is, what he thinks is her name. I'll dope out the letter yet to-night. If necessary he'll get a letter every day till the day of the bout."

"And then what?" says Nate.

"Why, nothing," says Jack. "What do you care, if it does the work?"

"It don't seem right," said Nate. "I don't want to break the kid's heart."

"You got as much chance of breaking his head!" says Jack. "What about the gal in Benton Harbor, that he was so stuck on and got over it in a day? But as far as that's concerned, we don't have to kill this gal off when we're through with Kemp. We can keep her going till he meets Britton. We'll have her tell him first that he's got to trim Kemp, and if that works, we'll send her to Europe or somewheres, leaving him a farewell note that she's been called away, but she'll be back in time to see him win the title."

"He's a sap," said Nate, "but I doubt if he's dumbbell enough to swallow this."

"You don't appreciate him," said Jack. "Where him and the fair sex is concerned, they's nothing so raw that he won't eat it up. But suppose he don't? You ain't got nothing to lose."

"Just him, that's all," says Nate.

"Well, he's no loss if he won't fight," said Jack. "And this may be the way to make him."

VI

Burke had started training at Daley's. When he got back from there the next afternoon, they was a special delivery waiting for him. It said:

DEAR MR. BURKE: You will probably be surprised getting a letter from one who you have never met, but still I suppose you get many letters from silly girls of my sex that has seen you and admires you. Hope you won't think bad of me for writing to you, but am a girl that acts on their impulse and sometimes am sorry afterwards that I done so and wished I was not so silly, but you know how girls are and especially in regards to affairs of the heart.

Well, Mr. Burke, you don't know me, but I was to the Garden last night with my daddy and set right near you and noticed you when I first come in, but didn't dast look at you and didn't know who you was till you was introduced from the ring. And then when you was returning to your seat I thought you smiled at me and I smiled back. Oh, Mr. Burke, was it me you was smiling at? If not I will feel very foolish for smiling at you and hope you won't think the worse of me for doing so.

Well, anyway, it's too late to mend and this A. M. I had my

secretary get where you are staying from Mr. Rickard and am writing you this letter and suppose you will say it's just another fool girl writing mash notes, but I flatter myself that I am a little higher class than most girls as I am a society girl and don't write these kind of letters as a rule. So please don't think I am a fool and tear this up. Am just a girl that sometimes lets their feelings run away with them.

Am going to make pa take me to see the bout between you and Willie Kemp, but am afraid you are going to be beaten that night, Mr. Burke, as have seen Mr. Kemp fight and believe he is going to be the champion. I admire him very much and up to last night, admired him more than any other man, but now am not so sure. There I am afraid I have been too bold and you will think I am a perfect fool.

Well, Mr. Burke, will not take up no more of your time though I don't suppose you have read this far, but hope you don't think I am a fool, but know you do. Pa don't approve of me writing to men to who I am not engaged and would be very angry was he to find out I had wrote to you, so can't let you answer this letter or call me up for fear he would find it out and be very angry. But maybe will write you again and certainly will see you fight Mr. Kemp and if you see me that night, please smile at me again so will not think you consider me a fool. But maybe you will not feel like smiling after you have boxed Mr. Kemp, as I think he is a wonder.

Well, Mr. Burke, good-by for this time and please don't think I am a fool.

Your would-be friend,
ESTHER FESTER.

Well, Jack Grace had guessed right. Burkey swallowed it whole. He begin reading it down in the lobby, but when he looked back and seen the name signed to it, he took it up to the room to finish it. And if he read it once, he read it twenty times—and looked sillier every time he read it. He surprised us one way, though. We was expecting he would show it to everybody. But he kept it to himself. Of course, we'd read it before it got to him. Jack had wrote it and had one of the phone gals copy it off.

Nate ast the kid at supper how he felt.

"Great!" he says.

"You want to keep working to improve your wind," says Nate. "This is your first fifteen-round bout and you may get tired."

"I won't have time to get tired," he says. "I'll knock him dead in a round!"

It was the first time he'd ever made a speech like that.

"Looks like you was right," says Nate to Jack, afterwards. "He's eat it up. The only thing now is to be sure and not overplay it. Just give him a couple more short notes between now and the bout."

"What shall I say in them?" says Jack.

"You don't need my advice," said Nate. "I think you wrote that one from memory. You must of got a few mash notes yourself."

"No," says Jack. "All the time I was boxing, I only got letters from one gal. And she always said the same thing: 'If you're a man, you'll pay me back that eight dollars and sixty cents you stole.'"

Well, Burke pestered the clerks to death asking if they was sure no mail had came for him; and he went for the phone every time it rung, and was scared to go out for fear a call would come w'ile he wasn't there. Finally it got so that Nate couldn't hardly drag him to Daley's for his work-out, and they seen they'd have to spill another note or he'd worry himself out of shape. The second one was short and said:

Dear Mr. Burke: It has been all as I could do to keep from writing you before this, but was afraid if I wrote too often you would think I was a fool.

Well, Mr. Burke, it's only five days now till your bout with Mr. Kemp and suppose you are excited. I know I am and can't hardly wait for the big event, though to be perfectly honest am in a funny position as I don't know if I want you or he to win. You see I am an admirer of the both of you. Suppose you will say to yourself I must be a funny girl to not know her own mind, but you see I have admired Mr. Kemp a long time and only seen you the other night for the first time, so don't know which I like best. Guess I will let you two decide the question for me and may the best man win.

Pa is going to take me to the fight and only hope I will not faint or something with excitement. Suppose you will think me a fool for feeling this way in regards to two parties who I have never met, but as I told you before, am a girl that always lets their feelings get the best of them, though sometimes am sorry when it is too late. Hope you won't make me sorry, Mr. Burke. That is, if you win. Am afraid for your sake, however, that you are doomed with defeat, as Mr. Kemp has a punch and you are just a boxer that can't hit hard.

Well, Mr. Burke, must say ta ta for this time as am going to a toddle party at the Ritz.

Yours, ESTHER.

And the morning of the big day he got this one:

DEAR MR. BURKE: Just a line to let you know am thinking of you and if you beat Mr. Kemp, will call you up and see if we can't meet somewheres and have a dance, or maybe you don't care for la dance, but we can have a little chat if you don't think me too much a fool.

Well, Mr. Burke, I won't bother you when you must be already worried and nervous over the bout and will just say that I will be at the Garden and will see you even if you don't see me and wished I could tell you where I will set but don't know.

Well, Mr. Burke, good luck and may the best man win.

ESTHER.

On the way down from the hotel that night, Burkey ast Jack and I if we'd bet on him. We told him no. So he says:

"If you want to make some easy money, bet some of these wise crackers that I'll stop this bird in a round. I'll slap him dead!"

VII

So I and Jack did get down a couple of bets, fifty apiece. We bet the kid would win by a knock out and we got three to one. The smart guys had looked over his record and didn't see how he could stop Kemp.

But when they got in the ring, I wished for a minute I hadn't bet. Instead of paying any attention to what was coming off, Burkey was looking all over the house trying to locate the little peach. I was scared he'd still be doing it yet when the bout started, and Kemp'd sock him before he got down to business. But Jack Grace seen the danger, and leaned over and w'ispered to the kid:

"You remember that Fester gal? She's up in a box with her old man."

"Where at?" ast Burke, all excited.

"It's pretty dark," says Jack, "but I'll try and point her out between rounds."

As you know, they wasn't no "between rounds." In the first

two minutes Kemp made five trips to the floor, and he liked it so well the last time that he decided to sleep there.

And in the excitement, Jack pretended he'd lost sight of the gal.

VIII

Burkey staid in the room all the next day, waiting for the phone call. The papers had went nuts over him and said he was the Benny Leonard of the welters, and that it was just a question of the date when the title would change hands. But for all the effect it had on Burke, they might as well of said he'd opened a bird store.

Meanw'ile, Nate and Jack Grace talked it over and decided to go through with Jack's scheme—keep Esther alive till the Britton bout, but send her to Europe, where she wouldn't be so much trouble. So late in the evening, w'ile Burkey was still waiting for his call, a special delivery come for him that said:

DEAR MR. BURKE: Have bad news or at least hope you will agree with me and think it is bad. By the time you receive this note, will be on the old pond with pa, bound for Europe. He got a cable this A. M. calling him to the other side and insisted on me going along. So we hustled round and got rooms on the ship that sails this P. M. I cried when he said I would have to go and hope you feel as bad as I do. But it's only for a short time and will be back in time to see you beat Britton and win the title. After that —well, Mr. Burke, I won't say no more.

You was wonderful last night and am proud of you. Wished I could tell you in person how much I admire you, but will do that later on. Will drop you a note just the minute we get back. In the mean time, don't forget one who is proud of you and wished I could meet my coming champion. ESTHER.

Well, it was a blow to the kid, but it would of worked out all right only for the toughest kind of a break. Nate had to hurry back to Chi, but before he left he seen Rickard and closed for the Britton bout. Burke's end was to be $10,000.

So the second day after the Kemp bout, they was taking the Century home, and I and Jack Grace was over to see them off. They'd just shook hands and was starting through the gate when Burke seen her, the gal he'd went wild over at Miss Morgan's show! She was saying good-by to another pip.

"Wait!" says Burkey, and before Nate could stop him, he'd grabbed the gal by the arm.

"Esther!" he says. "Miss Fester! You didn't go after all!"

The poor gal was speechless.

"Don't you know me?" said the kid. "I'm Burke, the boy that beat Kemp, the boy you been writing to."

She jerked her arm loose and found her tongue.

"I'm not interested in who you are," she said. "I don't know you and I don't believe I want to."

By this time, Nate had him.

"Come on, boy," he says. "You've made a mistake."

And he dragged him through the gate, w'ile the crowd stared goggle-eyed.

"Well," says our gal to her chum, "you're going to have a thrill —a trip with a crazy man!"

Burke was numb, Nate tells me, till the train was way out of New York. Then he said:

"Maybe she didn't recognize me. Or maybe she just didn't want her friend to know."

"That was probably it," says Nate.

"But why did she lie to me and say she was going to Europe?" says the kid.

After a w'ile he got up from his seat.

"Her friend's on this train," he said. "I'm going to find her and ask her something."

Nate tried to coax him out of it, but he wouldn't listen. So Nate went with him to see that he didn't get in no trouble.

They found the gal's pal a couple of cars back. The kid stopped and said:

"I beg your pardon, lady, but I want to ask you just one question. That gal that seen you off, is her name Esther Fester?"

The jane laughed and says:

"I'm afraid it's nothing as poetical as that. Her name is plain Mary Holt."

Without another word, Burke followed Nate back to their own sleeper. He didn't open his clam again till they hit Albany. Then he made some remark about wanting some fresh air, and got off the train.

That's the last Nate seen of him till the other day, when he showed up in Chi, after money.

So you see why the Britton show had to be postponed. They's no plot for it.

XXXIV

SUN CURED

It seems there were two New Yorkers, C. L. Walters and Ernie Fretts. They met on a train Florida bound. Fretts was in the insurance business, over in Brooklyn.

"I'm in the insurance business, over in Brooklyn," said Fretts. "Handle all kinds of insurance. I started when I was just a kid, twenty years ago, and now I've got it built up so's I don't need to worry. It runs itself. I guess that's the trouble. I mean I got too much time on my hands, and I play around too much. Why, say, it's a wonder I ain't dead, the way I been going. I bet I ain't been to bed before two, three o'clock the last six months. You can't go that pace and not feel it."

"It's bound to tell on a man after a w'ile," said Walters. "Now you take me——"

"So I'm about all in," said Fretts. "And the funny part of it is I didn't realize it. I wouldn't of thought nothing about it only for the girl I got in my office. You couldn't hardly call her a girl, either; she's a woman about fifty-three and looks like a Channel swimmer. That's the kind to have in your office. I had a regular Miss America once, the first year I was in business for myself, and we were so busy petting each other that we couldn't even answer the phone. I didn't sell enough insurance that year to keep her in typewriter erl. The smartest play I ever made in my life was getting rid of her.

"This woman I got now—well, you'd about as soon think of making love to a horse. And she's as smart as a man; you don't have to tell her nothing. And where do you think I got her? In an emplerment agency."

"Now you take me——" said Walters.

"So as I was telling you, I come in the office one day last week, along about noon, and hadn't been to bed in thirty-six hours, and Miss Clancy—that's the woman I got in the office—she give me one look and said, 'Mr. Fretts,' she said, 'don't think I am butting in on your private affairs, but you better be careful or you will kill yourself. If you will take my advice,' she said, 'lay off for a month or two and go to Florida or somewheres and rest up. Get away from these friends of yours for a w'ile.'

"She said, 'You know you can trust me to handle the business,' she said, 'and if you will take a vacation for a month or two, you will feel like a new man. You use' to play golf and tennis and enjer yourself in things that was good for you,' she said, 'and now look at you! I bet you ain't taken no real exercise in four years. And you don't sleep and you don't eat. Just pack up and go down to Palm Beach or Miami or some place and take a little exercise and lay around in the sun and read, or just lay there and relax yourself. You got nothing in the world to worry about and if something does come up that needs your personal attention, I will let you know. But I won't anner you,' she said, 'unless it's absolutely necessary and I don't think it will be.'

"She knows me so well that she could see what kind of shape I was in. I tell you I was a wreck, but wouldn't of thought nothing of it only for her calling my attention. I tell you I was a wreck."

"You and me both," said Walters. "Now in my case——"

"So I promised her I'd think it over and that night I went on another party—without a wink of sleep, mind you—and I told a pal of mine, Ben Drew—he's in the furniture business in Brooklyn, in partners with his brother, and a great pal of mine—I told him what Miss Clancy had said, and they was a couple of girls with us. Bonnie Werner, the girl I been going around with, she was with us, and a girl named Stevens that Ben had picked up somewheres; they were both along on the party.

"The Werner girl thinks I'm going to marry her. Fine chance!

"Anyway, she overheard me telling Ben about this Florida idear and she was all ears. She made some crack about Palm Beach being a grand place for a honeymoon. I guess she thought I was steweder than I really was. I kept right on talking to Ben and he was cock-eyed and got all steamed up over the idear and said he would go along with me. He would of been right on this train, too, only for his brother getting sick. But he's going to jern me next week."

"I tried to persuade a friend of mine——"

"We got rid of the girls and sat up all that night in a poker game and I was half asleep, and at that I win over seven hundred dollars. We was playing deuces wild and they was one hand where I had three deuces and drew to them and caught a five and nine of clubs. Well, I and a fella named Garvey bet back and forth and he finally called me and laid down a deuce and three tens. I was so gone by this time that I couldn't talk, so I just throwed down my hand face up and somebody said, 'My Lord! A straight flush!'

So they give me the pot and I thought all the w'ile that what I had was four nines. That shows——"

"I don't like deuces wild," said Walters. "What's the——"

"I finally got home about noon and called up the office and then slept five or six hours and by that time I was ready for another party. But when I showed up at the office on Wednesday, Miss Clancy bawled me out again and I promised I'd take her advice. Well, I hadn't played golf or tennis for years and meanw'ile I'd moved three or four times and when I come to look for my golf-clubs and tennis racket, well, they'd disappeared. And I couldn't find a bathing-suit either, or my fishing-tackle. So all this stuff I'm taking along, it's all new; I had to buy an entire new outfit—seventy-some dollars for a set of golf-clubs and a bag, fourteen dollars for a tennis racket, and thirty-odd dollars for fishing-tackle. And besides that, a bathing-suit that I paid thirty-two dollars for it, but it'll knock 'em dead.

"I don't know how my golf game will be after laying off so long; I expect it'll come back to me after the first couple of days. The last time I played was out on Long Island, at the Engineers'; must of been four, five years ago. I remember I shot an eighty-seven and win over a hundred dollars. Tennis is my game, though, and I can't hardly wait to get at it again. What I'm planning to do is get up early in the morning, have breakfast, play two or three sets of tennis, then go swimming and maybe lay around on the beach for an hour; have lunch and then get in eighteen holes of golf and another little swim; then have my dinner, probably up in my room, and go to bed around nine, ten o'clock. Three weeks and I'll be in the pink!"

"Now you take me," said Walters, "and——"

"Yes," said Fretts, "but you probably use some judgment, or maybe you're married and don't——"

"No, I'm——"

"I don't believe they's a man living could of went the pace I been going and stood up under it. Ben Drew—he's a pal of mine—he says I'm a marvel. He said, 'Ernie, you're a marvel!' Why listen: Here's what I did three weeks ago, just for an example. That was right after New Year's eve. Of course I was on parties morning, night and noon all through the holidays and wound up with a bat that started New Year's eve and lasted till Monday morning, the third. I slept a w'ile Monday forenoon and showed up at the office about three o'clock. Miss Clancy—the girl I got in the office—she give me a message to call up a pal of mine, Ben Drew.

"I called him up and he had a date with a girl he had picked up somewhere named Stevens, and would I and my girl come along. That's a girl named Bonnie Werner that I been going with. She thinks I'm going to marry her, and I suppose everybody's entitled to their opinion. Anyway, I couldn't leave Ben in a hole so I said all right and he and I got together around five o'clock and loaded up on cocktails and later we jerned the girls and made the rounds and wound up at a Black and Tan, and I and Ben both got pie-eyed and finally sent the girls home mad and we stayed and got in a crap game and I win two three hundred dollars. The game broke up at noon.

"I went straight to the office and Miss Clancy give me a message to call up Miss Werner; that's the girl I was with the night before, Monday. She was sore on account of me not seeing her home and said if I didn't take her out this night—Tuesday—why, it was all off between her and I. Well, Tuesday nights we always have a big poker game and I told her I couldn't get out of the game, but I would see her Wednesday night. I was praying she'd stay sore and carry out her threat and I wouldn't have to bother with her no more. But no; she backed down and said Wednesday would be k. o.

"So I got in the poker game and it not only lasted all Tuesday night and all day Wednesday, but all night Wednesday night. I got outside of five, six bottles of Ben Drew's Scotch and win a hundred and seventy dollars. I snatched three, four hours sleep Thursday forenoon and when I showed up at the office, the girl, the Werner girl, was waiting for me.

"To keep her from making a scene I had to promise to devote the rest of the week to her, and the next three nights, we made the rounds of all the different jernts, dancing and drinking rat-poison. Now that's just one week, but it's like all the other weeks. No wonder Miss Clancy said I looked terrible!"

"A man can't go that pace and not feel it. I know in my case——"

"So I need just this kind of a trip—go down there where I don't know nobody and no girls pestering me all the w'ile, and be out-doors all day and exercise and breathe God's fresh air. Three, four weeks of that life and the boys in Brooklyn and New York won't recognize me. And besides that, I never been to Florida and I'm anxious to look it over and see if it's all they claim. They tell me a man can pick up some great bargains there now and if I find something I like, I'm liable to grab off a piece of it, not for specu-lation, but maybe build myself a little place to spend the winter months. I hate cold weather and snow and they's no sense in a man in my position hanging around New York and freezing to death when I could just as well be enjering myself in a clean, wholesome way, in the sunshine."

"You take me, now——"

"You're probably a fella that uses some judgment and eat regular, or maybe you got a wife and family to make you behave. But I got nobody only my friends, though I guess I got more of them than any man in Brooklyn. That's one of my troubles, having too many friends, but only for them, I wouldn't be where I am, I mean in business. A man in my business has got to have friends, or they wouldn't have no business."

"In my business, too. I'm——"

"This must be Fayetteville we're coming to," said Fretts. "I've got to send a wire to a pal of mine, Ben Drew. He's in Brooklyn now, but he's going to jern me next week down in Miami."

It seems that the two New Yorkers happened to be on the same train a month later, northward bound from Jacksonville.

"Hello, there," said Walters.

"Fine," replied Fretts, regarding the other somewhat vaguely.

"I come down on the same train with you a month ago," said Walters.

"That's right," said Fretts. "We come down on the same train together."

"Well, what do you think of Florida?"

"No place like it in the world!" said Fretts, warming up. "Say, I could write a book! I wished I'd kept a diary of the month I been there. Only nobody would believe it."

"Where was you? Palm Beach?"

"No, Miami. That is, I guess we drove up to Palm Beach one night. I don't know."

"Where did you stop in Miami?"

"Over at the Beach, at the Flamingo."

"What did they charge you there?"

"I've got no idear. I paid them with a check," said Fretts.

"It's American plan, ain't it?"

"No. Yes, yes, it's American plan."

"And how was the meals?"

"Meals! I don't know. I didn't hear anybody say anything about them."

"I thought——"

"After this, I'm going to take all my vacations in the winter and spend them right there. That's the Garden Spot of God's Green Footstool!"

"So you bought yourself a place?"

"No, I didn't buy nothing; that is, no real estate. I met some guy the second day that was talking about a big bargain in some development he was interested in, and I promised I'd go out and look at it. He called up a couple of times to remind me of my promise, so to keep him from pestering me, I finally did go out there, but they was no moon, so I couldn't tell much about it."

"I thought——"

"Listen till you hear something funny. When I got to the hotel, they told me my room was still occupied, but the guy was just moving out and I could move in inside of an hour. Well, they made the fella pack up in a hurry and he overlooked two bottles of Plymouth gin. So there was the two bottles staring me in the eye and I was afraid he'd come back after them, so I phoned up to another fella's room that had rode over with me in the taxi from the station and he come down and we had ten, eleven Tom Collinses just as fast as we could drink them.

"Then we filled up the both bottles with water and fixed them like they hadn't been opened, and sure enough, the bird come back for his treasure. He said he was on his way to Key West and had got clear over near to Miami station when he recalled leaving the gin and he had enough time to come back for it and still catch his train yet. That's one thing about Florida trains—you can't miss them no matter what time you get there. He said it was a good thing for him that his room had been inherited by an honest man. I'd like to heard what he said when he took his first swig out of those bottles.

"Well, I and the other fella, the fella that split the gin with me—he's a fella named Leo Hargrave, from Cleveland; got a foundry there or something—the two of us went up in his room and polished off a bottle of Scotch and then it was time to dress for dinner. That's all I done about dinner the whole month I was in Miami—I dressed for it, but I never got it. Hargrave said he knew a swell jernt out near Hialeah and we hired a car and drove out there and it was a place where you dined and danced, but we wasn't hungry and we didn't have nobody to dance with. So we just ordered some drinks——"

"Did you have any trouble getting drinks?"

"Yes. You had to call a waiter. Well, we stayed there till pretty close to midnight and then drove back towards the beach and stopped at another jernt where you play roulette. There's a game I always been wild about and I'd of been satisfied to send for my baggage and settle right down for the month. But Hargrave was dance mad and he said we would have to find some girls to travel around with. He said he knew one girl; he would call her up in the morning, and maybe she had a friend.

"I told him to never mind about a friend, because it's been my experience that when you ask a girl to bring along a girl friend, the girl friend generally always looks like she had charge of the linen room at a two dollar hotel. So we stayed up till the telegraph office was open and then I sent a letter to New York, to a girl I been going around with, a girl named Bonnie Werner, and told her to jump in an upper and jern me."

"Did she come?"

"Sure, she come. She thinks I'm going to marry her. But she couldn't get there till two, three days later and in the meanwhile, I run around with Hargrave and his dame. I wasn't lonesome, though; not as long as they was plenty of Scotch and a roulette w'eel, and besides that, I found a poker game, to say nothing about a couple dandy fellas lives there at the Beach and love to just sit around and hit up the old barber shop harmony—Jim Allison and Jess Andrew.

"But I didn't really strike my stride till Miss Werner got in. From that time on, I went some pace! And of course it was even worse when Ben Drew showed up. He's a pal of mine, in partners with his brother in the furniture business in Brooklyn. He was going to come down with me, but his brother got sick and held him up a week. He brought a girl named Stevens that he picked up somewheres, and with Miss Werner and I, and Ben Drew and the Stevens dame, and Hargrave and his girl, that made six of us that stuck together all the w'ile; that is, for the first few nights. After that, we'd get the girls all wore out by one, two o'clock and chase them home and then I and Ben and Hargrave, we'd play the w'eel or sit in a game of stud.

"It was the same schedule, day after day, the whole time I was there. The party would start out along about seven, eight o'clock in the evening and go to whatever place we hadn't been to the night before. We'd dance till, say, one o'clock and then chase the women home and do a little serious gambling. The poker game generally broke up a little before noon. That would give us fellas the afternoon to sleep, w'ile the girls would do their shopping or go to the polo or waste their time some way another. About six o'clock, I'd get up and have the barber come in and shave me and then I'd dress and be all set for the roll-call."

"But I thought——"

"From the first day, I didn't wear nothing but dinner clothes. And I brought along a trunk full of white pants and knickers that I never even unpacked.

"You'd have to get Miss Werner or one of the other girls to tell you the different places we went. They all looked alike to me—just jernts, with tables and waiters and an orchestra."

"But the weather was beautiful——"

"So I heard somebody say. I guess it's a great climate, if that's what a man is looking for. They say California's another garden spot and that's another place I've always intended to go. But of course it takes longer."

"The California climate," said Walters, "is probably just as good——"

"I've always intended to go out there. But of course it takes longer. Four, five days on a train is too much. A fella don't get no sun or air. I always feel cooped up on a train."

"How was the golf?"

"I didn't get to play golf; never had my clubs out of the bag. But I heard somebody telling Ben Drew that they had four, five fine courses around Miami."

"Play any tennis?"

"No, I didn't have time for tennis. They got some swell courts right by the hotel, but even at that, when you change into your tennis clothes and play four, five sets and then take a bath and dress again, why, it means a waste of two hours."

"Go fishing?"

"Fishing! That's a whole day! And as far as bathing is concerned, why, it looks like they was a law that you couldn't swim only at noon time, just when a man's ready for the hay."

"How far is the ocean from the hotel where you stopped?"

"I don't know. I didn't get over there. You see you can't do everything at a place like that. It would wear you out. I'm thirty-eight years old and when a man gets that age, you've got to watch your step. You can't go in for athaletics like you was a kid.

"I'm in the insurance business in Brooklyn, and one of the things we learn in our business is that a man is taking chances if he goes in too strong for sports after a certain age. You can't be a youngster all your life."

"Did your friends go home ahead of you?"

"Do you mean Ben Drew and Miss Werner and the Stevens girl? No, Ben, he's back there in a compartment dead to the world and he said he'd shoot anybody that woke him up this side of Manhattan Transfer.

"And the girls—they look like they'd just stepped out of a waste-pipe."

"You look pretty good yourself, better than last time I seen you."

"I should! A trip like this was just what I needed—away from the office a whole month and longer and ain't even given business a thought.

"That's where so many men make mistakes—not taking a vacation; or if they do take one, they keep in touch with their office all the time and sperl the whole trip, worrying. I got a girl that can run my business pretty near as good as I can myself—not a girl, either; a woman about fifty-three years old; a Miss Clancy.

"She's the one that realized the shape I was in and insisted on me taking this trip. And how her face will light up when I walk in that office Monday morning—or maybe Monday afternoon—and she sees what this has done for me!"

XXXV

THE FACTS

I

THE engagement was broken off before it was announced. So only a thousand or so of the intimate friends and relatives of the parties knew anything about it. What they knew was that there had been an engagement and that there was one no longer. The cause of the breach they merely guessed, and most of the guesses were, in most particulars, wrong.

Each intimate and relative had a fragment of the truth. It remained for me to piece the fragments together. It was a difficult job, but I did it. Part of my evidence is hearsay; the major portion is fully corroborated. And not one of my witnesses had anything to gain through perjury.

So I am positive that I have at my tongue's end the facts, and I believe that in justice to everybody concerned I should make them public.

Ellen McDonald had lived on the North Side of Chicago for twenty-one years. Billy Bowen had been a South-Sider for seven years longer. But neither knew of the other's existence until they met in New York, the night before the Army-Navy game.

Billy, sitting with a business acquaintance at a neighboring table in Tonio's, was spotted by a male member of Ellen's party, a Chicagoan, too. He was urged to come on over. He did, and was introduced. The business acquaintance was also urged, came, was introduced and forgotten; forgotten, that is, by every one but the waiter, who observed that he danced not nor told stories, and figured that his function must be to pay. The business acquaintance had been Billy's guest. Now he became host, and without seeking the office.

It was not that Billy and Miss McDonald's male friends were niggards. But unfortunately for the b. a., the checks always happened to arrive when everybody else was dancing or so hysterical over Billy's repartee as to be potentially insolvent.

Billy was somewhere between his fourteenth and twenty-first highball; in other words, at his best, from the audience's standpoint.

His dialogue was simply screaming and his dancing just heavenly. He was Frank Tinney doubling as Vernon Castle. On the floor he tried and accomplished twinkles that would have spelled catastrophe if attempted under the fourteen mark, or over the twenty-one. And he said the cutest things—one right after the other.

II

You can be charmed by a man's dancing, but you can't fall in love with his funniness. If you're going to fall in love with him at all, you'll do it when you catch him in a serious mood.

Miss McDonald caught Billy Bowen in one at the game next day. Entirely by accident or a decree of fate, her party and his sat in adjoining boxes. Not by accident, Miss McDonald sat in the chair that was nearest Billy's. She sat there first to be amused; she stayed to be conquered.

Here was a different Billy from the Billy of Tonio's. Here was a Billy who trained his gun on your heart and let your risibles alone. Here was a dreamy Billy, a Billy of romance.

How calm he remained through the excitement! How indifferent to the thrills of the game! There was depth to him. He was a man. Her escort and the others round her were children, screaming with delight at the puerile deeds of pseudo heroes. Football was a great sport, but a sport. It wasn't Life. Would the world be better or worse for that nine-yard gain that Elephant or Oliphant, or whatever his name was, had just made? She knew it wouldn't. Billy knew, too, for Billy was deep. He was thinking man's thoughts. She could tell by his silence, by his inattention to the scene before him. She scarcely could believe that here was the same person who, last night, had kept his own, yes, and the neighboring tables, roaring with laughter. What a complex character his!

In sooth, Mr. Bowen was thinking man's thoughts. He was thinking that if this pretty Miss McDowell, or Donnelly, were elsewhere, he could go to sleep. And that if he could remember which team he had bet on and could tell which team was which, he would have a better idea of whether he was likely to win or lose.

When, after the game, they parted, Billy rallied to the extent of asking permission to call. Ellen, it seemed, would be very glad to have him, but she couldn't tell exactly when she would have to be back in Chicago; she still had three more places to visit in the East. Could she possibly let him know when she did get back? Yes, she could and would; if he really wanted her to, she would drop him a note. He certainly wanted her to.

This, thought Billy, was the best possible arrangement. Her note would tell him her name and address, and save him the trouble of 'phoning to all the McConnells, McDowells, and Donnellys on the North Side. He did want to see her again; she was pretty, and, judging from last night, full of pep. And she had fallen for him; he knew it from that look.

He watched her until she was lost in the crowd. Then he hunted round for his pals and the car that had brought them up. At length he gave up the search and wearily climbed the elevated stairs. His hotel was on Broadway, near Forty-fourth. He left the train at Forty-second, the third time it stopped there.

"I guess you've rode far enough," said the guard. "Fifteen cents' worth for a nickel. I guess we ought to have a Pullman on these here trains."

"I guess," said Billy, "I guess——"

But the repartee well was dry. He stumbled down-stairs and hurried toward Broadway to replenish it.

III

Ellen McDonald's three more places to visit in the East must have been deadly dull. Anyway, on the sixth of December, scarcely more than a week after his parting with her in New York, Billy Bowen received the promised note. It informed him merely that her name was Ellen McDonald, that she lived at so-and-so Walton Place, and that she was back in Chicago.

That day, if you'll remember, was Monday. Miss McDonald's parents had tickets for the opera. But Ellen was honestly just worn out, and would they be mad at her if she stayed home and went to bed? They wouldn't. They would take Aunt Mary in her place.

On Tuesday morning, Paul Potter called up and wanted to know if she would go with him that night to "The Follies." She was horribly sorry, but she'd made an engagement. The engagement, evidently, was to study, and the subject was harmony, with Berlin, Kern, and Van Alstyne as instructors. She sat on the piano-bench from half-past seven till quarter after nine, and then went to her room vowing that she would accept any and all invitations for the following evening.

Fortunately, no invitations arrived, for at a quarter of nine Wednesday night, Mr. Bowen did. And in a brand-new mood. He was a bit shy and listened more than he talked. But when he talked, he talked well, though the sparkling wit of the night at Tonio's was lacking. Lacking, too, was the preoccupied air of the day at the football game. There was no problem to keep his mind busy, but even if the Army and Navy had been playing football in this very room, he could have told at a glance which was which. Vision and brain were perfectly clear. And he had been getting his old eight hours, and, like the railroad hen, sometimes nine and sometimes ten, every night since his arrival home from Gotham, N. Y. Mr. Bowen was on the wagon.

They talked of the East, of Tonio's, of the game (this was where Billy did most of his listening), of the war, of theatres, of books, of college, of automobiles, of the market. They talked, too, of their immediate families. Billy's, consisting of one married sister in South Bend, was soon exhausted. He had two cousins here in town whom he saw frequently, two cousins and their wives, but they were people who simply couldn't stay home nights. As for himself, he preferred his rooms and a good book to the so-called gay life. Ellen should think that a man who danced so well would want to be doing it all the time. It was nice of her to say that he danced well, but really he didn't, you know. Oh, yes, he did. She guessed she could tell. Well, anyway, the giddy whirl made no appeal to him, unless, of course, he was in particularly charming company. His avowed love for home and quiet surprised Ellen a little. It surprised Mr. Bowen a great deal. Only last night, he remembered, he had been driven almost desperate by that quiet of which he was now so fond; he had been on the point of busting loose, but had checked himself in time. He had played Canfield till ten, though the book-shelves were groaning with their load.

Ellen's family kept them busy for an hour and a half. It was a dear family and she wished he could meet it. Mother and father were out playing bridge somewhere to-night. Aunt Mary had gone to bed. Aunts Louise and Harriet lived in the next block. Sisters Edith and Wilma would be home from Northampton for the holidays about the twentieth. Brother Bob and his wife had built the cutest house; in Evanston. Her younger brother, Walter, was a case! He was away to-night, had gone out right after dinner. He'd better be in before mother and father came. He had a new love-affair every week, and sixteen years old last August. Mother and father really didn't care how many girls he was interested in, so long as they kept him too busy to run round with those crazy schoolmates of his. The latter were older than he; just at the age when it seems smart to drink beer and play cards for money. Father said if he ever found out that Walter was doing those things, he'd take him out of school and lock him up somewhere.

Aunts Louise and Mary and Harriet did a lot of settlement work.

They met all sorts of queer people, people you'd never believe existed. The three aunts were unmarried.

Brother Bob's wife was dear, but absolutely without a sense of humor. Bob was full of fun, but they got along just beautifully together. You never saw a couple so much in love.

Edith was on the basket-ball team at college and terribly popular. Wilma was horribly clever and everybody said she'd make Phi Beta Kappa.

Ellen, so she averred, had been just nothing in school; not bright; not athletic, and, of course, not popular.

"Oh, of course not," said Billy, smiling.

"Honestly," fibbed Ellen.

"You never could make me believe it," said Billy.

Whereat Ellen blushed, and Billy's unbelief strengthened.

At this crisis, the Case burst into the room with his hat on. He removed it at sight of the caller and awkwardly advanced to be introduced.

"I'm going to bed," he announced, after the formality.

"I hoped," said Ellen, "you'd tell us about the latest. Who is it now? Beth?"

"Beth nothing!" scoffed the Case. "We split up the day of the Keewatin game."

"What was the matter?" asked his sister.

"I'm going to bed," said the Case. "It's pretty near midnight."

"By George, it is!" exclaimed Billy. "I didn't dream it was that late!"

"No," said Walter. "That's what I tell dad—the clock goes along some when you're having a good time."

Billy and Ellen looked shyly at each other, and then laughed; laughed harder, it seemed to Walter, than the joke warranted. In fact, he hadn't thought of it as a joke. If it was that good, he'd spring it on Kathryn to-morrow night. It would just about clinch her.

The Case, carrying out his repeated threat, went to bed and dreamed of Kathryn. Fifteen minutes later Ellen retired to dream of Billy. And an hour later than that, Billy was dreaming of Ellen, who had become suddenly popular with him, even if she hadn't been so at Northampton, which he didn't believe.

IV

They saw "The Follies" Friday night. A criticism of the show by either would have been the greatest folly of all. It is doubtful that they could have told what theatre they'd been to ten minutes after they'd left it. From wherever it was, they walked to a dancing place and danced. Ellen was so far gone that she failed to note the change in Billy's trotting. Foxes would have blushed for shame at its awkwardness and lack of variety. If Billy was a splendid dancer, he certainly did not prove it this night. All he knew or cared to know was that he was with the girl he wanted. And she knew only that she was with Billy, and happy.

On the drive home, the usual superfluous words were spoken. They were repeated inside the storm-door at Ellen's father's house, while the taxi driver, waiting, wondered audibly why them suckers of explorers beat it to the Pole to freeze when the North Side was so damn handy.

Ellen's father was out of town. So in the morning she broke the news to mother and Aunt Mary, and then sat down and wrote it to Edith and Wilma. Next she called up Bob's wife in Evanston, and after that she hurried to the next block and sprang it on Aunts Louise and Harriet. It was decided that Walter had better not be told. He didn't know how to keep a secret. Walter, therefore, was in ignorance till he got home from school. The only person he confided in the same evening was Kathryn, who was the only person he saw.

Bob and his wife and Aunts Louise and Harriet came to Sunday dinner, but were chased home early in the afternoon. Mr. McDonald was back and Billy was coming to talk to him. It would embarrass Billy to death to find such a crowd in the house. They'd all meet him soon, never fear, and when they met him, they'd be crazy about him. Bob and Aunt Mary and mother would like him because he was so bright and said such screaming things, and the rest would like him because he was so well-read and sensible, and so horribly good-looking.

Billy, I said, was coming to talk to Mr. McDonald. When he came, he did very little of the talking. He stated the purpose of his visit, told what business he was in and affirmed his ability to support a wife. Then he assumed the rôle of audience while Ellen's father delivered an hour's lecture. The speaker did not express his opinion of Tyrus Cobb or the Kaiser, but they were the only subjects he overlooked. Sobriety and industry were words frequently used.

"I don't care," he prevaricated, in conclusion, "how much money a man is making if he is sober and industrious. You attended college, and I presume you did all the fool things college boys do. Some men recover from their college education, others don't. I hope you're one of the former."

The Sunday-night supper, just cold scraps you might say, was partaken of by the happy but embarrassed pair, the trying-to-look happy but unembarrassed parents, and Aunt Mary. Walter, the Case, was out. He had stayed home the previous evening.

"He'll be here to-morrow night and the rest of the week, or I'll know the reason why," said Mr. McDonald.

"He won't, and I'll tell you the reason why," said Ellen.

"He's a real boy, Sam," put in the real boy's mother. "You can't expect him to stay home every minute."

"I can't expect anything of him," said the father. "You and the girls and Mary here have let him have his own way so long that he's past managing. When I was his age, I was in my bed at nine o'clock."

"Morning or night?" asked Ellen.

Her father scowled. It was evident he could not take a joke, not even a good one.

After the cold scraps had been ruined, Mr. McDonald drew Billy into the smoking-room and offered him a cigar. The prospective son-in-law was about to refuse and express a preference for cigarettes when something told him not to. A moment later he was deeply grateful to the something.

"I smoke three cigars a day," said the oracle, "one after each meal. That amount of smoking will hurt nobody. More than that is too much. I used to smoke to excess, four or five cigars per day, and maybe a pipe or two. I found it was affecting my health, and I cut down. Thank heaven, no one in my family ever got the cigarette habit; disease, rather. How any sane, clean-minded man can start on those things is beyond me."

"Me, too," agreed Billy, taking the proffered cigar with one hand and making sure with the other that his silver pill-case was as deep down in his pocket as it would go.

"Cigarettes, gambling, and drinking go hand in hand," continued the man of the house. "I couldn't trust a cigarette fiend with a nickel."

"There are only two or three kinds he could get for that," said Billy.

"What say?" demanded Mr. McDonald, but before Billy was obliged to wriggle out of it, Aunt Mary came in and reminded her brother-in-law that it was nearly church time.

Mr. McDonald and Aunt Mary went to church. Mrs. McDonald, pleading weariness, stayed home with "the children." She wanted a chance to get acquainted with this pleasant-faced boy who was going to rob her of one of her five dearest treasures.

The three were no sooner settled in front of the fireplace than Ellen adroitly brought up the subject of auction bridge, knowing that it would relieve Billy of the conversational burden.

"Mother is really quite a shark, aren't you, mother?" she said.

"I don't fancy being called a fish," said the mother.

"She's written two books on it, and she and father have won so many prizes that they may have to lease a warehouse. If they'd only play for money, just think how rich we'd all be!"

"The game is fascinating enough without adding to it the excitements and evils of gambling," said Mrs. McDonald.

"It is a fascinating game," agreed Billy.

"It is," said Mrs. McDonald, and away she went.

Before father and Aunt Mary got home from church, Mr. Bowen was a strong disciple of conservativeness in bidding and thoroughly convinced that all the rules that had been taught were dead wrong. He saw the shark's points so quickly and agreed so whole-heartedly with her arguments that he impressed her as one of the most intelligent young men she had ever talked to. It was too bad it was Sunday night, but some evening soon he must come over for a game.

"I'd like awfully well to read your books," said Billy.

"The first one's usefulness died with the changes in the rules," replied Mrs. McDonald. "But I think I have one of the new ones in the house, and I'll be glad to have you take it."

"I don't like to have you give me your only copy."

"Oh, I believe we have two."

She knew perfectly well she had two dozen.

Aunt Mary announced that Walter had been seen in church with Kathryn. He had made it his business to be seen. He and the lady had come early and had manœuvred into the third row from the back, on the aisle leading to the McDonald family pew. He had nudged his aunt as she passed on the way to her seat, and she had turned and spoken to him. She could not know that he and Kathryn had "ducked" before the end of the processional.

After reporting favorably on the Case, Aunt Mary launched into a description of the service. About seventy had turned out. The music had been good, but not quite as good as in the morning. Mr. Pratt had sung "Fear Ye Not, O Israel!" for the offertory. Dr. Gish was still sick and a lay reader had served. She had heard from Allie French that Dr. Gish expected to be out by the middle of the week and certainly would be able to preach next Sunday morning. The church had been cold at first, but very comfortable finally.

Ellen rose and said she and Billy would go out in the kitchen and make some fudge.

"I was afraid Aunt Mary would bore you to death," she told Billy, when they had kissed for the first time since five o'clock. "She just lives for the church and can talk on no other subject."

"I wouldn't hold that against her," said Billy charitably.

The fudge was a failure, as it was bound to be. But the Case, who came in just as it was being passed round, was the only one rude enough to say so.

"Is this a new stunt?" he inquired, when he had tested it.

"Is what a new stunt?" asked Ellen.

"Using cheese instead of chocolate."

"That will do, Walter," said his father. "You can go to bed."

Walter got up and started for the hall. At the threshold he stopped.

"I don't suppose there'll be any of that fudge left," he said. "But if there should be, you'd better put it in the mouse trap."

Billy called a taxi and departed soon after Walter's exit. When he got out at his South Side abode, the floor of the tonneau was littered with recent cigarettes.

And that night he dreamed that he was president of the anti-cigarette league; that Dr. Gish was vice-president, and that the motto of the organization was "No trump."

Billy Bowen's business took him out of town the second week in December, and it was not until the twentieth that he returned. He had been East and had ridden home from Buffalo on the same train with Wilma and Edith McDonald. But he didn't know it and neither did they. They could not be expected to recognize him from Ellen's description—that he was horribly good-looking. The dining-car conductor was all of that.

Ellen had further written them that he (not the dining-car conductor) was a man of many moods; that sometimes he was just nice and deep, and sometimes he was screamingly funny, and sometimes so serious and silent that she was almost afraid of him.

They were wild to see him and the journey through Ohio and Indiana would not have been half so long in his company. Edith, the athletic, would have revelled in his wit. Wilma would gleefully have fathomed his depths. They would both have been proud to flaunt his looks before the hundreds of their kind aboard the train. Their loss was greater than Billy's, for he, smoking cigarettes as fast as he could light them and playing bridge that would have brought tears of compassion to the shark's eyes, enjoyed the trip, every minute of it.

Ellen and her father were at the station to meet the girls. His arrival on this train had not been heralded, and it added greatly to the hysterics of the occasion.

Wilma and Edith upbraided him for not knowing by instinct who they were. He accused them of recognizing him and purposely avoiding him. Much more of it was pulled in the same light vein, pro and con.

He was permitted at length to depart for his office. On the way he congratulated himself on the improbability of his ever being obliged to play basket-ball versus Edith. She must be a whizz in condition. Chances were she'd train down to a hundred and ninety-five before the big games. The other one, Wilma, was a splinter if he ever saw one. You had to keep your eyes peeled or you'd miss her entirely. But suppose you did miss her; what then! If she won her Phi Beta Kappa pin, he thought, it would make her a dandy belt.

These two, he thought, were a misdeal. They should be re-shuffled and cut nearer the middle of the deck. Lots of other funny things he thought about these two.

Just before he had left Chicago on this trip, his stenographer had quit him to marry an elevator-starter named Felix Bond. He had 'phoned one of his cousins and asked him to be on the lookout for a live stenographer who wasn't likely to take the eye of an elevator-starter. The cousin had had one in mind.

Here was her card on Billy's desk when he reached the office. It was not a business-card visiting-card, at $3 per hundred. "Miss Violet Moore," the engraved part said. Above was written: "Mr. Bowen—Call me up any night after seven. Calumet 2678."

Billy stowed the card in his pocket and plunged into a pile of uninteresting letters.

On the night of the twenty-second there was a family dinner at McDonald's, and Billy was in on it. At the function he met the rest of them—Bob and his wife, and Aunt Harriet and Aunt Louise.

Bob and his wife, despite the former's alleged sense of humor, spooned every time they were contiguous. That they were in love with each other, as Ellen had said, was easy to see. The wherefore was more of a puzzle.

Bob's hirsute adornment having been disturbed by his spouse's digits during one of the orgies, he went up-stairs ten minutes before dinner time to effect repairs. Mrs. Bob was left alone on the davenport. In performance of his social duties, Billy went over and sat down beside her. She was not, like Miss Muffet, frightened away, but terror or some other fiend rendered her temporarily dumb. The game Mr. Bowen was making his fifth attempt to pry open a conversation when Bob came back.

To the impartial observer the scene on the davenport appeared heartless enough. There was a generous neutral zone between Billy and Flo, that being an abbreviation of Mrs. Bob's given name, which, as a few may suspect, was Florence. Billy was working hard and his face was flushed with the effort. The flush may have aroused Bob's suspicions. At any rate, he strode across the room, scowling almost audibly, shot a glance at Billy that would have made the Kaiser wince, halted magnificently in front of his wife, and commanded her to accompany him to the hall.

Billy's flush became ace high. He was about to get up and break a chair when a look from Ellen stopped him. She was at his side before the pair of Bobs had skidded out of the room.

"Please don't mind," she begged. "He's crazy. I forgot to tell you that he's insanely jealous."

"Did I understand you to say he had a sense of humor?"

"It doesn't work where Flo's concerned. If he sees her talking to a man he goes wild."

"With astonishment, probably," said Billy.

"You're a nice boy," said Ellen irrelevantly.

Dinner was announced and Mr. Bowen was glad to observe that Flo's terrestrial body was still intact. He was glad, too, to note that Bob was no longer frothing. He learned for the first time that the Case and Kathryn were of the party. Mrs. McDonald had wanted to make sure of Walter's presence; hence the presence of his crush.

Kathryn giggled when she was presented to Billy. It made him uncomfortable and he thought for a moment that a couple of studs had fallen out. He soon discovered, however, that the giggle was permanent, just as much a part of Kathryn as her fraction of a nose. He looked forward with new interest to the soup course, but was disappointed to find that she could negotiate it without disturbing the giggle or the linen.

He next centred his attention on Wilma and Edith. Another disappointment was in store. There were as many and as large oysters in Wilma's soup as in any one's. She ate them all, and, so far as appearances went, was the same Wilma. He had expected that Edith would either diet or plunge. But Edith was as prosaic in her consumption of victuals as Ellen, for instance, or Aunt Louise.

He must content himself for the present with Aunt Louise. She was sitting directly opposite and he had an unobstructed view of the widest part he had ever seen in woman's hair.

"Ogden Avenue," he said to himself.

Aunt Louise was telling about her experiences and Aunt Harriet's among the heathen of Peoria Street.

"You never would dream there were such people!" said she.

"I suppose most of them are foreign born," supposed her brother, who was Mr. McDonald.

"Practically all of them," said Aunt Louise.

Billy wanted to ask her whether she had ever missionaried among the Indians. He thought possibly an attempt to scalp her had failed by a narrow margin.

Between courses Edith worked hard to draw out his predicated comicality and Wilma worked as hard to make him sound his low notes. Their labors were in vain. He was not sleepy enough to be deep, and he was fourteen highballs shy of comedy.

In disgust, perhaps, at her failure to be amused, the major portion of the misdeal capsized her cocoa just before the close of the meal and drew a frown from her father, whom she could have thrown in ten minutes, straight falls, any style.

"She'll never miss that ounce," thought Billy.

When they got up from the table and started for the living-room, Mr. Bowen found himself walking beside Aunt Harriet, who had been so silent during dinner that he had all but forgotten her.

"Well, Miss McDonald," he said, "it's certainly a big family, isn't it?"

"Well, young man," said Aunt Harriet, "it ain't no small family, that's sure."

"I should say not," repeated Billy.

Walter and his giggling crush intercepted him.

"What do you think of Aunt Harriet's grammar?" demanded Walter.

"I didn't notice it," lied Billy.

"No, I s'pose not. 'Ain't no small family.' I s'pose you didn't notice it. She isn't a real aunt like Aunt Louise and Aunt Mary. She's just an adopted aunt. She kept house for dad and Aunt Louise after their mother died, and when dad got married, she just kept on living with Aunt Louise."

"Oh," was Billy's fresh comment, and it brought forth a fresh supply of giggles from Kathryn.

Ellen had already been made aware of Billy's disgusting plans. He had to catch a night train for St. Louis, and he would be there all day to-morrow, and he'd be back Friday, but he wouldn't have time to see her, and he'd surely call her up. And Friday afternoon he was going to South Bend to spend Christmas Day with his married sister, because it was probably the last Christmas he'd be able to spend with her.

"But I'll hustle home from South Bend Sunday morning," he said. "And don't you dare make any engagement for the afternoon."

"I do wish you could be with us Christmas Eve. The tree won't be a bit of fun without you."

"You know I wish I could. But you see how it is."

"I think your sister's mean."

Billy didn't deny it.

"Who's going to be here Christmas Eve?"

"Just the people we had to-night, except Kathryn and you. Why?"

"Oh, nothing," said Billy.

"Look here, sir," said his betrothed. "Don't you do anything foolish. You're not supposed to buy presents for the whole family. Just a little, tiny one for me, if you want to, but you mustn't spend much on it. And if you get anything for any one else in this house, I'll be mad."

"I'd like to see you mad," said Billy.

"You'd wish you hadn't," Ellen retorted.

When Billy had gone, Ellen returned to the living-room and faced the assembled company.

"Well," she said, "now that you've all seen him, what's the verdict?"

The verdict seemed to be unanimously in his favor.

"But," said Bob, "I thought you said he was so screamingly funny."

"Yes," said Edith, "you told me that, too."

"Give him a chance," said Ellen. "Wait till he's in a funny mood. You'll simply die laughing!"

V

It is a compound fracture of the rules to have so important a character as Tommy Richards appear in only one chapter. But remember, this isn't a regular story, but a simple statement of what occurred when it occurred. During Chapter Four, Tommy had been on his way home from the Pacific Coast, where business had kept him all fall. His business out there and what he said en route to Chicago are collateral.

Tommy had been Billy's pal at college. Tommy's home was in Minnesota, and Billy was his most intimate, practically his only friend in the so-called metropolis of the Middle West. So Tommy, not knowing that Billy had gone to St. Louis, looked forward to a few pleasant hours with him between the time of the coast train's arrival and the Minnesota train's departure.

The coast train reached Chicago about noon. It was Thursday noon, the twenty-third. Tommy hustled from the station to Billy's office, and there learned of the St. Louis trip. Disappointed, he roamed the streets a while and at length dropped into the downtown ticket office of his favorite Minnesota road. He was told that everything for the night was sold out. Big Christmas business. Tommy pondered.

The coast train reached Chicago about noon. It was Thursday noon, the twenty-third.

"How about to-morrow night?" he inquired.

"I can give you a lower to-morrow night on the six-thirty," replied Leslie Painter, that being the clerk's name.

"I'll take it," said Tommy.

He did so, and the clerk took $10.05.

"I'll see old Bill after all," said Tommy.

Leslie Painter made no reply.

In the afternoon Tommy sat through a vaudeville show, and at night he looped the loop. He retired early, for the next day promised to be a big one.

Billy got in from St. Louis at seven Friday morning and had been in his office an hour when Tommy appeared. I have no details of the meeting.

At half-past eight Tommy suggested that they'd better go out and h'ist one.

"Still on it, eh?" said Billy.

"What do you mean?"

"I mean that I'm off of it."

"Good Lord! For how long?"

"The last day of November."   –

"Too long! You look sick already."

"I feel great," averred Billy.

"Well, I don't. So come along and bathe in vichy."

On the way "along" Billy told Tommy about Ellen. Tommy's congratulations were physical and jarred Billy from head to heels.

"Good stuff!" cried Tommy so loudly that three pedestrians jumped sideways. "Old Bill hooked! And do you think you're going to celebrate this occasion with water?"

"I think I am," was Billy's firm reply.

"You think you are! What odds?"

"A good lunch against a red hot."

"You're on!" said Tommy. "And I'm going to be mighty hungry at one o'clock."

"You'll be hungry and alone."

"What's the idea? If you've got a lunch date with the future, I'm in on it."

"I haven't," said Billy. "But I'm going to South Bend on the one-forty, and between now and then I have nothing to do but clean up my mail and buy a dozen Christmas presents."

They turned in somewhere.

"Don't you see the girl at all to-day?" asked Tommy.

"Not to-day. All I do is call her up."

"Well, then, if you get outside of a couple, who'll be hurt? Just for old time's sake."

"If you need lunch money, I'll give it to you."

"No, no. That bet's off."

"It's not off. I won't call it off."

"Suit yourself," said Tommy graciously.

At half-past nine, it was officially decided that Billy had lost the bet. At half-past twelve, Billy said it was time to pay it.

"I'm not hungry enough," said Tommy.

"Hungry or no hungry," said Billy, "I buy your lunch now or I don't buy it. See? Hungry or no hungry."

"What's the hurry?" asked Tommy.

"I guess you know what's the hurry. Me for South Bend on the one-forty, and I got to go to the office first. Hurry or no hurry."

"Listen to reason, Bill. How are you going to eat lunch, go to the office, buy a dozen Christmas presents and catch the one-forty?"

"Christmas presents! I forgot 'em! What do you think of that? I forgot 'em. Good night!"

"What are you going to do?"

"Do! What can I do? You got me into this mess. Get me out!"

"Sure, I'll get you out if you'll listen to reason!" said Tommy. "Has this one-forty train got anything on you? Are you under obligations to it? Is the engineer your girl's uncle?"

"I guess you know better than that. I guess you know I'm not engaged to a girl who's got an uncle for an engineer."

"Well, then, what's the next train?"

"That's the boy, Tommy! That fixes it! I'll go on the next train."

"You're sure there is one?" asked Tommy.

"Is one! Say, where do you think South Bend is? In Europe?"

"I wouldn't mind," said Tommy.

"South Bend's only a two-hour run. Where did you think it was? Europe?"

"I don't care where it is. The question is, what's the next train after one-forty?"

"Maybe you think I don't know," said Billy. He called the gentleman with the apron. "What do you know about this, Charley? Here's an old pal of mine who thinks I don't know the time-table to South Bend."

"He's mistaken, isn't he?" said Charley.

"Is he mistaken? Say, Charley, if you knew as much as I do about the time-table to South Bend, you wouldn't be here."

"No, sir," said Charley. "I'd be an announcer over in the station."

"There!" said Billy triumphantly. "How's that, Tommy? Do I know the time-table or don't I?"

"I guess you do," said Tommy. "But I don't think you ought to have secrets from an old friend."

"There's no secrets about it, Charley."

"My name is Tommy," corrected his friend.

"I know that. I know your name as well as my own, better'n my own. I know your name as well as I know the time-table."

"If you'd just tell me the time of that train, we'd all be better off."

"I'll tell you, Tommy. I wouldn't hold out anything on you, old boy. It's five twenty-five."

"You're sure?"

"Sure! Say, I've taken it a hundred times if I've taken it once."

"All right," said Tommy. "That fixes it. We'll go in and have lunch and be through by half-past one. That'll give you four hours to do your shopping, get to your office and make your train."

"Where you going while I shop?"

"Don't bother about me."

"You go along with me."

"Nothing doing."

"Yes, you do."

"No, I don't."

But this argument was won by Mr. Bowen. At ten minutes of three, when they at last called for the check, Mr. Richards looked on the shopping expedition in an entirely different light. Two hours before, it had not appealed to him at all. Now he could think of nothing that would afford more real entertainment. Mr.

Richards was at a stage corresponding to Billy's twenty-one. Billy was far past it.

"What we better do," said Tommy, "is write down a list of all the people so we won't forget anybody."

"That's the stuff!" said Billy. "I'll name 'em, you write 'em."

So Tommy produced a pencil and took dictation on the back of a menu-card.

"First, girl's father, Sam'l McDonald."

"Samuel McDonald," repeated Tommy. "Maybe you'd better give me some dope on each one, so if we're shy of time, we can both be buying at once."

"All right," said Billy. "First, Sam'l McDonal'. He's an ol' crab. Raves about cig'rettes."

"Like 'em?"

"No. Hates 'em."

"Sam'l McDonald, cigarettes," wrote Tommy. "Old crab," he added.

When the important preliminary arrangement had at last been completed, the two old college chums went out into the air.

"Where do we shop?" asked Tommy.

"Marsh's," said Billy. "'S only place I got charge account."

"Maybe we better take a taxi and save time," suggested Tommy.

So they waited five minutes for a taxi and were driven to Marsh's, two blocks away.

"We'll start on the first floor and work up," said Tommy, who had evidently appointed himself captain.

They found themselves among the jewelry and silverware.

"You might get something for the girl here," suggested Tommy.

"Don't worry 'bout her," said Billy. "Leave her till las'."

"What's the limit on the others?"

"I don't care," said Billy. "Dollar, two dollars, three dollars."

"Well, come on," said Tommy. "We got to make it snappy."

But Billy hung back.

"Say, ol' boy," he wheedled. "You're my ol'st frien'. Is that right?"

"That's right," agreed Tommy.

"Well, say, ol' frien', I'm pretty near all in."

"Go home, then, if you want to. I can pull this all right alone."

"Nothin' doin'. But if I could jus' li'l nap, ten, fifteen minutes —you could get couple things here on fir' floor and then come get me."

"Where?"

"Third floor waitin'-room."

"Go ahead. But wait a minute. Give me some of your cards. And will I have any trouble charging things?"

"Not a bit. Tell 'em you're me."

It was thus that Tommy Richards was left alone in a large store, with Billy Bowen's charge account, Billy Bowen's list, and Billy Bowen's cards.

He glanced at the list.

"'Samuel McDonald, cigarettes. Old crab,'" he read.

He approached a floor-walker.

"Say, old pal," he said. "I'm doing some shopping and I'm in a big hurry. Where'd I find something for an old cigarette fiend?"

"Cigarette-cases, two aisles down and an aisle to your left," said Old Pal.

Tommy raised the limit on the cigarette-case he picked out for Samuel McDonald. It was $3.75.

"I'll cut down somewhere else," he thought. "The father-in-law ought to be favored a little."

"Charge," he said in response to a query. "William Bowen, Bowen and Company, 18 South La Salle. And here's a card for it. That go out to-night sure?"

He looked again at the list.

"Mrs. Samuel McDonald, bridge bug. Miss Harriet McDonald, reverse English. Miss Louise McDonald, thin hair. Miss Mary Carey, church stuff. Bob and Wife, 'The Man Who Married a Dumb Wife' and gets mysteriously jealous. Walter McDonald, real kid. Edith, fat lady. Wilma, a splinter."

He consulted Old Pal once more. Old Pal's advice was to go to the third floor and look over the books. The advice proved sound. On the third floor Tommy found for Mother "The First Principles of Auction Bridge," and for Aunt Harriet an English grammar. He also bumped into a counter laden with hymnals, chant books, and Books of Common Prayer.

"Aunt Mary!" he exclaimed. And to the clerk: "How much are your medium prayer-books?"

"What denomination?" asked the clerk, whose name was Freda Swanson.

"One or two dollars," said Tommy.

"What church, I mean?" inquired Freda.

"How would I know?" said Tommy. "Are there different books for different churches?"

"Sure. Catholic, Presbyterian, Episcopal, Lutheran——"

"Let's see. McDonald, Carey. How much are the Catholic

"Here's one at a dollar and a half. In Latin, too."

"That's it. That'll give her something to work on."

Tommy figured on the back of his list.

"Good work, Tommy!" he thought. "Four and a half under the top limit for those three. Walter's next."

He plunged on Walter. A nice poker set, discovered on the fourth floor, came to five even. Tommy wished he could keep it for himself. He also wished constantly that the women shoppers had taken a course in dodging. He was almost as badly battered as the day he played guard against the Indians.

"Three left besides the queen herself," he observed. "Lord, no. I forgot Bob and his missus."

He moved down-stairs again to the books.

"Have you got 'The Man Who Married a Dumb Wife'?" he queried.

Anna Henderson looked, but could not find it.

"Never mind!" said Tommy. "Here's one that'll do."

And he ordered "The Green-Eyed Monster" for the cooing doves in Evanston.

"Now," he figured, "there's just Wilma and Edith and Aunt Louise." Once more he started away from the books, but a title caught his eye: "Eat and Grow Thin."

"Great!" exclaimed Tommy. "It'll do for Edith. By George! It'll do for both of them. 'Eat' for Wilma, and the 'Grow Thin' for Edith. I guess that's doubling up some! And now for Aunt Louise."

The nearest floor-walker told him, in response to his query, that switches would be found on the second floor.

"I ought to have a switch-engine to take me round," said Tommy, who never had felt better in his life. But the floor-walker did not laugh, possibly because he was tired.

"Have you anything to match it with?" asked the lady in the switch-yard.

"No, I haven't."

"Can you give me an idea of the color?"

"What colors have you got?" demanded Tommy.

"Everything there is. I'll show them all to you, if you've got the time."

"Never mind," said Tommy. "What's your favorite color in hair?"

The girl laughed.

"Golden," she said.

"You're satisfied, aren't you?" said Tommy, for the girl had chosen the shade of her own shaggy mane. "All right, make it golden. And a merry Christmas to you."

He forgot to ask the price of switches. He added up the rest and found that the total was $16.25.

"About seventy-five cents for the hair," he guessed. "That will make it seventeen even. I'm some shopper. And all done in an hour and thirteen minutes."

He discovered Billy asleep in the waiting-room and it took him three precious minutes to bring him to.

"Everybody's fixed but the girl herself," he boasted. "I got books for most of 'em."

"Where you been?" asked Billy. "What time is it?"

"You've got about thirty-three minutes to get a present for your lady love and grab your train. You'll have to pass up the office."

"What time is it? Where you been?"

"Don't bother about that. Come on."

On the ride down, Billy begged every one in the elevator to tell him the time, but no one seemed to know. Tommy hurried him out of the store and into a taxi.

"There's a flock of stores round the station," said Tommy. "You can find something there for the dame."

But the progress of the cab through the packed down-town streets was painfully slow and the station clock, when at last they got in sight of it, registered 5.17.

"You can't wait!" said Tommy. "Give me some money and tell me what to get."

Billy fumbled clumsily in seven pockets before he located his pocketbook. In it were two fives and a ten.

"I gotta have a feevee," he said.

"All right. I'll get something for fifteen. What'll it be?"

"Make it a wrist-watch."

"Sure she has none?"

"She's got one. That's for other wris'."

"I used your last card. Have you got another?"

"Pocketbook," said Billy.

Tommy hastily searched and found a card. He pushed Billy toward the station entrance.

"Good-by and merry Christmas," said Tommy.

"Goo'-by and God bless you!" said Billy, but he was talking to a large policeman.

"Where are you trying to go?" asked the latter.

"Souse Ben'," said Billy.

"Hurry up, then. You've only got a minute."

The minute and six more were spent in the purchase of a ticket. And when Billy reached the gate, the 5.25 had gone and the 5.30 was about to chase it.

"Where to?" inquired the gateman.

"Souse Ben'," said Billy.

"Run then," said the gateman.

Billy ran. He ran to the first open vestibule of the Rock Island train, bound for St. Joe, Missouri.

"Where to?" asked a porter.

"Souse," said Billy.

"Ah can see that," said the porter. "But where you goin'?"

The train began to move and Billy, one foot dragging on the station platform, moved with it. The porter dexterously pulled him aboard. And he was allowed to ride to Englewood.

Walking down Van Buren Street, it suddenly occurred to the genial Mr. Richards that he would have to go some himself to get his baggage and catch the 6.30 for the northwest. He thought of it in front of a Van Buren jewelry shop. He stopped and went in.

Three-quarters of an hour later, a messenger-boy delivered a particularly ugly and frankly inexpensive wrist-watch at the McDonald home. The parcel was addressed to Miss McDonald and the accompanying card read:

"Mr. Bowen: Call me up any night after seven. Calumet 2678. Miss Violet Moore."

There was no good-will toward men in the McDonald home this Christmas. Ellen spent the day in bed and the orders were that she must not be disturbed.

Down-stairs, one person smiled. It was Walter. He smiled in spite of the fact that his father had tossed his brand-new five-dollar poker set into the open fireplace. He smiled in spite of the fact that he was not allowed to leave the house, not even to take Kathryn to church.

"Gee!" he thought, between smiles, "Billy sure had nerve!"

Bob walked round among his relatives seeking to dispel the gloom with a remark that he thought apt and nifty:

"Be grateful," was the remark, "that he had one of his screamingly funny moods before it was too late."

But no one but Bob seemed to think much of the remark, and no one seemed grateful.

Those are the facts, and it was quite a job to dig them up. But I did it.